PRELUDES

A MODERN PERSUASION IMPROVISATION

RIANA EVERLY

PRELUDES: A MODERN PERSUASION IMPROVISATION
Copyright © 2022 Riana Everly
All rights reserved.
*Published by **Bay Crest Press 2022***
Toronto, Ontario, Canada
No parts of this publication may be reproduced, stored in a retrieval system, or transmitted in any form or by any means, electronic, mechanical, photocopying, recording, or otherwise, without the prior written permission of the copyright owner.

This book is sold subject to the condition that it shall not, by way of trade or otherwise, be lent, resold, hired out, or otherwise circulated without the publisher's prior consent in any form of binding or cover other than that in which it is published and without a similar condition including this condition being imposed on the subsequent purchaser. Under no circumstances may any part of this book be photocopied for resale.

This is a work of fiction. Any similarity between the characters and situations within its pages and places or persons, living or dead, is unintentional and co-incidental.

Cover design by White Rabbit Arts, the cover designer of The Historical Fiction Company

ISBN- 978-1-7781297-2-8

DEDICATION

To music, those who make it, and those who love it.
If music be the food of love, play on!

Contents

Acknowledgements

This book, in many ways, has been a real labour of love for me. Although I am a musician by training, this is my first book where music has taken centre stage. Orchestras are my playground, symphonies are my favourite toys, and I want to acknowledge every composer who ever put pen to paper to create this wonderful music. Sammartini, Boyce, Haydn, Mozart, Beethoven, Brahms, Tchaikovsky, Mahler... it's impossible to complete this list. But thank you, all of you, for the music.

Then there are the individuals without whom this book would be a far lesser work. My gratitude is profound. Mikael Swayze, editor and proof-reader extraordinaire, deserves accolades. Also, a special thanks to my friend and brilliant author Liz Martinson, for her insightful comments. Further thanks go to Dr. Hedy Ginzberg for her assistance with the medical scenes, to Gavriel Swayze for his insight into legal matters, and to beta readers Nikita Sridhar, Anne Madison, Josanna Thompson, and Diane Andersen.

And I cannot neglect to offer my thanks to Dee Marley at The Historical Fiction Company for her beautiful cover design. If I made an extra effort on this book, it was to live up to the outside.

Cover design by White Rabbit Arts, the cover designer of The Historical Fiction Company
www.thehistoricalfictioncompany.com/book-cover-design

There could have been no two hearts so open, no tastes so similar, no feelings so in unison.

Jane Austen, *Persuasion*

CHAPTER ONE
Introduzione

The building was quiet. Everybody had gone home, the tech guys had turned off the lights, and the great hall stood empty and waiting. If Anne sat absolutely still, she could swear she still heard the faint echoes of music reverberating off the baffles and sound panels that banked the vast space. But it was not music that thrummed through her ears now. No silver cascade of the harp or brilliant gold triumph of trumpets. No iridescent swell of bows upon strings or undulating green cries of the oboe. Rather, it was the dull red tympanic throb of her heartbeat she heard as the blood rushed through her veins.

She tried to look away but her eyes returned again and again to the email open on her phone, bright and glaring in the dark auditorium.

Grand news, Anne dear! The orchestra has just engaged a new principal conductor and you will never guess who it is. Frederico Valore!

Yes, Fred! You must have known him from years ago. Isn't it wonderful? Remember the fuss we all made when he was starting his career? We knew he was good, but whoever would have imagined he would become the darling of Europe's music scene? What a coup to bring him back home. The musicians will be thrilled. The board will make the official announcement tomorrow afternoon. You will be there, right? We need you there. The press conference is at 2, with a spread afterwards. Wear something fabulous. Fred will join us on Zoom from Rome.

So thrilling! See you there,

Sophia

"Thrilling." Dreadful was more the word. After all this time, Fred was quite the last person she wanted to see. It had been a long time—eight years—and the pain was as acute as it had been that very last day before he left. Time had not healed these wounds, and they were about to be reopened.

She sighed and fumbled for the button on her phone. In a moment the screen went black, leaving her alone in the dark space, only the green glow of the exit signs left to cast their eerie light on the rows of chairs and empty stage.

"Ahem."

Someone cleared his throat by one of the back doors.

"Doctor Elliot? You still there?"

Anne grabbed for her coat and bag. "Yes, sorry Kostas. You'll want to be locking up and getting home too. I'm coming now." She slid along the row of seats and worked her way up the dark aisle towards the square of lights where the doorway was. "Give my best to your family." She waved goodbye to the custodian and wandered out into the dusk.

Marie was waiting in her SUV at the curb.

"Sorry to keep you." Anne leaned over from the passenger seat and kissed her sister on the cheek. "I had an... an unexpected email that needed attention."

"I don't know why you won't get a car, Anne," was Marie's response. "Look at this traffic. It took me half an hour to get down here, and it will take twice as long to get home. I had to leave the boys with my mother-in-law, and you know how she is with them. She spoils them so badly, they are total bears when I get them back. And Charles won't tell her to stop, and she never listens to me. Why does no one ever think about me?"

Anne collapsed into the padded seat. This was not a new conversation. "I told you I would take the bus. You didn't need to come for me. I wouldn't miss my nephew's birthday."

"What? And leave you at the mercy of the transit system, and with all those people? You might catch something, and pass it along to me, and you know how I come down with every single bug and get so sick, and no one believes me. Don't get me started about what the boys bring home from school. I can't move off the couch for weeks each fall."

A black sedan pulled in front of the SUV and Marie pressed her hand into the horn, sending a blast of noise through the vehicle. "Damned aggressive drivers. Aw crap, now it's starting to rain. Really, Anne, I wish you'd drive so I don't have to pick you up all the time." She turned north onto a busy street, already a sea of tail lights reflecting off the damp midnight-black road. "Look at all this traffic. At least you have time to tell me again about this project you're doing."

"I told you all about it when I won the position last spring."

"Oh, Anne, you know I never listen. Now was the first day, wasn't it? Tell me again. I'll listen this time. Out of the way, blue Honda! This is my lane! Turn on the radio, would you, Anne? I can't concentrate on driving without music. No, not that station. Here, I can sing along with this. Don't cut me off, red Subaru! It's my lane!"

Anne closed her eyes against the glare of lights and her sister's off-key belting and resigned herself to the torture of the trip back to Marie's house.

At last, they reached their destination. The dusk had, by now, settled into night and the windows were all bright against the darkness. Charles' car was in the driveway; he must have gone to collect the boys from his parents' place two blocks away.

"Anne!" He greeted her with a hug that spoke of genuine affection. "Come in. Let me take your coat. The kids are watching some nonsense on the TV. I've put on the kettle if you want something hot, and there's wine in the fridge. Jakey wanted pizza, and it's his birthday, so I ordered some."

From the corner of her eye, Anne saw Marie scowl, but Charles continued on. "I won't take your bag. That must contain your big new piece, right? You'll want to hold on to that. Let's have a drink and I want to hear all about your day. It's not every day that someone's sister-in-law becomes the composer-in-residence for the National Philharmonic. Mum and Dad are here too, and they'll want to hear all about it. Tell us everything!"

She followed her brother-in-law into the family room. Her two nephews sat in a nook off the main room, eyes glued to some animated show on the television. They jumped up and gave Auntie Anne a quick hug and kiss before returning to their show. Charles' parents were seated on the large, overstuffed sofa. Brenda Musgrove hoisted her large body up from the cushions to crush Anne in a generous hug. Tom, larger still and less mobile, remained in his place, but his greeting was no less warm.

"Annie! Look at you, the great composer. It's always a treat to see you. Come, these old bones won't move, but you can sit between us. You look cold. We'll warm you up. Shift over, Brenda dear, so Annie can fit. There."

At last, nestled between Charles' parents on the sofa and with a glass of sherry in her hand, Anne finally succumbed and talked about her new role.

"It's something quite new, really." She took a sip from her glass, allowing the sweet liquid to slide down her throat. "I am the composer-in-residence for the National Philharmonic—"

"That's an orchestra, kids," Brenda shouted through the television's din.

"Basically, we're trying a new idea. Rather than just writing music and giving it to the orchestra to play, we're going to do something more cooperative. I'll give the orchestra a first draft, in a sense, of my symphony, and we'll workshop it together. I'll work with the conductor and the musicians and together we'll see what works and what doesn't. It's a bit scary, but also very exciting. I'm nervous about what they'll all say, but I know this will push me to the next level."

"You're too modest, Annie. Nervous? Don't be silly!" Tom threw a fleshy arm around her shoulder. "You were on the front page of the newspaper's entertainment section last weekend! I showed all our neighbours the article. 'Look! Anne Elliot, the famous composer. My daughter-in-law, practically.' We were so proud. And you've written the background music for a movie—one that people have actually seen! What could these musicians say other than that you're amazing?"

"I play the piano too," Marie interjected from where she stood by the window.

"Of course you do, dear," Brenda gave a deep nod that set her chins jiggling. "And so beautifully as well. The boys are so lucky to grow up in a house filled with lovely music all the time. Now Annie," she turned back, "what was today's thing, then? What's in that bag that Charles wouldn't take from you?"

Anne laughed. "The bag is not nearly as precious as all that! Today was the first read-through of my symphony. We haven't really started doing anything yet. I just wanted to hear it. I made a few notes—that's what's in the bag—but the real work will begin after the new conductor arrives. Ultimately, it's his interpretation that the audience will hear, so his input is key."

She heard the words as she spoke them, so unaffected and disinterested. *The conductor.* So simple. Like *the baker* or *the guy down the hall.* It didn't sound at all like each syllable squeezed a fist around her heart.

"Yes, well, that's all very nice, I'm sure." Marie's jaw was tight and her eyes narrow. Why was she always so cross when people's attention was focussed somewhere other than on her? Anne let out a little sigh as Marie continued. "But we should start to get ready for supper. Come boys, let's wash up. We want to be ready to eat when the pizza arrives. Really, Charles, you know how bad pizza is for them. They won't sleep well and Dylan will be up all night with a stomach-ache. And there is so much sugar in the cake too. They'll be sick all weekend, and you know that I'll be the one who has to look after them, and you know how poorly I do when I don't get enough sleep."

And on she went. Charles threw a supplicatory look to where Anne still sat on the sofa, and she answered with a wry shrug. Marie was Marie, and nothing would change her.

CHAPTER TWO
Accelerando

"Anne, darling!" Sophia emerged through the crowd of people gathered in the reception room and rushed towards Anne. She kissed her on the cheek, then rubbed a thumb across her skin to remove some lipstick. "You look so smart, all dressed up like that. Now we just need to get a bit of colour in your cheeks. Like my frock?"

She stepped back and made a slow rotation. Anne watched the lights glint off the delicate sequins along the neckline and the edging of her friend's pale gold jacket. The sleeves ended just above her elbows; the dress beneath must be sleeveless. It suited Sophia's slim figure and blond pixie cut perfectly.

"It's lovely, but you always look like you've stepped out of a magazine. You must spend half your income on clothing alone."

Sophia laughed. "Not mine, darling, Jeremy's. But he likes to see me dress up, and so he doesn't complain. Here, let's look at you properly. Show off for me."

Anne struck an awkward pose. In the mirror along the far wall, she caught a glimpse of herself, pale face and dark hair, the 1950s-style deep teal dress looking not quite right on her frame. It was neither too large nor too small, but just looked... a bit off. "Stand tall, Annie, darling. Shoulders back. You've got a lovely figure. Don't be afraid to show it off. We can't all have such a curvy shape. Pretend you're happy to be here. You always hate the spotlight, don't you? Well, it's a lovely shade of blue, even if you could use a bit more colour in your cheeks. Shall we find a camera and smile?"

"Oh God, no! Anything but. Where is Jeremy, anyway?"

Sophia grinned. In the reflected image, Anne thought her friend looked younger than she herself, even though Sophia was ten years older. Or, Anne grimaced, she looked ten years older than she ought. She reached up to pinch her cheeks a bit to encourage a flush.

"My darling husband is being the media darling right now. There he is, by that gaggle of reporters. It was quite the coup getting Frederico here. He is such a splash in Europe these days; they can't get enough of him. And Jeremy convinced him to give it all up to come home. He's crowing, and who can blame him?"

Now Anne's chuckle was genuine. "Being the principal conductor of the National Philharmonic is hardly 'giving it all up.'

He's only thirty-four, after all. That's practically a baby in this field. And he'll still have time to tour the world's orchestras."

"Now, now, don't be lessening Jeremy's triumph." Sophia gave another exuberant smile. "The fellow from *The Times-Tribune* wants to meet you. Maybe do a feature. Wouldn't that be splendid? I'm so glad you dressed up."

God, Anne hated these events. She was not the sort to preen before a camera, but wished only to hide away in her studio and speak through her music. Let the notes be her words, the orchestra be her voice. Having to stand there, face-to-face with some eager reporter, trying to remember where she hid her public smile, was akin to torture. But it was a part of the job and, with great reluctance, she allowed Sophia to grab her hand and drag her through the elegant crowd.

"Shep?" Sophia called to a forty-something man in a blazer and dark jeans and wielding an iPad and stylus. He spun around and Anne felt his eyes settle on her. Then, in a moment of recognition, he grinned.

"Dr. Elliot! I was hoping to meet you today. Shep Choi, from *The Times-Tribune*. I can't get enough of your score from *The Butterfly's Kiss*, and I was hoping to do an exclusive on you. Maybe a short series, two or three articles. Your past, your music, where you see yourself going from here. When you got this position as composer-in-residence, I convinced my editor, and he is as excited as I am. No, no, don't decide now. Well, do decide now if the answer is yes. But perhaps we can talk sometime. Here's my card. Oh… no pockets. No problem. I'll email my contact info to Mrs. Croft here, and she can forward it to you."

He dropped his voice to a conspiratorial whisper. "Tell me, did you really use ancient Chinese folk melodies for your thematic material in the battle scenes? My mother insists she knows that tune. She's seen the movie four times, and she hates anything other than Hallmark movies."

Anne forced a smile, quashing her discomfort at being so openly the object of interest and admiration. "Thank you," she managed. Why hadn't the floor swallowed her up yet? "Your mother has good ears. I searched through hundreds of traditional Chinese melodies before finding one that spoke both to the rich culture of the area where the battles occurred, as well as to Western musical expectations. I wanted to incorporate elements that would be true to, and respectful of, both traditions. I hope I succeeded."

Shep had pressed the button on his tablet and was scribbling away with the stylus. "May I quote you on that?" He looked up with hopeful eyes. "I can keep it for the exposé... let me arrange a time for a first meeting. Okay? Fantastic. I look forward to it. My wife just can't get enough of your *Preludes*. She is such a fan."

It seemed Anne's actual agreement was not quite necessary. She did not mind; publicity was part of the job, after all. But why did it all have to feel like a rogue bulldozer, relentless and completely unstoppable?

"Anything will have to go by the committee," Sophia interjected. "If it relates to the orchestra..."

"Yes, of course, of course. Lovely to see you again, Mrs. Croft, and a real pleasure, Dr. Elliot. We'll talk soon! Gotta get to the front of the crowd for when the speeches start. I see Mr. Croft already making his way to the front of the room." And with a wink and a quick shake of the hand, the reporter was off, melting into the glittering crowd.

He was correct. The speeches soon began. First Jeremy Croft spoke in his role as president of the orchestra's Board of Directors. Anne had always admired Jeremy, and not just as her friend's husband. Jeremy was tall and handsome in a rough sort of way, not the sort of face you'd expect on a tireless supporter of classical music. But he wore a tuxedo as comfortably as most men wear jeans and he spoke with a passion and commitment that left few unmoved. He had been one of Anne's biggest supporters when she first started her career. It was he who had encouraged her to apply for grants and loans to further her career; it was he who had reached deep into his Rolodex (no matter that it was all electronic these days) and given her the contact information for a friend in the movie industry. That email had ultimately resulted in her being chosen to write the score for *The Butterfly's Kiss*, which had made her famous. And it was Jeremy who had proposed she apply for the newly created position of composer-in-residence for the National Philharmonic. He had, of course, taken a leave from his role over the months that the board interviewed and listened and considered applicants—their choice of Anne Elliot was not due to his influence—but it was no secret that he was her biggest fan. She loved him like a brother.

Now she watched him behind the podium, seducing the microphone, making love to the cameras. They loved him and he loved them.

He thanked the board, the executive team, and the press, and made a few opening remarks before continuing. "We are incredibly proud of the success our orchestra has seen these last few years. In an age when so many arts organisations are fighting for scarce resources and recognition, our innovative programming has enabled us to reach out to sections of the community that would not ordinarily find us, and the collaborative results have been astounding. The partnership with the Hip Hop Collective two years ago is still bearing fruit, with youngsters now coming to our concerts on a regular basis and our musicians working with rap artists in their new endeavours. And last year we announced our innovative new composer-in-residence program, which has brought rising star Anne Elliot into our midst." Heads turned in her direction and a soft wave of applause interrupted Jeremy's speech.

"You all know Anne, of course," he beamed as he gazed across to where she stood. Beside her, Sophia gave an excited shimmy that sent her drop earrings dancing and her armful of bracelets jingling. "Anne is that rare, rare creature whose music has captured both the minds of the critics and the hearts of audiences everywhere. Her *Preludes* have garnered nothing but critical acclaim across the world, and last spring's blockbuster hit *The Butterfly's Kiss* has made her a household name. We are beyond delighted that she will be working with the orchestra for the next three years.

"And now we will add one more brilliant name to our roster. The reason we are all here today. I am beyond thrilled to announce that the National Philharmonic has engaged a new principal conductor. This man is young but not green. He has burned up the stages of Europe, where he has been living for the last eight years, and is adored by musicians and audiences alike. He has recorded over a dozen albums with some of the world's finest orchestras, and his touring schedule is booked for the next ten years. But he is no stranger, because this is where he comes from, where he grew up. We are delighted to be bringing him back to his hometown. Ladies and gentlemen, our new principal conductor, local boy Frederico Valore!"

The room erupted into gasps and squeals and the hum took a long time to settle. Sophia was all but bouncing in her designer heels and calls of *Bravo* and *Congratulations* sounded from all around. Eventually, the buzz settled to a low murmur and Jeremy was able to speak again.

"And we have him with us today—in a way! Please direct your attention to the monitor in the corner," he gestured to a large television screen that had been linked to an Internet feed. "Here he is, our star of the day, Maestro Valore himself, joining us remotely, all the way from Rome."

The black square in the centre of the screen dissolved into a clear image, and at last Anne saw, for the first time in eight years, the face that had haunted her dreams every night since that awful day when he left her and broke her heart.

CHAPTER THREE
Doloroso

Anne pulled the throw blanket around her shoulders and nuzzled the warm fleece for a moment with her cheek. The drizzles of late November had ripened into the sleet and snow of February, and there was nowhere she wished to be right now more than deep underneath this warm blanket, with endless hot cocoa at her side. She had even moved her electric kettle to the round table next to the couch and set up a portable desk, so she really never needed to move. At one hand, her mug and hot chocolate powder; at the other, her computer, music manuscript paper, and a selection of writing utensils. All was good with the world.

Damn. The phone. It was all the way across the room on the little table at her front door. She shrugged out of her warm cocoon and shuffled across the cold floor, hoping to get to it before the caller gave up. Then she would have to listen to a message and return a call, and these things filled her with dread.

"Hello?"

"Anne. Phyllis Russell here."

"Professor Russell!" Anne slipped back beneath her warm throw. "How lovely to hear from you. How have you been?"

"Now, Anne, we have discussed this. It's been six years since you were my student, and you are by far more famous than me now. Phyllis will do quite well."

"Yes, er... I'll try. Old habits."

The older woman laughed, her alto voice ringing clearly through the mobile phone.

"I just saw the feature Shep Choi wrote about you in the *Times-Tribune*. Very nice. Very nice indeed. I've been meaning to call for a while now, and this made me pick up the phone."

Of course. Professor Russell always hated technology. She even eschewed the new music notation programs, with all the wonderful bells and whistles that came with them, in favour of musty sheets of paper and a pencil. Still, her music was first rate, and she had been the finest composition teacher Anne had ever had. She had instilled a deep knowledge of the form and theory of music while never crushing Anne's distinctive voice. She owed so much to this woman. A chat on the phone was a very small price to pay.

"It's wonderful to hear your voice. And thanks. I was pleased with the article. We spent a great deal of time together, and I wondered what terrible secrets I might have let slip. He's a nice man. I met his mother and his wife, and they even fed me. I could just imagine the headline: *Local composer spills soup*."

She chuckled and Professor Russell laughed with her. "Well, soup or no soup, it was splendid. He clearly likes you a lot and knows his music."

"He did his undergrad in music performance before switching to journalism. We got on well, even though I hate being interviewed."

They spoke for a while about the article and other sundry matters: the weather, a planned trip to Spain, their old associates at the music department of the University, the latest popular novel.

Then Professor Russell cleared her throat.

Uh oh. She always did this when she was about to say something she thought Anne might not like.

"I couldn't help but discover the news from the orchestra. I was in India learning Tabla when the announcement came out, as you know, but it was all over when I got back. Frederico... that's... news."

"Yes." Suddenly, the blanket wasn't so warm anymore.

"I never did understand what everybody saw in him. He seemed just another maestro-wannabe to me, more than adequate for some provincial orchestra somewhere, or a top community orchestra, but..." She paused. "The top stages of Europe? Does he really merit that? Is he that gifted a conductor? Or is it all about how the cameras love his face?"

Now the blanket was too warm.

"He is a very handsome man."

"You did the right thing, Anne. If you had gone off with him, you would never have completed your doctorate. You'd never have finished your *Preludes*. They're what made you famous."

"I think..."

"Anne?"

"I might not have written *Preludes*, but I would have written something else."

"Surely you don't regret staying to finish your degree."

Anne pulled the blanket back around her shoulders. "I don't regret the degree, but I do have regrets. I made a mistake—we both made mistakes—and I've regretted it every day since he left."

Over the next few weeks, the schedule for the orchestra's coming season settled into some sort of shape. Frederico mainly dealt with the orchestra's board of directors, but since he would, by the nature of their respective positions, work closely with Anne, she was often drawn into the meetings. Jeremy Croft, it transpired, knew Frederico well from his first years in Europe when Jeremy had been working with one of the German orchestras for a season, and the two were often found chatting on some video conferencing platform when Anne arrived. Sophia tended to stay out of orchestral management affairs, preferring the music to the politics, but announced over coffee one afternoon that she had joined in some of her husband's chats with the new conductor and found him more charming than when she last had spoken to him. She referred to him often, Fred this and Fred that. "I knew him just a bit before he left," she explained, "not so very well, but enough to chat at functions. He was so young then, but he's really grown into himself.

"You knew him too, of course," she smiled behind her latte. "I think I remember you two talking at a few events. Did you work much together? This was back when we had just met, you and I. I know you were in different fields, but the doctoral music program must be pretty small, right?"

So she didn't know. This was a relief.

"Yeah, we knew each other."

"Were you close?"

How to answer this? Anne took a deep drink of her tea while she scrambled for an answer.

"We all were, in different ways."

"It must be so exciting to have him back. I wonder if he's changed much in person. He's a rather handsome man."

Handsome was not the beginning of it. From that day of the press conference, when she had seen him for the first time in nearly a decade, his face was all that she saw when she closed her eyes. The years had taken some of the boyishness and left strong masculine lines in their place. But his dark eyes had lost none of their depth and sparkle, and his curly hair looked as thick and black as ever. Would it feel the same now as it did then? Would her fingers remember the spring of his curls as she touched them? Or had the passing of years taken those tactile memories from her, just as they had taken the light from her own eyes?

Sophia was staring at her. Right. It was her turn to speak.

"Yes, he is handsome. He always has been. He is not so different. I would have known him anywhere." An ache began to grow in her heart. What had she lost?

She took another drink of her tea to disguise her distress. So many memories were lying buried, barricaded behind a wall she had constructed to keep them hidden and away. She could not weaken now. Like a dam holding back a mighty river, the slightest crack—the first recollection—would shatter the entire barricade and she would drown in the deluge.

"Anne?" Oh. Sophia was still speaking.

"Sorry. Daydreaming. I've been up late working on the last movement. It was so informative hearing the orchestra play through the first two movements last November; I've been reworking some of my ideas to take advantage of some particular strengths. The oboist is absolutely amazing..."

"You can tell me tomorrow night. Jeremy will want to hear it, too. This is what I was saying while you were in La-la-land a moment ago. Come for dinner tomorrow. It's too long since you've been over and Jeremy was saying he hardly sees you outside of board meetings. Seven o'clock?"

"OK. Thanks. That will be nice."

"And dress up a bit. We have a treat. Guess who else is coming. Frederico! Weren't we both surprised when he called yesterday to let us know he was on his way. He flew in from Rome only this morning, and Jeremy is running around with him looking at apartments. Isn't that wonderful?"

The teacup shook in Anne's hand and the table swam out of focus. Was she about to faint?

Wonderful.

Shit.

CHAPTER FOUR
First Theme

He was there. Sitting in the large armchair, one leg thrown casually across the opposite knee, laughing at something Jeremy had said. Anne stood just behind the doorway leading into the sitting room, wanting to see but not to be seen. "Give me a moment," she had mouthed to Sophia, who shrugged and went to put Anne's coat and purse away.

Fred, not on the screen, not some dissociated image that she could pretend was no more real than a television character, but there. In person. Larger than life. Anne's heart pounded and she wiped her damp palms over her thighs. Oh, God - had she stained her skirt? Her eyes flickered to the large mirror above the hall table. There was no colour in her face and the deep blue shirt she had chosen at home now made her look washed out, a black and white sketch in the midst of a rich oil painting. Even her lips, so carefully outlined and coloured in with lipstick, seemed wrong. And her low ponytail, which looked so elegant and understated in her own bedroom, now looked harsh and austere. Even her eyes seemed flat to her gaze. She was a shapeless, styleless mess. Not like him. Like Fred.

He had always dressed beautifully, and time overseas had honed his style. He was wearing slim charcoal trousers and a light turtleneck that shimmered gently like woven silk and he looked very European. If she had not known him, she would expect him to speak with an accent.

Italian, of course. His family was from somewhere near Florence and he had just come from a stint with one of Rome's leading orchestras, and he spoke the language as fluently as if it were his native tongue. Which, of course, it was. It was the language he spoke with his parents and siblings at home. But he had been born here, in Toronto, and went to school and university here, and was as comfortable in a big modern North American city as he was in an ancient and tradition-steeped city in Europe. He was a man of two worlds. In this intimate setting, he would have to speak to her, but surely he had outgrown her. Her name might be known around the world, but with every new level of fame, she felt her own universe shrink, each new commission sending her further into her mind to coax out the music, pulling her further away from the greater world. For Fred, it was the opposite. Each step upwards for him propelled him further into the world. If she had gone with him, would she have expanded past her cocoon too?

Would she have grown wings and learned to sip wine under a Parisian sky?

More memories. More regrets. She slammed the door on her thoughts.

"Anne, darling!" Jeremy glanced up and saw her. He rose from his seat to pull her into the room. "Come, come in. What are you standing there for? Come, you must meet… oh, but you know each other already, don't you?"

Fred rose as Jeremy stepped out of the way, but his eyes were full of questions, not recognition. Oh God. He didn't even recognise her. After all they had been to each other, and he didn't even recognise her face. She tried to smile, to be friendly, and could tell the exact moment he realised who she was. Hadn't they told him she was coming tonight?

"Anne." His voice was deeper than she recalled it, more sonorous than on videoconference. "How have you been?"

No comments about it being good to see her again, or whether he had missed her. Just a polite "how'dye do?" like any almost-stranger would ask.

"Well, thank you. Congratulations. The orchestra is lucky to have you."

"And to you as well. You are famous. Your music is spectacular." Such polite nothings.

A beat.

"You look… different. Your hair?"

"Oh. Yes. I find it easier to pull it back. I'm not twenty-three anymore."

"No. Of course. None of us is."

Silence.

"Well, what a treat this is!" Sophia had entered the room, and she was in full-out hostess mode. Anne knew that tone of voice. "Have a seat, Anne, and let me get you something to drink before dinner is ready. Fred was just telling us about some of the places he saw today..."

From here, Anne allowed herself to fade into the background, letting the conversation flow around her like a stone in a stream. She was there; she was acknowledged. But the water continued on its relentless course despite her presence. Sophia was garrulous enough to continue a conversation unaided, and Fred was equal to her. With Jeremy's sporadic interjections, there was no need whatsoever for her to utter a word, other than an occasional "yes" or "of course."

As for Fred himself, he seemed to be revelling in the spotlight. It was his milieu, after all. Unlike a composer, who completes her work in solitude, pouring out her soul to a sheet of lined paper or a computer screen, a conductor lives his art in public. One does not lead an orchestra in solitude; rather, every nuance and every emotion must be made grand and public, to be received and made apparent to all. How different they were, but how well they worked together.

At some unseen signal, they moved from the living room to the dining room. Sophia and Jeremy were both excellent cooks, and for tonight, they had brought in their housekeeper's daughter to serve and clean up. She was a university student studying urban design, and Anne had met her before and liked the girl. But for now, it allowed the four to dine uninterrupted by the need to get up and bring in the next course or refill the water jug.

"Are you here for good, Fred?" Sophia asked as she waited for her soup to cool. "Surely you still have commitments at your old gig in Rome." She blew gently on the fragrant soup. Anne took a sip of her own: pear, squash, and the perfect amount of ginger, with a swirl of crème fraîche. She had never had a bad dish in the Croft home. She savoured the combination of flavours as Fred finished his own spoonful and answered.

"I need to be back at the end of June. This is the time of year when they usually bring in guest conductors, anyway. I have a couple of engagements in Chicago, one in Montreal and one in Vancouver, and each of those will take me out of town for about a week. Then it's back to Rome for the final concert of their season, but I'm making this my permanent address pretty much immediately. I'll pack up when I'm in Rome in June, and hopefully I'll be able to move into my own apartment here as soon as I'm back. I liked those two we saw again today—the one on St. Clair Avenue and the one near High Park—so hopefully I'll get a lease signed for one of them before I have to fly off to Chicago next week."

"Where are you staying now?" Jeremy asked.

"My parents!" Fred chortled. "Yeah, I know. Thirty-four years old and living in my mother's basement again. If I weren't going to be dashing all over the continent for the next couple of months, I would find something short-term, but for a week at a time, I can put up with it. Besides," he mused, "I've missed them. I loved being in Europe. I loved being the star and the man of the hour and everything this amazing career has given me, but the spotlight gets tiring after a while. I miss hanging out with my dad in front of the TV to watch soccer, and I miss my mom feeding me tastes of her tomato sauce, and I miss just being me. I'm not going to slow down my career, but I'm ready to take another step in my life and find a home, somewhere I can stay and put down roots."

"Looking to find someone and get married?" Jeremy teased.

Fred gave a great laugh. "I'm not going about it like a project or some mercenary venture, but the thought had crossed my mind. I want a family and a stable life. Find me the right woman," he grinned, "who loves music and who can stand my travelling, and she can have me for a song, as long as she stays in key!"

His eyes did not even flicker once towards Anne.

"Anne?"

Anne fumbled with her phone. It was six thirty in the morning. What was Marie thinking?

"Yeah..." she mumbled. "It's early, Marie. What's up?"

"Charles just left on his business trip a few minutes ago. He had to get to the airport early. So I thought I'd see how you're doing."

"It's six thirty in the morning."

"I know, but I was up anyway to help Charles." Anne could hear the slurp of coffee. "Where were you last night?"

"Oh God, Marie. Are you Mom now? I was out at the Crofts. Sophia asked me for dinner."

"Why didn't she ask us too? I'm the one who introduced you to her, after all. I mean, it's Charles who works for them, not you. Well, never mind. Look, Anne, why don't you come over today? Maybe this afternoon, when the boys are back from school. They love hanging out with you. Maybe I could set up the spare room if you want to stay over."

"So I can look after them, you mean? Don't sputter, Marie. It's too early for games."

"Well, I just thought, since they are your nephews, you know!"

"And I adore them. But I'm not their full-time babysitter."

"I thought you'd want to spend some real time with them, because it's not like you're likely to have your own kids, now, are you?"

"Can this possibly wait till after I've had coffee? Or maybe a drink or two?"

"Well, it's true, isn't it? You're nearly thirty-two and I don't think you've gone on two dates in the last eight years. You do know how babies are made, don't you, Anne? Anyway, it's not like you have anything to do."

"Marie!" Anne had to restrain herself from throwing the phone against the wall. She lowered her voice; it would do no good to disturb the neighbours with her shouts this early in the morning. "I happen to have a lot to do. I need to get the final movement done in draft before the play-through in May, and then I need—"

"Oh really, Anne, how hard can that be? You just think of tunes and then write them down. You can do that while helping get the boys ready for bed."

"Sorry, Marie. Gotta go. Bye."

Anne pressed the disconnect button on her phone before her sister could say anything else and rolled over. She pulled the covers over her head in hopes of sleeping a bit more, but a few minutes of tossing and shifting proved that this would be impossible.

She dragged herself upright and slipped on her gown before padding to the kitchen to make some coffee. She would have to find another place to plug in her phone at night. No one else called at such unreasonable times. She had her phone set to do-not-disturb for most people, but she had flagged Marie as an accepted caller in case something urgent came up with the boys or with their parents. Perhaps she ought to change that to Charles' number rather than her sister's.

Was it true, though? These were not thoughts she welcomed as she waited for the coffee maker to come to life, but they would not be silenced. Was she destined to live out her life alone? She had tried to date after Fred left. She had met some very nice guys, and she was... she used to be... not unattractive.

There was Anton, the PhD student, with his wry sense of humour and his invariably poor taste in clothing. He was smart and interesting and more than a little bit cute, and she went out with him two or three times. But she could never think of him as anything other than a friend. At another time, if things had been different, perhaps something could have developed between them. They certainly got on well enough. But it was clear that he was, as they say, friend-zoned from the start.

Then, a while later, there was Rajiv. He was not a musician at all, but an architect whom she met through some mutual friends. Again, he was a terrific guy... for somebody else. His ready laugh and willingness to embrace every new experience were charming and more than attractive—not to mention that gorgeous black hair! Whoever ended up with him would be a lucky woman. But Anne's heart refused to open to the possibility, and they soon parted ways.

Had she dated anybody since them? Other than the occasional coffee with somebody at Marie or Sophia's urging, she could not recall a single one. Her soul had withdrawn deep into herself; she had locked away her heart. When Fred had left, she had sealed it off with a wall of pain and had not released it since.

And now Fred was back, and he seemed to have lost all interest in her.

Marie was right. She would likely remain single forever.

CHAPTER FIVE
Repetizione, più forte

April melted into May, and then June. Anne had not seen Fred since the dinner at the Crofts, although she heard about him everywhere she went. Jeremy had, at some point, introduced Fred to Charles, and the two had formed quite a fast friendship. At every turn, Marie talked about Fred coming over to watch the baseball, or of him and Charles taking in a pre-season football game at the stadium, or of the fabulous stories he told about his years in Europe.

"You should come over after the game sometime," Marie urged, but Anne always found some excuse. Seeing Fred only tore at her wounded heart, and he clearly had no interest in her anymore.

Sophia, too, talked all the time about the new conductor. She and Jeremy had gone with him to decide on the apartment he would take for the next year, and had appointed themselves a sort of older brother and sister to him. They went to art exhibits and plays in town, as well as day trips in the surrounding areas.

Anne heard about bike trips and hiking excursions and visits to wineries and local historical sites. She was invited along for none of these.

"I don't remember Fred being such an outdoors type," she mused to Sophia over one of their regular coffees. "He always seemed happier doing inside things."

All manner of memories came unbidden to her mind. She remembered him grimacing at the idea of ice skating outdoors. "It's cold out there, you know?" he would grumble. "People invented inside for a reason." But still, they would go every now and then and do two or three laps around some frozen rink, then hurry into the lodge for a hot chocolate. Later on, they would curl up together on a lumpy IKEA sofa, wrapped up in a single blanket, talking, laughing, and getting lost in each other. His hands would wander and she allowed it with great pleasure, stopping him only to tease him about something or to change the music on the CD player.

Then came the flood of memories of him talking about his one and only attempt at camping. His family were not the sort for roughing it in nature, and he had gone on his first trip with friends in university. She remembered him complaining about the heat and the insects and the discomfort. "The air mattress I brought along was like a pancake!" he had grumbled. "A roll of bubble-wrap would have been more comfortable. And the washrooms! Oh my God, Annie! Literally a hole in the ground! There was a shower, but it was so awful I just dunked myself into the lake at six in the morning when there was no one around to see me!"

They had laughed together, and suddenly, she could almost feel his arms as he pulled her closer to nestle along his side. Then he had smiled at her and she had smiled at him and he had kissed her in that wonderful way he had, and ended up in bed, and they never talked of outdoor adventures again.

But Sophia was privy to none of these recollections, nor was she even aware of their previous relationship, and so replied in a matter-of-fact voice.

"I suppose people change over time and discover new things. Jeremy asked if Fred did a lot of cycling, and he said he got into it in Europe. It was a way to get into shape. He realised he needed to be in top physical shape to conduct—it's hard work, you know, waving your arms around like that for an hour or more at a time. He told us a few stories about his first attempts along the Seine in Paris, and how he found he really enjoyed it. It sounds like he ended up doing a few long rides each year, up and down the rivers and through the countryside. I have to say, by the time he finished talking, Jeremy and I were about ready to drive straight to the airport and fly off to Italy or somewhere with our bikes.

"Hmmmm." What was she to say? That she wished she had been along on those rides? That these were her dreams that Fred had ended up living without her? The invisible hand squeezed tighter around her heart.

"Do you ride, Anne? Going to Niagara was Fred's idea, and it was a great one. The side roads are empty and flat, and it's very pretty there. Are you up for an adventure? Let's go sometime, you and I.

When do you have your next date with the orchestra? We could go the following week."

Anne sipped her tea. "They're playing through the last two movements next Thursday. We've got two sessions booked, so I can have them go over passages I want to hear again and so I can talk to the musicians about them. I've never worked this way before, so collaboratively with the orchestra. Usually we just give them the music and they play it. But this process is fascinating, and I'm learning a lot from how they react."

"Then the following Monday! You can take the weekend to make your notes and whatever it is you do, and we'll drive down after that. Do you have a bike? I'll rent you one. But I'll buy you a helmet. You don't want someone else's. Lice, you know? Hmmm..." She stared into the distance. "Pity Fred will still be in Italy. I think he'd enjoy coming along. His last concert with his orchestra there is on Saturday night. But he said he needs to pack up his old flat there and have everything shipped over. I think he'll be glad not to be flying all over the map for a while. Is your tea finished? Let me get you another."

So he was back in Rome. She had known he had some final engagements there, but hadn't known the date. Once, she would have known his schedule down to when his rehearsal breaks were.

Her eyes followed Sophia as she walked to the counter to order more drinks. She really must find a way to stop thinking of Fred all the time. But it seemed that it was becoming impossible to avoid him, and soon enough, they would be working together. She brushed away that invisible hand around her heart and locked her feelings away behind yet another wall of ice. And she felt another five years settle onto her shoulders and etch themselves upon her once-pretty face.

This was the day. A thrill of excitement tingled its way up Anne's spine as she made her way into the theatre. She had not been here since that first play-through last November. How long ago that seemed. She waved a cheerful hello to Kostas, the theatre custodian, and asked briefly after his family.

"Thank you, Dr. Elliot. You are always kind to ask after them. My daughter is enjoying her high school very much. She is in the visual arts program, and her poster design was chosen to be the official poster for the school's winter concert."

"You must be very proud of her!" Anne had seen pictures on Kostas' phone of his daughter's designs, and the girl was very talented.

"We are. Very much. And my son! How hard he has worked. Only last week, he was accepted into his first choice of university." Kostas beamed and puffed out his chest. "He was not a good student when he started high school, but this last year and a half, he has changed and worked so hard, and now this is his reward."

And Anne mirrored his great smile. In the short time she had known Kostas, she had heard a great deal about his two children and felt as proud of them as if she were an honorary aunt. "I am delighted. I truly am. Offer him my heartiest congratulations."

She was still beaming when, a moment later, she swished through the heavy double doors into the theatre space itself where the orchestra was setting up.

Most of the people here she knew, some quite well and others by sight. She had attended a handful of rehearsals before submitting her proposal for the composer-in-residence position, wishing to know what forces were at her disposal: their strengths, their weaknesses, their personalities. She smiled quietly at one or two as she scanned the banks of seats for a place to sit.

Her eyes stopped for a second on an unexpected figure. There, in the far aisle, was somebody she did not know. He was not one of the musicians, that was clear. He had no instrument or case and he stood quite still at the side of the auditorium. Furthermore, he was wearing a suit and tie. The orchestra members were all dressed far more casually, some in jeans and t-shirts, some in shorts, others in skirts and blouses. He was staring at the cluster of chairs and music stands under the bright lights and seemed quite unaware of her. She took a moment to examine him better.

He was a fine-looking man, handsome even, no more than forty, with thick wavy hair whose colour she could not quite determine under these lights. Light brown? Auburn? He seemed to be examining the stage quite intently, glancing now and then to the musicians still gathered in the front rows of the theatre, then back to the chairs and music stands that were set up for them. Whoever could he be? It didn't matter; she was there to write the music. It was not up to her who did or did not attend rehearsal, although she must make certain he wasn't recording any of her new piece.

"Hi Anne!" An arm shot up from a clump of musicians and waved at her. She isolated the face attached to the arm and waved back, the stranger quickly forgotten.

"Xi, hi!" She made her way over to talk to him. She had known the violinist since their university days, and while they had never been particularly close friends, they had always been friendly, and she was happy to catch up for a moment.

He introduced her to the people around him. Caroline was a cellist, a pretty young woman in her mid-twenties, with long dark hair pulled back into a ponytail. Then there was Viktor, who played the bassoon, tall and lank like his instrument, and Louisa, the French horn player. Anne had taken note of Louisa at the previous rehearsal because she had written an extended horn solo into the second movement and had been pleased at how Louisa had executed the difficult part. She was short and spunky looking, with huge earrings dangling from her earlobes and bright blue hair cut into a spiky pixie style.

The musicians all raved about the first part of the symphony, which they had played those long weeks ago, and expressed their excitement at reading through the rest of it at this rehearsal. They were friendly and enthusiastic and responded to Anne's relaxed grin with their own.

They chatted for a moment about timbre and cadences and the trouble humidity played on different instruments. This was her world; these were her people. She was content.

A ruffle of movement at the periphery of her vision caught her attention. It was Jean-Michel Tremblay, the interim conductor, making his way down the aisle.

"Excuse me, everyone," she nodded to her new acquaintances. "I need to check a couple of things with the maestro, but hopefully we can chat later. I enjoyed meeting you all." She parted with another warm smile and made her way to the rotund conductor.

As the musicians assembled on the stage and the comforting din of them all warming up filled the air, she went over her manuscripts and the printed parts with Jean-Michel, pointing out something here and asking his thoughts on something there, until it was time for the rehearsal to start.

"One thing," she remembered. "That man over there..." She glanced to where the stranger was still standing by the mirrored walls at the side of the room. "Do you know him? I can't have this recorded at all."

"Yes, he's alright. That's William Barnett. He's new on the board. I said he could come, but I will make certain he knows."

"Thanks."

The conductor wandered over to speak to the newcomer, and then, with a nod to Anne, headed to the stage. He climbed the stairs to the stage and stepped onto his low podium, and immediately the chaos of strings and horns and flutes fell silent, everyone anticipating his opening remarks and the first flick of his baton.

But instead of inviting the musicians to turn to the third movement of the music before them, he cleared his throat.

"Bonjour," he began, and acknowledged the murmured replies. "Today we have the honour of doing a first reading of the second half of Anne Elliot's new symphony..." He paused for a rush of applause and the sound of bows tapping on music stands. "Anne, come give us a bow. I know I introduced you when we read the first part last November, but let's welcome you again."

Anne climbed the stairs to the stage and nodded to the orchestra. She was not built for the spotlight; she was no fan of crowds. But here, with an orchestra, she was at home, and the seventy-odd faces smiling back at her were far from intimidating. It was, she had to admit, a rush like none other to hear her music come to life under the talented fingers of this gifted crew of musicians. From the corner of her eye, she noticed the stranger's eyes fixed upon her. *A rare sighting of the elusive composer in its natural habitat.* She grinned at her internal joke and the man grinned back.

Her smile still in place, she found herself a seat in the auditorium and took out her score and her tablet and stylus, ready to take notes, and waited for the downbeat.

The first hour passed in a heartbeat. From the first note, Anne had been transported into her own world, listening, writing, floating on cushions of sound. The music swirled about her like a river wending its relentless way to the sea, now tarrying in a wide pool of gentle melody, now swirling along in a rush of cascading scales or whipping into the rapids of staccato counterpoint. An eddy here, a chute there, the river nonetheless never varied from its course until at last it reached its destination in a series of grand chords that rang from the baffles at the back of the stage, resonating long after the final notes were played.

In that moment of silence, as Jean-Michel rested his arms and the musicians took a collective breath after the roiling finale, a lone voice rang from the back of the hall.

"Bravo! It's a masterpiece. Bravo!"

Her heart all but stopped. She knew that voice. But wasn't he supposed to be in Rome?

"Mesdames et messieurs," Jean-Michel beamed, "here is another treat for you today. We weren't sure whether to expect him, but here he is. Your principal conductor for next season, Maestro Valore."

Another wave of taps and claps filled the hall as Fred jogged down the aisle and all but leapt onto the stage. He belonged there like a fish belongs in water or a bird in the air. He seemed bigger, somehow, even just standing there and acknowledging the welcome.

"We'll take a break now, and come back in twenty to go over some of these passages again. Maestro? If you wish...?"

Jean-Michel and Fred huddled off together, and the musicians rose from their seats to stretch and chat before the rehearsal resumed.

A group of the musicians swarmed towards her.

"Anne, it's fabulous!"

"Ms. Elliot, what an honour to play this for the first time."

"You've created a masterpiece!"

The adulation continued and Anne could not stop her wide grin, even as she blushed. Tim, one of the violinists whom she had known for a while, pulled an arm about her shoulders and gave her a brotherly hug. "Looking good too, Anne! Genius becomes you!"

She glanced up to where the man, Barnett, had been standing before the rehearsal, and caught her reflection in the mirrors by the loges. With her smile and pink cheeks, she did look a bit... fresher than usual. Almost younger. A movement caught her eye. Mr.

Barnett. He had taken a seat just off the aisle, and now stood up and nodded to her. She dipped her head at him in acknowledgement; he was a member of the board, and was being friendly. No need to be stand-offish. Her smile still in place, she turned back to Tim just as Jean-Michel came over with his score. It was time to go over her notes before the rehearsal resumed.

From what she could see, Fred was the centre of his own little galaxy of star-gazers. He was still on the stage where he looked so much at home, and his admirers were mostly women. Of course. He was a very handsome man, after all, as well as being the new maestro. Anne noticed Louisa's peacock-blue hair among the heads, standing very close to Fred. She ignored the twinge of jealousy that taunted her and turned her attention back to Jean-Michel and the score.

"Here… I'd like to go over this section again, to see if I need to rework the parts to bring out the cross-rhythms. They're getting lost in the brass and I might need to thin out the parts. And here, at rehearsal letter C, can we try to bring out the middle voices in the strings? The violas have a key part, and the violins are just a bit too loud…"

They conferred for a while until the break was over and the musicians reassembled in their seats on the stage.

"May I?" Fred stood in the aisle, gesturing to the seat beside her. In the distance, Mr. Barnett was watching, his expression lost in the dim lighting.

"Yes, of course." He slid into the chair.

"What were you talking about with Jean-Michel? He's very good. He's been an excellent interim conductor for them. It's good to have different voices. But I think he'll be pleased to be back in Montreal full time."

Anne nodded. "His wife and kids are there. Here," she brought out the score, "this is what we were going over." She found the passages and pointed them out to Fred, who nodded and hummed a passage or two as he read along.

"Yes. I see… and there, you want more clarity in the horns. And I think… Hmmm…"

He leapt up while the orchestra was tuning their instruments before the downbeat, and called to Jean-Michel, who crouched down to chat to him for a moment. Then he returned with a cocky smirk on his face.

"What was that about?" Anne asked.

Fred winked. "You'll see."

What was this? Suddenly, after all those weeks of him all but pretending she didn't exist, Fred was giving her his attention again. Sitting next to her, talking to her. Smiling, even. Teasing. She recalled him standing up on the stage during the break, surrounded by the cloud of women, Louisa all but hanging off him, and she could see the smug satisfaction on his handsome face. He must know she had seen him. Was he deliberately rubbing her nose in his success with the women? Was this his new form of revenge? But his friendly smile seemed genuine, not vindictive.

She had been the one who ended their relationship, after all; it had been she who refused to join him in Europe. He had been angry. Bitter. She could not blame him. And he surely had no thoughts that she still cared about him. It had been eight years, after all. Perhaps now that he was the centre of other women's attention, he felt that he could let go of some of that rancour and acknowledge her again.

He had, it seemed, put the past in the past, and her along with it. She meant nothing to him anymore, other than as a colleague. She wasn't even important enough to raise his disdain.

She gave a sad smile and returned to her score.

Jean-Michel led the orchestra through some of the passages they had discussed, and Anne made her notes. The violins could be trusted to give room for the middle voices in the strings, but the brass section needed some reworking to allow the cross-rhythms through. From time to time, Jean-Michel turned around to ask her a question or two before returning to his musicians.

And then the unexpected happened. Fred stood up and gave her a wink before heading to the stage.

Jean-Michel addressed the orchestra. "Friends, our new conductor has asked to take you through one or two passages before we finish today. You are in excellent hands. Maestro." He bowed and passed his baton to Fred, then stepped off the podium.

He bowed his head to the smattering of applause and taps and waited for silence to reign again before addressing the musicians. Anne could not see his face, but his head of dark curls moved eloquently, his broad shoulders commanded even without moving. She could only imagine the impression he made upon those graced with a view of his expression.

"Thank you. Now, we'll have a chance to get to know each other later, but for now, let's go back to the third movement." He gave the exact place in the music and flicked the baton. The orchestra responded, and they played a few bars before Fred stopped them.

"Excellent. For reading, this is fabulous. We are going to be a world-class team next season. I couldn't be more thrilled to be working with such a terrific group. I'd like to do that again, with more attention to the dynamics, and then let's go back to that theme. I'm not sure we realise at first just how brilliant this music is. You see, in measure 48, where it seems like we're coming to the end of a phrase, how the harmonic rhythm moves at a different pace. Let's look at it not as the end of the phrase, but as an elision between two phrases, where the last notes of the previous phrase are the first notes of a new one. Sort of like a portmanteau of sentences. 'The boy ate the cake is a delicious treat.' The word 'cake' fills two roles. It's like that with this measure." And on he spoke before raising the baton again.

Anne was amazed. She had spent weeks working out how this passage would come together, and Fred understood it in a moment. He was the one who would conduct the orchestra for the premier of the piece next season. She could imagine no one better for the task.

When they had worked through that section to his satisfaction, he asked the orchestra to turn to a passage in the last movement.

"The melody is expansive and lush, but there's an insistent rhythm in the horns that turns up the tension a bit, and I'd like that to come through, but without breaking up the cathedral of sound Doctor Elliot has constructed. Horns... Louisa." There was a hint of something cheeky in his voice at the sound of her name. "Is there some sort of tonguing technique that would allow for that articulation while not stopping the sound?"

Anne saw the blue-haired horn player's saucy grin. "Sure. It's a fast enough passage that it will take some work, but there's always something we can do. I'll make sure to do lots of tongue exercises. I'm known to be pretty good in that area."

The orchestra laughed. Anne could not see Fred's face, but his posture took on a cocky aspect that suggested he knew exactly what Louisa was saying and approved of it. She imagined the horn player and conductor would be spending quite a bit of time together working on her... tonguing technique.

Yes. He had got over her completely, and this was her punishment. For the thousandth time, she regretted that awful decision she had made eight years before. Why had she let Professor Russell persuade her to stay?

CHAPTER SIX
Con Moto

Anne had to admit it: Sophia's idea to go biking was an excellent one. After a wet and windy weekend, Monday dawned bright and clear, with crystal blue skies and perfect temperatures. It was usually Mother Nature's cruel joke, saving the great weather for when people had to be at work, but today Anne had no other obligations, and she was looking forward to the outing.

Sophia had told her to dress appropriately but to bring nothing other than sunblock, a water bottle, and her new biking helmet. She would take care of the rest.

Anne could just imagine what her well-to-do friend had in mind. A gourmet picnic, all packed in ice, perhaps? Reservations for two at the local ice cream factory afterwards, with a custom-built banana split waiting for them? She smiled at the idea. What she knew for certain was that Sophia had rented two good bicycles that they would collect once they arrived in the area, and that she had a route planned out.

Anne hopped off the city bus at the stop by Sophia's building and sauntered inside. She nodded to the doorman, who tipped his head in reply. "Morning, ma'am," the young man gave her a professional smile, and she asked politely after his health. "I'll let Mrs. Croft know you're on your way." It seemed she was a frequent enough visitor here that the desk staff knew her; that Sophia had dragged her along once while hand-delivering Christmas presents certainly had not hurt, and she was treated to the same welcome as the residents of this lovely building. She smiled to herself as she rode up the elevator, all gleaming brass and tinted mirrors. She had done well enough at her art to afford a small condominium unit in a nice building in this expensive city, but it was nothing like the towering midtown palace where the Crofts made their home.

Sophia was waiting at the open door. "Anne, darling, come in. All dressed for the day. Perfect. Give me two minutes while I finish getting ready. Won't be a moment."

Sophia bustled off, leaving Anne alone in the living room with just her reflection for company. She looked, well, like she was set for a day of biking. A bright pink polo shirt offered some protection to the back of her neck, and her blue cargo shorts had zippable pockets for things like her phone and keys. She had debated bringing her camera, but decided that the extra weight about her neck wasn't worth it and her phone would have to do in the case of a photographic necessity. In a small backpack, she carried her water bottle, sunglasses, and a tube of sunscreen, and the new helmet Sophia had purchased for her the previous day hung from her wrist by its straps.

She glanced down at her legs. They were shapely enough, she supposed, but were blindingly white. Should she get more sun? No. The sun was bad for the skin, but right now she looked like a ghost in a snowstorm. In a bright pink polo shirt. No matter. She was not trying to impress anybody with a gorgeous tan, anyway. The birds would have to live with her pasty limbs.

Sophia reappeared from her room. "That pink is a good shade on you. I know you like blue, but this brings colour to your cheeks. All ready? We just have one stop on the way."

"A stop? To get food?"

"Oh no, dear. I've ordered lunch from a new local caterer that I've heard such wonderful things about. Didn't I tell you? Jeremy decided to come along. I reserved two more bikes. We'll take the SUV and pick him and Fred up on our way."

Her heart stopped.

"Fred? He knows I'm coming?"

"Oh, yes. Since it was really his idea in the first place, we thought he might want to come along. Do you mind?"

Anne opened her mouth, but no words came out. Did she mind? How could she possibly answer that? Did she mind spending a day in close proximity and enforced friendliness with a man whom she had hoped to be over, but whom she feared she still loved, despite the fact that he clearly had no further interest in her at all, other than the purely professional? Oh. And he would spend all day staring at her glaringly white legs. Did she mind?

"No, not at all. It will be lovely."

Sophia gave her *that look*. "One day, I think, there is a story you have to tell me. But never mind. We'll be late. Ready?"

With a sweep of her hand, Sophia grabbed her own supplies and ushered Anne out the door towards the garage and whatever the fates decided to throw her way on this bright summer day.

The drive down to Niagara was only slightly uncomfortable. Since Sophia and Anne were already in the front seats of the SUV, the men took the back and Anne was able to avoid too much conversation. Most of the drive was rather ordinary—endless suburbia followed by light industry followed by featureless highway—but as they approached their destination, the scenery grew lovely. The lake, when it was visible through the banks of buildings or the trees, threw back sequins of bright sunlight to the crystal blue sky, and the late June foliage was fresh and verdant.

Sophia had rented bikes from a place on the outskirts of Niagara-on-the-Lake, a small town dating back to the late 1700s and which still held a great deal of Georgian charm. Anne knew the town well and was a frequent visitor, especially when the local theatre festival was in full swing during the summers. It was one of Anne's favourite places to spend an afternoon wandering through quaint shops and down picturesque laneways before tracing the shoreline along the lake. Today's route, as described by Sophia, would take them through country lanes and along the river instead, and Anne was eager to explore a part of the area she did not know so well.

They parked and soon were on their bicycles, heading out of town towards one of the wineries in the region.

"That helmet matches your shirt!" Sophia called. She and Anne were riding beside each other; the men were a few metres ahead, giving Anne a rather pleasant view of Fred's back. He had worn regular shorts in the car, but had changed into biking shorts at the rental shop. He had invested in proper gear when he started biking in Europe, he explained to Jeremy's raised eyebrows. Why not be comfortable?

The tight latex shorts gave the ladies a rather clear idea of what lay beneath them. Biking shorts might be excellent for the sport, all sleek and aerodynamic, but they left little to the imagination. Not that Anne needed her imagination for this. Her memory served quite well.

It wasn't just his obvious endowments that drew her eyes. The years and his time on a bicycle had added welcome bulk to Fred's physique. He had always been attractive, but he was broader now, more solid, and his lanky arms and legs had become toned and nicely muscled. Not too much. Just enough. His legs, long and lean and beautifully shaped, pumped up and down on the pedals, and his calf muscles flexed and released in perfect rhythm, a magnet to Anne's eyes.

She wrenched her attention back to the road and to the surrounding countryside. This was wine country. Field after field of vineyards surrounded them, the long straight vines sporting bright leaves and clusters of young grapes, broken up by orchards of tender fruit or tracts of hay and other farmland. There was something soothing and reassuring in the even spacing of the vines, like the regular harmonic progression of a Bach cantata, a walking bass line, predictable and comfortable, leading inexorably from tonic through a musical path back to the tonic.

But the leaves greening on their stems were something different again. Lush. Unpredictable. Growing where they wanted, a riot of life upon the carefully manicured vines. The exotic, free-flowing melody that crested and swept along, anchored by the harmony but not bound to it, moving where it would, twisting here and there, but always returning to its roots.

Yes. This was beautiful country indeed. Perhaps she should have brought her camera after all. Her phone would suffice but it was a poor substitute.

"Stop for a drink?" Jeremy called out from his bike.

The four pulled to the side of the road and dismounted for a moment. Anne pulled her helmet from her head to allow the breeze to cool her damp hair, and then took a gulp from her water bottle.

Although the weather was pleasant, the sun was hot on her back and she was unaccustomed to this sort of activity. Fred looked cool and comfortable. Of course. After biking through hot Italy, this must be nothing to him. A mere bagatelle of amusement for an afternoon.

As if picking up on her thoughts, Jeremy turned to Fred and said, "You never did tell us why you're back so soon. We're thrilled you're here, but we didn't expect to see you till the end of the month."

Fred rummaged in his backpack for his own water bottle. "It's nothing, really. I did my final concert and was just packing up my flat. But I don't have so much stuff. I was a student for a while, and then when I started getting engagements, it was a week here and two weeks there, and my flat in Rome was really just a place to sleep between gigs. It was like living out of page twenty seven of the IKEA catalogue. It's not like I had anything—or anyone—to come home to."

Now he sent a cruel glance towards Anne. He might as well have slapped her, and she looked down at her feet. White legs. Blue socks. Black running shoes. He must be congratulating himself for having avoided this 'prize.' She stepped backwards.

If Fred noticed, his voice didn't show it. He continued as if nothing had happened. "And so, after my final concert, I boxed up everything meaningful and sent it ahead. I covered the rest of the stuff with sticky notes—things to pack, things to donate, et cetera—and I hired a company to deal with it all. They'll send over the few items I've labelled. But I'll want new furniture for my new apartment anyway, so there's very little from Rome that I need. And with that done, I thought I'd rather be here. I have one or two details to take care of in Rome this summer, but I left a mattress on the floor. It will do."

He took a drink. When he spoke again, his voice had softened. "I'm glad I came. I was able to drop in on Anne's rehearsal last week. It was lovely to see you there, Anne."

This was the first time he had directed his words directly at her. Had he realised how much his last comment hurt? Was he trying to make amends? He had a right to be angry with her, but he had never been a cruel man. She didn't know where to look. Her shoes were getting boring.

"What did you think?" Sophia asked.

"What am I supposed to say?" Fred laughed. "The composer is right here. I can hardly say anything bad. But I don't have to lie. Her symphony is brilliant. Knowing that I'll be conducting the world premier is a thrill like I cannot tell you. Let's talk more later. Should we get back on our bikes? There's a winery a couple of kilometres down the road that makes a lovely Riesling."

They biked for another hour, stopping here and there to admire the scenery or take a drink of water, and a couple of times at one of the area's wealth of wineries to do a tasting. Sophia bought a case of a white blend she particularly enjoyed, arranging to pick it up in the car later on, and with this example in mind, Anne added three bottles to her own meagre collection.

"Right at the next crossroads, and then it's just another kilometre or so back to the parkway. If I've set my route properly, we'll come out exactly at the park where I've arranged for lunch." Sophia was always happy to organise everybody's life, but she acted with every good intention and she was generous with both her time and her money. If she had arranged for lunch to be delivered to the park, it would be ready and it would be excellent. Of that, Anne had no doubts.

Her expectations were met. When they crossed the parkway a few minutes later and flung themselves off their bicycles, there was a van waiting with the name of one of the local catering companies emblazoned on the side. The attachment to the roof suggested the interior held a fridge, and probably a warming station, too. No mere cold picnic for Sophia and Jeremy Croft.

Within moments, two perky people hopped out of the van and began setting up one of the picnic tables under a large tree. Anne watched in awe as the wooden bench and table were transformed with soft pillows, an elegant tablecloth (secured down with weights at the corners), and a full place setting for each. Then came the food. It was simple enough fare—salads and sandwiches—but the salads were ice cold and the grilled vegetables on focaccia were hot, and the iced tea and lemonade had not been sitting out in the sun. Or in a hot backpack. Anne suspected there would be hot coffee afterwards for those who wanted.

"Did you bring enough for yourselves?" Sophia asked the caterers. "Good. You enjoy yourselves till we're done." Always thinking of others. Always generous. She was a good friend.

The four cyclists settled themselves onto the cushioned benches. For someone not used to being on a bike, Anne was very grateful for this bit of thoughtfulness. She would hurt for a couple of days, but it was well worth it. The ride had been a welcome break from the city and the feast before them looked spectacular, all the more so after a morning spent exercising. At Sophia's invitation, they all helped themselves to the food and sat in silence for a few moments as they took their first bites.

Then Fred turned to Anne again. "I've been following your career, Annie." He took a bite of the bean and corn salad. That he used the affectionate form of her name was not lost on her, and she wondered if he realised what he had said. "I've never told you how much I was blown away by your score for *The Butterfly's Kiss*." He put down his fork to grab a piece of focaccia.

"Oh. Thank you. I didn't know you'd seen it. You were never much of a movie-goer." Anne saw Sophia's eyebrows shoot up towards her hairline, and Jeremy cocked his head. Uh oh. There would be questions later.

"I'm not. But when I heard it was your score, I had to go. Not a bad movie. But the music! I went out and bought the soundtrack and listened again and again, and then I went to see the movie a second time."

Now his words came more quickly, and his eyes bored into hers.

"Anne, what you did was genius. Having distinct thematic material for each character or place is lovely, but not new. But what you did next was fantastic. Taking that thematic material and reworking it in different keys and modes to reflect the action was just inspired. Setting the lovers' themes in counterpoint with a pentatonic scale... well, I was in awe. And to do all of this, keeping it so technically perfect, and still make it sound effortless and natural, and, well, beautiful! I hardly have words."

Anne suddenly felt very warm. God. She was blushing. She took a bite of the bread in her hand to hide her embarrassment. "Thank you," she mumbled into her sandwich.

"No, Annie, don't be coy. Tell us more. I've always wanted to pick your brains about how you write, but never felt I should ask. Trade secrets and all, I suppose." Sophia leaned forward, elbows on the elegant tablecloth, leaning over her glass of iced tea. "I know something about music, but I thought it would all go right over my head. But if you tell Fred, I'll probably understand enough that it will make sense to me, without turning you into a kindergarten teacher. Please. I'm really interested."

Jeremy also sat forward, his eyes eager. As the president of the orchestra's board of directors, he had more than a passing knowledge of music. He was here as a friend and was one of her biggest fans already, but it could never hurt to talk to him more about her technique and ideas. Her tenure as composer-in-residence was only for three years, after all, and then she would be out looking for more commissions. She would need all the cheerleaders and contacts she could find, and she would have to get used to talking about her art. Here was as good a place to start as any.

So she poured herself another glass of lemonade and took a bite of the warm focaccia and began to talk.

By the time she had finished, the salad and sandwiches were long gone, and had been replaced by warm apple pie topped with cold ice cream. And yes, there was coffee. Fred leaned forward, nodding and murmuring his approval or agreement at various comments, and Jeremy and Sophia sat with amazed grins on their faces. Anne broke off her monologue and gaped at her friends.

"I'm sorry! I didn't realise I had that much to say. It... it must have been a bit much. I forget, sometimes, how much I work in my own head and how my thoughts don't always translate well into words."

"On the contrary, dear," Sophia licked some ice cream off her spoon, "it translated incredibly well. I had only thought of your music as interesting and pretty—"

"Which really should be enough to keep a listener happy," Jeremy added.

"—but now I see something about how it's constructed. It's like a building, I suppose. We see the facade and the paint and decorations, but never think about all the stuff going on underneath that keeps the stairs in place and lets the light in. Or a painting, which is as much the science of mixing colour as it is the art of a pretty picture."

"You should write a book, Anne." Fred looked quite serious. "You have described some of the techniques of composition exceedingly well. Others could learn a lot from you."

"I did." It came out as a mumble.

"'Scuse me?" Jeremy asked.

"I did. I did write a book. My doctoral thesis. Part of it was the composition itself, part was an analysis of my work, and part was a treatise on composition as an art form."

Fred's demeanour went cold again. "Right. The thesis. Of course. You must be very pleased you stayed to finish it. Well," he rose from his cushioned bench, "I think it's time to get back on our bikes and return to the car. We don't want to get caught in too much traffic on the drive back to the city."

If he had slammed the door in Anne's face, his import could not have been clearer. Another layer of bricks went up around the damage that was Anne's soul.

CHAPTER SEVEN
Agitato

Seven o'clock in the morning. Ugh! Why did Marie always have to call at the crack of dawn? Anne rolled over and groped for her phone.

"Mmmfphh."

"Anne, are you awake? I need you today."

"Do you always have to call me so early, Marie? Isn't it school vacation already? Why are you up so early?"

"That's why I need you. I need you to watch the boys. I'm going out."

Anne rubbed her eyes with her free hand. It was late June, and the sun had been shining for a while, but only a thin bright line shone through the crack in her window blinds.

"Going out where? And why are you only calling me now? I might be busy."

On the other end of the line, Marie laughed. "Oh, Anne! Be serious. You're never busy." Anne heard some shouting in the background. Charles yelling at the kids?

"Why are they awake so early?"

"I know, right? Every day they were at school, I had to pry them out of bed, and now that it's summer, they're up with the sun. I don't know why they don't sleep in, or at least nag their father. No one ever thinks of me. I need my sleep too, you know. But yeah, this afternoon. Charles and Fred decided to get tickets for the soccer game today. It's not a big sport here, so it's easy to get tickets. And I decided I wanted to go with them. They're always having fun without me, and I like to go out too. I deserve some fun as well as them, and no one ever thinks to ask me. So when Charles went on-line to get tickets, I told him to get one for me as well. We're going to get lunch before the game, so I'll need you here by about eleven. That gives you plenty of time."

The line went dead. Anne groaned. She had not been sleeping well of late, and had hoped to be able to take an easy morning. Who went to a soccer game on a Tuesday afternoon, anyway? Wasn't Charles working?

She dragged herself out of bed and stumbled to the shower. *Fred.* His name echoed through her head as she rubbed the shampoo through her dark hair. *Fred.* Was there no escape from him? She would have to work with him in the autumn, this she knew, but could she not have the summer to try to shore up her crumbling heart?

It had been a week since the awkward bike trip. It had started well. They had both enjoyed the ride, even though Fred was so much better on a bike than she was, and they had, for a while, conversed easily and comfortably. It was almost—almost—like before. Before her decision. Before he left. He understood her like no one else did. He understood her art; he breathed the same rarified air. She had seen the lights in his eyes as she had described her new symphony, and she had responded similarly to his comments about his own metier.

And then the door had slammed shut and the lights went out. They had finished their lunch almost in silence and had said not another unnecessary word to each other for the entire drive home. He was pleased to see the end of her. She didn't need another reminder.

Oh well. She rinsed the shampoo and slathered on some conditioner, then let the fruity scent of her body-wash trickle down from her shoulders. At least she wouldn't see him today. Even if he came to the house, she could arrange to be busy somewhere until he left. Washing dishes, tidying the boys' toys. Something. Somewhere else.

She lathered the body-wash on one leg to shave it, then repeated her actions on the other leg. No one who cared would come close enough to tell whether she sported a sprinkle of leg stubble, but little Dylan always teased her when she was prickly, and if she couldn't shave for her four-year-old nephew, who could she shave for? She smiled at the thought. He was a handful, but a sweet kid nonetheless, and she adored him and his brother to the moon and back.

Time now for a coffee or two, and maybe a walk around the block, before heading to the subway for the trip out to the Musgroves' house. It was another fine day, perhaps just a tad hot, but nice enough to enjoy the short stroll between her destination subway station and her sister's home. Maybe she could take the kids to the local park and let them run off some energy. She threw a book and her tablet into her tote bag and started on the way.

It had grown hotter as the afternoon progressed. Even sitting here under the shade of a large white oak and sipping cold water from a thermos, perspiration dampened Anne's forehead under her sunhat. Perhaps she should have stayed at the house and let the boys play in the backyard, close to air conditioning. But the boys wanted to run and climb, and here, at the park, they might see their friends. And, to be honest, it was easier for her to be here. At home, she had to step in every two minutes to moderate some disagreement, some territorial assertion over toy trucks and hula hoops and soft balls that couldn't damage the windows. Here at the park, there were enough climbing structures to keep the kids busy and apart.

A trickle of sweat dripped down between her shoulder blades and she took another sip of water from her insulated bottle. How the boys managed to run around in the full heat of the sun, she could not understand. But kids are kids, and beneath their sunblock and protective hats, they seemed not to have the first concern about the rising temperatures.

There were a few other families at the park. A couple of women sat chatting on the bench across the way, one or the other of them leaping up every now and then to tend to one of a group of young kids on the climbing structure. There was another woman sitting alone on the next bench, looking like a nanny rather than a parent, gabbing on her mobile phone to some distant friend. A dad stalked around the see-saw, pushing or prodding one of two similar looking children about the same ages as Anne's nephews, and three teenagers hung out at the picnic table under another tree, each with a tall plastic cup of something that needed a straw to drink. Slurpees? Frozen coffee? Both sounded lovely to Anne right now. A bit further along, a few kids were kicking a ball back and forth and one or two people strolled by with dogs on their leashes.

A perfectly ordinary day at the park.

Something teased at Anne's ears, soon to materialise into a recognisable and not entirely unwelcome sound. That awful tinny tune could only mean one thing: an ice cream truck. Someone had very good business sense. The driver would almost certainly make a few dollars here, especially so if the teenagers at the table were to judge by, each rooting through her pockets for something, presumably enough coins for a frozen treat.

"Ice cream!" Six-year-old Jakey came running. "Annie, can we get ice cream? Can we?"

"Please, Annie!" Dylan echoed his brother's pleas. He was a precocious four years old, always eager to do just what Jake could do. "Ice cream! I want chocolate. With sprinkles!"

"Does your mama let you get chocolate with sprinkles?"

Jake shook his head, but Dylan looked up with the innocent eyes of childhood. "No. But Papa does. Please!"

"I don't know, guys. We had a treat before we left the house, and we'll have a cold drink when we get home. In fact, it's getting warm. Why don't we head back now? Maybe we can walk past the corner store and get a tub of frozen yogurt."

Jake nodded his agreement, but Marie's temperament came out in her younger son. "No!" Dylan stomped his little feet on the dry ground. "I want ice cream. I want chocolate ice cream. With sprinkles!"

And before Anne could stop him, he dashed off in the direction of the ice cream truck, which had just pulled to a stop on the other side of the road, since the near side was lined with cars. A chorus of shouts from the playground bounced off her and the heat of the sun faded to nothing. All she saw was her nephew running towards the garish white van with the tinny speaker.

She had to stop him. Now.

"Jake, stay here. Don't move. Dylan! Come back!" Anne leapt to her feet to run off after her errant nephew. Her foot got tangled in her tote bag's straps and she fought to free it so she could hurry after the little boy. "Come back right now!"

But the boy either didn't hear, or didn't care, and kept running. Those little legs were fast, and he was already at the street. The seconds it had taken Anne to free her feet were too much for her to catch him. It was normally a quiet neighbourhood road, little travelled by anyone other than local residents and the occasional ice cream truck. But not today.

Anne saw it all as if in slow motion, part of some bad movie. The van that came around the corner, not speeding but faster than it ought. The parked cars, lining the sidewalk at the edge of the park. Strange, unrelated images like the red bike leaning against a tree and the small plane flying overhead, the drone of its propeller a distant buzz above the everyday sounds of children at play. And Dylan, short, too short to be seen, dashing out into the street from between two of those parked cars, just as the minivan hurried along its way. Anne tried to force her legs to move more quickly, but she too was caught in this timeless, endless, relentless progression towards disaster.

And then, like in that imaginary movie, the slow-motion pan ended and events sped up to their horrible conclusion. There was a screech of brakes, a sickening thud, and a scream that Anne would recall for the rest of her days. The world crumbled beneath her.

"Dylan!" Was that her voice? Could she shout like that? Panic propelled her faster than she thought she could ever move, but it was too late. The minivan stood still in the middle of the road; a small blond body lay crumpled on the ground before it, blood pooling from under one shoulder. The universe reeled around her.

"I've called 911," someone shouted. Who was that? She tried to spin about to see, but she could not move. The world was a kaleidoscope of whirling images. Nothing made sense. What had she done?

She had to do something, take some action. She was Anne, the one everyone relied on in a crisis. But every rational thought was gone, the world a senseless whir of motion and dread.

"I'm a doctor. Can I look?" A shape came into focus. One of the two chatting women, breathing hard.

A doctor. That was good. Anne nodded. She was numb, paralysed in her terror. Her nephew. Little Dylan. Oh my God.

The woman knelt down by Dylan's inert body and did some things Anne could not see. "He's breathing fine," the doctor looked up. "I won't move him. I hope the ambulance gets here soon. Are you okay?"

Time stood still, a mess of chaos and inertia, as people buzzed about. The doctor stood by Anne with her arm around Anne's shoulders. At last there was a distant wailing, and then a closer one, as Jake ran up and threw his arms around Anne's neck, his hot tears mingling with the sweat that now had nothing to do with the hot sun.

"Stand back. I'll direct the EMTs. Here they come now. That was fast." The doctor. Thank heavens someone had done something useful, had been able to think.

Anne stood there in a daze. She should act. She should do something. But still, she remained rooted to the ground as activity erupted around her. There was a wall of sirens, a cacophony of flashing lights, and people who hadn't been there before. The paramedics were now there, tending to Dylan, asking questions, saying things that didn't quite coalesce into words.

The doctor was talking to them now. "...ran away... parked cars... tried to catch..." Nothing made sense.

And then there was Jake. Who would look after Jake? The little boy was sobbing at her side, calling out his brother's name. Anne took a deep breath and pulled her nephew to her side in a crushing hug. In a voice steadier than she thought possible, she reassured him. "He'll be okay, sweetie. Don't worry. We can go with him to the hospital…"

"I'm Sylvia," the doctor approached her again. "Marie's neighbour. Hi Jake." Her voice was calm, a cool, still place in the midst of a cyclone.

"Hi, Doctor Alvirez," the little boy replied, all but inaudible in the din. Good. He knew her.

The doctor looked up. "You're Anne, Marie's sister. I've seen pictures of you and she talks about you. Look, I can take Jake if you want to go in the ambulance with Dylan. They won't let you both go. My daughter is in Jake's class at school. He often comes over."

Jake nodded again. "Kailey's my friend." He pointed to where a little girl stood at the edge of the green space. She gave him a timid wave in return.

Alright. She had to make a decision. She had neglected one child and let him run in front of a moving car. How much worse could it be to abandon the other to the care of a stranger? "Can I get your phone number?" There. That was responsible adult behaviour, right?

Sylvia Alvirez reached into a pocket and pulled out a business card, listing her clinic and pager number. She found a pen somewhere and scribbled another number down on the back. "My cell. Marie has it, but here it is again."

Numb. She was numb. A hand snaked out to accept the card. It was her own. She stuffed it into her tote bag. "Thanks." She forced out the word.

"Ma'am?" The paramedics called her over. They had transferred Dylan to a gurney and were ready to load him into the back of the ambulance. "Coming with? You can tell us what happened again on the way."

Another nod.

Marie would kill her. If she didn't die of horror and self-recrimination first.

Anne heard Marie and Charles before she saw them. They came rushing into the hospital waiting room in a cloud of wails and moans. Or, rather, Marie was the source of the lamentations. Charles was deadly silent. She had called them as soon as the ambulance had arrived at the hospital and a small army of white-coated doctors and nurses swarmed around the little boy. Marie's protestations at being disturbed at the game quickly dissolved into cries of horror before Charles took the phone. Once Anne explained things, he cursed once and hung up. She knew she would see them soon enough.

There was little enough to do now. Dylan was still unconscious, and he was being shuttled from place to place for tests and imaging and procedures that Anne could not start to comprehend. *Cervical spine... Trauma routine... CT scan...* The terms hovered in the air like a swarm of noseeums that she could not avoid but equally couldn't quite catch. Things were attached to his head, his arms; machines beeped and whined; the smell of disinfectant was everywhere. And all Anne could do was sit in the cold, sterile waiting room until they returned him to... wherever.

Soon enough, Marie's wails sounded through the hallways. She stormed up to Anne, her face a red mess. "My baby! Anne, what did you do to my baby? Why did you offer to watch them if you couldn't keep them safe? My baby!"

"Marie…" Charles growled. His voice was quiet but fierce. "It's not Anne's fault. Dylan runs." His face was white, his hands clenched at his sides. He turned to Anne. "How is he?"

She pulled her sister into a hug as she answered. "He'll be fine. The doctors won't tell me much since I'm just his aunt, but there's no serious injury. The driver slammed on her brakes as soon as he dashed out from between the cars, and it hardly tapped him at all. Most of his injuries are from where he fell, not from being hit. He scraped up his back pretty badly and he broke his arm when he landed on it. They're just keeping him because he hit his head. The doctors will tell you more."

At that moment, an impossibly young man in a white coat walked through one of the doorways. "Mr. Musgrove? Mrs. Musgrove? I'm Dr. Chiu. Come with me. Your son is sleeping normally…" He led the two anxious parents down a long hallway. Anne knew she wouldn't see them again today. She sent a quick text to Marie asking her to call when she got home and turned to collect her tote bag from the seat behind her.

A shadow emerged from the corner of the waiting room by the nurses' station, all long limbs and worried lines on his face.

"Fred."

He must have been there all along, not wanting to intrude. Of course, he had been with Charles and Marie at the game, and had probably driven their van to the hospital. Neither of the Musgroves would have been in any state to negotiate Toronto traffic.

"Annie. He's okay?"

She nodded. She was still numb. He walked up to her and let her fall briefly against his chest, pulling her close with one arm. Then, just as quickly, he released her and stepped back. He would comfort her, but only so much. Fine.

"How are you getting home? Walking? I'd offer to drive you, but we took Charles' car and he'll need it to get home later. I can call a taxi or an Uber."

Another nod. "No, that's fine. Walking is good. It's not so far. I'm just out along Queen Street, past Spadina. It's only about 20 minutes. I need... I need time to think. If only I'd acted a moment sooner. If only I hadn't tripped on these damned straps. If only he hadn't been so fast. Why didn't I expect him to dash off like that?"

The words flooded out of her before she could stop them.

His entire stance softened. "It's not your fault, Annie. Charles was telling me in the car how impulsive he can be. Let me walk you home. You can yell at me the whole time."

He walked over and took up her bag, then put an arm about her shoulders again. She leaned into him for a moment before following him out of the hospital.

She hardly spoke on the walk, and Fred did not push her. Before, so long ago, he had always understood her so well. He knew when she needed to vent and when she needed to process things internally. He knew when she needed physical contact and when she needed to be left alone. Now he seemed to sense her need for silent companionship, and he walked beside her, not too far and not too close, until they arrived at her building. Anne knew the walk took about twenty minutes, but it could have been seconds or hours, such was the unsettled mess in her mind.

She would never stop berating herself for what had happened, but Fred's presence was somehow comforting. Even in her distress, even now that he was back and clearly wished to be far away from her, he grounded her. Now he stood there by the big set of doors to her building, neither moving inside nor shuffling away to take his leave. Waiting... waiting to see what she needed.

Anne spoke before she could think. "Come up? I could use a drink." They were some of the first words she had said to him since they left the hospital.

"Sure." He followed her up the elevator and down the hallway to the one-bedroom unit she called home. She fumbled in her pocket for the keys and unlocked the door, stepping aside to let him enter.

As she closed the door behind them, he stepped towards her with his arms wide. She needed a hug. He knew that, too. She collapsed against him, and at once the dam burst. All that dry numbness, all that paralysis and horror, dissolved at once into a flood of pain and despair, and heavy sobs racked her body. She hadn't even realised until now that she had not shed a single tear so far. Until now, when it all came out in a horrible torrent. Fred held her close and let her cry, and then when she stepped back to take a breath, he found a tissue in his pocket and handed it to her so she could dry her face before bursting into tears once more.

In time, the tears ran dry and Anne's choked breathing started to settle. Fred pulled her closer, wrapping her in his arms, a warm blanket to reassure and to soothe. She laid her head against his chest to let him stroke her hair. His hand was gentle, each stroke hinting at affection, bringing back all those buried memories. The constant beat of his heart was comforting, grounding. A solid rhythm, steady and sure, holding the universe together.

Out of instinct, she responded by enfolding him in her own arms. He would leave soon enough, but for now, she welcomed the comfort.

"There, there," he murmured into her hair. "It's okay. It's alright." She felt the soft pressure on something against the crown of her head. Not his hand. One was on her back, the other at the back of her head. He was nuzzling his face against her hair. Another murmur, another caress. Was that a kiss? She burrowed her face into his shoulder and let him cocoon her in his arms.

Another kiss on her hair, a tightening of his hug about her shoulders. One large hand moved down her back to press her into him and she sniffed back a tear and looked up at him.

Those lips that had, moments ago, nestled in her hair now came down to kiss her forehead right between her eyes. He moved his other hand to wipe the tears from one leaky eye, and then he leaned forward to kiss her head again. Then her cheek. Then those lips that she had once known so well moved again and touched her mouth.

Just a brush.

A butterfly's kiss.

They both pulled back and gasped at each other, but before Anne could say anything, Fred growled, "Damn it," and leaned forward again with much more amorous intent. Anne met him halfway in a passionate kiss.

It had been eight long years since they parted so badly. Almost a decade since they had indulged their passion. After Fred had left, Anne cauterised her wounds with endless work and had wept out her pain in the notes of her *Preludes*. With every passing day, she had fortified the wall growing around her heart, dampening her distress, dampening her joy as well. She had cultivated that wall, tended it, kept it strong, so nothing—no one—could hurt her again.

Now, with every touch of his hands and every caress of his lips against hers, that wall started to weaken. All those years of repressed emotion pressed at the barricades, crying for freedom, and right now, with Fred kissing her like she was everything in his world, she didn't care.

Her fingers threaded themselves in his thick dark hair, even as his hands ran up and down her back, those long fingers playing arpeggios with her nerves, bringing her senses to a crescendo that threatened to overwhelm her. Promised to overwhelm her.

When they moved to the couch, she echoed his touch. When they moved to the bedroom, it was she leading the way. And when their symphony reached its crashing climax and every brick around her heart crumbled into dust, she revelled in the release and the freedom.

It was not just her body that thrummed with the echoes of their lovemaking; her soul, too, was freed. After so long in its fortress, as much a prison as a stronghold, it soared and gloried in its expansiveness. Now she saw the heavy dungeon in which she had buried herself, and now she understood the joy of escape. And she knew that no matter what happened, she would never again trap her essence behind those artificial walls. Be the reward pain or exaltation, she would no longer sublimate her emotions in her life or in her music. Now she could let her art soar as free as her spirit in glorious creations, even greater than what she had done before.

She nestled against Fred's chest, revelling in the feel of his arm around her. Her fingers swirled through the hair on his chest and he purred in satisfaction. Just like before. This was new and familiar, a revelation and a coming home. Recapitulation—the return to the grand themes that begin a work. Home. The world was back on its axis.

She had been so wrong; Professor Russell had been so wrong. She had lost nearly a decade, but she need mourn no more.

Fred was back.

They stayed in bed all night, talking about music, talking about Dylan, making love again.

But in the morning, when Anne opened her eyes to the crack of light slicing through the blinds, Fred was gone.

CHAPTER EIGHT
Lacrimoso

His note had been simple.

Sorry, Annie.

We shouldn't have done that. I know you want to put the past to bed, but not so literally.

Forgive me?

Fred

And that had been that.

No flowers, no promises, no confession of a lifetime of regrets.

Just "sorry."

Anne felt her heart had been ripped out once again. But this time would be different.

A steel thread of anger pierced through the pain, stiffening her spine. Anger at herself for succumbing so quicky to Fred's charms. Anger at Fred for treating her so coldly, for leaving again with nothing but a few words on a piece of paper. Eight years ago, when they parted ways, she had crumbled into herself, but not now. Now she would step on this experience and climb higher. There would be memories, yes, and regrets too, but they no longer defined her and held her down.

She had spent too long in her self-imposed emotional exile, too long in her box. She had been set free and she would not return. Right now, she would mourn for what might have been, but only for now. She would indulge these reminiscences, and then move past them.

For that moment yesterday, after the devastation of seeing her nephew's injured body rushed to the hospital, after their desperate reconnection, she thought that there might be another chance for her and Fred. He had initiated the kiss that led to their night together; he must have known she wanted it too. Why would he think she had left him in the past if she had welcomed him into her bed so willingly?

Images from eight years before came flooding back. Their deep love for each other; Professor Russell's relentless urging; Anne's decision to remain in Toronto. And Fred's furious response.

He had been so excited about his invitation to study with a world-renowned maestro in Italy. Giancarlo Buscagni had accepted him as a member of his orchestra; Fred's skill on the cello was undisputed, and Anne knew he could have succeeded as a performing musician. But the orchestra was Fred's true passion. Why play one instrument when one can play a hundred, all at once? Buscagni's invitation was a dream come true, a once-in-a-lifetime opportunity. He was all but finished his Doctor of Music degree and had one last performance to conduct before he was done. It would mean leaving the city and the internship he had arranged with a second professional orchestra in town, but really, there was no choice to be made other than when he would leave.

Anne, at first, had been delighted. She could, of course, write her own music anywhere, and she could take a leave from her own studies for a year or more. Fred's career was about to take off, and he would reach stellar heights. Think of those great conductors over the years: Van Karajan, Ozawa, Toscanini, Mehta, Boulanger, and now Valore. It was their dream come true.

And then Professor Russell had stepped in. Slowly, persistently, relentlessly, she had gone after Anne again and again until at last Anne relented. Professor Russell was correct. If Anne wished to succeed as a composer, she needed her degree. Of course her music could stand by itself, but the weight of a doctorate, that extra time studying and honing her art, the contacts she could make through her professors, would make the difference between being a gifted composer no one heard of and being a household name, one of the brightest musical lights of half a century.

Fred would find his fame in Europe; Anne would find hers here, at the University.

And Anne, reluctantly, agreed. She would stay.

Fred, on the other hand, was less pleased with Professor Russell's efforts.

"I can't believe this, Annie. This is everything we've hoped for. If you really loved me, you would come with me. Just for a year. You can still finish your degree later. You said you loved me!"

He had begged but, with Professor Russell's words and admonitions still ringing in her ears, she had refused.

"I do love you, Fred. But it's not just your career. It's mine too. We can both do this. This doesn't have to be the end. We're not in the nineteenth century anymore. We can email, we can Skype. I can fly over to see you every couple of months. You can come home. You'll want to see your family, anyway. It will only be a couple of years. Then I'll have finished my degree, and I can move to be with you permanently. Surely, we're strong enough to make this work for a couple of years."

But it had not been enough. The discussion degenerated into a row, and it soon became clear that Anne had a decision to make: her man or her career. Professor Russell constantly in her subconscious, Anne chose her career.

And Fred had stormed out of the apartment, never to return other than to pack his stuff one day when Anne was out.

Eight years ago... nearly eight years.

Later, she would be strong. But now, Anne wept.

"Anne? Want to talk about it?" Sophia handed her a tall ceramic mug. "Chai, just the way you like it, with vanilla sugar on top."

They were sitting in their usual places at Percolations, their favourite coffee shop, the one where the friendly counter staff put your order on a tray with little pieces of chocolate beside each drink. Outside, the sun was blistering. Inside, the air conditioning kept everybody comfortable, allowing them to sit at the window and people watch without the inconvenience of exposure to nature. It was a busy downtown corner in the part of town where daytime commercial enterprise blended into funky streetscapes and upscale residential buildings. Anne's condo was not too far away, on a somewhat less funky and upscale street. But Sophia loved this spot. It was trendy and interesting and close enough to the financial core that Jeremy could stop by for a coffee if he knew she was at her chosen table.

"Anne? You've been in the dumps all week. Is it your nephew? How is he?"

Once again, Anne hid her face behind her drink while she scrambled for a response. The warm spicy notes of the chai tea stimulated her senses, all cinnamon and clove and cardamom, and she breathed deeply before taking a small sip of the creamy hot liquid. Something in the warm drink soothed as it titillated and she squashed the memory of panic enough to answer her friend.

"Poor Dylan. I can't stop feeling I should have been able to do something. I guess it's something I'll have to live with forever. But he'll be okay. He needed surgery on his broken arm and he was unconscious for a while, but he's definitely on the mend. He's coming home from the hospital today, thank heavens. Marie will probably never talk to me again, though." She buried all her conflicting emotions in another sip of the chai.

Because it wasn't really Dylan who dwelt constantly in her mind. It was Fred. And she was not at all ready to talk about that.

Sophia gave her another of *those looks*, but just smiled serenely. "I am pleased to hear that. About him coming home, of course. And I'm sure Marie will forgive you soon enough. She is still traumatised. Who wouldn't be? I'll send over a little something for the boy this afternoon. Something soft. Does he still like teddy bears? I think I saw one that's three feet tall. He should like that. And flowers for Marie and Charles. And of course, something for Jake. Maybe some building blocks? No, no flowers. A meal. After all this, the last thing they need is to have to cook."

"You are generous to a fault. Thank you. They'll appreciate it." Another sip of tea.

She fell silent for a moment as a young mother sidled by in search of a table, one hand pushing a baby stroller that looked like it cost more than a small car, the other holding a toddler's hand. A renewed pang of guilt stabbed her in the gut. Everything reminded her of Dylan and her utter failure to keep him safe. No wonder Marie had threatened never to allow her near the boys again. That hurt almost as much as her disastrous outing the other day.

The woman settled her toddler on the bench and started fumbling with the stroller brakes. There was a high chair in the corner. Anne slid from her seat and approached the woman, gesturing to the chair with her head.

"Would you like me to get it for you?"

Great, dark, thankful eyes blinked at her and the woman's shoulders dropped two inches. "Would you mind...?"

In two seconds, Anne was back and the woman set about loading her little girl into the chair.

"What's your name?" Anne asked the frazzled mother. Then, realising how this might be taken, hurried to add, "When I hear it, I'll go and get your tray." If she couldn't help Marie and Dylan, she could at least help a stranger with a young child.

"Suri!" the barista at the counter called out.

"That's me. Here's my receipt if they need it."

Anne sidled through the tables to collect the tray and brought it to where the woman and her children sat.

"You're a lifesaver." Suri beamed at her. "I can't thank you enough. It's been quite a day."

A lifesaver... The furthest thing from it. But Anne just mumbled something about having spent enough time looking after her nephews and wished the woman a lovely day before returning to Sophia.

"You done good, kid."

"She would have managed. I don't know how, but she would have."

Sophia reached over to touch Anne's hand as it rested on the table. "Yes, she would have managed. But she didn't have to. You made a difference. She'll smile more tonight."

And after several days of the most dreadful self-recrimination, these were welcome words. Like Suri, the weight on Anne's shoulders eased a touch. Was she blushing? Oh, God. She would make a terrible poker player. Still, she felt lighter. Brighter somehow. That smile on her face was there of its own accord, not forced, and it felt good.

Another sip of tea, although it was getting cold.

"It's a gorgeous day today, if a bit hot." Anne changed the topic. "I brought my camera with me to try to get some photos in the parks, or maybe some streetscapes. Are you planning on a walk later?"

Sophia shook her head. "Not today. I'm meeting Jeremy here later on. He's bringing someone he wants me to meet. He's new to the orchestra's board of directors and he wants to talk about fundraising ideas. They'll be along in..." she checked her watch, "about half an hour. You can stay if you'd like. I'm sure he'd be pleased to meet you, too."

Was it that man who had been at the rehearsal those short weeks ago? She had hardly given him another thought afterwards, although he had made the effort to look friendly and nod at her whenever their eyes met. He was the only new board member she had heard of, but she had not exactly been paying attention to the orchestra's press releases regarding its board members. Fred's desertion last Tuesday still left its mark on her psyche and clouded out all other thoughts, despite her determination to move forward.

"I'm not sure I'm up to meeting a new board member right now. I'm not quite feeling all sparkly and brilliant like I should. And look at me. I didn't dress to meet anybody; I'm a bit of a mess."

Her eyes dipped to take in her dark blue t-shirt and patterned broomstick skirt. More than adequate for a coffee with an old friend. Less than impressive for meeting a new member of the board. Her hand crept up to her hair, which she was certain was a mess from being crammed into her sun hat.

But Sophia laughed away her inadequacies with the wave of a manicured hand. "Nonsense, Anne. You are in fine spirits today, and you look lovely. I know I tell you not to wear so many dark colours, but that blue suits you. Your cheeks look positively rosy today. Only your eyes are sad. Something else is the matter, I know it. You're sure you don't want to talk about it? Here, have a taste of this cake. It's got just the slightest hint of burned caramel in the icing. Chocolate helps everything."

Anne took the offered tidbit. "Yeah. I'm sure. Just processing. Tell me more about the trip you were planning."

"Ah, the trip. That requires more cake and another latte. Back in a jiff!"

Sophia slipped out of her chair for a moment and returned with a grin. "They'll bring it right away, since they know me. Well. About our plans... We wanted to go to Venice, but Jeremy has a former colleague who once rented a villa near Dubrovnik..."

By the time Sophia finished talking about her ideas and plans, two more mugs sat empty on the table between them and the cake—with two forks—had been reduced to a few stray crumbs decorating the white plate.

The recitation must have taken longer than Anne thought, for just as she was about to slip out of the coffee shop, Jeremy's voice sounded through the place.

"Soph, my love! And look, Anne is with her. Come over, William, and meet my two favourite ladies."

In a moment, Jeremy was standing by the table, another man at his side. It was, indeed, the same stranger who had been at the rehearsal not so long ago. Sophia shifted over and the two men pulled up chairs to sit as well.

Jeremy started to make the introductions, but the newcomer reached across the table with an open hand. "William Barnett. A delight to meet you, Dr. Elliot. I saw you at the rehearsal, of course. Your symphony is just wonderful."

"Call me Anne, please." She shook the offered hand. His skin was warm and soft and his nails neat, the hand of a man who takes good care of himself. She looked up at his face. It was, as was her first impression, rather handsome, with light brown wavy hair and an easy smile. His entire appearance matched his manicured hands: elegant, very well tended, suave. Now, in the full light of the bright window, she could see his eyes were light blue, and that they crinkled at the corner when he smiled. Which he did a lot.

"William has just joined the board," Jeremy explained as he introduced him to Sophia. "He is a property developer, and a true lover of the arts."

"Indeed!" William interjected. "Music, theatre… I was a clarinet player when I was younger and almost went into music, but, well, the lure of business was too strong to resist. Then I discovered I could use my business experience to support the performing arts organisations I love so much."

"It's such a win-win," Jeremy nodded. "Let me put in an order, and then we can talk about ideas. William comes to us with so many ideas, Soph. What will it be? Latte? Tea? Cheesecake?"

He was up in a moment, leaving the others to smile at each other and comment on the weather until Jeremy returned, to be followed a minute later by a barista carrying a large tray.

"Black coffee and cheesecake," she placed them down in front of Jeremy, "and espresso and the double-dip biscotti for you, sir?"

"Not a cheesecake fan, Mr. Barnett?" Sophia laughed as she picked up her fork to attack her husband's treat.

"Need to keep my boyish figure," he joked in reply as he patted his stomach. He certainly looked trim and fit. "And it's William, please. We're all friends here." His eyes flickered to Anne, and she thought his eyebrows rose suggestively when she caught his glance.

For a few minutes, the conversation was general, as William addressed his comments to the group. Had they seen the latest Van Gogh exhibit at the art gallery? What were their thoughts on the new theatre season? A particularly famous local author was doing a reading of her latest novel at the main library; what had they thought of the book that was garnering so much press?

He was witty and articulate, and when he spoke of the arts, Anne could hear the passion in his voice. If he approached the orchestra with this sort of zeal, he would be an asset to the board indeed.

As the topics veered towards the fundraising ideas he wished to broach with Sophia, Anne began to shift in her seat.

"Pardon me, but I should get going and leave you to your business. I'm afraid this sort of thing goes over my head." She found the straps to her tote and checked to ensure her camera was inside.

"Must you go so soon, Anne?" William cocked his head just enough to give the hint of boyishness to his polished demeanour. It was very attractive. Then his eyes lit on Anne's camera. "Oh! Are you a photographer too?"

She felt that blush creep across her face again. "No, not at all. I enjoy it as a hobby, but I have no real training. I find it a good way to relax, almost like—"

"Almost like meditation," he supplied. "Yes. Walking through a park is a pleasure in itself, but walking with the focus of searching out beauty in unexpected places, that brings you to a very different level of consciousness, doesn't it?"

Anne blinked at him. She felt her lips curl into a slight smile, and he answered it. "Yes, I suppose that is so. I'd never really thought of it that way before. Searching for beauty where it's not expected. That is what we do, isn't it?"

He leaned back in his chair and let his head fall back just a touch as his eyes caressed her face. "Fortunately, I do not have to look very far to find beauty now. Perhaps, Anne, we might go out together one day. I don't have a particularly fine camera, but it's a hobby of mine too. One evening, when it's a bit cooler? If it's late enough, we might hit that magic golden hour light."

It was high summer; sunset was close to ten at night. That sounded almost like...

"I wouldn't want to bore you with my ramblings," she mumbled, but he would not be deterred.

"Bore me? No! I don't go out with my camera often enough, and my friends aren't interested at all. They'd rather watch some game or play pool. It would be a delight. What do you say?"

He pulled out his phone and his fingers danced across the screen for a moment. "There. What about Wednesday? The forecast is perfect, if you believe what they tell us. Can I call you or send you a text to make plans?"

Wednesday. That was usually the night she went to the Musgroves to have dinner and then watch the boys while Marie and Charles went out for an hour or so together. She was persona non grata with Marie, this week at least. She had no plans for Wednesday.

That little thread of steel worked its way through her once more, and she made her decision. It was time to move on. She met his gaze with a smile.

"Yes, thank you. That sounds lovely. I'm looking forward to it."

They exchanged numbers and emails on their phones and said their goodbyes for now.

Anne didn't even mind the very pointed *look* that Sophia sent her way.

CHAPTER NINE
Second Theme

Every so often, the unimaginable happens. Contrary to every expectation or every seeming possibility, forces in the universe seem to align to bring some unanticipated phenomenon to fruition. Sometimes it's an uncanny coincidence of events that brings two long-lost friends together. Sometimes it's putting your hand into a pocket that you thought was empty, only to find a five-dollar bill just when you're itching for a cappuccino, or finding an empty parking spot right in front of your destination. And sometimes, just sometimes, the weather forecast is accurate.

Wednesday was one of those unusual days. The evening proved to be lovely. The afternoon had been warm but not too hot, and as the day began to drift towards night, the air cooled that little bit further until the temperature was perfect for a ramble in the park. It was still bright daylight when Anne stepped off the subway to meet William at High Park as they had arranged, but it would only be an hour or so before sunset would extend its fingers through the few clouds.

Meeting by the subway station had been her idea. He had offered to drive by her building to pick her up, but she had insisted she was happy to meet him at their destination. Stay cool, stay independent, she reminded herself. She was quite prepared to enjoy William's company, but Fred was never far from her thoughts—or her heart. She would have to exorcise him eventually, but it was still too raw to make that effort now.

And so, she would just cover her wounds with the balm of a handsome and interesting man's attention. As long as she made certain he knew she only wished for friendship, there should be no trouble. She hoped.

She stepped out of the subway station and checked in her bag for her equipment. Camera, telephoto lens, tablet, phone, notebook... yes, everything was there. Perhaps, if they tried this again, she might bring a tripod. But tonight was more for enjoyment than any particular artistic effort.

She scanned the street and saw him waiting. He answered her wave, and she hurried in his direction. To her surprise, he leaned in to press a kiss to her cheek. Nothing intimate, more European than familiar, but it took her aback. She didn't think she said anything, but perhaps she stiffened. He clearly sensed her surprise.

"Oh, forgive me." He stepped back with an embarrassed laugh. "I forget that we're still all but strangers. I feel like I've known you for so long." He shuffled his feet. "I promise to be a perfect gentleman! Shall we, my lady?"

Those feet, Anne noticed, were encased in light walking shoes today. Gone were the jacket and tie of last Friday, but even in casual beige chinos and a white polo shirt, William looked like he had stepped off a magazine cover. Give him a sweater draped artistically around his neck, or a tennis racket in his hand, and the image would be complete. Although, Anne considered, the camera around his neck filled the spot rather perfectly, too.

They crossed the street into the park itself and wandered down the main path for a while. High Park was a huge expanse of parkland, about 400 acres, reaching almost two kilometres from Bloor Street to the lakefront. It had something for everyone: picnic grounds, an outdoor theatre, sports facilities, hiking trails, a zoo, and a large pond that was home to all manner of local waterfowl. This pond, as they had discussed by text, would be their destination.

But with that detail already cleared up, Anne felt her social awkwardness around her shoulders, heavier than her camera and backpack. Should there be conversation? Surely, she must think of something witty to say. "Nice camera" was not exactly the sort of thing one said to impress a man like William Barnett.

"That's a nice camera." Oh heavens. She couldn't stop the words in time.

But instead of sneering, he beamed in pride.

"It's fairly new. I got it a couple of months ago for my niece's birthday party, but I haven't put it through its paces yet. I spent so long at the camera shop, looking at every model they had and asking a thousand questions, the poor salesman must have rued the day he first saw me. I think I had him on speed-dial for a while. We discussed different lenses and the relative benefits and disadvantages of DSLR and mirrorless, and how many megapixels I really needed, and eventually I got this little toy." He cradled it like a newborn babe. "And what have I done? Taken snapshots of a seven-year-old eating cake."

His laugh was low and appealing, the gentle sounds of a wooden marimba, warm and inviting.

"What equipment do you have?" He gestured to Anne's bag with his head, and she fished out her own camera as they walked.

"It's nothing particularly fancy, but it has a rather nice lens and it's not too heavy. I chose the mirrorless for that reason. I don't really need too many fancy bells and whistles, and I do a bit of post-production on my computer, anyway. But the lens is what's important for me. We can always play with the superficial appearance, but unless there's a good clear core to the picture, there is little point in dressing it up."

He turned his light eyes on her and cocked his head. "I'd never thought of it that way. You are, of course, correct. You've thought a lot about this, haven't you? Brains and beauty in one package. And talent. So very much talent. I am truly in awe of you."

How to respond to this? She mumbled something self-deprecating in return and asked where he wanted to start.

"There." William gestured to one side of the path. "There's a track there that I think leads down to the pond. The light is lovely now. Shall we see what we can spot? The swans might be out on the water."

The path they had chosen was narrow and uneven as it led down a hill towards their goal. There was little conversation as they picked their way down, other than the occasional "careful of the branches" or "watch for that root."

"Wait!" Anne whispered just before they reached the bottom. "There, up in the tree. Do you see him?" A flash of red had caught her eye. "I don't think he's close enough to photograph, but let me try. I hope he doesn't fly away."

With quick practised motions, she changed her lens to the telephoto and then crept forward. The cardinal was posed perfectly, brilliant red against the deep green of the tree behind him, the sun that slipped through the foliage illuminating him like some chiaroscuro painting. Caravaggio in the wilderness. She raised the camera to find the best angle, praying that the bird would remain posed until she had taken at least one shot.

Click. Click. He was still there. Hardly daring to breathe for fear of alerting the bird to her existence, she fiddled with some settings, moved a bit to the side, and tried again. *Click. Click.*

At last, the bird seemed to realise he was the model in a photoshoot and took wing. But he had remained still for long enough that one of those photos might turn out. She looked forward to getting home to download the images onto her computer.

"You're very patient." She had almost forgotten about William, so intent had she been on getting the shot. "What settings do you usually use? How do you compensate for the uneven light?"

They walked down the last section to the wider path that skirted the pond, talking about ISO settings and F-stops and depth of field. A man stood by the water's edge where a heron perched proudly on a log. The camera in his hand made Anne's look like a child's toy, its massive lens a good eighteen inches long.

William hurried her along a bit. "I know they say that it's skill and not equipment that makes the art."

He winked at her. Was that some sort of double entendre?

Without missing a beat, he continued, "But I suspect that his snapshots will be better than anything I could ever produce with my camera. Perhaps I should have gone a level up."

They walked slowly, scanning the area for more things to photograph. A patch of moss on a tree branch, interesting shadows coaxed into existence by the setting sun, an unexpected patch of wildflowers complete with dancing butterflies.

"There. That's the shot." Anne put her hand on William's arm. She pointed towards the pond, where the angled light was hitting the wind-ruffled surface, painting golden ripples across the surface of the spangled water. Two mallards floated on the small crests, black silhouettes against this display of light and water. The scene was made complete by a frame of leafy branches and artistically fallen logs.

He nodded and the two set about the task of selecting apertures and angles to capture the image. This might be one to enlarge and frame, if Anne's expectations matured into reality. As the ducks floated up and down, in and out of the frame, they snapped dozens of shots each, moving this way and that, playing with angles, exposures, and other settings.

It had been a long time since Anne had felt so comfortable with a stranger.

By the time their walk was over, the sun had all but set. It was a beautiful time in the city. "Let's get a coffee. My treat. Then, if you wish, I can drive you home."

The idea was most appealing. "Thanks. That sounds lovely."

They were soon settled on uncomfortable chairs in a noisy coffee shop, each with a cup of tea steaming in front of them. They discussed photo editing software, what sorts of adjustments and processing they liked, and then talked about setting up a Flickr account to share their finished images. William pulled out his phone and looked up apologetically.

"Do you mind? Normally I would never do this in company, and especially not such charming company, but..." he shrugged, the playful little boy appearing again. "I'm already on Flickr, to share photos with my brother, so this will just take a moment."

"Of course. Don't worry about it."

This man could be very charming. He was attentive, considerate. So many people put their phones ahead of their in-person company and thought little of checking email and texting with others while supposedly out with a friend.

In a minute, he put the phone down and smiled. "There. That was easy. I've emailed you the link. Since we took photos of the same things, it will be interesting to see what sorts of differences there are in our pictures."

"Here's to photography." She raised her mug in a toast.

"And to new friends," he replied.

She beamed at him in response.

Anne set about uploading and tinkering with her photographs the next morning. She was working on a commission for a local choir, but part of the music was not coming together in her head and she knew, from experience, that a change of activity could let the musical ideas coalesce without her conscious intervention. Photoshop was an excellent choice. It kept her creative and thinking, but it involved such different ideas and skills that there was no interference with the burbling notes that tickled the back of her brain.

The photographs of the cardinal were, at first, disappointing. The light was good, but the composition was lacking. It took a great deal of cropping and shifting the focal point of the image before she settled on a result that pleased her. She adjusted the exposure and the black and white settings and played with the channel corrections to bring out the red. There. Now to play with selective focus, to leave the bird itself in sharp relief against a slightly blurred field of greenery, just like a bed of off-beat syncopations in the altos and sopranos would allow the tenor melody to emerge.

"Ha! That's it." She abandoned her photos for a while to work on her choir piece. It still needed a lot of work, but this was a good start. It would provide the technical foundation on which to base the rest of the piece. She worked for a couple of hours, then made herself a quick lunch and sat down at the computer again to upload the cardinal to William's Flickr account.

He had already put up some of his photos. They were good, well-composed and thoughtful. He could still use the abilities of his camera to better advantage, but it was clear he had a good eye. She sat down to jot him a quick email, explaining how the photograph had helped her solve the problem of her choir piece, and returned to the other shots she had taken.

The pictures of the ducks against the bright water of the pond were more promising still, and soon she was lost again in her world of light and contrast and leading lines. At last, she was satisfied and uploaded her pictures, only to see a reply email from William.

Not only lovely and a brilliant composer, but a skilled photographer, too. Anne, my hat is off to you.

She sat down to compose a reply, and they chatted back and forth for a while before William suggested another outing the following week. This time, it was an exhibit of street art in an old warehouse near the railway tracks. It was not Anne's normal style, but the idea was tantalising nonetheless, and she accepted.

Once again, he met her at the closest subway station and they walked the last few blocks together, following a crowd of people heading in the same direction. The area had once been full of light industry and storage facilities; now it was a pocket of old empty buildings surrounded by a gentrifying neighbourhood that had, not so long before, been home to working men and women. Their particular destination had been chosen for its large inner spaces that could house the large pieces the exhibit showed.

"Look at these buildings." William's eyes roved from side to side. "So much potential, so much of it untapped. Most people see empty shells that had their best days half a century ago. But imagine, Anne. Imagine these turned into combined ateliers and living spaces? Those ugly windows? Imagine the light they'd let in for a painter. Those dull concrete floors? So easy to soundproof for musicians. They could probably add performance and rehearsal spaces to the ground floor, and leave the upper storeys for studios."

His eyes were bright with possibilities.

Anne peered at him.

"This is what I do," he explained. "You haven't asked, but it will come out soon enough; it's why I'm on the board, after all. I'm a property developer. That's the business that drew me away from my clarinet. Most of the time we work on new developments, but retrofitting old spaces is a bit of a passion of mine. The space is there. The buildings are there. They're cheap and unused, and they have such potential. Infill is what the city needs, rather than this endless sprawl that we're seeing. I need to look into this area."

She gave a tight moue.

"I'm boring you. I'm sorry."

"No, no, I'm not bored. It's just something I know so little about."

"It's like your photographs, I guess. You see beauty in unexpected places in the parks. I see it in unexpected old factories. We have a lot in common, Doctor Elliot, and I'm delighted I've met you."

CHAPTER TEN
Con Brio

Over the next weeks, Anne found herself more and more in William's company.

If there was a show on some small stage, he knew about it and was able to get tickets; likewise, he was in the loop for a wider variety of art exhibits than she knew existed. At times he would suggest something more casual, like a stroll along the lakefront or an outing to one of the more interesting parts of town, or a farmer's market, or another photography excursion. And each time he made a suggestion, Anne was pleased to accept.

He was excellent company. He was intelligent and witty, and his love of the arts was clear. Nor did it hurt that he was a handsome man, one that any woman would be pleased to have walking at her side. Anne was not a vain woman, but she could not help but be satisfied by the glances that others cast in their direction when they were out together. At times she would catch a glimpse of their reflection in some shop window and think, *what a lucky couple,* before realising she was seeing herself. It went a long way to heal her wounds after Fred's desertion and to bolster her ego.

She found her horizons expanding as well as her social calendar. As she and William talked, over a stroll or over drinks or a picnic lunch somewhere, she learned more about property development than she ever imagined she would know. He spoke with pride about the high-end condominium and townhouse project he was working on north of the city, up on Lake Simcoe. He boasted about the design of the project and how well it would be incorporated into the local community rather than replacing it, helping to bring new vibrancy to a small moribund town, and promising new custom for the town's shopkeepers and a revitalisation of the existing school in the area with the new residents' children.

"The ground floor of the condominium building is set up as a sort of community centre for the development," he explained, as gazed absently over a marina down at the lake. "There will be a swimming pool and gym, of course, and the expected communal rooms and party space, as well as tennis courts behind the building. We are thinking of opening up membership to the whole town, or possibly building some other facilities in the town itself, where there is space. Perhaps in the empty field behind the high school, or near the library. We want this to benefit everybody. We are also putting in three additional banquet rooms on the first floor, but these will be high end, the sort you would expect to see in a world-class hotel. Crystals, floor to ceiling mirrors, marble, the works. Nothing but the best. And the largest of these rooms will be a full-sized ballroom."

He executed an elaborate mock bow, ignoring the gulls that shrieked overhead. "Do you wish to recreate your favourite Regency dance, my lady? We'll have all the space you need for that, and more. We could hire a band and I could be Mr. Darcy to your Miss Bennet!

"In fact," he dropped his voice conspiratorially, "I have an idea of using the space for orchestra functions. Do we want a gala dinner? The kitchen will be top-flight; any caterer would be thrilled to work there. There can be dining and dancing, and an art auction if we want. Plenty of parking, not too far from the city... We are even discussing setting aside one floor of the building as private hotel space so a select few guests can stay overnight. This is all provisional still, but we are really excited about the possibilities."

He had the same infectious enthusiasm when he mentioned another development in the Caribbean. This project was further from fruition, but the prospectus had been distributed and they had a healthy group of buyers ready to take possession of their specially designed units as soon as the construction permits were complete.

"The islands, you know..." he shrugged. "Things take time. We expected this, of course. It's just another way of doing things and I don't fault them. But I cannot wait until I can invite you to fly down with me for a long weekend at this luxury private beach resort."

Still, for all his invitations and flirtation, he was the perfect gentleman at all times. Anne grew accustomed to his friendly peck on the cheek, and reciprocated in kind, but other than a gentle hand on her elbow or the touch on her shoulder, he made no physical overtures whatsoever. The more she thought about it, the more she found it odd.

Did he know about her past with Fred? She had heard no rumours about herself and the new conductor, for all that she was not plugged into the local rumour mill. Still, it would not take a lot of digging to learn that she and Fred had been together all those years ago. If William had looked into her background even a bit, he must know this. But of course, even Sophia didn't know. Or at least, she didn't know the details. Neither she nor Fred had been famous then; no one cared about who impoverished grad students dated or lived with. It really could be that there was nothing to find.

Was William being a gentleman out of consideration? Was he giving her the time and space to decide when—if—to take their relationship further? Or, she now wondered, was it a relationship at all? Was he, perhaps, just being friendly, with no other intentions at all? By day, she looked forward to their next outing, but by night, when she was alone with her thoughts, she analysed them, perhaps a bit too much.

She flopped down on her bed and stared at the ceiling. Marie was right. It has been so long since she had been involved in anything like a relationship, she hardly knew how to read the signs anymore. Those long walks, the dinners out, the cosy conversations—all seemed to suggest that William had a romantic interest in her. Perhaps he was just taking things slowly. Perhaps she should make the first move.

But... the awareness hit her. She was happy as things were. Did she want there to be a move? Did she want things to progress? Or was this gentle friendship enough for now? If she was honest with herself, Fred's actions still hurt more than she wanted to admit. He had come to her, had made love to her, and then left her without a backwards glance.

Her heart was not ready for another amour. She did not want William to move any more quickly than he was, for all that she enjoyed being with him. She would take his friendship as it was offered, and if, in time, he suggested becoming something more, she would consider her heart then.

Still, for the moment, he seemed as happy as she with a friendship, and from time to time their photographs would appear on the *About Town* pages of one or another of the local newspapers. If she did not find them, Sophia made a point of telling her.

As Anne and William were seen about town together, so were Fred and Louisa, the horn player from the orchestra. Fred was more of a public figure than was Anne; his very career propelled him into the greater world, for he worked his art in front of the crowds. As such, his social life was somewhat under the public lens. Where Anne and William made only an occasional appearance in the newspaper and on social media, images of the conductor and musician were more common, and someone had even set up an Instagram account just to document where they had been and had been seen. Sophia sent Anne these links all too often; she likely meant well, but had no idea how much it hurt to see Fred, whom she had loved so much, cavorting with another woman before the eyes of the city. And Anne would not tell Sophia to stop. That would involve baring her heart, which she had no intention of doing.

Louisa had changed her image somewhat. The bright blue hair was now a darker burgundy shade, still vibrant and edgy, but veering more to the elegant than the playful. She was dressing up too, if the photographs could be believed, putting on the glam to match Fred's natural style and good looks.

With every photograph that passed under her eyes, Anne felt her heart ache, but she was determined no longer to let the conductor under her skin. He had made his choice. He made it eight years ago, and he made it again earlier this summer, and she would not suffer for it any longer.

Her life was hers to live and enjoy, and enjoy it she would. She tried to convince herself of this every day.

So it was that when an unexpected email appeared on her computer screen at the end of July, she was delighted.

From: Jasmine Smith
To: anne.elliot@torontomusicians.net
Subject: Reaching out, was Jasmine Hamilton

Hello Anne,

I hope you remember me. I'm Jasmine Hamilton, and we were friendly at university all those years ago during our undergrad. You were majoring in performance and composition and I was in the music education program, and we studied music theory and history together. Wow, that seems like a long time ago.

I saw the exposé on you in the Times-Tribune a few months ago, and I've been thinking ever since that I should reach out. I kept second guessing myself, but I finally decided to do it.

I hope you don't mind. Your email was on the orchestra's web page, so I thought it would be alright.

I'm looking forward to hearing from you if you want to reconnect,

Jasmine

A hundred memories all sprang up at once of the bubbly young violinist. She had been pretty and slightly chubby, with that thick black hair that Anne could only dream about. They had never been particularly close, but they were certainly often found together after class or sitting together on the lawn outside the music building with their books open and ignored around them as they chatted about everything under the sun. Perhaps Jasmine had never been one of her closest soulmates, but she had been a lovely person to hang out with and all of Anne's memories were good ones.

Smith... So Jasmine had married. What else was she up to now? If Anne was to embrace a new attitude to life, where better to start than by reconnecting with an old friend, a link back to an earlier time when they had all been happy and carefree?

She poured herself a glass of iced tea and sat down to reply.

From: Anne Elliot
To: Jasmine Smith
Subject: Re: Reaching out, was Jasmine Hamilton

Jasmine!

What a wonderful surprise to see your email. Of course I remember you. After all those hours trying to figure out those harmonic progressions, how could I forget? I've thought about you often over the years and I'm so pleased you reached out.

What are you doing these days? Are you teaching? Do you have a family? If you are still in town, perhaps we could meet for a coffee and talk in person. I'd love to see you again.

Best,

Anne

Jasmine wrote back within the hour. She was back in Toronto after several years out of town and was very pleased to make plans. They settled on the coming Thursday afternoon near High Park, where Anne and William had gone for their first... date? Outing? Photography walk. It was an old but vibrant neighbourhood, and if the coffee shop proved too noisy, there would be plenty of places to walk around outside.

On Thursday, Anne dressed carefully. Her closet was a forest of dark blues and blacks, even her summer clothes, and she decided it was time to buy something a little brighter. Time to *be* a little brighter. Still, with the options before her, she chose a smart silk t-shirt in the dark blue that Sophia liked on her and paired it with a mosaic print broomstick skirt. Smart, but not fussy. Casual but still put together. A pair of gold stud earrings and a chunky necklace completed the look.

Then she went to the bathroom and found the blush she had bought for her outings with William, and dusted a bit on her cheeks. It was a soft pink, more a hint than a colour, but it helped her feel a bit more like the young musician Jasmine would have known all those years ago. A quick swipe of tinted lip gloss and a touch of mascara and she was ready. Easy but put together.

Still, she had changed a lot over the years, and not for the better, and she hoped Jasmine would recognise her.

When she entered the coffee shop, she knew Jasmine in a moment. If the years had been hard on Anne, they had been more so on her friend. But despite the drawn look about her mouth and eyes, her face was still pretty and her amazing hair tumbled down her back in an ebony waterfall, with not a streak of grey in it.

The moment their eyes met, Jasmine rose, and the two hugged each other like long-lost friends. Which, of course, they were.

After some preliminary *how are you*'s and the necessary ordering of lattes and snacks, they settled in to catch up with each other.

"You're looking good, Anne." Jasmine should have been a singer with her melodic voice. It was a gentle mezzo soprano, all smooth caramel and lilting cadences. "The photos in that newspaper spread were good, but they made you look older than you look in person. I guess the photographer wanted to emphasise your experience rather than your youth."

"My youth!" Anne laughed. "That, my friend, has flown."

"Ahem, but I'm three years older than you, and I still consider myself a babe, so you must be young. I'll hear nothing else."

Jasmine did look older. But it would not do to comment. Instead, Anne said, "So what have you been up to? I can't believe it's been so long."

The other woman shook her head. Her smile was sad. "It's been... it's been a bit rough. I won't lie. I went back to India for a while after

I got my MEd. I had grand ideas of teaching music in the schools there."

Of course. Jasmine inherited her British last name from her English father, but her complexion and features from her Indian mother. If Anne recalled, her grandfather had been the concertmaster of the New Delhi Symphony Orchestra—a venerable heritage for her violinist friend.

"Was your time in India what you hoped for?"

Now the smile was lighter. "Yes. I lived with my aunt and cousins and really loved it there. But when my father became ill, I moved back to Canada. He died two years later, and I stayed."

Anne mumbled the appropriate condolences.

"Then I met Connor. That's the Smith part of my name. We've been married for six years. No kids, before you ask."

"You don't seem happy." In Anne's limited experience, a wife should smile when talking to somebody about her husband for the first time.

"Oh, I am. That is… we are. Look, I won't bore you with these messy details. Connor is great and I'm very happy with him, but we've fallen on some rough times and it's taking its toll. But enough about me. We didn't get together after all this time to listen to me moan.

"You! Annie Elliot, my study buddy, are a world-famous composer. I should ask if I can rub your hand. I want to hear all about you! Tell me about this new piece the newspaper article mentioned."

And so, Anne told her about the composer-in-residence position and her symphony. "The real joy," she added, "is working with the orchestra, having them as a partner in the process. What I hear in my head isn't always what I hear from the stage, and their comments are helping me shape this symphony into something I'm very proud of."

From here, they drifted into reminiscences of people they had known back in school. Anton, the cellist, Christina the guitar player, Monica the soprano. She had gone far—her fabulous voice now rang from some of the world's best concert stages, not bad for a girl who grew up singing in her church choir in a small town in the Maritimes.

"What about that fellow you were dating? Fred. He was a couple of years ahead of us, right? He's also made it big. He's back in town too, isn't he?" Jasmine's eyes were wide. Did she really not know? "You two seemed made for each other. I guess it didn't work out, eh?"

No. She didn't know. Jasmine had done her master's degree in education rather than in music and had rather disappeared from Anne's life by the time she and Fred...

Anne swallowed a sigh and searched for the appropriate version of the tale. "We were together for a while. All through grad school, really." That sounded okay. "But life took us in very different directions, literally. He went to Europe and I didn't, and that was the end."

Jasmine pinched her lips, her head shaking slightly. "That's too bad. Is it strange having him back in town? You'll be working with him at the orchestra, won't you? Or are your roles so different that you don't really have much to do with each other?"

A sip of coffee. Her usual avoidance technique.

No, she would not hide anymore. No more fumbling to protect her damaged soul. She sat up straight and looked her friend in the eye.

"It was uncomfortable at first, but we have established a good working relationship. We're both in it for the music, so we're on the same side. I wish him well in his life, wherever that leads him."

Jasmine reached over to cover Anne's hand. "You were always such a good egg, Annie. I'm so thrilled we've reconnected."

They talked for an hour before Jasmine made her excuses. "I'm really sorry I have to go. I have my violin students coming. That's how we're making ends meet these days. But can we get together again soon? I've missed you."

"Of course! I have my work, but my time is more flexible. Let's make another date quickly."

Both drew out their phones and in a matter of moments, a second coffee date was scheduled, to both women's satisfaction. Perhaps, Anne considered as she walked back to the subway, the rest of the summer would not be so dreary after all.

Her prediction was accurate.

No sooner had she arrived home when her phone binged its notification of a text. It was from William.

Heading up to see the new development tomorrow. Join me?

She stared at the phone for a moment. Was this the move on his part that she had been wondering about? Until now, they had met in public near to their destination. She was usually coming by public transit, he by car. She had never been alone with him in his vehicle, other than the occasional quick drive home; at most such offers she had demurred and had returned by bus or subway. Perhaps that was the reason he had held back so much. Now that she thought about it, she was definitely sending messages that she was not ready to be alone with him for anything more than a few short minutes.

This invitation, though, was something very different. There was no question of her getting there by herself. Even if some sort of regional transit were available—a bus or a commuter train—the final leg of the trip would have to be by car. She could rent her own vehicle, she supposed, and drive herself, but that seemed contrary to the intent of the request.

William had always been everything polite and proper. What was making her so nervous?

She ignored his message for the time being and called Sophia instead.

Her friend answered on the first ring.

"Annie! You've been the busy creature of late. I was thinking you'd forgotten your old friends."

"Hi Soph. I could never forget you! But you're right. I've been out a lot recently."

"Making up for lost time? The grapevine tells me you've been seen with William Barnett a lot."

"Mmmm. He's very attentive and we seem to have a lot in common."

"And handsome. Don't tell me that doesn't make a difference."

"You're teasing me." Pause. "That's actually why I called. What do you know about him?"

On the other end of the line, Sophia hemmed for a moment. "I don't know a lot, really. Just what I've seen on the official biography from the orchestra and the few minutes I've had to talk to him. Give me a moment." Anne heard the phone being set down and then the sounds of somebody rustling around in the background, followed by the familiar clicks of hands tapping at a computer screen. Then Sophia's voice was back, the tinny sound suggesting she had put the phone on the speaker setting.

"Right. He's local, born in Toronto, educated in the UK and Montreal, thirty-eight years old, married once."

Oh.

"You didn't know?" Sophia sounded surprised. Had she heard Anne's surprise over the phone?

"No. We've never really talked about our pasts that much. Mostly, we discuss art and our plans and ideas."

It was true. Was this also a sign that his interest in her was purely platonic? Or was he once more giving her the space to bring up the past? Why were men so confusing?

Sophia clucked over the phone. "I see. Well, that's fine. Better to know where a man is going than where he's been. Do you want to know about his wife? If he hasn't mentioned it... But then, it's hardly a secret. A quick web search will tell you everything you need to know."

"Just the basics, I guess."

There were a couple of moments more of hemming, then Sophia continued. "She was from Montreal, from a wealthy and well-connected family. Part of the circles most of us never aspire to. Friends with the You-Know-Whos." She didn't elaborate, but Anne could imagine her eyebrows rising suggestively. The You-Know-Whos were probably some big political dynasty or something.

"It doesn't look like it was a very happy marriage. Hmm.... from what I'm reading, they spent more time apart than together. You know the thing, she's in Cancun, he's skiing at Tremblant, that sort of stuff. But that's when he started really getting involved in the big development projects he does now."

"Yes. I know about that. We've talked about some of his developments. So, when did they divorce? I guess he got enough of a start that he didn't need her money anymore."

"Oh, they didn't divorce. She died. Car crash. It was one one of those trips she took. Her car went off some mountain road. Sort of like Grace Kelly, but in Saint Lucia and not Monaco. It left him sitting pretty. Whatever she had, it's all his now."

Oh. "No wonder he's never brought it up. Those must be hard memories to relive. Was he with her?"

"Give me a moment." Another moment of hemming while Sophia clicked at her keyboard. "No. He was visiting some building site near Vancouver. She was with... let's see... a friend. A man. He also died. I can't find anything else right now. It was just one of those tragedies, I guess."

"Wow. I wouldn't want to talk about that either. But he's okay? He's asked me to go to see one of his developments up north tomorrow."

"You're being very Victorian, Anne. Are you asking if you can trust him? Of course you can. He's on the board of the orchestra. The last thing he needs is for something to happen to the best thing that's happened to the organisation in years. You're his bread and butter right now."

"That's not very flattering, Soph."

She heard a chuckle from the other end of the line. "You know what I mean. No, I've heard nothing against him. No rumours of nasty goings-on in the back rooms or the bedrooms, no whispers or allegations. No Reddit threads. You really haven't been alone with him? It's been weeks since you started going out."

"We're not 'going out.' We're just... doing things together."

If you could hear somebody roll her eyes, Anne heard Sophia. "Potato, potahto, Annie dear. Go. Enjoy the day. You can call me from the car so he knows that I know, if it helps. Tell me about it when you get home."

CHAPTER ELEVEN
Allegretto

William came by Anne's building at ten o'clock the next morning. She had risen early to work on the suite for choir she had been commissioned to compose, and was happy with her progress so far. The second movement was all but complete, with its delicate trills in the sopranos and its syncopated rhythms in the tenors. It was bright and cheerful, an ode to spring, a counterpoint to the stately first movement. It was ready to be set aside until the third movement was complete. Then she could listen to the entire composition as a whole and work on the changes and reworking that would be needed to bring it all together.

Now for the third movement. She had her text, excerpts from a poem by nineteenth-century Canadian author and poet E. Pauline Johnson. She had read and absorbed the words until she knew them by heart, had picked apart the poetry for meaning and rhythm, and had spoken to an English professor at the University about the piece in case she had missed something of import in the words. Now she only had to wait for the music that would arrive to set them to their best advantage.

> *There's a spirit on the river, there's a ghost upon the shore,*
> *They are chanting, they are singing through the starlight evermore,*
> *As they steal amid the silence,*
>   *And the shadows of the shore.*

There was a beauty and power to the words, one she did not want to disturb with forced melody. It would come to her. She hoped. In the meantime, she would allow her subconscious to work while she enjoyed the day with William.

He was already there when she stepped out of the elevator and into her building's lobby. This was not a man to make a lady wait. He opened the car door for her and waited until she was seated to close it. In a moment, Anne thought jokingly, he would lay his cloak down across puddles so she could cross without getting her delicate feet wet in the mud. Still, while it was very old-fashioned, it was nice to be treated with such attention.

"Do you listen to music when you drive?" he asked as they merged onto the highway heading out of town. "I usually have something on, but I didn't want to presume... music probably means something very different to you than to me. I just enjoy the pretty sounds. For you, it might be something of a busman's holiday."

Considerate again.

"Some music would be fine. What do you like?"

He nodded to his phone, which sat in the well between them. "The playlist is up. Feel free to scan through it. It's hooked up to the Bluetooth, so when you find something you like, just hit play."

She did as invited, and soon the sounds of Bach's Brandenburg concertos filled the car. They were beautiful and intricate, but comfortable, like an old friend. Perfect driving music.

The highway slipped through the city, a long grey ribbon that carried with it all manner of vehicles from low sleek sports cars to hulking rigs and trailers. From the luxurious comfort of William's car, it seemed as if they were staying still with the city and its inhabitants all rushing past them. The cabin allowed in only the barest trace of noise from outside; instead of the sounds of the road, all they heard was the soft cushion of Bach and the gentle ebb and flow of conversation. Outside their insulated bubble, the world rushed along at its relentless speed. The tall buildings of downtown gave way to lower structures and light industrial parks, which in turn tapered to parkland and vast fields. And through it all, the highway carried them, first along the lakefront and then northward and out of town.

They talked of everything and nothing, that pleasant but meaningless conversation that simply passes the time but then is forgotten. The weather, the upcoming summer music festival, the annual September book fair that took over the city's streets. Had Anne ever gone to a reading? What did she think of crowded outdoor patios? Was a cloudy day preferable to one sunny but too hot?

It was all perfectly appropriate conversation for a drive, interesting enough to keep both parties engaged and satisfied, not so deep as to distract the driver from the road. It was comfortable. The silver road slipped through the countryside, and the time passed quickly.

"Nearly there," William exclaimed as they passed a signpost. "Just another few kilometres to our exit."

He was a good and confident driver, and within minutes, he guided the car into the exit lane and off the highway. A right turn here, a ten-minute drive, a left, and soon they were entering a small town. As they crested a low hill, Anne could see the blue lake in the distance, sunlight dimpling off the bright water.

"The development is on the far side of town, with access to the little harbour." William turned down a street that led through a small downtown. It was, in many ways, typical of small-town Ontario. The commercial area was perhaps three blocks long, lined with rows of three- and four-storey buildings that looked to date from the early 1900s. Some were older, some were newer, but it was clear that very little development had taken place in over a century. Until now.

There, in the distance, just past the 1950s school building, and down the road towards the lake, towered a huge yellow crane. As they came closer, Anne noticed rows of cars and SUVs—belonging to the work crews, she imagined—and then a veritable armada of work trucks and other construction vehicles. They passed a small kiosk at the side of the worksite, where William waved at the person inside, and they entered the area.

"Well?" William beamed as he helped Anne from the car. "What do you think?" He gestured to the work-in-progress around them with the puffed pride of a new father showing off his offspring.

It was, to Anne's eyes, a forest of steel and concrete. The bones of the buildings were there, waiting for the cladding of organ and muscle and skin—pipes and ducts and walls—to be completed.

The townhouses were closer to completion than was the taller condominium building, looking very much as they would when families began to move in. They lacked nice gardens and paved drives, but from the outside, at least, the buildings were finished. The tower—all eight storeys of it—was more of a work-in-progress. There was no gaping pit, but the structure was still very much in its skeletal stages, tall shafts of steel protruding from the solid concrete that formed its base. Like high, stacked chords emerging from a thick bed of supporting sound, a sturdy framework on which to hang the luxuries of walls and electricity, melody and ornament.

> *Mine is the undertone;*
> *The beauty, strength, and power of the land*
> *Will never stir or bend at my command;*
> *But all the shade*
> *Is marred or made,*
> *If I but dip my paddle blade;*
> *And it is mine alone.*

The words of Pauline Johnson's poem were already in her mind. Now, as the leaves swirled in the imagined landscape of the evocative passage, so did the notes in Anne's head, a note here, a leaf there, until they came together in an eddy of light and sound and colour and tone. The strong power of the land, the undertone of permanence and solidity, the tall reaching trees, stretching to the opal-hued heavens of the first verse.

Where softly swings
The music of a thousand wings
That almost tones to sadness.

She could hear it, a single descant soprano voice soaring above the lush forest of harmony like a bright bird against the midsummer sky, looking down on the peacefulness of this landscape. She closed her eyes and committed the melody to memory, and then, to be safe, reached into her tote for her tablet and stylus to make some notes.

"Anne?"

How long had she been standing there? Had she been staring into space like she had lost her senses? Was it seconds? Minutes? She blinked and called the world back to her.

"Anne? Everything alright?"

"Yes. Sorry, William. It's a piece I'm writing. It just came to me, seeing this…" She turned slowly in place to take in the sights that surrounded them.

"This?" He chuckled. "It's hardly picturesque. In a few months, perhaps, or when the marina is complete and we're out on the water…" He gave a quick shrug. "But all I see now is dirt and girders."

He was correct, of course. There was little beauty in the harsh steel and rough concrete. But there was promise. The seeds were there. The inspiration.

"It was more the idea than the reality. The pilings are a foundation of sound. The beams are strong shafts of chords... It's hard to explain. Sometimes ideas come, almost from nowhere."

"That is a true gift."

"Only sometimes. They don't always come. Then I need to go hunting for them. That feels almost rude, like I'm disturbing a melody when it just wants to lie hidden. But I have to force it out into the open, and they don't always like that."

He was staring at her.

"You must think I'm mad."

He pulled her into a one-shoulder hug. "Mad, in the most charming way possible. We should all have your sort of madness, Anne. What a beautiful place the world would be then."

He released her and caught her hand with his. "I have a surprise for you. It's August ninth today."

She nodded at him. A little black rock settled in her stomach. She had hoped nobody would know.

"You hadn't said anything, and I didn't want to presume, but according to the orchestra's website, it's your birthday. I was presumptuous enough to order some cupcakes from one of the local bakeries. Do you mind?"

He asked with such concern in his eyes she could only forgive him. It was not his fault that she disliked the fuss that usually accompanied birthdays, and if the full extent of his presumption was a plate of cupcakes, that she could well stand.

"Thank you. That was very thoughtful."

He led her past the nascent condominium building to where a lonely picnic table sat overlooking the harbour. A young man in jeans and a yellow t-shirt and matching hardhat was setting out a few small things, and at William's wave, he nodded and walked away. This was not like Sophia's grand spread in Niagara those few weeks ago, but it was welcome, nonetheless.

Two steaming paper cups of coffee stood waiting for the addition of milk and sugar, and a plastic box posed proudly between them, the clear casing showing off the towering piles of swirled frosting underneath. There were no ribbons or balloons, no edible sequins or birthday candles, just two rather elegant cupcakes. If she had to celebrate her birthday at all, this was perfect.

She told him as much with a huge grin and pressed a kiss to his cheek. It was, she realised, the first time she had initiated any sort of real intimacy, even as tame as this.

He beamed back at her and invited her to sit so they could enjoy their late morning treat.

But all through the snack and the tour that followed, all Anne could think of was the snatch of melodic inspiration that had struck her earlier.

Later on, Anne had only fragmentary recollections of the day. She retained flashes of the semi-complete townhouses, of the concrete-walled tower, of the embryonic marina. A map-like image of the wide crescent of homes flitted through her mind, melding into the plotted out community centre and the posted plans and charts in the portable that housed the site office. William had spoken on and on about his project, and she hoped she had responded suitably. Her face hurt from trying to smile all day.

It had been a monumental effort to appear interested when all she wanted to do was come home and compose. The music had taken root in her brain, in her soul, and it screamed to be set free. The seeds had germinated and the plant must burst out of its casing and push through the soil into the light, to strive for the sun. To refuse this was to condemn it to death.

He had asked her once or twice on the drive home about the piece and she had answered the best she could. It was a suite for choir, based on the poetry of a Canadian poet, suitable for an advanced amateur group with strong singers. Her music was all original, not based on existing folk songs, but she hoped to evoke the feeling of traditional melodies through her use of modalities and strong rhythmic patterns.

He nodded and asked some more questions, and she could see his interest was genuine, yet she knew he didn't understand. Not really. No more than she understood the allure of an empty lot, begging to become a cottage community, or the need to pursue wealth for its own sake rather than for the comforts a good income could provide. She understood, sort of. But not really.

Fred would get it. He would understand completely. The translation of concrete to harmony, of sunlight to melody, of steel to chordal progressions. The way the music filled her body and her mind until it was bursting. The compulsion to write it down, to work on it, to coax it into its best possible form. He would understand every bit of it. This was his life, too.

But Fred was gone.

She worked on her piece all that night and through the next day. Sophia left a message wishing her a happy birthday and asking about her day, which she ignored for the time being. She also ignored an email from Jasmine to finalise their coffee date. There was nothing from Marie.

By the second evening, she had enough of her piece written down that she could now step back and let it bubble for a few days. Like a stew on a slow burner or a wine that needs ageing, the space of time here was the magic that let her approach her creation anew and massage the raw form into something neater, tighter, more perfect. Like the mythical bears who licked their infant cubs into shape, she could now caress and stroke and guide her new movement into something approaching its polished form. But for now, she would let it sit.

"Anne, I wondered what happened to you," Sophia gushed when Anne finally returned her call. "So? William? How was the trip?"

"It was fine." How was that for damning with faint praise? "I mean, it was interesting. I've never been on a building site before. Things are closer to finished than not, but still, walking through a building before it's put its clothes on is something new to me. Did he tell you about the ballroom?"

"The ballroom? Oh, at the condo tower. Yes. He's offered it for fundraisers and functions. Did you see it?"

Anne laughed. "There's not much to see now, but if you use your imagination, it's wonderful. It's a huge space, and they're putting in a surrounding balcony and even an orchestra gallery so the music can come from above. I think he sees it as a venue for weddings as well as community needs, and it's going to be wonderful. He tried to describe his vision for the clothing—the decor, I guess—but all I could see was some fabulous ballroom scene from a Jane Austen production. You know - those pastel dresses and tight breeches and long sets of dancers with the crowds drinking punch along the walls. Throw in some pale celandine-green walls and crisp white columns and trim, and I'll be writing minuets for them to dance to."

"And William himself?"

"Really, Soph, you're a yenta."

"Nonsense. That was my grandmother. I just want you to be happy. I know, I know. You *are* happy. But are you really, Annie? I always feel like there's a light that's gone out somewhere in your past. I wish you'd tell me about it sometime. So? William? Spill already."

Another chuckle. "He is very nice. He was everything a gentleman should be. He had even arranged a very small birthday celebration with cupcakes. Apparently, my birthdate is on the orchestra's website, which I should ask to be removed. He really was so excited to show me the place, he was like a little boy with a new pet. I hope I was enthusiastic enough about it. But I got an idea for my choir commission, and I'm afraid my mind was focussed elsewhere."

"If your mind was lost in your music, I don't think he noticed. He called to talk to Jeremy last night, and he spent most of the time talking about you."

"What? Jeremy told you this?"

"Not necessary. He had the phone on speaker since he was working at his painting. I heard the whole thing. If you were distracted, our Mr. Barnett didn't notice at all."

Was this supposed to reassure her? Anne gave a little sigh. The man was charming and excellent company, to be sure, but it seemed he didn't really understand her at all.

CHAPTER TWELVE
Sforzando

The days turned into weeks, and before long, September was on the horizon. With the orchestra's season starting so soon, announcements and advertisements were all over the press, and Frederico Valore's handsome face was plastered all over the city. On flyers, on posters in the subway and bus shelters, in the newspapers, he was there wherever Anne looked.

She thought she was immune by now, that all this recent exposure had inured her to him. But every glance pricked another hole into her heart. Anger at his cruel departure; pain at the loss. She had sworn never to put up those walls again, but she also felt she would never really heal.

The concert season was also being broadcast far and wide.

THE NATIONAL PHILHARMONIC ORCHESTRA

Introducing our new conductor

FREDERICO VALORE

In a special concert of favourite pieces

ELLIOT ~ PRELUDES
BEETHOVEN ~ SYMPHONY NO.5
HOLST ~ THE PLANETS

Anne was, of course, thrilled to be featured in this first concert of the season, and she had arranged to be at the rehearsals. The first one was shortly after Labour Day, once the arts seasons and schools were starting back again after the summer break. There was nothing much for her to do at this rehearsal—the piece had been performed countless times over the last seven years, and recorded twice, and it was past the point where Anne could change any part of it even if she wanted to do so—but she had been asked by the orchestra's board to attend, and it was always a thrill to hear how a different conductor would interpret her notes.

Her stomach jolted at the understanding that this conductor was Fred, who had been so intimately involved in the piece's inception, and with its composer. He was far too much of an artist and a professional to allow any personal baggage to colour his interpretation, but the notion disturbed Anne, nonetheless.

Thank heavens she would only be at some of the rehearsals. In addition to her duties with the orchestra, Anne was on faculty at the University's music school and her classes were starting up again as well. She only taught two courses on composition, but she worked with three students in the composition program and she was expected to be available at certain times. Some of those obligations conflicted with the rehearsals, but she had communicated this to the board, which in turn had cleared the matter with Fred.

She gave a bitter laugh. Not so long ago, they would have just spoken face to face and resolved such a minor issue in seconds. Now it involved formal communications through a third party.

Damn, she missed those old days.

"You must be so excited!" Jasmine fixed her with bright and curious eyes. "Does it ever get old, Anne, hearing your music being performed live on the concert stage?"

The two friends had met a couple of times since they reconnected and were now sitting by the boardwalk along Lake Ontario, watching the world go by. On the split pathway, people walked this way and that, some alone, others in pairs or in groups, some dragging along children or pushing strollers. Beside this path, there ran a separate one dedicated to bicycles and rollerbladers, allowing them to race without disturbing those on foot. Just beyond them, Lake Ontario glistened in the hot August sun. White gulls hovered in the air right at the edge of the water and water fowl bobbed up and down on the ripples that marred the smooth surface of the lake. Further out in the water the drone of a Seadoo ripped a swath through the water and someone on skis came tearing after it, while out in the far distance a small armada of sailboats poked their white masts and sails up into the air as their crews enjoyed the last days of the summer.

But Jasmine's eyes weren't on the bikers or the boats. They were fixed quite firmly on Anne.

Anne shrugged, trying to look nonchalant. But really, she just barely kept the huge smile that threatened to break free. At last, she gave in and giggled like a schoolgirl. "It is, really. I keep thinking that I'm still dreaming, that the CDs are little figments of my imagination."

"And that movie!"

"Is it real?" She laughed.

The friends shared a great smile. Then Anne continued. "I have to be at the first concert, and at the reception afterwards, but the real fun is watching the rehearsals. Say, Jaz, do you want to come along to one of them?"

Her friend's eyes shone even more brightly, if such a thing were possible.

"Really?" Then her smile broke. "Oh. I would love that, but it depends on when it is. My students, you know…"

"Even during the daytime? I thought they would all come after school."

"Oh, most do. But some parents pull their kids from school for music lessons, and I teach a lot of very young kids during the day and do a preschool music class at a daycare. Anything to pull in a few dollars. Connor still hasn't found work…"

Anne had wondered about this. Jasmine had never mentioned her husband's work in any specific terms, but it seemed like he was between jobs, and not intentionally. This was the first time her friend had actually said anything, and she wasn't sure how to respond.

Jasmine saved her from an awkward blunder. "I didn't want to say anything. I didn't want you feeling sorry for me, and I certainly didn't want it to seem like I was asking for anything. I know that even famous composers don't live in fancy mansions. And it's a bit embarrassing. I'm sorry."

"Do you want to walk and talk about it at all?"

They got up from the bench and found some freezies to sip on. Then they strolled with the other pedestrians until they found a bit of a pier, nestled amongst the condominiums and marinas down on the waterfront.

"We were doing well, really. Connor had a great job as a financial advisor, and I was bringing in a bit of extra teaching violin. We saved everything we could to buy a house. Then one of his friends told him about this amazing investment opportunity in the Caribbean. Some fantastic project that would quintuple its value in a couple of years, a hotel complex in a very popular spot. The plan was to buy in and keep our small apartment in the meantime until the dividends started coming in, and then we'd buy our dream house.

"Connor was so confident about it. He worked in investment, after all, and he did his homework. It looked absolutely like a sure thing. So we put in everything we had, and more. And then, just before the project was to get going, something happened. The original conglomerate sold out to another company, who immediately changed everything about the project and demanded twice what we had put in to keep our investment. We couldn't afford that. We had nothing left, and a load of debt."

"But surely the first group had to give you your money back. Isn't that how these things work?"

Jasmine sighed. She sat very still, her eyes fixed on the small toy-like boats bobbing out in the vast lake, white miniatures against a background of varied blues. She did not turn to look at Anne as she spoke. "Yes, in theory. But then things got tied up in legal and appeals, and time just ticks more slowly in some places than in others. Our lawyer keeps promising we'll get every penny back, but he can't guess when. When Connor's clients found out he'd been hoodwinked, they all abandoned him, and no one else wants to hire an investor who lost a half a million dollars of his own money overnight. So it's just me and the violin lessons now." She stared over the glimmering water. "I'm sorry, Annie. I'm being a downer. I just wanted to celebrate your success."

Anne wrapped an arm around her friend's shoulder. "I'm sorry, Jaz. I really am. If I hear of anyone wanting lessons, I'll mention your name. But listen, you should come along to the dress rehearsal if you can. I'll get you the time, or come to one of the others if that's better. And I want you to meet my friend Sophia. She and her husband move in rather elevated circles and they may know of things."

"Oh no! I would never ask anything like that. I don't want charity!"

"You're just talking to them. Leads aren't charity. That's all it would be. You never know who knows someone who might know someone. And you'll love Sophia. Maybe after the rehearsal we can all go for lunch or a drink."

The smile was back, even though it was quieter and sadder now. "Thanks. You are such a wonderful friend. I wish we hadn't drifted apart the way we did. I'm so glad we've reconnected."

Soon it was the last weekend of the summer. Monday would be Labour Day, the temporal portal that stood sentry over the year, separating the two months of summer and relaxation from the following months of work and effort. It was a rare person who was not somehow affected by this transition. Schools would start up again for those with children; performing arts seasons would begin; work became more serious.

As might be expected, this long weekend was often one of revelry, a sort of *Mardi Gras* before a period of Lenten restraint. Everybody was back in town from wherever they might have spent the summer or part thereof; everybody was looking forward to a final celebratory bash before buckling down to the serious work ahead. Anne was no exception.

She had been invited to three such parties over the long weekend. All of these invitations, she knew, were due solely to her position as composer-in-residence and not to her personal charms, but this was not unexpected. She was not a habitual party goer. But she looked through the invitations with a professional eye and accepted everything that she could fit into her schedule.

The first party, which she had little real desire to attend, was a backyard affair and barbecue on the Saturday afternoon. One of the orchestra members whom she knew from university had invited her, along with the rest of the orchestra. Trina was a gifted musician who had the fortune of having married into a wealthy family, and the grounds behind their suburban home were more than sufficient to hold the entire orchestra. There would be excellent food as well, Anne knew, and the company of people who spoke her language.

But the afternoon would be either hot and humid or rainy and humid, and no amount of beer and potato salad would make up for having to come up with enough pleasant things to say to all those people who likely saw her as either an interloper or some sort of other-worldly creature, now condescending to spend time with mere mortals. If not for the real desire not to seem, frankly, like a snob, she would have begged off. She wondered if Fred would be there. If Louisa, the horn player, was going to attend, he would almost certainly join her. Local social media had, after all, been twittering all summer with photos of the two together at this function and that, the magenta-haired dynamo hanging off his arm with a possessive glint in her eyes.

The idea was painful, and she wished, once more, that she had some perfect excuse not to attend.

On Saturday evening, there was to be another event, this much smaller and perhaps easier to get out of. Jasmine and Connor were going to a club to see a small jazz band and had invited her along. In theory, it was a wonderful plan. She knew relatively little about jazz, but always enjoyed it in the background, and moreover, she loved live music in its proper setting. And what better place for a jazz band than a cosy pub?

But after an afternoon in the sun, surrounded by the din of a hundred people all talking and calling to each other, drinking warm beer and smelling over-done burgers and greasy chips, she was certain that she would want nothing more for the evening than to sit at home. Home would be quiet and peaceful. She could have a cool drink of lemonade and eat fresh fruit and ice cream from the tub and not worry about finding more suitable things to say, even if it were to people she liked.

Still, it was such a delight to have Jasmine back in her life. She had forgotten how well they had got along at university, and the casual friendliness of their school days was maturing into the more intimate friendship of mature adults. She was eager to meet Connor, and did not want to do anything to suggest that she felt otherwise. And so, to the club she would go. At least Fred would not be there.

The only party that held any real appeal to her was the Crofts' affair, to be held in the large party room in their building on Sunday evening. This was a welcome-back celebration for the orchestra's board and staff and their partners. In true Sophia style, it would be formal and very elegant. Fine wine would be served instead of cold beer; tuxedos and cocktail gowns worn in place of shorts and flip-flops. Anne had not seen Sophia in a couple of weeks, but she could well imagine her friend buzzing about in her accustomed methodical manner, organising a small crew of waiters and prep staff to help out the caterer she had almost certainly engaged for the event.

It was not the food or the elegance of the evening that made this a welcome-ish event, but the company. Sophia had the gift of making everybody feel comfortable and welcome, and Anne loved watching her at work. And William would be there. This she knew for certain because he had called to ask if he might pick her up and attend with her. They were not a couple, *per se*, but arriving and departing together would send a certain message to anybody who had not already noticed.

This devolved into another session of staring at her bedroom ceiling, trying to work out what, exactly, she hoped for where the handsome William Barnett was concerned. She was not in love with him, not now, at least. This she could say for certain, and wondered if she hoped that might change. Still, while she enjoyed his company greatly when they were out together, she didn't miss him at all when they were apart. He had been away for a week now, seeing to some project somewhere down south. Or, at least, Anne thought it was a week. He had mentioned something when they met for an outdoor concert shortly after the trip to his development up north. After the concert, he had suggested they grab a coffee and then, over chai and cheesecake, had mumbled something about an upcoming trip before asking if she would accompany him to Sophia's function. She smiled and wished him a good and productive time while away, but she had not really taken much notice of the details. The light was suggesting an unusual harmonic progression and her mind was miles away, buried deep in the lines of some imaginary manuscript paper, subverting the cycle of fifths.

It was funny. She and William had been out several times together, sometimes to the parks, sometimes to a show. But it was almost always somewhere public, and despite the growing friendship between them, it lacked... something. Intimacy, perhaps. Not the physical sort, although he was a handsome man and the idea was not unpleasant. Should he make some more suggestive overtures, she might well accept them, and with pleasure. Perhaps, rather, there was a sort of emotional intimacy that she was missing. She didn't really know him. Despite all the time they had spent together, she still did not sense she knew the inner man beneath his suave veneer. How strange. The thought flitted across her mind not for the first time.

She had finished a morning's worth of work on her choir commission and was pleased with her progress. Now she was wandering around her apartment, debating going outside into the sticky heat or sitting at home eating ice cream from the tub. Both had their appeals and their drawbacks.

She replaced her manuscript paper into the drawer where she kept it and sharpened her pencil, ready for the next day's work. It was an old habit she had, preparing her tools for the next time she picked them up. Pencils sharp and lined up, eraser at the ready. A book of composition techniques faced her from the bookshelf, and Pauline Johnson's poetry stared at her from where she had pinned it to her corkboard. In front of all of these, Fred's face flashed before her, a figment of her imagination and more real than the physical objects before her. That's what she always saw when she was thinking of something else. Fred, not William.

She sighed.

Would he ever leave that space he had carved out in her heart? There was no avoiding him professionally, but surely, she could learn to live without him emotionally.

Still, Fred would be at Sophia's party, and if Fred was in attendance, Louisa would be likewise. Now, for the first time, she longed to see William again. His presence at her side would make her feel far less like the rejected lover, the spare wheel.

Oh, why was this all so complicated? She flopped back onto her bed and ran her hands through her hair.

Hair. She needed a haircut. Something for Sophia's party. It was a week away, and she just had time to make an appointment. It was something to do, something to keep her busy. Maybe she would even be brave enough to try a different style for a change.

Before she could convince herself otherwise, she picked up the phone to call her salon. New season, new style, new Anne. It would be done.

CHAPTER THIRTEEN
Tremolo

"Oh my God, Annie! Look at you!"

Jasmine rushed up to Anne's table at the coffee shop and stopped just short. She held her hands in front of her in a mock picture frame to capture Anne's face and beamed. "What brought this change about? You look fabulous, like a different person. Oh... not that you didn't look good before, but..." She caught her lower lip between her teeth, but didn't stop smiling.

Anne fluffed her newly shorn hair. At least, it felt shorn. It still fell to her chin, with long layers framing her face and giving the ends a bit of bounce and texture. Jessica, her hairstylist, had kept the colour its natural dark brown, but had added just a bit of apricot gloss to make her tresses glow with hidden golden depths. Not a new colour, just... more colour. The apricot brought out the blush in Anne's cheeks, and she felt, if not younger, fresher.

"You like it?" Jasmine nodded, her eyes wide. "I've had that old style for so long. It was easy—just wash and pull back into a ponytail. I can still pull it back and have those fashionable wispy things around my face, but now it looks okay loose as well. This takes some work, but I feel like a grownup for a change. I've even bought some mousse!"

"You look like a movie star," her friend agreed. "Smart, outrageously talented, and gorgeous, too. Think about what you're doing to us mere mortals."

Anne had to laugh. Jasmine had one of the prettiest faces she had ever seen. "Mere mortal, nothing. If I'm a movie star, then I'm in perfect company. What can I get you? No, no arguing. I just got my cheque from my choir commission and I insist. Latte? Chai?"

"Pah, chai! No one here makes chai like back in India. A vanilla latte will do fine."

"Biscotti? No. Cheesecake. It's a cheesecake sort of day. I'll be back in a moment."

A few minutes later, Anne returned with two tall steaming cups and two plates on a tray. The friends contemplated the choices of strawberry and chocolate cheesecake, and eventually decided to split both down the middle.

For a moment the chatter fell silent, all due reverence being owed to the cheesecake. Rich, creamy, sweet... and that bright tang of sweet strawberry, followed by the gentle bitter tones of the chocolate. It was prayer on a fork.

"Mmmm. Thank you." Jasmine leaned back against her chair, eyes closed and a beatific smile on her face. She picked up her latte and took a small sip. "It's a good thing I don't do this often. I'd be three hundred pounds." She drew her fork over her strawberry cheesecake and looked up at Anne. "So why is it a cheesecake sort of day? Not that I'm complaining at all." Now she picked up a sliver of cake and popped it into her mouth.

Anne mirrored her movements, moaning in pleasure at the taste of the chocolate treat. "Why? We need an excuse?" She licked a bit of cheesecake off the side of her mouth. "I just finished that choir commission I mentioned. I'm really pleased with it. I wasn't expecting to fall so much in love with the poetry, and the music just flowed around the words. I tried some new things too, and I think they really work well with the poetry and the mood I want to create. I hope I didn't make it too hard for an amateur choir, but I've heard this group and they are good. So now the work is over and I have a few days to sit back and relax before the orchestra season starts after the long weekend."

"How are you going to celebrate?" Jasmine's eyes twinkled with suppressed mischief.

"Celebrate? With my haircut, and with cheesecake! Did you have something else in mind?"

Jasmine let out a puff of air and cocked her head. "Let's see. You've been all adventurous with the music and your new haircut. So we should stay with that and do something else adventurous. What have you always wanted to do? Come on, Annie. Be wild!"

"Wild? That's just the opposite of me. We could go shopping in Little India or at Pacific Mall."

It had been a long time since she had wandered the streets of Little India, eying those beautiful silk saris through large shop windows and stopping into small corner stores for some of the spices she loved so much. A trip to that part of town could be interesting. Or Pacific Mall, with its rows upon rows of booth-like shops, all neat and organised, offering everything an Asian shopping centre could promise. New phone case? A hundred stalls beckoned. Silk scarves? Over that side. Those delicious papaya hard candies or a set of beautiful chopsticks? Right that way. She was thinking of the best way to get there by transit when Jasmine stopped her thoughts with a snort.

"No. Not shopping. Something crazy. Okay, maybe not totally crazy, but different. Adventurous. Something you've never done. This is Annie-breaks-out-of-her-comfort-zone time. What about...?"

"Water skiing? No. Scratch that."

"Zip-lining?"

Anne shook her head. No.

"Axe-throwing?"

"A cake decorating class?"

"An escape room!"

Silence.

Then Anne saw Jasmine raise her eyes to something she saw outside. They were just on the outskirts of downtown, near where Queen Street roared to life with its trendy boutiques, galleries, and cafes, and in the near distance, the CN Tower soared skyward. Once the tallest free-standing structure in the world, it still dominated the city's skyline.

Anne turned around to see what Jasmine was looking at with such a grin. "Oh no! I'm not a fan of heights. Besides, it's such a touristy thing to do. I've lived here all my life. I'm not a tourist."

"And how often have you gone up?"

Anne chewed her lip. "Never," she mumbled.

"Then it's time to fix that. Come on. We'll have a blast." Jasmine pulled out her phone and tapped at the screen for a couple of minutes. "There. We can get tickets to go up this afternoon. I ate the cheesecake. Now this is my treat."

Anne shook her head, her new hairstyle bouncing and swaying around her face. "Oh, no... I mean... well..." She stopped, then smiled. "You know, you're right. Let's do it! I need to break out of this rut I'm in, and this is my next step."

They finished their treats and walked through the busy city streets towards their destination. The tower, in its massive plaza, loomed up ahead of them, a monolith of concrete thrusting heavenward from the earth, piercing the sky with its needle top. In a few minutes, they had navigated the grid of streets and waded through the crowds to enter the grey stone square. Behind them, massive and squat with its iconic dome, stood the baseball stadium. A short distance away, on the other side of the plaza, was the aquarium. Anne had not been there either. Before them, signed in red and white, was the tower itself.

Anne craned her neck to try to see the top. Two little bugs that were the elevators raced up and down the massive structure, seeming to defy gravity as they clung to the concrete walls. She was going to go in one of those? Her heart started to race.

"Nervous, Annie? Don't be. And look, what a gorgeous day it is! There's hardly a cloud, and we'll see for miles. I bet we can even see right across the lake today. It will be amazing. You've got your camera, right?" Jasmine grabbed Anne's hand and pulled her towards the canopy that led to the ticket windows. In a moment, the deed was done, and they were heading down the corridor to the waiting elevators that would bear them upwards, upwards, to the observation floor over a thousand feet up. Anne's stomach twisted again.

"Connor has had a bite on one of the resumes he sent in. If he gets the job, we'll treat you to a dinner at the restaurant." Yes. Of course. The tower had a revolving restaurant with fabulous views and sky-high prices. How could anybody eat a thing, that high up? Anne gulped. What was she thinking when she agreed to do this? But no: She said she was going to spread her wings, and this was part of it. She forced a smile, although she felt more than a little green.

Eventually, they reached the front of the queue and crowded into the lift. The tour guide started her spiel as the doors closed and the contraption began its ascent.

"Construction began in 1973, and the tower was opened three years later…" The young woman's canned speech turned to drones in Anne's ears as she fought the panic that threatened to consume her. Up… up… up… She was not made for heights.

No. She reprimanded herself. You're safe. You're going to enjoy it. Breathe in, breathe out. Feel the floor under your feet. Relax and just go with the flow. She had squeezed her eyes closed, almost unaware of Jasmine's hand still holding her own. Now she took a deep breath and slowly let her eyes open, just a crack. The excited faces around her bore no signs of panic or fear, just wonderment. She let her pupils dart to the side. The world was racing away from them, growing ever smaller through the glass walls of the elevator car. It was terrifying. It was unnatural. It was… rather interesting.

Her eyes opened a bit more.

"You okay?" Jasmine squeezed her hand once, a reassuring pulse.

Anne nodded. "I think so." Swallow. "I've just about convinced myself to have fun. But I might hug the ground when we get down."

"Don't worry. We're not doing the glass floor or the walk around the edge, where they tether you to the building." Anne felt her face go white. "Next time." Jasmine giggled and Anne relaxed just a little more.

The ascent took only a minute. "…climbing at 22 kilometres an hour," she heard the operator say. Soon the lift slowed down and in a moment the doors opened, spilling the travellers out onto the observation floor. Anne glanced down at her feet. The floor looked solid enough, so she stepped forward with what she hoped was confidence. Thank heavens they weren't on the glass floor right now. Her stomach could not handle that.

Jasmine was right. The day was fine and the vistas glorious. Far below them, tiny toy cars scuttled along grey ribbon roads and highways, while the lake twinkled its deep blue around the islands protecting the city. To the other side of the observation area, the city's grid of streets spread out in every direction, broken here and there by a river, a park, or some other feature natural or constructed. It was fascinating. Almost exhilarating.

Eventually, Anne relaxed enough to truly enjoy herself as she and Jasmine pointed out landmarks they knew and could identify from this enormous height.

"Look, there's the University. You can see the music building, just past where the road circles around Queen's Park. And there's the concert hall, and there's the park where we used to hang out."

"Oh," Jasmine added, turning a bit. "Can you see that way, past the river? Just by where the road crosses the Don Valley, that's my old high school. I wonder if I can see my parent's house."

And so they went, laughing and reminiscing, until Anne felt quite comfortable despite her initial trepidation. At last, they decided to head back down to earth. Anne needed to get started on her dinner, and Jasmine had some violin students that evening.

"Before we go, Annie, we need photos. Pics or it didn't happen, right?"

"Uh, sure. Why not? I can't avoid the camera in this job."

"And you look fabulous. That hairstyle really suits you. Fun, young, fresh, but sophisticated. There. Stand there. Try to look happy. Okay, smile!"

In a couple of minutes, the photoshoot was complete.

"Send me those two?" Anne asked her friend as she scanned the screen. "I should probably put something on Twitter."

"Can I upload these to Instagram? I can pretend to be all fancy by association."

The ride down to earth was a lot less terrifying than the trip up, and for half a moment Anne even thought she might try this again sometime.

Perhaps, just perhaps, spreading her wings would not be so hard after all.

The weekend came quickly, and with it the spate of parties.

First was the barbecue in the Dalrymples' spacious back garden. Trina, the violinist, had set up tables and chairs all throughout the wide lawn, and had erected a small tent near the house to keep the food out of the sun. As the guests arrived, they placed their pot-luck offerings on the appropriate table there—salads, snacks, drinks, desserts—until it looked a veritable feast, fit to feed hundreds. Carter, her husband, manned the barbecues off to the side of the stone patio right by the deck. There were two such appliances—one for meat and one for vegetarian alternatives—and he moved between them like a seasoned chef. The hot food was their contribution to the affair, plus the buns and condiments. No one would go hungry.

The garden was already busy when Anne arrived. Trina welcomed her warmly and showed her where to put her offering of cookies, then disappeared into the house as someone called for her. Anne looked around. She knew several people, some rather well, and drifted in the direction of Xi and his family. She could see Kevin Walters chatting up Carter Dalrymple by the phalanx of barbecues, his wife Penny looking bored at his side.

Of course, the CEO would want to chum up with Carter. The Dalrymples had deep pockets, as this large house and massive garden evidenced, and he would be a good person to whom to appeal when the next fundraiser came up. Anne hoped to say hello and thank you to her host, but she had little desire to be caught in a conversation with Kevin and Penny Walters right now, so she made a point of not catching his eye as she wandered further into the growing crowd.

She waved at a friend here, said hello to an acquaintance there, and generally acknowledged the people who came up to her. But in all the gathered masses of musicians and their families, she did not see Fred and Louisa anywhere, and was unsure about whether she felt relieved or disappointed that he was not there.

The second event of the weekend—the jazz band at the club with Jasmine and Connor—was better than she expected. She had heard a lot about Connor, but this was the first time meeting him. She selected what she hoped was a suitable outfit: loose dark blue linen trousers and an asymmetrical ivory silk shirt that dipped lower over one hip than the other and that framed her face with a neckline that angled to the opposite shoulder. This shirt brought syncopated rhythms to mind, not quite here, not quite there, always dancing around the beat without alighting upon it. It was just the thing for jazz. She added a pair of dark flat shoes and some chunky gold earrings to make it an outfit, and then bounced around in front of the mirror for a moment, watching the earring disappear behind the long layers of her new hairstyle before peeking back out again. She liked it.

Now for a touch of makeup. A sweep of black eyeliner, a touch of mascara. There. She had eyes again. She reached for her usual neutral pinkish lipstick, but her hand wavered. Just behind that tube was a rich red that Sophia had convinced her to buy on a shopping expedition a while ago. She had worn it once. If a night out at a jazz club wasn't the place to wear it again, where was? She picked up the red instead of the pink and put a careful layer on her lips. It was a bolder look than her usual one, but with the neutral palette of her clothes and eyeliner, it worked. She was ready for a night on the town.

Connor was not what she had expected. He was very tall and thin, almost to the point of looking unhealthy, a contrast to his wife's soft, round figure. His face, in repose, was stern, his eyes dark slashes under heavy brows. But when he smiled, Anne could see exactly why the two were so well suited. The forbidding mien dissolved in an instant, revealing a warm and inviting soul within.

"I am so pleased to meet you!" He rose from his seat to shake Anne's hand, towering above her. "Jaz has talked about you for years, since I met her. She always used to talk about her study buddy who made it big, and now I actually get to meet you." He stepped aside and pulled out a chair at their little table. "Please." He gestured and Anne sat down.

"And I've heard so much about you. The pleasure is all mine. I'm delighted to meet the man my friend has chosen."

The waiter came by with menus, and the three pondered their options for a few minutes before deciding. The musicians were to begin their set in about 20 minutes, and the little bar was quite full. "How did you know about this band?" Anne picked up her dark ale. She was so used to hiding behind her drinks. She must learn to move away from this habit.

Surprisingly, it was Connor who answered, rather than Jasmine. "I know Jamal, the bass player, from work. He's a lawyer in daylight, if you can believe that. This is what happens when the moon comes out."

Anne cast her eyes to the small stage at the side of the space. The musicians were setting up, adjusting mics and amps and all sorts of things she knew little about. There was a large string bass, leaning its carved side against a tall stool, a keyboard that looked full size, and a couple of stands that suggested the third musician played a variety of wind instruments. Sax and clarinet? She was eager to find out.

Jamal must be the fellow tinkering with the electrical cords leading to the bass. He was a short, round man, clad in the *de rigeur* black expected of a jazz musician, with a deep complexion and thick natural hair, closer to an afro than a buzz. He looked up and his eyes stopped when they reached Anne's table. He smiled and waved at Connor, who waved back.

By the time the food had arrived, the band was ready to begin their first set. Anne and her friends had decided to split a platter of flatbreads and dips, some mozzarella sticks with a tangy salsa, and a groaning plate of nachos. It was no health food, but it fed the soul perfectly. Anne toyed with a greasy, crispy spear of fried cheese as the band did its final sound check and launched into their first number.

They were good. She knew little more about jazz than the average music lover, but she knew good music and good musicians when she heard them, and the set passed more quickly than she would have imagined. The three friends ordered more beer while the band took their break, and discussed getting something sweet for the second set.

Jamal now put down his bass and wandered through the bar to their table. "Connor! Thanks for coming. Good to see you."

"I hardly recognised you without your suit and tie. Come, you know Jaz, of course, but let me introduce you to our friend, Anne. Jamal, this is Anne Elliot...."

The bass player's eyes went wide. "Anne Elliot? *The* Anne Elliot?"

"I'm sure there are others," she mumbled.

"The composer Anne Elliot?"

Jasmine leaned forward. "The very one! She's amazing."

Anne's face went hot.

"It's a pleasure, Ms Elliot. I'm a huge fan. I cannot just let your music play in the background. I'm always drawn to actively listen. I love how you use tonality and modality in your music, and how you paint such colours with the orchestra. May I?" He gestured to the empty fourth chair and sat down. They talked about music for a short while before he looked up. "Ms Elliot, would you mind if I introduced the others to you? I know they'd be thrilled."

In a couple of minutes, the other two jazz musicians were at the table, paying homage to the superstar composer in their midst. Marisol played keyboards and the front man, a nondescript fellow who introduced himself as Stick, played everything with a reed, and very well at that. He had started on saxophone, moved to clarinet, then oboe (jazz oboe!), and back to sax.

Just before their second set was to begin, Stick leaned forward to Anne and whispered something to her. No! He couldn't. He wouldn't!

Jasmine had heard his request. "Come on, Annie! The new you, right? Go for it."

The ocean of eager smiles around her finally wore through her reluctance. "Well, alright. Just for a minute."

The band returned to their stage and Stick took the microphone. "Ladies and Gents, I know you're here to hear jazz. At least, I hope you are. Otherwise, you're in the wrong place. But I have just discovered that we are in the presence of greatness. Who here has seen the movie *The Butterfly's Kiss*?"

There was a wave of hands in the air and a pattering of applause.

"Who liked the soundtrack? No... who LOVED the soundtrack?"

More hands, and a roar of applause.

"Fucking loved it!" someone yelled out from the floor. More applause.

"Then you will love this surprise. The composer herself, Anne Elliot, is right here with us today. Come up, Ms Elliot. Take your bows. You deserve them."

Anne pushed back her chair and swivelled through the islands of tables to climb the two short steps to the stage. She was not one to hog the limelight, but there was a certain satisfaction in receiving such acclaim. She smiled in what she hoped was a gracious manner and waved. But Stick wasn't finished.

"Ms Elliot has agreed to take just a couple of minutes to join us here. This is totally unrehearsed, so you'll forgive us, but jazz is all about improvisation, and that's what we're going to do. You heard it here first, folks."

Marisol stood back and Anne took her place at the keyboard. "Nothing tricky, okay? I'm winging it here. Let's start simple. Scarborough Fair?" Jamal and Stick nodded. "In D Dorian?"

She began to play. Just a simple melody with a traditional harmony supporting the tune. It was pretty, but nothing special. Until she reached the end of the first verse. "Now, à la Bach." Immediately, she launched into a very different piece, the same tune, but arranged extemporaneously to reflect the counterpoint and figured bass style that so epitomised the genius Baroque composer. From the corner of her eye, she saw Jamal's face break in half with a wide grin, and Stick picked up his sax. As Anne approached the end of her rendition, she looked up at the jazz musicians and nodded, and passed the piece to them as smoothly as if they had rehearsed it for weeks.

They took over now, improvising their own magic over the ages-old tune. Stick's sax wove intricate chromaticisms and thematic arabesques while Jamal provided the walking bass that gave structure and solidity to his musical wanderings. It was silver lamé spun over deep brown, golden threads ornamenting the structural warp of harmony. It was lovely.

Just as smoothly, they passed the melody back to Anne. "Mozart," she called out, her fingers starting an Alberni bass line upon which to situate the tune. By the time they had completed a version in the style of Beethoven and one (pushing Anne's improvisational limits to their utmost) of Gershwin, and the jazz musicians had added their own spin between Anne's verses, the crowd was all but stunned. There was no talking, no eating, not a sound. It was the silence of awe.

And then, as if on cue, the place broke into thunderous applause. People leapt to their feet, and whistles and cheers sounded from the patrons. How many phones were there snapping pics of this? Anne shuddered to think of the next day's Twitter feed.

It took five minutes to quieten everyone enough for the band to resume their set. She thanked them all for a terrific experience, and made sure she got their contact information. "You never know," she explained, although already an idea was forming in her mind.

Eventually, she made her way back to her seat. "Oh my God, Annie, that was fabulous. Isn't she amazing, Con? Don't sit yet. We need selfies!" Out came the phone, and Connor took a few photos of the two friends before someone offered to include him in the pictures.

These would be all over social media by morning. Oh well. It was part of the job, wasn't it? No such thing as bad publicity, just spell my name right.

It was a while later, after some dark cinnamon coffee (perfect for a jazz club), a plate of sweets, and more adulation from the crowds than she had ever imagined, that Anne and her friends finally left the place. It had not been the quiet evening she hoped for, but it had been a lot of fun nonetheless, and she was glad she went.

Chapter Fourteen
Serenade

The third and final do of the weekend was Sophia's soireé the following evening. This was not for the orchestra members, but for the board of directors and some select donors. Fred would certainly be attending, as it was one of his extra-musical obligations to the orchestra. No doubt he would be his most charming self, flashing that winning smile everywhere and gaining a new following of adorers. Anne imagined Louisa would attend with him. She was prepared for it, and would be gracious.

William called that morning to make plans. He had left a message for her the previous night while she was at the jazz club.

Back in town. What a long flight. Talk tomorrow around 10?

Ten o'clock should be fine; it was late when she arrived home from the club, but not so late that she would sleep the morning away. And so, at 10 o'clock, when her phone rang, Anne was ready with a smile. She asked about his trip and then let him talk as she puttered about the kitchen, making coffee and toasting a bagel. With the phone on speaker, she could move around and get ready for the day while chatting.

Where had he been again? Barbados? The Dominican Republic? Right. The Caymans. He mentioned it a couple of times as he talked. He spoke very little about his current project, other than to say that it was going well, and dwelt mostly on the island itself with its gorgeous scenery and rich cultural heritage. He spoke with great animation, and it was like listening to a polished travelogue as she sipped at her morning brew. She asked some questions here and there and made the appropriate comments when suitable, but in all, he was happy to talk and she was happy to let him.

"Do I still have the pleasure of taking you to Sophia Croft's do tonight?" he asked at last.

What a strange question. They had made their plans before his trip.

"Yes, of course. Did I say something to make you think otherwise?"

He laughed now. "No, not at all. I just turned on my computer as we were talking, and I see you have been quite the busy lady. You are all over Facebook. You seem to have made quite an impression last night. I hoped that somebody hadn't come along to steal you away."

"Oh Lord! Last night at the jazz club—what was I thinking? I haven't dared to check online. It seemed fun at the time, but upon sober second thought, perhaps I should have just stayed in my chair."

"Don't be a silly goose. The people who were there are all gushing, and those who weren't are jealous. If I'd known, I would have flown home early. Let me see… I'm scrolling through some pictures. Every single comment is positive, and you know how rare that is."

Could a blush be heard over the phone? "That's a relief."

"So tonight? You'll arrive on my arm? I could not be prouder. The invitation said eight o'clock, so I'll come for you at about quarter to. It's formal, and I'll be in my dinner jacket. What colour are you wearing?"

She had thought a lot about this, and had two options she was playing with. It was time to make a decision. "I have a black dress that I often wear…"

"You looked very good in that light colour in the photos."

"Oh. Thank you. I don't have any ivory, but my other dress is green. I never wear it, but maybe I should. I need to wear more colours."

"That sounds lovely. I'll see you downstairs at quarter to eight."

The dress was, thankfully, where she thought it was, safe in its garment bag from the last time she had it cleaned. It was a simple gown, a strapless underdress with elegant princess seams in a rich green between emerald and forest, not so bright as to be garish, not so dark as to be sombre. The skirt was full and fell to the floor, and it swirled about her ankles when she moved. She felt like a little girl twirling about. But what made the dress special was the lace overlay. It followed the line of the underdress exactly, but for the higher scoop neckline that was perfect for a simple and elegant necklace, and long lace sleeves. The lace itself was a modern, intricate pattern with a hint of sheen, that touch of look-at-me that turned the understated frock into something really eye-catching.

She rooted through her jewellery box for the right accessories. The dress was striking enough that it needed very little adornment.

Emeralds would be too much. She selected a thin gold rope chain that her grandmother had given her for her graduation, and some plain gold studs for her ears. No bracelets, no rings. She would let the lace do all the shining. A light touch of gold on her eyelids with black liner and mascara and a layer of the rosy peach lipstick she saved for special occasions completed the look. As for her hair, her new style was perfect, the long layers framing her face with delicate tendrils.

William seemed to approve. He greeted her with appreciative eyes and a satisfied smirk. As he came around to her side of the car to open the door for her, Anne noticed the green flecks in his tie and pocket square. He had dressed to match her. The thought both pleased and alarmed her. What would people think? Hell, what did she think?

Sophia noticed at once. She said nothing, but Anne knew the meaning in those raised eyebrows. *That look.* She welcomed her guests into the elegant space and graced Anne with an air kiss on both sides. One must not disturb the lipstick, no matter how delighted you are with your company!

"Come in. About half the guests have arrived, so go and mingle and have fun. I'll find you when I have a few moments." She glanced over at William again, but his eyes were elsewhere, scanning the room with detached interest.

Kevin and Penny Walters stood near the bar and William gestured in their direction. There was no avoiding the orchestra's CEO this evening, and they might as well get the inevitable conversation over with.

Walters was an efficient administrator, and while he had no great creativity of his own, he possessed the gift of discovering it and appreciating it in others. It was under his leadership that the orchestra had had such success in recent years, both with its community and youth outreach programs and with this new composer-in-residence program. But, to his credit, he was the first to admit that the ideas were those of his program developers. "I'm just the guy who puts the train on the track," he would joke.

He was a handsome man—perhaps a little too handsome, judging by the way he always managed to find himself in any mirror around—and even in his late sixties, he cut a fine figure. He dressed to the very best advantage, and he had allowed himself to age gracefully in that way that some men manage, not attempting to look younger than his years but striving to make the very most of what nature had bestowed upon him.

His wife, Penny, was something of a different story. She was far closer to Anne's age than to her husband's, and she always looked like she was trying a little too hard. Her hair was that smidgeon too blonde, her makeup that bit too heavy. She was a very attractive woman, but would probably look better if she did not try to look ten years younger than she was. Tonight she had on a silver evening gown that was almost too tight and clung just too well to her well-toned curves. Diamond earrings dangled from her shell-like ears and more clusters of the clear gems sparkled at her throat, wrists, and fingers. It was just too much to be truly elegant, Anne decided, and then reprimanded herself for her catty thoughts.

She did not know Penny particularly well. They had met on previous occasions such as this and had exchanged a pleasant word or two, but Anne always said her good-byes with no particular desire to further the acquaintance, and she well suspected that Penny felt similarly.

Now, as Anne and William approached the couple, Anne saw Penny's eyes first light upon William and then herself. She turned on her Bosses' Wife's smile and Anne could all but hear her form the appropriate sentences in her head.

"Anne Elliot! How lovely to see you!"

Yes, that was pretty much word for word what Anne would have imagined.

"And William. A pleasure to see you again, too."

Of course, although William was new to the board, he surely would have met the CEO's wife before now. This was a social event, not a business one, and everybody knew everybody else already. Penny brought out the usual safe topics. What lovely weather we've been having. How was your summer? Are you looking forward to the upcoming season?

The four chatted meaninglessly for several minutes, all superficial smiles and insincere compliments. Walters could turn on the charm as well as anybody, and prided himself on his smooth social manners as much as on his physical attributes, but it was all on the surface. He was a pleasant companion for ten minutes' worth of conversation; there seemed to be little substance beneath his suave exterior.

Anne wondered what William thought about him. William's smile was easy and his eyes seemed engaged, but he, too, was adept at these interactions. Surely he played the game as well as Walters, if not better. If the two had to work together, he definitely would wish to establish, if not a friendship, then a friendly relationship with the CEO.

As the men began to talk about matters relating to the orchestra, Penny fluttered her hand suggestively, which prompted Anne to ask about her bracelets. "Oh, these? Aren't they lovely? I got them on a recent trip to the Islands. If you know where to look, one can get such excellent deals on jewels there. I don't always want to be so flashy, but sometimes a woman just wants to sparkle." Pause. "As I'm sure you know."

On she prattled, and Anne nodded and agreed as the conversation required. Yes, she had heard wonderful things about St. Maarten. Yes, the upcoming book festival looked exciting. No, she hadn't tried that new restaurant on the Danforth. The usual time-eating, expected chatter.

And then she felt it. Something in the air changed. It wasn't a sound, or a scent, or anything tangible, but the very feel of the room that shimmered for a moment, as if adapting to a different reality.

He had arrived. She knew it without turning around. Frederico Valore had entered the room.

Beside her, Walters was facing towards the door and he clearly saw what Anne had felt in her soul. He gave a shake of his head and his eyebrows rose as his lids lowered. He turned and proclaimed in his bass voice, "Behold, our maestro!"

At once, the room quietened down. Choruses of *Maestro* and *Signore Valore* sounded from every direction, as well as the occasional familiar *Fred*. Anne shifted so she now faced the door, too. There he was, tall and elegant in his beautifully cut black dinner jacket and bow tie. He needed no embellishments. His face and figure and that fine suit were all he needed, and a breath caught in Anne's throat. William was an attractive man, to be sure, but Fred always made her heart skip a beat.

She stepped backwards. Could she hide behind Penny? Disappear into some other room somewhere? After all, the last time she had seen him was the night of her nephew's accident, when they had ended up in her bed. When he had vanished and left her that note telling her it was all a mistake. She had known he would be here tonight, but the sight of him was more than she was prepared for. That surge and anger and loss threatened to pull her off her feet, and she was uncertain which of the two was stronger.

But it was too late to disappear. Fred had clearly heard Walters' boom and turned at once in their direction. He smiled at the CEO, a warm, open expression. Anne saw when his eyes settled on William for a moment, and then, a couple of steps away, on Penny, who stood interposed between them. And then he stopped. Just for a moment. His step stilled for that infinitesimal moment of time and his face lost all expression. In the blink of an eye, all was back to normal, and had she not been so aware of him, she might not have noticed. Certainly no one else seemed to think a thing was amiss. But he had seen her.

Still, his path was committed, and he continued to sail his path across the room. "Kevin," he reached out to shake Walters' hand. "Mrs. Walters," he took the lady's offered hand and pressed an old-fashioned kiss to the back of it. Then he greeted William with a polite, "Mr. Barnett," and only then did he turn his eyes to Anne.

"Anne. A delight to see you again." He leaned forward to kiss her cheek. Ah. So that was the game he was playing. Old, familiar friends. Only friends. As long as she knew what to expect, she could handle it.

But he did not step back as she expected and remained close to her side.

The conversation was general for a moment. Walters made the predictable comments about the exciting upcoming season and the buzz in the music world about Fred's new leadership of the orchestra. Anne straightened her back and plastered her smile on her face, and tried to look interested as Fred made the predictable replies.

"And your summer, Maestro? I hope it was very restful, since we will be more than busy once rehearsals begin." He chuckled at his little joke.

"Alas, not restful at all, although I am more than ready to get back into the music."

"Not restful?" Penny asked. "Was it exciting, at least?"

"Ah, that is a matter of opinion." His voice was smooth, the velvety tones of a clarinet in its low register, full of burgundy and chocolate. "An international move is never a calm affair, and yes, I suppose it was interesting. I am delighted to be back in Toronto, and finding and setting up a home is exciting, I suppose. But it has been busy. I just returned from Rome a couple of days ago. I was there for much of August."

"Oh!" Anne didn't realise she had spoken until she heard her own voice.

"I had a few unexpected odds and ends to tie up there," Fred explained. "The usual business matters—ending the lease on my old flat there, selling some unwanted items, taking leave of friends, you know the sort of thing. In fact," he now stepped closer to Walters, although Anne could see his eyes settle for a moment on William, "one of my friends has decided to join me in Canada for a few weeks. He's an English chap, a journalist, but he's lived in Italy for several years. He's just coming off a very rough time, and I thought the change would do him well. I'm grateful now that Jeremy suggested getting a place with two bedrooms, because Benjamin is staying in the second one for the time being."

He turned his eyes to Anne. "Perhaps, while he is in town, you would like to meet him. When he isn't chasing down the next big story, he writes poetry. Some of it is really rather good."

"Yes. Yes, of course. It would be an honour."

"Excellent! I have told him so much about you, he is quite eager to meet you. I might have gone on a bit about how there really is no one to compare to you."

What was this? Such kind words, when he had all but washed his hands of her only a couple of months before, with not a word in the interim? Now Fred turned to the others. Their expressions asked all the questions they did not voice.

"Anne and I go back quite a way," he explained to William and Penny. Kevin Walters surely knew this much already. "We were at university together; we were quite good friends."

Well, that was one way of putting it. Anne strove to keep her smile from wavering.

At this, William's stance stiffened, and he shifted closer to her; strangely, Penny Walters' face went hard for a moment. Surely she wasn't jealous of Fred. Was she? Had she envisaged some sort of... dalliance with the new conductor? Anne gave herself a mental shake. No, she must be imagining things. But then it occurred to her to wonder where Louisa was. The horn player and the conductor had seemed to be a couple; if Fred had just been in Rome for the last few weeks, surely they would want to be together now. Was she worried about not being welcomed at the board of directors' party? It might not be cricket for the maestro to be carrying on with the principal horn, but far worse things had happened, and as long as the music didn't suffer, no one would say a word.

Well, this was not her matter to worry about. She would find out all the sordid details soon enough. Sophia had a way of wiggling these tales out of even the most stony people.

She was so wrapped up in her thoughts that she almost missed Penny's question. "Where is your friend now? Didn't he join you? I'm sure Sophia would gladly have extended an invitation."

Of course. Everybody was interested in his friend, not Louisa. Only Anne dwelt on that.

"I did suggest it," Fred replied to Penny. "But Ben insisted he would be happy just relaxing and catching up on some sleep. As I said, he's had a rough time recently and I don't think he's quite up for this sort of function right now."

The deep brown eyes flickered towards Anne and she wondered what had happened to Fred's friend. Did he think she might be able to help at all? Perhaps he would tell her later.

Walters now reclaimed control of the conversation. He had this idea in mind, and that program to discuss, and perhaps they could meet at some convenient time... William seemed quite interested, but Anne found her attention drifting, and when Jeremy waved at her from across the room, she made her excuses and went to find her friend.

He gave her a quick hug. "Looking good, Anne. Are you having fun yet? It's always a bit of a working vacation, these things. You want to enjoy yourself, but you're also on display. I'm sure all the board members will want a moment's chat with you, and probably a selfie too, for their Facebook pages."

They chatted for a few minutes about this and that. All of the guests seemed to have arrived, and there, like a butterfly flitting from flower to flower, was Sophia working her way through the room. She hovered around each little group of people as if they were the most important people on the planet. Dressed as she was in pale gold, she almost left a visible glow along the path she had visited. Anne had never particularly wished to be more of a social creature, but at times like this, she envied her friend's true gift in this sphere.

"Finally, a moment to breathe!" Sophia slid into place to join Anne and Jeremy. Her bright eyes belied the exhaustion suggested by her words.

"Liar, Sophia. You love this stuff. You're in your element." She looked around at the smartly dressed crowd in the room. Silks and satins and smart black evening garb were everywhere. The space was abuzz with the sound of a hundred conversations while some carefully selected music—Mozart string quartets—provided the aural cushion to support but not overwhelm the sound. Waiters in their black and white uniforms wove through the room offering finger food and drinks to the guests in their suits and cocktail dresses, and the bar, where Kevin Walters and William still stood talking, was surrounded by a loose cloud of people hoping for a brandy or something other than sparkling wine. It was a smart and elegant affair, a testimony to Sophia's talents as hostess.

Sophia's perfectly arched eyebrows rose quickly at Anne's jibe. "Perhaps. I do rather enjoy a good soirée. But you, Miss Annie, seemed to be in your own element last night. Why didn't you tell me?"

"Oh, no! Don't tell me you saw something about the jazz club." Did a red face go with a green dress? Or did she look like some sort of grotesque Christmas tree?

Jeremy was grinning. "I'll leave you ladies to talk. Time to make myself useful as host." He winked at them as he walked away.

"Did I see 'something?' Not at all. I saw the deed itself. Some enterprising person uploaded a good amount of your little adventure to YouTube. There was something on TikTok too, but those clips are too short to really hear what happened. You looked like you were having a marvellous time. You should get out there more often."

Et tu, Sophia? "That's what Jasmine said. She's the one who convinced me to go. I've told you about Jasmine and Connor, haven't I?"

"Your friend from school, yes. I thought you were with William."

"He was out of town until yesterday." She explained about his business trip in a few words, then described the chain of events that convinced her up onto the little stage at the club. "I wish I had known. I would have dressed up... or not gone at all."

"Nonsense. You looked great. You really do, you know. This summer has been good to you. You've got colour in your cheeks and your eyes seem brighter, somehow. It's like a little lost piece of Annie has been found and put back into place. This isn't your first big adventure, either. I saw those pictures from the CN Tower. You have been busy."

"Are we talking about Anne's new career as a jazz musician?" Fred's voice sounded from behind Anne's shoulder, and she turned to see him walking up. "Don't be shy, Anne. The video is everywhere. It was my friend Ben who noticed it first and pointed it out to me." He took a step back and his dark eyes moved from Anne's head to her toes. "It becomes you. You've let your light go out a bit, and I'm pleased to see it back." Then, in a hushed voice that maybe even Anne was not supposed to hear, "I've missed you."

CHAPTER FIFTEEN
Variation One

It had been three days since Sophia's grand farewell to summer. Anne cracked open her eyes and rolled over in bed. A glance at the clock told her she had a few more minutes to sleep, but wakefulness was upon her. Today was the first orchestra rehearsal of the season, and the schedule included her *Preludes*, the piece that made her famous. It was impossible to deny the excitement she felt at the idea of it.

There would be no more sleep today. She pushed off her blankets and staggered to the kitchen to set the coffeemaker, and then took a shower while the machine worked its magic. She dressed quickly in a simple skirt and t-shirt before going to have her morning drink. Her phone told her she had some messages, which she checked as she waited for her bagel to toast.

There was one from Fred.

Coming to rehearsal? Hope to see you. Maybe go for coffee afterwards and meet my friend Ben? Think about it and tell me later.

This was a surprise. When he had first mentioned his friend at Sophia's soiree, Anne thought he intended to arrange a meeting, but since he had said nothing else about it all evening, she changed her mind. She was certain it had just been making meaningless small talk, but apparently, he was serious. It was a strange sort of message too; there was no intimation that he felt bad about his abrupt departure in June, no suggestion of apology. It was as if their night together meant nothing at all to him. Was her former lover trying to set her up with another man?

She laughed at the thought. No, that was not like the Fred she knew. He was just hoping to introduce two people who might get along. She really should read nothing into it. Besides, didn't Fred know that she was sort-of seeing William Barnett?

She cast her mind back to the party. William had arrived with her and had spent some time with her before they left together, but he had not danced attendance upon her, or at least, no more than might be expected of a board member. She recalled him talking to Kevin Walters, then later on to Jeremy, and then—for quite a long time—to Penny Walters, whom he seemed to know quite well from some previous board events to which she had not been a party.

But he had not doted upon her, and any people who had not seen them arrive and depart as a couple would be unlikely to consider them a couple. Fred certainly had not said a word, nor had even glanced at them after his initial assessment. If he had been so busy during the summer and had spent a good deal of it in Italy, he might have no idea that William had been taking her out.

Anyway, meeting Ben might be nice. She sent back a quick reply to that end and then checked the rest of her messages.

There was the usual collection of notifications, semi-legitimate advertisements, and newsletters, and a reminder of the morning's rehearsal. Still nothing from Marie. She had not heard from her sister since the accident in early summer, despite her periodic emails and calls. The little boy was fine, she knew from Charles, but her sister still refused to speak to her. She rolled her eyes. Marie would come around in time, but if there was drama to be found in any situation, she would milk it to its utmost.

The rehearsal itself went well. The orchestra members were all first-rate musicians, and they seemed to be putting forth their best for the new conductor. No matter that he had taken up the baton with them once before; this was their first official time together and everybody was on point and seemed to be taking great care to please and be pleased. The musicians knew their parts and played well, and Fred was friendly and encouraging, coaxing his own interpretations and ideas from eager bows, reeds, and brass.

Anne's *Preludes* had never sounded better, and she was delighted by Fred's subtle inflexions. He understood the music perfectly. Of course he would; he was there when she had first started to compose it. He was part of its inception; it was his piece almost as much as it was hers. How fitting that he should be the one to conduct it now.

Anne sat in her seat in the auditorium, listening but not making notes. Her role was now over, and she could enjoy the process as an observer. It was liberating, if a little intimidating. She let her eyes rove over the musicians. There was Xi in the second violins, there Caroline behind her red cello, and there, up on the risers behind the woodwinds, was Louisa with her shiny horn. She had changed over the summer. Her hair was blue again, but now it was a deep sapphire rather than the peacock blue of last spring, and her earrings were small enough that Anne could not see them from her seat in row G. But the satisfied smile on her face was still visible when she put down her instrument to look at the conductor. Why, Anne wondered again, had she not been at the party last weekend?

It seemed just a moment before the orchestra took their break, and once more Anne was surrounded by friends and admirers, all gushing about her piece. More than one person also mentioned the video of her performance at the jazz club, which only served to increase her appeal. How strange that a few minutes of improvisation could have spurred so much buzz!

Then the rehearsal resumed. Anne had nothing to do now, other than sit back and enjoy the experience. She closed her eyes and allowed the music to wash over her. They started with Holst's *The Planets*. Fred took a few minutes to go over some of his ideas with the orchestra, and the musicians put down bows and horns in favour of pencils, to mark down these points. Then they were ready to play.

"Alright, folks, let's read through it and we'll stop where necessary." Fred lifted his baton and at once the orchestra was at attention, instruments prepared.

The first movement was "Mars, Bringer of War," with its unsettling five-four time signature. First came the percussive *col legno* notes of the strings and the low tones of the brass, followed by the brighter sounds of the trumpets. The music, undulating orange and brown and gold, never failed to send a thrill through her. Triplet-quarter-quarter-duplet-quarter. Brass and timpani and power.

Next, after the God of War, was "Venus, Bringer of Peace," all shimmering high winds and harp, blue and silver, allowing the melody in the cello and solo violin to float on its bed of sound. Then playful Mercury, all cheeky yellows and greens, exuberant Jupiter with its reds and gold, and through to the end of the piece. Fred stopped the musicians every so often to clarify something or to go over a specific section, but for the most part, he let the orchestra play, saying they would focus on the details at subsequent rehearsals. For Anne, it was as good as a vacation. What a treat to sit back and relax with good music in the air and no demands on her time. She closed her eyes and let the music wash over her, a warm hug of sound, all enveloping and familiar. Her happy place.

"All ready?"

The rehearsal was over and everybody was packing up. Fred stood in the aisle by her row, his scores and baton in the messenger bag he had slung over his shoulder, his hands in his grey trouser pockets. He cocked his head just a touch as he looked at her. The smile on his face was open and friendly.

"Yes. Give me a moment." In a trice she had packed up her own few things and walked out of the theatre with him, waving at Kostas on the way. "Where are we going?"

"I told Ben we would meet him at the coffee shop near your building." He named a popular local chain. "It's halfway between here and my place, and seemed like a suitable spot. Is it okay?"

"Oh. Yes, of course. Are we walking? That's how I got here."

They loped along the street, side by side, like old friends. Which, in a sense, they were. The day was warm, and the sidewalks were busy and they spoke only a little, and then only about the music from the rehearsal. What did Anne think of the Holst? Did she have any insights into the Beethoven that might keep it fresh? The fifth symphony was a bit of a warhorse, a terrific piece, but one that everybody knew so well it was all but tired. What about the next concert in the season? He had included a piece by the brilliant Canadian composer Vanore Voaklander, and he asked if Anne had ever met her. It was easy conversation and quite impersonal, and she appreciated this.

Ben was waiting at the coffee shop when they arrived. He had taken a table in the far corner and sat with an empty cup in front of him, peering into his tablet. He turned the device off when Fred called his name and set it face-down on the table before standing up to meet Anne.

Fred made the introductions. Benjamin James was English, from York, and he sounded the part. If Anne were later asked to describe him, she would have fumbled for words, because physically, in almost every way, he was average. Average height, average build, neither pale nor dark, neither handsome nor plain, and with no distinguishing characteristics or marks.

His garb and deportment, however, were another story. His hair was long, not quite to his shoulders, and loose, with a sweep that fell over his face. He would push it back with his whole hand, only to have it flop forward over his eyes again a moment later. He was wearing black jeans, despite the hot late summer weather, and a loose black linen shirt—almost a tunic—that was buttoned to the neck and at the wrists. There was something about the intensity of his gaze, the studied melancholy of his expression, that put Anne in mind of some tortured poet from ages past. Would he have been a Romantic-with-a-capital-R back in the nineteenth century? One of Lord Byron's set, all angsty and passionate about passion, with a flair for the dramatic and an eye for the ladies?

Despite the air of gloom that hung over him, he was a personable enough fellow. He had studied both art history and international relations before moving into journalism as a career, and seemed ready enough to talk about his experiences.

"I spent some time as a foreign correspondent in South Africa," he explained, "before moving to freelance. I do investigative stuff. You know, the sort where I follow a paper trail to its bitter end. There are a few politicians and business people out there who do not like my name very much."

He pushed the curtain of hair out of his face again. "I was looking into some monkey business with an Italian company once a few years back and decided I liked the place so much that I wanted to stay. Since I'm not tethered to an office, I did exactly that. I stayed in Rome. My Italian is reasonable, good enough for the necessaries. Not as good as Frederico's, mind you, but good enough."

Fred shrugged in modesty, a very European gesture. "I spoke it at home with my family, growing up. It's my first language, after all." Now he told his part of the story. "I'd been in Rome for a year or so, studying with Buscagni, but I tried to see everything the city had to offer. It is so different, living in a place rather than being a tourist. Now I had time for all those little things, the exhibits and the shows and the events that don't make it into the guidebooks. I met up with a few people in the expat Anglo community, and we got together from time to time to take advantage of what was on offer. Through some of these folks, I'd heard of this English poet in the city, but I had no idea who he was until we were both at a gallery opening. Ben here was flirting with the artist—"

"And she was lovely, you must admit!"

"—by extemporising poetry for her. But she's Italian and didn't understand some of the English turns of phrase, so I stepped in to translate."

"You were trying to shoulder in on my date." Beneath that flop of hair, a scowl crept over Ben's face.

Fred laughed. Anne had missed that sound so much over the years. "In the end, neither of us left with the artist, but we two ended up talking and that's how we became friends."

Ben rolled his eyes. "Imagine my surprise when this chap spouting flawless native Italian then turned to me and spoke in flawless native English, and sounding like a Hollywood actor, all New York and Los Angeles, whatever that might mean. I was shocked to learn he was Canadian. Never really gave much thought to Canada before, other than hockey and maple syrup. Italian conductors never occurred to me at all."

Anne asked after Ben's poetry. Rhythm and cadence were part of both of their vocabularies, after all.

"I used to write about my travels, the places I've visited." The gloomy face was back. "There is so much beauty in this world, but also so much pain. And too often, the two are juxtaposed rather too starkly for comfort. Recently, however, I find the words will not come. My talents were adequate for other people's agony, but not, it seems, for my own. I am a poor sort of artist who cannot come to terms with his own psyche."

Anne made a sound that she hoped was sympathetic and understanding. What was she to say? Fortunately, Ben did not need much encouragement to tell his tale of woe. This, at last, was what Fred had alluded to before.

"I don't want to bore you with the details, but, well, I am not quite myself these days. You see, I was engaged to be married to a wonderful woman. At least, I thought she was wonderful. She was Italian, but had studied in Australia and had perfect English. She was beautiful, intelligent. She was my muse. Was she not lovely, Frederico?"

Fred murmured his agreement. "Indeed. Claudia was very attractive."

"And smart and witty, and so funny." Ben gave a great sigh that all but echoed off the coffee shop's high ceilings. "She travelled with me for some of my assignments, where it was safe. She was everything to me." He lapsed into silence. Anne could all but see the grey fog gather around his head.

She had to ask. "What happened?"

Another deep, shuddering sigh. "We were engaged to be married, as I said. Everything seemed perfect. Then I accepted a commission for a story in central Africa. It was riskier than anything I had done before, and I told Claudia I wasn't comfortable with her joining me. She was an artist. I do have a thing for artists, I admit. She could work anywhere, and she begged to come along, but in the end I refused. I could not risk her safety. And so off I went." The grey clouds above his head intensified with his long sigh.

"But while I was chasing my story, it turned out that she was chasing some new fellow who came into her gallery one day. And when I got back, she had moved out."

"You poor man. Did you have no idea?"

Ben slumped. "Not the foggiest clue. Her emails were all normal. When we talked, she sounded absolutely like always, right up until the last week. Then she was always out when I called, or busy. I came home to an empty flat and a Dear Ben note."

Anne tutted and consoled. She really did feel for the Englishman. At least she had some sort of warning when Fred had left so cruelly all those years ago. Ben, on the other hand, had been completely blindsided. As she cooed her empathetic words, she felt Ben warm to her more and more. "And when did this all happen?" she asked at last. "Was it recent?"

"Last spring." She had to strain to hear the words he all but whispered. "April. Before Frederico left. He was the one true friend I had, and he left, just like Claudia did."

"Now Ben, that is not quite fair. You seemed to be doing alright."

"Grief follows no schedule. I pushed through the initial devastation, but after you abandoned me and all Rome, the pain grew greater and greater." He glanced up as if realising he had an audience. "I do apologise, Anne. I'm baring my soul here and we have hardly met. Forgive me."

Fred leaned close to Anne to explain, sotto voce, "When I returned to Rome last month to finalise my move, I had quite the shock. I got back to find Ben sleeping on the floor in my empty flat. There was no furniture, just a mattress and an old carpet that I needed to dispose of. He hadn't showered or eaten in a week. That's why I stayed so long. I would have come back sooner, but, well, I needed to get him straightened up a bit."

"I should curse you, Frederico. You should have let me die."

"Not in that flat! Can you imagine the clean-up fee I would have had to pay? No, Annie, instead of letting him die on my lovely old carpet, I brought him here with me instead."

"So now I can die on your new carpet." The hair flopped back over his face, and this time he left it. "Still, this is my first visit to Canada. It's rather nice. Perhaps it was worth living for."

"I'm glad to hear it." Anne reached out to put a hand on Ben's arm. "I know how painful a heartbreak can be." She kept her eyes away from Fred. "Time, they say, heals all wounds. Or," now she could not help but dart a glance to the dark-haired man at her side, "it at least softens them. I hope that it won't be too long before life is worth living again."

Ben glanced at her hand, then picked it up with his free one and kissed the back like some gentleman in an old movie. "Thank you. Frederico has spoken of your kindness and empathy. He was not wrong. You are a gentle spirit. Perhaps, if I ever write poetry again, you will inspire my first words."

She felt, rather than saw, Fred stiffen in his seat beside her.

"Er, thank you." *I think.* A pause. "What do you think of Toronto?"

From here, the conversation became lighter. Ben spoke about the things he had seen and the places he still wished to visit. "Niagara Falls, of course, because it is one of those places a person should see if he can possibly manage it. And parts of the city I have heard people talk of. Chinatown—you have three? Remarkable!—and Little India. I thought London was cosmopolitan, but this place is a veritable kaleidoscope. And of course, I would like to see a lot of nothing. Those tracts of empty land of which we have so little in Europe, where there are no villages and no farms and no people, only trees and rivers and wilderness."

"You will have to travel some distance for that. It's pretty built up around the city. But if you can rent a car, you should head north to Algonquin Park. It's only a three-hour drive or so." Ben snorted out a laugh. "There you can see all trees and lakes and rivers you like, and it's quite unspoiled. For something a bit closer, and especially if you are an art lover, the McMichael gallery is lovely.

"But if you are a poet, I think you would enjoy some of the material I've been working with. I recently completed a commission for choir, and the text I was setting recalled exactly that. Have you heard of Pauline Johnson? Here, let me find some of her poetry. Her words sing to me." Anne reached into her tote bag to retrieve her tablet, and soon the three were reading the beautiful words that transported them to a time long ago, to a world that had disappeared and yet that was timeless.

Three cups of tea later, they were still engrossed in their conversation when Fred sat upright with a start. "My goodness! The time." He gestured to his watch. "I have an appointment this evening." A date with Louisa? What else could it be? "I need to get going. Ben? Coming?"

But his friend shook his shaggy head, that curtain of hair flopping over his face. "If the lovely Anne has no objections, I'll stay here to talk some more. Or, perhaps, you know of another place we might converse about poetry and nature." He turned to his friend. "I can find my way back to the flat. You gave me a key. I'll be alright."

Fred's eyes narrowed, and his jaw went tight, but he nodded his acquiescence.

"Okay. Have fun."

But his glance all but screamed, *but not too much fun.*

CHAPTER SIXTEEN
Concertante

The first performance of the new season was now at hand, and Anne's *Preludes* was to open the program.

She had enjoyed her time at rehearsals. Fred's acclaim as a conductor was not exaggerated. His time in Europe, Anne had to admit, had been very well spent. He had a deft hand with the orchestra, coaxing as much as commanding, and the group had never sounded better. The musicians were all world-class individually. Together, under Frederico Valore's baton, they were exceptional. When added to his sensitive and nuanced understanding of the music, the result was pure magic. Even

Beethoven's workhorse, the Fifth Symphony, sounded fresh and new, while remaining true to Classical sensibilities.

She had attended all the rehearsals, and twice more had joined Fred and Ben afterwards for tea and sympathy. Ben was ever the gloomy Gus in the room, but Anne had started to think his melancholy was now more a habit than a genuine despair. He was talking about renting a car to see Algonquin Park, and once or twice his eyes almost shone with excitement.

"How long will you be here?" Anne asked. "If you stay a few more weeks, you might time your trip to see the fall colours."

"Ah, those glorious hues of autumn that I hear so very much about.

> *October's orchestra plays softly on*
> *The northern forest with its thousand strings,*
> *And Autumn, the conductor wields anon*
> *The Golden-rod—The baton that he swings.*

"Indeed, Anne, I have been making a study of Ms. Johnson's lyrical poetry. She does sing. I have six months of leisure here before I need to return to the ruins of my life. I've let my place in Rome as a holiday rental, so I suppose I shall have to return to my parents in Yorkshire. But I have until February to make that move, by which time, so Frederico tells me, I shall have had my fill of Canadian winter weather and shall be most happy to go back. Is it that dreadful? One hears tales."

"Our winters are... enjoyed by some." That was the best Anne could manage. "If you like skiing or skating, there is a lot to do. But you will certainly be here when the leaves change colour, and that is always lovely. I'm sure there's an app that will suggest the best times to see them."

And through it all Fred had sat as silent as an old oak, and as disapproving.

William Barnett had also attended a couple of the rehearsals. He found his way through the rows of seats to take his place next to Anne. He was the perfect companion; he knew when to whisper his comments and when to remain silent, and his opinion, when he voiced it, was informed and relevant.

With the coming of September, his calendar had filled up, and he was often busy in the evenings with meetings and business matters, and he had only called Anne once to see if she was free. That was the night, it turned out, that she had already accepted an invitation to Sophia and Jeremy's place for dinner. These quick and quiet chats, therefore, were all the time they had to spend together for the next while.

"After this concert, maybe we can find a day when you have some time," he whispered as the orchestra tuned after their break one day. "The Island should be lovely these days. Perhaps we can take the cameras." He had left this invitation hanging, and while Anne had agreed to the idea, they had yet to settle on a date. For some reason, she had never mentioned the post-rehearsal tea times with Ben and Fred to William; somehow, these little gatherings that tended to extend past tea-time and into dinner somewhere seemed so separate from whatever she had going on with William that she didn't even think to say anything.

Dinner with Fred and Benjamin, coffee with Jasmine, photography with William, and whatever Sophia had planned, these filled her calendar. For someone who had been all but a hermit for eight years, she was now quite the busiest person she knew. The thought amused her.

At last, it was opening night. There was a reception after the performance for the orchestra and a select group of donors, and Anne was expected to attend. William called the day before asking if he could accompany her, and Ben sent her a text that afternoon saying he would be there as a guest and that he was looking forward to seeing her. Sophia and Jeremy would attend, of course. The only friend who was missing was Jasmine. Anne had another coffee date planned with her in a couple of days to go over the whole event.

The concert itself was wonderful. The orchestra was in top form, the music note-perfect, bringing Fred's interpretation of the pieces to full glorious life. Anne was pushed up onto the stage at the end of *Preludes* to take her bow before the raving audience. Waves of applause filled the cavernous space of the theatre, growing even louder and more insistent as she dipped her head and accepted a huge bouquet of flowers from a little girl in a sparkling party dress—the daughter of one the musicians, she presumed.

Calls of *Bravo* and *Encore* floated on top of the acclaim and it was several minutes before the audience fell quiet enough for the concert to continue with the Beethoven symphony. Thank heavens Anne had decided on her black dress tonight. From the heat in her face, she must be so red that had she worn the green, she would look like a Christmas tree!

Sophia came to rescue her at intermission, standing sentinel between Anne and the adoring masses who hovered about in hopes of conversing with the great composer. Anne almost feared that someone would try to rub her head for luck, but her friend was an admirable bodyguard. Then came the second half of the program—the Holst—during which she could relax and enjoy the performance, and then, the reception.

The space was crowded. The audience had all departed, leaving only the invited guests to mingle with the orchestra members and staff. White-aproned servers snaked between clusters of chatting donors, bearing trays of nibbles and sweets and glasses of sparkling wine. Coffee and tea flowed from urns set out along a long table by one wall, and the lights of the city twinkled through the glass walls of the reception area in the concert hall.

Anne could not see Fred, but she knew where he was. He was in the middle of a crowd of devotees, hidden from view but nonetheless the star of the evening. Ben was there, standing by himself, just a bit apart from the gaggle of admirers. He had done something with his hair that kept it off his face, and he wore a smart-looking black t-shirt of sorts (was it silk?) under a tailored Italian-styled suit. The look was not formal, but it was very smart and it made his unremarkable face almost handsome.

He held himself very still, all but motionless, with his hands in his trouser pockets and only occasionally shuffling his feet. Anne felt the urge to move to his side to introduce him around, so he wasn't all alone.

Her eyes scanned the space again. There, to the other side of the galaxy of fans, stood Louisa, her midnight-blue hair blending well with the black dress that was her orchestra outfit. She glared at the mob surrounding Fred, eyes narrow and jaw tight. She was not pleased at what she saw. But really, Anne thought as she rolled her eyes and then hoped no one had seen her, what did Louisa expect? If you travel next to a star, expect to be outshone from time to time.

Her own little circle of admirers had dissolved with the latest offering from the waiters, and she started to move towards Ben.

"There you are!" William's voice stopped her. She had glimpsed him a while back, when the guests first started to fill the space, but he had been talking to one of the donors and she had not spoken to him since they had arrived at the theatre earlier. He was a busy man, it seemed, always being called over to meet this person and to greet that one, and generally to schmooze. It was part of his role on the board, Anne supposed. She would have been pleased to have someone at her side through all the socialising so as not to feel so much like a spare wheel or an exhibit at a zoo, but she did not require his company specifically.

Still, here he was, apologising for neglecting her and hoping she was enjoying the reception. "Come," he took her by the elbow with a manicured hand. "You really must meet the Harvilles. They're old money and have been big donors to the orchestra. Rochelle, in particular, is a huge music lover." He guided her over to where a pleasant-looking couple stood. They looked to be in their fifties, beautifully dressed in understated fashions, and very well preserved.

"Dr. Elliot," Rochelle Harville shook Anne's hand as William performed the introductions. "I am so delighted. I didn't want to presume by coming over to talk to you uninvited, but now that you're here, let me gush for a moment." She did just that, but in so genial a manner that Anne hardly minded it at all. As Rochelle poured out her admiration for *Preludes* and *The Butterfly's Kiss*, Anne heard William talking to Gregory Harville about some real estate, presumably the development up north, or the one in the Caribbean. Oh well, better to be discussing music with this sophisticated woman than trying to make more sense of property development at an orchestra reception.

By now, of course, any thoughts of speaking to Ben James were long since set aside. He would have to make his way through the evening alone. She glanced over to where he had been standing. He was still there, but he was no longer by himself. Louisa, the horn player, had made her way to his side, and the two stood chatting. That was a relief. For some reason, Anne felt responsible for the Englishman, and seeing him engaged like this was a relief, a burden lifted from her.

Before she turned back to Rochelle, however, another sight snared her attention. Fred had emerged from the centre of his nebula of admirers and stood there, a solitary figure, tall and still in the sea of whirling bodies. His eyes caught hers and his face went hard. What was he glowering at? Not the Harvilles, surely...

Then Anne realised that William's hand was still on the back of her arm, a proprietary gesture. *She is mine.* As she looked over at Fred, William turned to her and whispered something. She didn't hear what it was, but he laughed and, as an automatic response, she echoed his laughter. He leaned in closer to her and moved his hand from her elbow to her back. It was all perfectly innocent, all completely decent. But the storm clouds over Fred's head intensified. Was this what her old lover disapproved of so greatly? Surely he wasn't... jealous! The notion was laughable, and yet the scowl on Fred's face was very real.

Before she could excuse herself to go and talk to him, he stiffened his jaw and turned away, stalking through the mist of guests in the direction of the bar. What was that all about?

The reception did not go on too late. It was a weeknight, after all, and many of the guests had work the following morning. William drove Anne home, talking all the while about the people he had met and the connections he had made. This world of constant networking was one which Anne abhorred. It was important, though, this she knew, and it was exactly why William was on the board of directors. It had been a long day and the excitement of the performance of her *Preludes*, then the stress of the reception, had caught up with her. Anne tried to respond to his monologue, but the words all washed through her mind without sticking long enough to make much sense.

"Wealthy donors... good connections... right sort of people... interest in my developments... support the arts..."

She plastered on a smile and tried to respond with appropriate enthusiasm and non-committal sounds, and William seemed not to notice. Still, she was most relieved when, after what seemed like far too long a drive, they arrived at her building. Never had that cold glass entrance looked so welcoming. The elevator, just past the lobby desk, beckoned to her, a warm invitation, a vertical passageway to long-desired solitude.

Did William expect her to ask him up? She never had before. No, he had pulled up into the little loop off the street, but he could not stay there. It was only a place to stop for a moment to let somebody in or out of a car. He clearly had no such expectations, else he would have parked on the street.

She squeezed her tired eyes closed for just a moment, then turned to him to thank him for the ride and say her goodnights.

"I'll call you tomorrow," was his reply, and he leaned over to kiss her on the cheek. But he didn't get out of the car to open her door, and he did not wait outside long enough to watch her get into the elevator.

Perhaps she should have been miffed, but deep down, she was relieved.

Morning, as happened so often, came too early. Anne winced against the insistent sunshine that invaded her bedroom and, when it became clear that there was no escape, shuffled out of bed and to the kitchen to start her coffee machine before heading off to shower.

Soon enough, clean and more awake, she sat with her steaming mug of wakefulness and a freshly toasted bagel and reached for her tablet to check her mail.

There was a quick note from William that said nothing of any real importance, a message from Sophia suggesting a time for coffee in a couple of days, and to her surprise, a short email from Marie.

Anne,

I am sad that you have not called once to check on Dylan. He is all recovered, not that you seem to care, and he is proud of his scar. If you had called to check in on me, you would know how much I need a night out. Come at seven tonight.

Marie

She glared at the screen. Pouring her hot coffee over the device would not help matters at all, and would only result in a damaged tablet and a loss of precious coffee. Of the two, the latter was more concerning to her right now. Of course, she had checked on Dylan. She had emailed Charles every day that first week, and then twice a week since. He had replied politely, even affectionately, but had insisted that Marie would not appreciate her calling anytime soon. How like her sister, only to reach out when she needed something.

She glared at the tablet for a moment longer, wondering how to respond. A certain string of bad words crossed her mind, but calling her sister out would not improve matters at all. Tonight. Marie wanted her to babysit tonight, and had not given her the choice to agree or not. It was a command, not a request.

As she considered what to say, the machine made its little pinging sound, a chime of bright pink that meant she had a new message. Was it from William again? His first note has just said good morning and that he'd be in touch later.

To her surprise, it was from Ben.

Hallo Anne,

Are you going to the concert tonight? If not, join me for a cuppa somewhere? I'd like to talk to you about something.

Ben

Tonight was the second performance of the season's first program, with another performance scheduled for tomorrow. Fred would be on the podium, but Anne had not planned to attend, having made her bows at the very first concert. So Ben would be at a loose end, she understood, but what did he want to talk about? Something about his poetry? He had mentioned something about finding inspiration in Byron recently, despite Anne's suggestions that he perhaps find some time to read more uplifting prose. A good novel with a happy ending can, after all, go a long way to raising gloomy spirits.

Still, this was as good an excuse as any to give to Marie, and she sent off a quick note to her sister.

> *I'm glad Dylan is all healed, but I'm sorry I can't come by tonight. I have an important meeting.*

There was no need to say that the meeting was with a friend over coffee to chew over poetry. The response came a minute later.

> *An important meeting? What can anyone want to talk to you about?*

She did not reply.

One further message appeared later that morning, shortly before she dashed out the door to teach her classes at the university. This one was from Fred. It was a rather formulaic note, congratulating her on her *Preludes* and thanking her for being at the concert and at the party afterwards. It could all have come from a how-to guide, except for the final sentence.

> *You looked really nice last night. I was proud to be on stage with you.*

If she didn't know better, she would think that Fred was trying to flirt with her!

She met Ben as they arranged that evening. Instead of coffee, they chose to meet for dinner at a casual place near Fred's building, close to High Park. It was on a less busy street, one enterprise in an eclectic collection of family homes, law offices, mosques, and the like, but it had good reviews and an interesting menu that suited her tastes. Ben was wearing his usual long-sleeved tunic-type shirt and black jeans despite the continuing summer heat, but something about him was very different. It was there, on his face: a smile!

They exchanged all the standard greetings and ordered their meals before Anne could control her curiosity no longer.

"Tell me! What has happened that has dispelled the grey cloud that usually hovers over you?"

"Ah, Annie, and I thought I was the poet! Yes, you're exactly right. That is what I wanted to talk about tonight. I think I have met somebody who's exorcised the ghost of Claudia from my mind and my heart."

Anne's brows rose. "Oh yes?" Who could it be? Ben had certainly carried his accustomed aura of gloom at the reception last night. She searched her memory, trying to work out what might have happened between then and now. The only person she had seen him talking to was...

"Louisa. The horn player. Do you know her well?"

Oh! Her face must have gone blank for a moment, because Ben peered at her with concern on his face. "Is everything alright? Did I say something I shouldn't have? She's not... touched in the head or anything, is she?"

"No, no! It's fine. Yes, I know her a bit. But I thought she and Fred were a bit of an item."

Ben screwed up his forehead. "That so? Frederico never said a word to me. I think they went out a few times in the summer, but he hasn't mentioned her once since I've been staying with him. Maybe the attraction was more on her part than on his. She did talk about him quite a bit, the new handsome maestro and all that. I'll ask him when he gets home tonight. I don't want to be 'that guy' who steals his chum's girlfriend."

This was a surprise. Maybe Ben was right. Anne had only seen Louisa staring at Fred, not the other way around. Was it all on her part? She could hardly ask Fred himself, could she? "That sounds like a good idea." Then, unable to help herself, "Let me know what he says."

"Will do, Annie. He does go on about you a lot, though. I've asked him some rather pointed questions, and he just gives me that glower that could peel paint. Is there a story I should know?"

"He hasn't told you? No, I suppose not. We were... we were together eight years ago, before he went to Europe. It ended badly."

Ben's mouth twisted into something like a sad smile.

"Sorry to hear that. He certainly doesn't act like it was bad. He seems rather wistful, really. Sad rather than angry. But let's not reopen old wounds. What can you tell me about Louisa the lovely? We started chatting about poetry last night. Did you know she writes as well? She has a few pieces that have been published in literary magazines and she's collecting material to get a book together. I suggested we get together to read to each other..."

"Is that what they're calling it these days?"

Ben laughed. "You are a naughty one, Annie. No, just reading. But if she and Frederico were at all together, I shall suggest another location. Maybe an evening by the lake? Let nature make besotted fools of us all? Is she the sort who would enjoy that?"

They talked for a while about Louisa, music, poetry, and hair colours. They seemed an odd couple, Ben so contemplative and reserved and Louisa so exuberant and obvious, but stranger things had happened. While a certain degree of commonality was good in a relationship, sometimes opposites did attract, if Louisa's interest in Ben matched his in her. If these two could find that connection in their poetry, who was Anne to throw water on budding affection? And, after all, one meeting to read poetry was hardly tantamount to a lifelong commitment. Some lighthearted banter and frivolity would likely do sombre Ben a world of good.

"That was a fabulous concert last night. We loved the Holst and Beethoven. Your friend the maestro really breathed fresh life into them. I never knew that old chestnut of a symphony could sound so new. But the real treat was hearing your *Preludes* live. I boasted to everyone I could see at intermission that I knew the composer. Annie, you are just amazing!"

Anne and Jasmine were sitting at their favourite coffee shop, Percolations, near Anne's condo. The early afternoon sun was bright on the streets and glared through the window, and Anne had pulled down the window blinds to block the rays before they even took their seats. Autumn would be on them soon enough, but summer was not giving up her reign without a fight.

The friends hadn't seen each other since the night at the jazz club and had been looking forward to catching up. Now Jasmine grinned across the table at her, a cup of hot tea in front of her, her phone in her hands. Anne had been unable to get her friend comps to the first night of the season but had given her friend and Connor tickets to the second performance last night.

"So tell me about the reception," Jasmine went on. "I saw all the photos on the orchestra's Facebook page, but we all know that's just a sliver of what happened. Was it fun?"

"You have stars in your eyes, Jaz. These things are never fun. Sometimes they're more tolerable than other times, that's all. This one was okay. It was a good thing that Fred was there. He's the new darling and everyone was falling over themselves to flock around him, which meant they left me mostly alone."

"You never were one for parties, were you? But you made your way into a few pictures. You looked really good. That dress is a great style for you, and your new hairstyle looks fabulous."

Anne mumbled something she hoped sounded like thanks. One of these days, she really must learn to accept a compliment with grace.

"Here's one of you with your friend Sophia. Who is that man next to you, the one with his hand on your back? He looks so familiar, almost like someone I once knew." From the tightening of her eyes, this was not a welcome association.

"His name is William. William Barnett. He's on the board of directors."

Jasmine's eyes tightened even more. "Oh." Definitely not a good association. "Then it is him. He looks... he looks like he's quite close to you."

Was this suddenly an interrogation? "He's been around since last spring. We've been out a few times."

"You're dating?" Her voice was quite cold.

"I don't know if I'd call it dating. He's asked me out a few times for things like gallery shows and bird-watching, but he's never been romantic about it, if that makes any sense. He'll be very familiar at one moment and then act the Regency gentleman the next, all formality and distance and whatnot. I don't quite know how to label it."

"Do you... like him?"

Anne laughed. "What are we, Jaz? In middle school? 'Like him.' It's another case of I don't know. I enjoy spending time with him. He's intelligent and sophisticated and very interesting. I don't know if I'd say no to something more, but I'm certainly not head over heels or anything."

There was something in her friend's face that made her ask, "Why? Is there something I should know?"

Jasmine gave her head a quick shake and her expression cleared. "No, no. Just some business stuff. Nothing to worry about."

"Oh, okay. You'd let me know if he's a serial killer or something, right?"

Now Jasmine laughed. "No, no, nothing like that at all. He's just someone Connor rubbed up against once."

This made more sense. If Connor had been involved in investing, it was not unreasonable that he might have had some dealings with William's world. And sometimes things didn't work out so well, so there might be some bad associations. Still, it was one more little burr that niggled at the corners of Anne's mind.

CHAPTER SEVENTEEN
Recitativo

The day held one more surprise.

Fred was waiting for her when she got back to her building later that afternoon. He was sitting in one of the comfortable chairs in the lobby, one argyle-socked ankle balanced upon his opposite knee. The concierge kept sending sidelong glances his way, and visibly relaxed as Anne walked up to him to greet him.

"Fred! What are you doing here? Don't you have another performance tonight?" This was the last of the three concerts of the opening program.

He got to his feet and gave her a quick hug and a kiss on the cheek. The concierge sent them another glance, eyes narrowed. To reassure him, Anne responded with the traditional European greeting, a kiss to one side, then the other, lips not quite touching his face. She felt centred when she was so close to him. Even his scent grounded her, something undefinable and warm, with a hint of cologne.

"I have to be at the theatre at half past seven, but there's nothing really to do before the performance at this point. The musicians have to warm up, but we all know the music by now. I wondered if you'd like to grab a quick dinner before. It's only five. It's still a touch early to eat, but..." he shrugged. "Maybe just keep me company or have something light? I've got my tux at the theatre, so I'll change there."

Anne cast her eyes down at her shorts and t-shirt. "I just had coffee with Jasmine. Remember her from university? Jasmine Hamilton." Fred's eyes widened in recognition. "Now she's Jasmine Smith. We got in touch over the summer. I'm sure she'd love to see you again too, sometime."

"Yes. Of course. Dinner?"

"I'll keep you company. Mind if I go up and change first? I'm dressed for the beach more than for a restaurant. You can come up if you want."

Why had she offered that? William had never so much as been inside the building, let alone to her apartment. Of course, she shared a very different past with Fred than with William. When you had lived with somebody, the boundaries changed a great deal.

Fred followed her into the elevator with the easy gait of someone who was completely at home. He had, after all, been to her flat once before. And had left it once before as well. He made some meaningless comments about the decor and the carpet, and then stood in silence by her side while she unlocked her door and let him inside.

"Just a moment. Make yourself comfortable. I think there's iced tea in the fridge. Glasses are above the microwave." Thank heavens she had tidied up a bit this morning. She had the habit of leaving her dishes strewn all over the counters before washing everything in one load at night, and dangling her robe over the back of whatever chair looked lonely. There was still a pile of note paper on her desk in the corner and a book of crossword puzzles splayed open on the coffee table, but the place was presentable.

She slipped into her bedroom and shucked her shorts and t-shirt in favour of a light summer dress, and then grabbed a cardigan in case the restaurant was cold. She pulled a comb through her hair, dabbed at her nose with a powder brush, and tapped on some tinted lip balm. The whole production had taken less than five minutes. Cinderella's fairy godmother would be proud.

"Looking good, Anne." Fred's eyes slid up and down her form as she emerged. He had not found anything to drink, but stood at the sliding door to the postage-stamp sliver of a balcony. "Nice view. Do you like it here?"

A bit of an odd question, but he was probably just trying to be polite. The last time he was in her apartment, after all, they had not exactly been discussing the scenery. "Yes. It's just the right size for me and it's convenient to everything. A little noisy, sometimes, being in the middle of the city, but I have good noise-cancelling headphones for when I need silence."

He turned his body to take in the flat. It was small but comfortable. The living room was just big enough for a couch and chair and her desk along one wall, with another area that made do as a cosy dining room before the counter that marked off the kitchen. His eye seemed approving.

"I've got more space, but I'm further out, closer to High Park. I think you met Ben nearby last night. You know the area. You should come over sometime. Jeremy helped me find it, and Sophia gave it the nod of approval. I think you'd like it."

She blinked. Why was he being so warm? He was the one who had left her last July, after all. But she said nothing about that and smiled. "Sure." What else could she say?

They found a small trattoria part way between her building and the concert hall. It was off the main street and a little poky, but it had the tremendous advantage of being quiet so they could talk and not shout at each other over the din of bad music and loud patrons.

"I've been here a few times," Fred explained. "It's not much to look at, but the food is fabulous."

He ordered some fish; Anne got a salad. They shared some bruschetta to start. It was, as Fred suggested, excellent.

"Did you have something you wanted to talk about?" she asked as they started on their food. "Or am I just convenient company?"

He looked at her, his fork part-way between plate and mouth. "You're never *just* anything, Anne. I did have something I wanted to talk about, but I also wanted to see you, ask how you're doing. We didn't have a chance to chat at the reception." His fork resumed its journey, and he took a bite of his meal. "So, how have you been? Were you pleased with the performance?"

They talked for a while about the concert, about how the performance built upon her original vision of the piece and how the orchestra brought so many little details to life. The conversation ranged from there to the Holst and the Beethoven, and from there to Anne's current projects. Finally, they got back to the reception, just as the waiter brought Fred his espresso and Anne her cup of tea.

"I saw Louisa hovering around you. I never wanted to ask, since it's none of my business, but were you two, well, you know. Were you together?"

Fred scrunched his brows for a moment. "No. Not really. I mean, she was always hanging around when I first got here, and she found my email address pretty quickly. I guess we did go out together a few times, and there were often cameras. I sometimes wondered if she arranged for that." His eyes lost focus for a moment. "I can see how that must have looked."

"I wasn't asking because I was upset. You're both adults, and it's none of my business."

He stared down at his coffee. "I think she wanted more than I was willing to give. She's full of energy. It makes her a valuable member of the orchestra, and she is fun to be with, but she doesn't have the depth that really draws me." His intense gaze bore into her, as if he were looking at her soul. It was just for a moment, a hair's breadth of time, but it lasted an eternity. The cup of hot tea disappeared beneath her touch; the restaurant vanished and time stood still. It was just her and Fred, alone in the universe, linked irrevocably by that gaze and the cord that connected their hearts.

Then, just as quickly, the moment was gone. Fred withdrew his glance and the cup and the restaurant and the entire world snapped back into being, and Anne wondered if she had imagined everything. Was still imagining everything.

"... still calls often, but I've been busy." She missed the start of his sentence. He must be talking about Louisa still. "Between rehearsals and meetings and showing Ben about the place, I've put her off a lot. I don't think she's too pleased about it. I don't know if she's looking for a relationship or just sex, but she's looking in the wrong place if she's still got her eye on me."

He looked at her again and started to laugh. "Am I shocking you, Anne? Are you surprised? You shouldn't be. You should know I'm not that sort of person. When I'm in the game, I'm in for keeps. Or as much as I can be." His voice went cold again, just for a moment.

"Besides," he warmed up again, "Ben spoke to me last night when I got back from the concert. It seems like you and he have been getting together behind my back."

"Fred! You don't think... anyway, would it matter? I mean..." She stumbled with her words. Was he angry? He didn't look angry. More amused.

"Don't worry, Anne. I was joking. I know why you met. Ben also asked about Louisa. It looks like everyone thought we were a couple."

"You were photographed all over town together in the summer." She cocked her head and watched him. He didn't turn red, but he let out a huff of frustration.

"I think I was flattered by her attention. Yes, Anne, I know. I'm not a child anymore. But for the first time in quite a while, it felt like someone liked me for myself, rather than for a chance to get in with the maestro or for a photo-op. Even in Italy, most people I met seemed far more interested in the cachet of being seen with me than in actually knowing me as a person. It feels a bit like tooting my own horn, but I understand something about those characters in the books you used to love so much. You know what I mean, the men who worry that the ladies only want them for their twelve thousand a year or whatever it was, or for their fancy estates. Would your Elizabeth Bennet have fancied that Darcy fellow as much if he was a bricklayer? Or an impoverished music teacher?"

"Now you're being silly. I think she would have, really. She learned to value the man himself. She joked about being attracted by his estate, but if she only wanted security, she could have had that before. She had a perfectly good offer from her slimy cousin, and from Darcy himself, the first time he proposed. And while Mr. Darcy did use his wealth to save her family, I think he would have found another way to do it if he hadn't been so rich. It was his character that was his real wealth, for her at least."

Just like you.

Instead of voicing this thought, she added, "Do you think Louisa just wanted to sleep with the conductor?"

Fred drained his coffee. "I wouldn't be quite so blunt about it, but I never had the impression she was interested in me as a person. She never asked those important questions, you know. Do I like camping? How do I feel about baseball? What do I like to read? Do I agree with Plato or Aristotle?"

This was some of the most honest conversation Anne and Fred had engaged in for so long. Eight years, in fact. Even though they were talking about another woman, she was touched that even now he felt he could confide in her. Almost without thinking, she replied to his rhetorical questions.

"Only for a night or two, love it, the classics and modern literary fiction, and you see the merits in both."

He put down his cup and reached across the table to gather her hands in his. "After all this time, you remember. You know me better than anybody in the world. I was..." He stopped short. Grand pause. Subito.

"I'm not sure Louisa even knows who Plato and Aristotle are. Some musicians are powerfully intellectual with a wide range of interests and a wider breadth of knowledge. Some are more focused in their pursuits, all about their music and their instrument, but with little other background. Louisa is closer to the second group. She is fun and attractive, but I want more than to discuss the latest movie or who wore what better."

"From what Ben told me, she writes poetry as well. There must be something more to her."

"Perhaps." He let go of her hands and glanced at his watch, then called for another espresso.

"Perhaps there is something more to her. But I didn't see a lot of it this summer. I hope Ben knows what he's doing. To be honest, I think he could do far better than her. He's an educated man, a thinking man. And for all her musical talent, I really don't see much else in her. But, unlike some people," the voice went cold again, "I'm not about to tell my friend who should or shouldn't make him happy. If he wants to see her, he has my blessing. Not," he scowled, "that he needs it."

The waiter brought over the small demitasse, which Fred drained in one gulp. "I need to go. I have a brilliant piece of music to conduct tonight. Thanks, Anne. You're a gem." He pulled out a credit card and refused Anne's protestations over splitting the bill. "I invited you. My treat."

"You said you wanted to talk about something," she reminded him as they were about to head in their different directions.

"Yes. Of course. We'll just have to do this again. I'll call you." He leaned forward and gave her another kiss on the cheek before striding off into the crowds that filled the busy sidewalks. Anne stood for a long time, watching him grow smaller and smaller as he disappeared into the distance.

CHAPTER EIGHTEEN
Molto Agitato

"**A**nnie, I've had a fabulous idea!" Sophia's voice rang from the telephone. Anne had the phone on speaker while she fixed her coffee, and her friend's bright tones filled the space. "Jeremy was talking to William about his new development up north, and the possibility of using the hall as a concert venue, or for fundraisers. William invited us to see it, and Jeremy suggested Fred come as well. So why not make it a party? William is looking for some dates that will work."

The coffee was hot in Anne's hands and she placed the mug on the counter. Was this a good idea? "I'm pretty busy these days, Sophia."

"Nonsense. I know you teach your classes, but we can find a time that doesn't interfere. Jeremy thought it might make a useful article for the orchestra's website, maybe one of the business pages in the paper. *Business and the Arts Working Together*, that sort of thing. Maybe have one or two orchestra members join us, get some photographs. I'll arrange a lunch. Now, what about next Tuesday?"

When Sophia had an idea, very little could stop it, and so it was that a small procession of cars trailed their way up to the development site the following week. Anne rode with the Crofts and Shep Choi, the journalist who had written the exposé on Anne the previous spring. William was already at the site, and Fred and Ben had hired a car for the day. In the end, six other musicians were coming as well—Louisa, an oboe player named Henrietta, and four string players who were going to perform a string quartet on the site for a short video. Sophia had even arranged for perfect weather, with clear skies and pleasant temperatures, everything a late September day should be.

William greeted them all with the smooth manners and practised smile of a businessman. He knew he was on display and was playing his role, with grand gestures, elegant words, and flashing white teeth. He welcomed the Crofts with a hearty handshake, and Anne with a kiss on the cheek that seemed a bit more for the camera than for her. But he whispered in her ear, "I'm so delighted you joined them." *Them*, not *Us*. She nodded her understanding. This was as much his public performance as *Preludes* was hers, and anything personal was best left for another place and time.

Fred, when he arrived, wore a forced smile. It would look fine in photographs, but Anne knew him too well to believe it was sincere. Whether he was unimpressed with being dragged to a construction site in the middle of nowhere, or unhappy at being pressed into William's company, she didn't know. But his eyes softened when he spotted her, and he strode over, across the gravel site, to greet her with a quick hug.

Before long, everyone had arrived, introductions were made, and they gathered for the tour. Shep was included in the group as a guest, as welcome as the others, despite the professional camera slung about his neck and the tablet and stylus in his jacket pocket. Every so often he would snap a photo, or ask William to repeat something as he recorded a short video.

Anne was surprised at how much progress had been made in the few weeks since her first visit to the site. The townhouses looked all but complete, and the naked bones of the tower now were mostly hidden behind walls and concrete. Piles of construction materials decorated the brown lot, which was marked by the tire tracks of countless heavy vehicles as they carried and hoisted and rearranged these metal bars, coils of cable, and sheets of siding into buildings where people would soon live.

It was an unlikely place for a gathering of classical musicians, and more unlikely still for the short performance that the quartet would give after lunch, but the incongruity of it would make for an eye-catching series of videos. Anne only hoped her presence in these would be as small as possible.

"Watch the warning signs and tape," William remarked as he began the tour. "The whole place is an active construction site, and we have to take appropriate safety precautions. And please, do not remove your hardhats or boots until we are out of this zone." He indicated a series of noticeboards, and Anne watched as everybody's hands crept to their heads to ensure that the heavy protective caps were still in place. "Let me give you an overview, and then we'll move into that building there..."

He described his vision, as he had to Anne on their previous visit, talking about the community, the school, the marina, and the performance space he envisioned. They wandered through those structures that were deemed safe enough for the group, down to the waterfront, where the slips and wharves were already hosting a handful of recreational boats, and at last, to one of the scaffolding elevators that would take them to a platform where they could survey the site from several stories up.

Anne's stomach dropped to her ankles as she watched the lift approach them with its open cage. Her recent adventures up the CN Tower notwithstanding, she did not enjoy heights at all. In her own building, where the elevator was a safe little box that started in one place and ended in another, she could forget that it was carrying her up and down a shaft, that its system of cables and cranks were hoisting her up and down so many unthinkable metres of nothingness. Here, in the open air and with no comforting walls and mirrors to distract her, this fiction was impossible to maintain in her mind.

"I'll stay down here, thanks," she murmured to whoever was listening.

"Anne? You okay?" Sophia was at her side.

"Yeah, fine. I'm... I'm happy to stay here on the ground. I'm not crazy about heights."

William must have overheard, and he stepped in close. "You'll love it once you're up there. I won't let anything happen to you. It's all perfectly safe. We've got rules and regulations we need to follow as well." He placed a hand on the small of her back and began to guide her in the direction of the contraption.

"No, William, please, I'll be far happier here. I have my tablet. I can entertain myself quite well while you're up there. No need to hurry back." She turned to face him directly, refusing his gentle nudge.

"Don't be silly, Anne. We need a photo from the platform. It won't be the same without you." His blue eyes did not quite meet hers and his smile was one for the newspapers and not for her. A sliver of discomfort edged its way into her consciousness. Is this what being involved with William would entail, whether that involvement was romance or friendship? Would she always be pressured to grin and perform for the camera despite her own inclinations? She stiffened under his hand and felt it drop an inch towards her backside.

"Annie? Is everything alright?" Fred now turned towards them from where he had been chatting with Louisa and Diego, the violist. It was a small enough group that no conversations were private.

"Yes, yes, just fine, Maestro." William's public smile flashed in his direction, and Anne let herself feel a moment of relief. "Our lovely composer is anxious about the height, and I'm assuring her. You'll come, won't you, Anne?"

"I would really prefer to stay down here." She was an adult. They could not force her into that lift, could they?

"There you have it, William." Fred turned his hand palm-up in a very European gesture. "She's an independent person and can make up her own mind about this." He let out a small chuckle and smiled at the other man, but his eyes were hard.

"Of course, Anne. I would never make you do anything you don't want. You can sit on any of those crates there, or the cement blocks in the shade. Just keep away from those girders." His smile was as friendly as Fred's, and he turned away to address the rest of the group.

"You okay, Annie?" Fred's voice was soft in her ear. "Was he pressuring you?"

She shook her head. "He just wanted the group photo. He's just in his Property Developer role. He's the star of today's show and he wants it to be perfect."

Fred's icy eyes softened. "Just let me know if you're not comfortable. Mind if I go up? I'm curious to see it all from up there." He gave her a quick hug and pressed a kiss to her cheek before moving back to the group, who were now filing into the cage.

"Should I stay with you?" Sophia slid up beside her. "I don't mind."

"No, I'll be fine here. You know you want to see it. Have fun," she called out as she waved to the group. She smiled at the sea of excited grins as the lift began its ascent. What she was not expecting was the scowl on Louisa's face, a scowl directed right at her.

Lunch was an uncomfortable affair, for Anne, at least. The food, as ordered by Sophia, was excellent and the excited conversation among most of the group animated. But now there was an awkward dynamic, and Anne felt in the middle of it all. William was busy enough showing off his site that he was not able to spend a great deal of time with her. But when he did, just enough for the others to raise their eyebrows but not enough to comment on it, Fred's face grew hard. And now, when Fred turned his attention to her, Louisa glowered in response. Ben seemed intent on engaging Louisa in conversation, with mixed results, and Sophia sat back with *that look* and a small smirk, as if watching a melodrama on television.

From her conversation with Ben recently, Anne had thought that Louisa was as smitten with the Englishman as he seemed to be with her, but perhaps he was mistaken in what he had seen. Despite his, and Fred's, assurances that there was nothing between the conductor and the horn player, Louisa still seemed quite focused on him. Anne watched over her lemonade and chocolate-caramel cookie as Louisa smiled at something that Ben said, then reached over and laid a hand on Fred's arm to draw him into the conversation. Was she flirting with both men? Or was this a show for some reason? Anne let out a soft sigh and tried to focus on Jeremy's description of the view from the platform.

After a while, the members of the quartet went to find their instruments, which had been kept in the temperature-controlled site office, and prepare for their performance, while Shep set up his own equipment to capture the show on video. The others got up from their tables to wander around the permitted area and stretch their legs. Fred, Ben, and Louisa were strolling back in the direction of the least-complete building, while Diego and Sophia were discussing something about Renaissance art, from what Anne could hear. She was content to sit and enjoy a few moments of solitude, even in the middle of this busy gathering. No music filled her head today; she was happy enough for the silence. Her legs were getting cramped from sitting on the uncomfortable bench and she rose to wander over into the shade by the skeletal structure, letting her eyes drift to the lake that sparkled just past the construction site.

Then a shout came from somewhere behind her. "Louisa, no! Don't be silly."

That was Fred's voice, followed quickly by a laugh. Anne spun around and her eyes widened. A short distance away, Louisa was balancing on one of the metal girders William had warned them about, arms outstretched like a tightrope walker, head thrown back with laughter.

"It's fun! Come and join me."

She jumped down, but immediately rushed back around the pile to repeat her climb. All the while, both men yelled to her to come down. She walked to the very edge, a diver about to do a swan dive into a pool with no water. "Come up with me, Fred. You can see for miles. You can keep me safe. It's fun!"

"Louisa!" Fred called again, his voice tight.

"It's dangerous! We were told not to get close to those." Ben's voice echoed Fred's, but Louisa laughed again.

"Come down, Louisa." This was Fred at his most serious, the voice that had student orchestras quaking in their collective running shoes. "Come down now."

As Anne watched in horror, Louisa called out, "Spoilsport!" and leapt off the metal beam from a much higher point than she had before. But rather than landing neatly on her feet, she caught her hand on something as she jumped and she twisted terribly in the air.

Once again, the world slowed into that dreadful, fatal loop where action slowed but help was hopeless. Anne watched in horror as Louisa's body seemed suspended in midair for a moment, quite off-kilter, impossible to correct, and then, just as suddenly, plummeted to the ground below. She landed in a pile on the hard stone-strewn earth, her head making a sickening sound as it made contact.

The horn player didn't move.

Somewhere by the tables, somebody screamed, and the horror of Dylan's accident rushed back at Anne, threatening to drown her. The world swam, the sound of her nephew's head and Louisa's merging into one dreadful cacophony that turned black and pulled Anne's stomach to her feet.

No! This could not happen again. She had to act. Memories of Marie's friend, the doctor, filled her mind, and almost without thinking, Anne reached into her pocket and fumbled for her phone. Numb fingers stabbed at the screen until the number pad appeared and she dialled 911 for emergency services.

"Don't move her," she yelled to anyone who would listen. One ring. "She might have injured her back."

Two rings. Oh, when would someone pick up the phone?

Almost at once, somebody answered the call.

"An ambulance!" she shouted. "Send an ambulance. There's been a terrible accident!" Louisa was still motionless on the hard earth a few feet away.

A calm voice on the other end started asking questions, that even, measured voice leading her through the information needed. Where were they? Who was the patient? What was her name? Was the patient breathing? Somehow, Anne managed to answer the questions, determined that this time, she would hold herself together. Breathe in, breathe out. Breathe in, breathe out. Her world narrowed to that steady voice and the rush of blood in her ears, staying by Louisa's side and giving updates on her breathing and responses as requested. Yes, she is breathing evenly. No, she is not conscious. No, her eyelids don't seem to be flickering. Yes, there is blood under her head. She suspected the questions were designed more to calm her than to assess Louisa, but she kept talking, until at last, the blessed sound of sirens replaced the din in her head.

As the EMTs took over, the world swam back into focus. The black haze that had closed in ebbed gradually backward to reveal Louisa being tended to and moved, so slowly and carefully, onto a backboard, with the paramedics calling out to each other and taking down measurements and vital signs as they worked. Sophia and Jeremy were gathered with the rest of the group, trying, it seemed, to keep everybody calm and arrange for a quick return to town. William was standing apart, talking furiously into his phone. The liability issues must be horrendous for him; she would offer to inform anybody who needed to hear that he had warned them all and that Louisa had acted recklessly. Ben was pacing up and down, hand clenched, and Shep's fingers fussed with his camera and tablet, but—Anne noted with admiration—he did not take either out.

A presence at her side coalesced into a most welcome shape. Fred. He said not a word, but held out his arms and she fell into them, feeling his distress and his strength in his embrace. There was nothing intimate about this; it would cause no knowing glances. These were two friends comforting each other. But oh, how she needed this comfort.

"You okay, Annie? You were fabulous. I heard you answer those questions, as calm as I've heard anybody. You knew exactly what to say and what to do. We were all standing around too shocked to move, and you acted. There's no one as level-headed or reliable as you."

"I didn't feel level-headed at all. I felt about to dissolve into dust."

"You held us all together. Is this what happened with Dylan?" She nodded, and he gave her another squeeze.

"It was all in my head. It all came back, like I was watching Dylan's accident again. I was afraid of falling apart again."

"But you didn't. You're a rock, Anne. You might have saved her life. I'm proud of you."

Anne spent the night in Sophia's spare room. She promised her friend that she was quite fine to be by herself, but Sophia insisted and she really didn't feel like objecting. They had a quiet dinner and an early night, and when Anne woke up, it was to the aroma of brewed coffee and fresh cinnamon buns.

"William just called with news about Louisa," Jeremy announced as he pulled the tray of pastries from the oven. "She'll be fine. They kept her in hospital in Newmarket overnight for observation, but she'll probably be released today. Ben took the rental car up there this morning so she isn't alone, and he'll bring her home when they spring her. He said he'll stay the night in a chair if necessary."

"Thank heavens for that!" Sophia breathed, and Anne concurred. Any sparks of jealousy she might have felt towards the horn player were nothing now. What was important was the woman's health. "Let me find her address, and I'll send over a big bouquet of flowers." Sophia was always so thoughtful.

"And some bubble bath," Anne added. "I imagine she'll be achy for a while after that fall. Was nothing broken?"

Jeremy pursed his lips. "Seems not. A scrape on the side of her head, and we know how much those can bleed, but everything else seems fine. She'll have to sit out the next concert or two until the doctors give her the all-clear, but then she'll be back to her old self." He ran a knife between the rows of cinnamon buns and placed one on a plate for each of them, then spread a dollop of cream cheese icing on each.

"Here you go, Anne. By the way, William wanted to speak to you. He said he needed to apologise, although for what, I don't know. Call him when you're ready."

This she did, and was greeted with a sigh of relief. "I am so pleased to hear your voice, Anne. Can you ever forgive me? I should never have suggested that outing. I was up all night worrying about everything. I am so sorry."

"Sorry?" Her confusion sounded in her voice. "It wasn't your fault. You warned us all, and she ignored everyone who tried to stop her."

"And I ignored you. When you said you didn't want to go up the elevator, I didn't listen. I see now that in my way, I was as bad as Louisa, thinking that I knew best. Forgive me?"

She nodded, then realised he couldn't see her. "Yes, of course. You were showing off the site, not catering to me. I understood that. And the others seemed to love it."

"I'd love to make it up to you, but my schedule is swamped with meetings and business trips. I'll call when I get back."

She wished him well, he reiterated his apologies, and they rang off. When Anne finally returned home later that day, it was to find a large bunch of roses in a crystal vase at the concierge's desk, from William. There were no hard feelings at all, it seemed.

CHAPTER NINETEEN
Parlando

With the new season underway, everybody grew busy. Anne, of course, had her classes to teach and composition students to supervise. Jasmine had a full schedule of students and had only a few hours in the week to meet for coffee, Ben was spending a lot of time with Louisa as she recovered, and William was kept occupied with his various projects.

Between his evening meetings and a couple of trips back to the Caribbean to oversee some issues with his development there, Anne saw him only twice in the course of almost a month. He sent messages and emails, and once another bouquet of flowers to her flat, but the man himself was scarcely to be seen.

Sophia, too, was running about doing a hundred different things. She took her volunteer work seriously and was on the committee for this organisation and that, arranging fundraising lunches and bike-a-thons and poetry readings.

This left Fred as Anne's main source of social interaction. The classes she taught at the University and her new commission for a documentary short kept her busy during the day, but her evenings often stretched out before her as solitary ordeals to be endured as best she could. Once she arranged to visit Charles and the boys when Marie was out with friends, and a couple of times she attended a show or a play on her own, but it was Fred and his frequent calls that kept her from lapsing into the pastel-hued melancholy that had so often haunted her over the years.

"We have an afternoon rehearsal," Fred called to say one morning the following week. "We finish at five, and then I have some business to go over with Kevin Walters, but what about dinner afterwards? At seven, maybe? Ben is taking Louisa out. He's been to see her almost every day since the accident, keeping her company while she's still on reduced activity."

"How is she doing? We're hardly close enough for me to call often, but I did speak to her once or twice."

Fred's voice sounded his relief. "She was lucky. She's been given the all-clear to play in the next concert. Her doctor wants her to stay quiet for a little longer, but in all, she seems fine. She only has occasional headaches, and those, so Ben tells me, are easing all the time. We are all very relieved." He took a breath, and Anne exhaled with him. "So, dinner?"

"Oh? I'm the back-up plan?" She laughed. "Should I be honoured or offended?"

"Definitely honoured, Anne. My other thought was the baseball game. It's down to the wire between the Blue Jays and the Red Sox. But if you're free, I'd rather eat with you."

"If I'm taking precedence over baseball, then I feel very special indeed." She was enjoying this easy banter they had recovered. Hopefully Fred would always be a good friend, even if nothing else.

They made their plans. There was a little Chinese place Anne had always loved, a hole-in-the-wall restaurant with the best food she had ever tasted. What it lacked in decor it made up for in flavour, and they could enjoy a quiet conversation while they ate.

She met Fred there as they had arranged. He had his satchel slung over one shoulder. It was stuffed full and Anne could see the tops of the music scores through the gaps at the edges where the flap did not quite close. She had been dabbling at ideas on her own tablet while she waited for him, and she put her device away as he sat down.

"What's on the program?" She gestured to his bag.

"We're starting with a suite from Weill's *Threepenny Opera...*" He reached into his satchel and opened the flap to withdraw the thick pile of scores. They alternated looking at the music and the menu until, some indeterminate time later, the young woman who served as hostess and waitress alike in this small place brought a tray with their food.

Fred put the music away with a wistful look on his face. "Can't get hot-and-sour soup on the Mozart, can I? I'd love to have your thoughts on the Schumann. Maybe later...?

At that moment, Anne's phone pinged from her tote bag. She waved her hand, a sign that she meant to ignore it, but Fred nodded at her. "It's okay. You can check it. I don't mind. It might be important."

"No one ever wants me when it's anything important," she returned, but reached into the bag anyway to see who had texted her. "Oh, it's just William. I can answer him later. We were only confirming some plans for when he's back in town."

"Plans?" He looked hurt. "Is this William Barnett?"

"Yes. He's been away on business."

The look on Fred's face suggested the acquaintance was not entirely a pleasant one. The young waitress put the dishes on the table with all due speed and disappeared. When she was gone, Fred continued.

"I didn't want to ask after the day at the development, but he seemed... familiar with you. Are you dating?"

"We've been out a few times." She picked up her chopsticks, more for something to hold than because she was ready to take some of the food.. "Like you and Louisa were during the summer."

"Except," he countered, "I'm not seeing Louisa anymore, even as a friend. It sounds as if you and Barnett are still a thing, if he's texting you to make plans."

Now she laid the chopsticks down on the table again. "And if we are?" She took a deep breath. "Look, let's not ruin a nice dinner. You asked me here as a friend and I am more than happy to be here with you. Let's talk about something else. But..."

His eyebrows rose in question.

"What do you know about him? About William? We've been... acquainted since the spring, and I've gone to all manner of shows and walks and whatnot with him, but I hardly feel I know the man himself."

Fred helped himself to some rice from the large bowl on the table, and then to some of the fragrant dish of vegetables and bean curd. "I never took to him. Even up at his building site, he was more concerned about the photograph than about you not wanting to go up to the platform, and when Louisa was hurt, he was more worried about his insurance than about her. He's one of those types that's all about prestige and money."

Anne gave him an assessing stare. "That's exactly what he's supposed to be. That's what the board of directors is all about. Don't roll your eyes at me. You know it's true. That's how they pay for your not-quite-exorbitant salary. And my less-than-exorbitant stipend."

He huffed. "You're right. I still don't like him. But if you do..."

"I'm just trying to figure him out a bit. I find him charming and well-informed, but I might be missing something. I'm not so blind as to brush off what other people think. Jasmine also gave me that strange look when I mentioned his name."

"Jasmine Hamilton? What's her name now? Smith? You mentioned her a while ago. I should drop her a line to say hello. I do remember her a bit."

"She'd appreciate that, I think. And her problem with William was with her husband, really. Connor worked in finance and had some business deal go bad. William was involved somehow. But that happens, I suppose. It's just part of the game. I'm sure it's nothing."

"Yeah. Probably nothing." He finished filling his plate and Anne took her own helpings of the shared dishes. With their bowls full of food, the mood changed. "So, Annie, let's talk about your symphony. We're doing another play-through in a couple of weeks, and I had some questions."

"How is Ben doing? I haven't heard anything from him in a while."

Anne and Fred were wandering through the Ontario Art Gallery, which was near the concert hall, before a rehearsal. Anne was not required to be at the practice, but Fred would need to be there in a couple of hours. Not for the first time, she was pleased she had a gallery membership so she could stop in whenever she wished, even for a few minutes or to look at one hall.

Right now, they were wandering through a vast collection of small paintings depicting early life in Canada. The pictures were sometimes poignant, sometimes comical, and always fascinating. Fred stepped back from one particular piece, an indoor scene of a country dance with a fellow on a fiddle and two people doing a jig in the middle of the kitchen.

"Ben! I hardly know how he's doing, because I've hardly seen him. It's like he's a different man. I don't think I've ever seen him smile so much."

"Are things going well with Louisa, then?" Anne peered at the next picture along the wall. This one depicted a horse-drawn sleigh racing through the snow-covered countryside, as people leapt out of the way.

"It looks like they're going very well indeed. After the accident, he was there every day to visit her, and she hasn't glanced at me since. And as for Ben, he's almost never home. When I'm not at rehearsal, he's usually out, and when he is in, he's always talking about her. Perhaps I was wrong. Maybe there is more to her than her French horn. It seems she's quite a gifted poet too, at least from what Ben tells me."

"Have you seen her poetry?"

Fred laughed. "I'm afraid it would make little difference if I had. I know music and a bit about art, but poetry? I'm afraid that unless it's the text for some music I'm conducting, I'm still back at the level of limericks.

> *There once was a very glum poet*
> *Who tried to get wed but did blow it.*
> *Then he met a musician*
> *Who changed his condition*
> *And now he's all fun, don't you know it!"*

She laughed. This was the Fred she had missed so much over the years. Funny, bright, confident, but self-deprecating where appropriate. She gave him a playful punch on the arm and he responded with a quick shoulder hug before dropping his arm.

"Also," Fred dropped his voice, "and I shouldn't tell tales out of school, but there have been a few nights when he didn't come back to the apartment. He never said where he was, just sent a text saying not to worry. I can only imagine that he was at her place."

Anne raised her eyebrows. Fred scowled.

"No, we're not comparing notes. I never even kissed her, let alone slept with her. I think she was more than ready to move on to someone a bit more... in the game, so to speak. There were no hearts broken when she moved on from me to my friend."

"So that's taking up all his time, then? When does she have time to practise?"

They moved on to another wall of the delightful little paintings. Fred exhaled, an audible sound. Besides the two of them, there was only one other person in the room, perusing the pictures on the far wall. Fred's words wouldn't be heard. "He's not busy with her all the time. As much as I'm pleased he's out of his funk, that would be unhealthy. He's been exploring the city a lot. I don't see him much, but there's evidence of his rambles. A bag of spices from Little India or some fruits I can't identify from Chinatown sitting on the kitchen counter. He's also been working on a project..." He let that drop.

"Oh? More poems?"

Fred's face clouded for a second. Then he replied, "No, some investigative piece that fell into his lap. He is a journalist, after all. That's his bread and butter. I think he enjoys the research and the digging as much as the writing. When he *is* at the apartment, as often as not, he has his head buried in his laptop, looking up this or that. That's all I know right now."

It was clear he didn't have anything else to say about it, so Anne moved her remarks to the paintings, and they wandered through the gallery until it was time for Fred to head off to his rehearsal.

Hi Anne, it's William. I'm finally back in town. Dinner tonight? Maybe somewhere fancy? Call when you have a moment.

She had returned his call, and they chatted about nothing for a while before making their plans. A nice restaurant, somewhere smart enough for her to dress up and put on more than her usual light makeup. Eyeshadow, mascara, and some lipstick that promised to stay on even through a meal. She found an elegant skirt in her closet, all black lace over a satin underskirt, and matched it with a silk blouse in a soft peach colour. Sophia had insisted it was a lovely shade for her complexion, and she had bought it solely on her friend's recommendation. A pair of pearl earrings and a pearl necklace completed the ensemble, and she hoped William would approve.

When he arrived to pick her up, his smile suggested her efforts were appreciated. He was in a dark blue suit, not too formal for a weeknight out, but certainly smart enough that he would not be out of place anywhere but at the most high-toned of events. Once more, he was the perfect gentleman. He got out of his car when he saw her coming through the lobby and opened her door for her, planting a kiss on her cheek before handing her into the passenger's seat.

His hand on the small of her back felt familiar now, comfortable even, and she liked how secure it made her feel. But there was no thrill. She was still waiting for the thrill. Still, comfort and gentle satisfaction were not things to reject, and she was pleased to be out with him again.

They made their way into the elegant restaurant William had selected. The maître d' led them through the gently lit space, their feet all but silent on the carpeted floor, wending between well-spaced tables with crisp white linens. All about them the ambiance whispered of the belle époque, all art nouveau in warm tones with gothic touches to give some whimsy, and a fabulous, vaulted ceiling.

"Your table, sir," the man pulled out a chair for Anne. But William did not sit. Instead, he lifted his head to glance at a couple at a table nearby. The man there waved and William walked over.

The couple were an elegant pair, possibly in their 60s, very smart and handsome and beautifully dressed. He had thick white hair cut exactly to bring out his best features and wore a beautiful dark grey suit; she sported a stylish short haircut that made no attempts to allude to lost youth and a long-sleeved pearl-coloured dress. Both smiled at William and gazed with curiosity at Anne.

William exchanged a word or two with them, then called Anne over. The maître d' nodded and returned to his station and Anne rose to join William at the other table.

"Anne, please meet a business acquaintance of mine, Pierre Gaultier. Pierre, Madame Gaultier, my dear friend Anne Elliot. You have surely heard of her. She's the brilliant composer behind *Preludes* and the movie score for *The Butterfly's Kiss*."

"A pleasure." Pierre rose to shake her hand, and his wife's face broke into a radiant smile.

"Enchantée! I have, of course, heard of you. It is really you? You are so young and beautiful." The lady spoke with a marked French accent, although her English was perfect. "What an honour to meet you."

"Say, William," Pierre now remarked, "we have just arrived. We only have our drinks. This is a large table. Will you join us? Or is this a, er, more intimate dinner?"

William turned to Anne, who shrugged and smiled.

"Thank you, Pierre. We'd be delighted."

"I'll see about having more places set." Pierre strode off to make his request, and in moments the maître d' had returned with a waiter and the table was transformed to seat four with comfort.

By now Madame Gaultier had insisted she be called Monique, and the four settled in with their menus to make their selections. William insisted they refrain from talking about his and Pierre's business dealings, but encouraged Anne to talk about music. The Gaultiers were both great music lovers, and their intelligent comments and insightful discussion were the perfect accompaniment to a delicious meal.

They lingered over dessert and coffee, and it was very late when they rose at last. "I'll call you tomorrow, Pierre. We can talk about the project then." William gave his associate's hand a firm shake.

"Very well. And let's discuss that development you have going on again. I'm very interested. A real pleasure, Doctor Elliot. Anne. With your permission, I'll dine out on this evening's conversation for months. I shall be the envy of all my friends."

The car ride home was not long, the day's heavy traffic long since having disappeared as people returned to their homes and families. William drove skillfully, as always, a contented grin upon his face.

"You charmed them, Anne. You always do. One word and you have people enchanted."

She fought a blush, although she knew he couldn't see it. Why did she always turn red at the first compliment? "I don't always feel that way. I'm usually so tongue-tied I can hardly remember my name. I don't have the gift of the gab some people have, yourself included."

"Perhaps we can arrange a trip to Ireland. Kiss the Blarney Stone. But you really don't need it. Your intelligence and thoughtful opinions are a far greater gift than being able to shape words into pretty sentences. Anybody with the first bit of sense will hang on your every utterance."

They arrived at her building, and once more he motioned for her to stay in her seat as he leapt from the car to open her door and hand her out. This time, instead of the expected peck at her cheek, he put a finger under her chin and touched his lips to hers.

It was nice. It was comfortable. It felt pleasant. But there was no spark.

"Call you tomorrow, Anne. Thanks for a really delightful evening."

And he was off.

As she puttered about in her apartment, washing off the day and getting ready for bed, her thoughts wandered through the evening. She had liked meeting the Gaultiers, had found a great deal in common with Monique, had enjoyed an exceptional meal. And she had been flattered by William's kiss. But when she turned off the lights and closed her eyes, it was still Fred's face she saw.

CHAPTER TWENTY
Appassionato

This scene was replayed several times over the next couple of weeks. William would invite her out to dinner, to a gallery, or to a show, and each time he would greet her with displays of growing affection. The hand on her back became a more serious embrace; the peck on the cheek became a kiss on the lips. Always careful, never too demanding, but more intimate all the same. When they met people William knew, as almost always happened at such events, for this was where *that set* were to be found, he introduced her as tenderly as he would a lover and doted upon her with an obvious adoration. If there began to be more noise going around concerning their relationship, William was the orchestrator of it.

And all through it, Anne did not object to his intimacies, but she was still waiting for that spark.

"When did you know Jeremy was the one for you?" She and Sophia were sitting on Sophia's expansive balcony near the end of October, gazing out over the ravine below and the towers of the city centre in the near distance. "Was there a single moment or was it something that grew slowly?"

It was early evening, and the sky was showing off to the world with its fiery display of golds and reds and blues. Trumpets, trombones, and lush strings, with the sultry swing of jazz lurking just beneath the surface. They were sipping cocktails tonight instead of their usual tea, letting the warmth of an outdoor heater and warm jackets protect them from the growing chill of the autumn air.

Sophia lowered her crystal glass to her lap. "Why do you ask? Are you... are these rumours about you and William Barnett true?" She assessed her friend from under carefully plucked eyebrows. "I knew at once with Jeremy. He came into my life like a piece of a puzzle that I didn't know was missing. I was happy before I met him, but when I did, he just fit. And once he was there, I could not imagine life without him. William...?"

Anne shook her head. "I'm trying to work this out for myself. I've been going out with him now and then since June. I like him, and I always enjoy the time we spend together, but when he's busy or away, I don't miss him. Not like—"

The eyebrows rose again. Oops. She shouldn't have said that.

"Not like who? Come on, Annie. Fess up. You've been keeping something secret for too long. What, exactly, is your past with Frederico the Beautiful? Did you two once date or something?"

"Something." It came out as a mumble. She took a sip of her drink, hiding behind the brim again.

"Anne?"

She sighed. She would have to divulge her great secret sooner rather than later. Now was as good a time as any to start. "We were together, back when we were at university. It was... It was pretty serious."

Sophia gave her *that look* again. "How serious? Anne, I can't believe you never said anything. What happened? Was it just another case of young love not lasting?"

"No. We were really committed." She would not say just how much. "I thought it was forever. Then Fred was invited to study in Europe and I was all set to drop my degree and go with him. I told my supervisor and she, well, she started working on me. You've met Professor Russell. She can be persuasive."

"Overpowering, you mean," Sophia huffed. She clearly knew and did not much like the professor.

"I was young and easily led. Too easily. I know that now. I'm glad I finished my doctorate, but I've learned a lot about myself since then. I'm not that insecure girl anymore, the one who could be swayed with talk of prudence and responsibility. She told me it would never last with Fred, that I deserved more than to be second fiddle to a conductor, that I was throwing away my future. And at the time, I believed her. But now I see it was wrong. My future is wherever I want it to be. I can write anywhere I have a thought in my head and a scrap of paper. I don't need to choose between my profession and my heart."

She blinked back tears that had suddenly gathered in the corners of her eyes. "I've realised over the years that I could have had success *and* romance. That I could have been happy. But it's too late now."

In an instant, Sophia had put down her glass and was at Anne's side to wrap her in a hug. "Oh, Annie. Why didn't you ever say anything?"

Sniff. "What would have been the point? It was over. So badly over. Nothing could be done, so I just moved on. Or rather, I tried to."

"And here we've been, Jeremy and I, rubbing him in your face all this time."

Anne grabbed a piece of the paper serviette that sat beside her drink and mopped at her eyes. "It's alright, Soph. We're both adults about this. One of the things that I loved about Fred was how fair he is, how genuinely good. He'd never take out his feelings on me professionally. And really, those first days of bitterness are gone. We've become friends again."

Sophia returned to her seat, and the two sat in silence as the sun dipped below the horizon, taking its multihued mantle with it. The darkness was warm and comfortable, the ceramic heater warding off the breeze that brought more than a hint of the winter to come. It was a soft blanket for the soul, a place to hide and heal, and neither woman made any attempt to move, or even to speak. The peace between them was eloquent in itself.

The tranquillity was broken by a sound from inside the apartment, and Jeremy appeared at the balcony door.

"Ladies," his voice carried through the glass. "I wondered if I'd find you there. Isn't it cold? Come inside. I brought cheesecake, and a guest."

Anne and Sophia looked at each other, eyes alight. "Cheesecake!" they exclaimed in unison and hurried inside.

There was Jeremy, a grin on his face, and a large strawberry-covered cheesecake on the table next to him. And just behind him stood Fred.

Anne did not need to look at Sophia to know what she was thinking.

Fred stepped forward to greet Sophia with the European-style double cheek kiss; his similar greeting to Anne was less perfunctory, his hand moving around her shoulders to pull her into a brief embrace as his lips touched the edge of her ear. She shivered at the contact, and not from the cold.

"What are we waiting for?" Was Jeremy really oblivious to the change of energy in the room? Or was he overcompensating? "Soph, my love, will you do the honours? I'll put on some espresso."

The two Crofts bustled about for a moment at their respective tasks, refusing all help from their guests. "Nice to see you, Annie. Now that you've had a chance to go over things in your mind, what did you think of the rehearsal the other day? Are you pleased with how the orchestra is doing with your symphony? We should schedule a proper meeting sometime to talk about details, but I'd love your general impressions."

Shop talk was safe, and they batted about some vague ideas for a minute until Sophia and Jeremy had the table all ready. Beautiful tiny espresso mugs, each decorated with the image of a famous piece of art, sat evenly spaced around the table, the steam rising from them, redolent with the rich aroma of the strong coffee. Beside each was a plate, its pattern obscured by a rather too-large slice of the cheesecake and some extra strawberry sauce.

Anne sat by the Monet cup; she was certain that when she finished her cake, which she had no doubt she would do, the plate would shine up at her with the same image as the cup. Jeremy took his seat by the Picasso, Sophia by the Renoir, and Fred took the Klimt. *The Kiss.* Of course he would.

"I was at the orchestra's offices to talk to Kevin Walters, and Fred came in to confer with him about something for next year's program. I waited and then brought him home." Jeremy preened, a cat proud of his conquest.

"Your friend William arrived just as we left." Fred's voice went icy as he said the name. "He said something about a committee of some sort."

"The corporate outreach committee," Jeremy explained. "I'm more interested in building bridges with different arts organisations and with youth. Good thing we have folks like Barnett on board to do the boring business talk. He's good with that lot, schmoozing with the presidents and owners of this company and that. The man certainly knows where to find money. Like the nose on a bloodhound, that one. Just sniffs them out."

"Yes..." Fred still did not sound impressed. "Just like a dog."

They turned their attention to the treat before them, as oohs and ahhs replaced all talk of finance and management. Anne had no hopes that Sophia would let her confession out on the balcony drop completely, but perhaps she would leave the topic for tonight, at least. Anne glanced at the ornamental clock on the wall. When would she be able to leave and not seem rude? Maybe after one more sip?

Her hopes were dashed when Sophia glanced up from the rim of her whimsical espresso cup and turned her gaze directly at Fred.

"I've heard rumours, Maestro, that you and my friend Anne here are not new acquaintances."

Fred's face went white. Anne wanted to fall through the floor. "No," he tested the word. "The rumour is true. We... We knew each other at university. That's no secret."

"The rumours also say that you were rather more than just classmates."

"I was a few years ahead of her. We were never classmates."

"Let me tease you, Fred. I've wheedled some of this out of Annie already. So you two were an item? What did they call it then? It's not so long ago. She was your girlfriend? Your 'significant other?'"

Fred put down his cup and squared himself to the table. Anne knew what was coming, and the room swayed around her. He wouldn't. He couldn't. But he did.

The great conductor's voice was so low it was almost inaudible, but there was no question of what he said.

"She was my wife."

CHAPTER TWENTY-ONE
Variation Two

The impromptu party broke up very soon thereafter. Fred wouldn't divulge anything more, but explained that he had an early rehearsal and needed to go over his music. He said polite goodbyes and left with scarcely an extra word. Anne, likewise, scrambled for excuses to leave.

"We'll talk about this soon," Sophia murmured to Anne as she put on her light autumn coat. Was this a promise or a threat? No matter which, there would be no escape from her friend's well-intentioned curiosity.

Anne spent the next morning working on a new piece. This was another component of her position as composer-in-residence for the orchestra. Rather than a full symphony this time, she was asked to write a shorter work, something suitable for the first piece on a concert program. Often, this would be an overture or a symphonic poem. Or a set of songs or dances. Just as her *Preludes* had opened the season and her symphony would close it, she would welcome audiences back in January with another short introductory piece. She had several ideas in mind and had been jotting down notes and themes for months, and the piece was all but complete in her mind long before she began to set it out in her computer program.

She was enrapt enough in this task, so consumed by the tones and melodies that filled her head, that she quite lost track of time. Only when her stomach began to nag at her did she realise that she had taken only a bite of her oatmeal and had completely missed lunch, half of her morning coffee now cold in its mug.

Two o'clock! How did that happen? She pushed back from her chair and rubbed at complaining muscles in her back, then grumbled to the kitchen to put on the kettle and make a sandwich. A glance at her silenced phone informed her that she had missed a few messages. One was from Fred.

> *Sorry about last night. I didn't know what else to say. Forgive me? But we should talk. I'll call when I'm finished rehearsal.*

There was also an email from Marie, explaining how she had finally forgiven her sister for her gross negligence last summer, and how she really needed a night out. She would expect Anne at seven this evening.

Anne massaged the back of her neck. It was Wednesday. William always had meetings on Wednesday nights, and Fred's message had said nothing about plans. She replied to Marie, agreeing to the command, and then sent a separate message to Charles saying that she had to be home by ten, so he should keep any plans for the evening appropriately short. It was useless trying to talk to her sister about things like that.

She had a quick meal and returned to her work with a happier stomach. She had all but completed the outline for the short set of miniatures when her phone rang. It was Fred. She hit save on her computer and took the call.

"Hi. You must have known I was just about finished thinking for the day."

"Hi yourself." He sounded tired. "What are you working on?"

"The concert opener for January. I've had these ideas floating around for a while. Instead of an overture, I'm writing a three-part set of images. Think Monet, but in music. I don't have a title yet, but I might just call them *Impressions*. It should be about fifteen minutes long in total."

She heard some clicks from the other end of the line. He must be looking something up on his laptop.

"That sounds perfect. It will go nicely with the Mozart clarinet concerto, which is about half an hour." He paused. "Look, Annie, about last night…"

"Don't worry about it, Fred. She was bound to find out at some point. We should talk."

Another pause, much longer this time. Was he still there? Just before she drew breath to ask, he cleared his throat. "Yeah. I suppose we should. But here's something else. Do you want to come over tomorrow night for a bit? Ben has been complaining he hasn't seen you in ages—"

"He's the one who is always busy!"

"—and he wants to have you over. I'll be your chaperone."

She spat out a laugh. "Yes. We definitely need a chaperone."

"Will you come? You haven't seen the place at all and I've been here for months."

Now she paused. Going to her ex's condo carried with it all sorts of strange associations, but this was just a friendly get-together. Besides which, Ben would be there. It was his invitation, after all.

"Sure. What time? Send me the address so I know I'm going to the right place."

Fred had taken a suite near High Park, where Anne and William had gone with their cameras so many months before. It was not a shiny new building, but neither was it old, and it spoke of a quieter elegance than some of the more recent flashy buildings that had sprung up around the city like dandelions after a spring rain.

His apartment, when she entered it, was welcoming and chic, decorated with a discerning eye. This was a far cry from the tiny place they had shared so long ago, with paper posters on the walls and blankets tacked up over the windows because they couldn't afford curtains.

Ben welcomed her inside as if it were his own home. "Anne, love, come in. I've put on the kettle for a cuppa, but we have wine and cider in the fridge, and all sorts of yummies to eat. I hope you came hungry. Frederico just got home. He'll be out soon. Let me take your coat." He bustled about, divesting her in moments of her jacket and scarf.

Now she had a moment to take full stock of the place Fred called home. She looked around as Ben hung up her outerwear. The apartment was larger than she expected, with a separate kitchen and a dining room nook off the main living space, and a tiny room by the balcony that looked to be a study. She glanced down a short hallway. There were three doors. Two bedrooms and a bathroom? It must be so, if Ben had been staying here for so long.

The living room, eggshell white and wood with a dark green couch and set of chairs, was dominated by a black baby grand piano in one corner. Fred's cello was propped up on a chair beside it. A music stand, almost lost behind a pile of music, filled the space by the wall. She smiled at the sight of it. She hadn't realised he still played. What memories that brought back, the two of them in their tiny flat, playing through sonatas and concertos and their own compositions, he on his cello, the sound damped by a heavy mute, she on an electronic keyboard with the volume turned low. She closed her eyes, lost in the past, until Ben's footsteps recalled her to the present.

"Come, help yourself. I took the liberty of pouring you something."

He led her to the nook that was the dining room. The table, as promised, was laden with treats sweet and savoury. Ben handed her a glass of sherry and had just suggested they sit when Fred emerged from one of the rooms down the hall. He must have showered when he came home, because his dark hair was still damp where it curled over the collar of his white linen shirt.

He greeted Anne with a hand on the back of her arm and his accustomed double cheek kiss. Fresh from the shower, he smelled good. He was not one for cologne or fragrance, but she recognised the citrus aroma of his shampoo. Funny that he still used the same product all these years later. She took a deep breath, enjoying the scent. She missed that. She had never noticed how William smelled, but then she had never seen him fresh from the shower.

They helped themselves to heaping plates of snacks. Being with two men, Anne felt no shame in the large portions of chips and dip and baked cheese buns that she took. There would be no judgement. She was not one to be embarrassed by her enjoyment of good food, but she was aware of taking smaller helpings when out with her women friends. Now she could go back for more without a second thought, and later would help herself to the cookies and two-bite brownies that taunted her from their plate in the centre of the little feast. Satisfied with her selection, she took a seat on the comfortable chesterfield and let Ben direct the conversation.

They chatted for a while about his adventures in the city and the new areas he had discovered. "I borrowed Frederico's bike for a day," he explained around a mouthful of corn chips, "and followed the path along the Humber River. We have a Humber too, back home, but it's a rather different creature. Ours is wide and flat and open; yours snakes along, hidden behind tall trees and mossy paths. It was a great adventure and I'm going to do it again, hopefully with Louisa, if her head allows it. She doesn't get dizzy anymore. I'm not a great rider like our friend here, but I'm adequate for a trip in town. Lou has a bike, so when she has a break, and feels ready for an adventure, we'll make a day of it."

The conversation moved to Anne's new composition, which she had made good progress on earlier in the day, and then to Marie.

"Charles sent me a note and mentioned you were going there last night. How did it go?" Fred explained the situation to his friend in a few short words and then sat back to listen to Anne.

"It was fine. Marie acted like nothing had ever been wrong, other than that I haven't been doing my aunt-like duty by coming to babysit every week. The boys seemed happy to see me, though, and Charles was gracious as ever. Luckily, they had school today, so I didn't have to entertain them all night. We played for a bit, had a story, and I put them to bed. Then I started scoring the second movement of *Impressions*. I hope you'll like it, Fred. It's based on that bike ride we did with Sophia and Jeremy last spring, just after you came back. The vines and the grapes and the river all called to me until I turned them into music. May I?"

She gestured to the piano. Both men nodded. Anne put down her plate and moved to the bench. She tried a few chords and, satisfied that the instrument was in tune and that the action of the keys was comfortable, she began to play. It was only a few bars, two or three minutes at most, but it would give the men a sense of her idea. The steady, regular progression of the staked vines, the riotous glorious abstract growth of lush leaves and fruit, the mighty and relentless press of the great Niagara River broken up with little waves and splashes upon its banks, all these were now notes and melodies and harmonic progressions, sometimes separate, sometimes layered, other times in counterpoint. She spoke up above her playing, explaining something here or there.

"This section will be brass, with a strong bass line... here I'm going to let the winds take the melody, with the strings *con sordino* and a whisper of tympany... I was thinking of solo cello here, with commentary from the English horn and bassoon...."

She finished and returned to her seat, then went to refill her plate.

"Bravo, Anne. I can hear exactly what you mean. It will be terrific." Fred's words were warm and genuine. Ben just sat there with a goofy smile on his face.

"I am in awe. I knew you were famous, but now I've realised what rarified company I'm keeping. Fabulous!" He took a sip of his beer. "What's that solo cello part again, Anne?" he asked. "Do you have the music for that?"

She pulled out her tablet and called up the program she used. She handed it to him.

"Oh, not me, dear. I can't read a note other than Middle C, and then only if it's circled in red with an arrow pointing to it. Show it to our friend here. He bashes that great ugly guitar from time to time." He winked and looked over at the cello.

Fred took the tablet and hummed a couple of notes, his fingers moving up and down as he did so, pulling phantom music from the air. Then he took the tablet to the music stand beside the piano and picked up the cello and settled it between his knees. He tightened the bow and plucked the strings. It was in tune with the piano. He must have played it earlier today.

He put the bow on the strings and in a moment the room was filled with the lush sounds of the instrument, chocolate and velvet, the reddish-tinted tones of the notes a perfect complement to the wood and green of his decor. Anne had forgotten how gifted he was. Had he not taken up the baton, he could have had a good career on the concert stage as a cellist.

"Play with him, Annie," Ben invited. It sounded like an acceptable idea, and she did so, joining him with the murmuring undercurrent of harmony, punctuated by the contrapuntal comments from the cor anglais and bassoon lines.

"You two sound wonderful together. What a treat this is. If I were less scrupulous a gent, I'd have you do it again, and I'd record it and upload the whole thing to YouTube in a moment. But say…" Ben paused. "Come back and pour yourselves another drink each. I have an announcement that needs celebrating, and then, perhaps, a great favour to ask."

"An announcement?" Fred's arched eyebrows matched Anne's surprised thoughts.

Ben's expression now became sheepish. "I should have had Louisa here too. But she preferred I just tell you by myself. We'll want a drink with this one. Those glasses are empty." Anne poured herself another sherry and then sat while Fred refilled his glass as well.

"Louisa and I," the Englishman blurted with a smile that all but split his face, "are getting married."

There was a moment of absolute silence. Then Fred leapt up to give his friend a shoulder clap. "Congratulations, old man! That's wonderful news."

Was it? Anne supposed it was, although Fred's response seemed forced. Perhaps it was just her own internal turmoil that clouded her impressions. Ben and Louisa. Louisa and Ben. She supposed it was good news after all, and she joined in the celebrations.

"It's a bit sudden, though," Fred continued. "You've really just met."

Ben shook his head. "Not at all, man. When it's right, you know. Have you never been in love? Have you never met the person you didn't know you were missing? No, I suppose not, otherwise she'd be here with you right now."

I am! Everything in Anne's being wanted to shout this out. She could not look at Fred at all, for fear of what his eyes would say. Would he be looking at her with disdain, full of relief that he had escaped a lifetime tied to her? Or would he be full of longing for what he had given up? She remembered those words, whispered so long ago. *You complete me. You are what I never knew I needed. You are the music my soul craved.* She didn't know which would bring her greater pain.

She sensed Fred tense up beside her, but he didn't say a word. What could he say, after all? It was evident Ben knew nothing of their history, and it was probably better that way. The man's biggest concern was probably that Fred and Louisa had been something of an item only two months ago. The tension in the room was all but palpable to Anne and seemed to last an eternity. But Ben seemed oblivious to all of this. Why should he notice, after all? It did not involve him at all, and he was all wrapped up in his own joy. He had no reason to expect so much drama to be playing out in silence around him.

"We were hoping," the prospective groom went on, "that the two of you would help with the music for the wedding. Would you play something? I knew you were both fabulous musicians, but hearing you play together, well, it was magical. Would you? Perhaps you know of some suitable piece of music. Some Bach, or Ave Maria, or something else that you like."

"As long as it's not Pachelbel's Canon," Fred groaned, breaking the tension between them. Anne laughed. That popular piece was the bane of cellists everywhere, those same eight notes repeating again and again until the poor musician's fingers were ready to fall off from sheer boredom.

"I'll do you one better." Anne spoke without thinking. Where did this idea come from? She groaned to herself, but the offer was already being made. "I'll write you something. When is the wedding?"

Now Ben went red. "You can change your mind, Anne. I know you're a busy creature. My six months as a visitor come up in late February, and we need to get some legal stuff out of the way, either here or in England. Probably both. We were hoping for late January, maybe mid-February if necessary. We need to find someone official to do the official necessaries. I'll go home over Christmas to see the folks, and then, when I get back, we'll make it all legal."

"Late January or February?" She did a quick mental tabulation of her commitments. "I can manage that if you don't expect anything too long. It's only for two instruments. Fred? What do you think?"

He walked to her side and put an arm around her shoulders. "I think we can manage. We'll make time to rehearse. Ben, I'd be honoured."

They celebrated for a while longer before Fred went serious. "Where will you live? How long will it take to get the paperwork sorted?"

Bed shrugged. "We'll live wherever we can. I know you want Louisa for the final concert, for Anne's symphony. We've already discussed this. If we have to move to the UK, she won't leave till after the season is over. Even if we have to be in different countries for a while, we're prepared to manage. Maybe I can get some sort of temporary residency so I can fly back and forth for a while.

What's important is that we'll be together in the end. What happens in the short term is just a detail. We're in this for the long game. We won't let a bit of inconvenience get in the way."

Anne went cold and Fred went silent. This was exactly what they had not done. If they had Ben's attitude... if Fred had Ben's attitude all those years ago, they would still be together.

But now was no time for uncomfortable memories. Anne plastered a smile on her face and said all the right things and the little party continued until she had to leave to return to her home.

CHAPTER TWENTY-TWO
Lacrimoso

Anne had hoped to spend the next few days working on *Impressions*, but Sophia would not give her another moment of respite and, to be honest, by noon on Friday, she had all but given up any hope of making progress. Her mind was everywhere but on her music, her thoughts awhirl and her emotions too loud to let her concentrate.

And so when Sophia called for the fourth time after lunch, Anne agreed to meet her friend for coffee at Percolations. Sophia was there waiting in her favourite seat when Anne arrived, with two large mugs of tea and two plates of treats on the table before her.

"You're always exactly on time, so I knew the tea would still be hot. Now no more excuses. You and Fred. What else haven't you told me?"

Sophia, as always, looked elegant and sophisticated. Her shirt was a crisp button front, blindingly white under a navy blue jacket, and her trousers were dark grey wool. She would look like a model for a boys' school uniform but for the silver and pearl jewellery that decorated her earlobes and throat and the large pin on her lapel. On someone else, it would be crystal and paste; on Sophia, Anne was sure the gemstones were real. But as cool and urbane as Sophia looked, her eyes sparkled like those of a child who had just been promised more chocolate.

"Spill it, Annie. Or no cheesecake for you."

There would be no hiding behind a chai latte today. "Okay. But there's not much more to tell. You really know most of it already."

Sophia just raised her eyebrows again. *That look.* Anne told her story.

"We met at university. Fred was finishing his undergrad when I started, but we were in a couple of ensembles together. He was still a performance major then, concentrating in cello, and I was a piano performance major. We, well, we hit it off and went on a few dates. Then he went away to do his Masters. We kept in touch." She didn't tell Sophia about the long passionate letters between them, written in ink on paper, too precious to commit to the ephemeral whims of email. "He came back when I was in my final year. He had taken up conducting, and I had decided to do my graduate work with Professor Russellin composition.

"It was like he never left, except that it was better. Before he went to Oberlin, we had just gone on a few dates. Now we were both ready for a serious relationship. We lived together for three years."

She took a sip. It was definitely time to hide behind a cup of something hot, even if only for a moment.

"Three years? That's not just a whirlwind relationship. Then what happened, Anne? Have a piece of the caramel shortbread. It's really good."

"What happened was that Fred finished his doctorate in conducting and began to wonder what to do next. Then he got an invitation to study personally with Maestro Buscagni in Rome. Buscagni had seen him on a guest conductor stop in Toronto with the Philharmonic and was impressed. Fred was over the moon. The arrangement was that he would play in Buscagni's orchestra, but also start to take on some conducting duties. Some rehearsals, some youth orchestra concerts, some regional orchestra gigs, all under Buscagni's tutelage."

Sophia laughed. "I have never heard anyone use the word tutelage in conversation. You're one in a million, Anne. Carry on." She leaned forward, elbows on the table, chin resting on her hands.

"Tutelage. There. I said it again. Anyway, it was clear that Fred would be going to Europe, and we thought I would join him. It seemed to make sense for us to get married. It would make all the official stuff around study visas and whatnot easier. And really, it just seemed so natural for both of us. I think we both wondered why we hadn't done it before."

"But why didn't anyone tell me? It's hardly the sort of thing you keep a secret. Is it?"

Anne shrugged. "We didn't try to keep it secret, but for all everyone knew, we were already an established couple. Having documents to confirm it seemed, well, almost silly. It was just for legal purposes. And so we got married at city hall one day between my morning seminar and Fred's afternoon rehearsal.

"But then Professor Russell found out about our plans. Or rather, about my plans. I was going to leave school to go with Fred. I thought it might just be for a year or two, but then it became clear Fred would be in Europe for a while. I knew I could finish my piece - that's what became *Preludes* - anywhere, but Professor Russell had a fit. I had to stay. I had to finish my degree, and she wouldn't hear of me going to Europe with Fred. I had to be in town to lead the workshops she insisted were integral to my progress. I had to meet the people she knew who would sit in on rehearsals to help me hone the piece. For every suggestion I had, she had five arguments. And, of course, she could get me the exposure I needed to really succeed. And perhaps she was right.

"The upshot was that I decided to remain in Toronto. Fred was not happy with this. Even when I explained that I could be finished in a year, that I would join him afterwards, it wasn't enough. And so when he left Toronto, he left me too. That was the end for us. Coda. Curtain call. No encore."

Unaccountably, tears had gathered in the corners of her eyes and she sniffled. Sophia was there in an instant with a paper serviette and then fished in her purse for a tissue. "You poor thing. What a rat..."

"No, Soph. Don't make him the bad guy. He might have done better, and he might have broken my heart at it, but he was never the bad guy. He's one of the best people I've ever known. He was hurt by my decision to stay, and he felt I was too much under Professor Russell's thumb. But we were young and the world seemed impossibly large and our futures too far off to imagine. We couldn't see how it would work. And we did both find success even though we went in different directions."

More tea. And a bite of shortbread. It did help.

"How long were you married? How long before he left?"

She swallowed hard.

"Three weeks. We were married for all of three weeks. And then he left, and I never saw him again until he arrived here last spring."

Over the following few weeks, Anne's schedule was full. Her mornings were mostly taken up teaching and with her music, for she needed to have the score to *Impressions* completed soon. The first performance would not be until January, but the orchestra members would want some time to learn the music, and Fred planned more than the usual number of rehearsals for it because it was new to everybody and because he wanted it to be an outstanding performance. He had scheduled some dates before the Christmas break, and Anne had to meet that deadline.

She was also working on the piece she had promised Ben for his and Louisa's wedding. This was easier, being both shorter and for only two instruments, but she still intended to give it every bit of the attention it deserved. There would be no second-rate piece dashed off in a hurry for her friend.

These intense days of work were punctuated by the occasional coffee with Jasmine, as her friend's teaching schedule allowed, and with Sophia; her evenings were often claimed by her renewed babysitting obligations for her nephews. This latter she did not mind at all. She adored Marie's boys and was delighted to spend time with them again, although she still felt the sting of Marie's coolness over the summer and the mercenary change of her sister's heart when she wanted a free babysitter once more.

The other claim on her time was William.

He was almost as busy as she, he explained, between travelling for his work and frequent evening meetings with clients and investors, but he tried to make plans at least once a week, when he was in town. And every time he called, Anne felt that strange sense of dissociation. Never had she felt so confused about a man. She liked him. She liked him a great deal. She enjoyed their evenings out together. She loved dressing up and going to nice restaurants or interesting plays, and then discussing things afterwards over coffee or drinks at some upscale bar. She loved the galleries and then exhibits, and even when she didn't quite understand the intricacies of what he was talking about, she found his tales about his business deals absorbing.

But what, exactly, was there between them? Was this comfortable relationship just friendship? Or could it grow into something else? It hadn't done so yet, and she wondered if it ever would. And what did William want? He hovered dotingly when he saw people he knew, and his kisses had progressed from a slight brush of the lips to something more intense, but not that much more. Was he moving slowly to see if she would respond with some ardour of her own? Or was it just another friendly gesture, more intimate perhaps than what she would expect from someone firmly in the "friend-zone," but still more platonic than passionate?

She couldn't help but remember that awful day of Dylan's accident, when Fred had come home with her. There was nothing platonic about their kisses. She had long since rationalised the evening to herself. They were both overwrought with distress and anxiety over the little boy's mishap. Emotions had been high, the need for reassurance great. They had taken comfort in each other when they were too upset to think straight. Or, at least, she had. She never had asked Fred about his reactions that day. And even after so long, Fred was familiar, something solid and reliable, a rock in the sea of turmoil that threatened to sweep her away. But that—what had happened between them—*that* had been passion.

With William, no matter how much she enjoyed his company, there was no passion.

And she did not know whether he wanted it that way or not.

Still, when he called asking if she wanted to make plans, she was always happy to accept.

It was now mid-November, and the air held strong hints of the winter to come. William called after lunch one blustery, rainy day, and talked for a moment about the change in weather from his last visit to the Caribbean for his development there, and how Anne's voice helped him warm up again. Then, as always, he made his invitation. This time he suggested a play, an unusual production of one of Shakespeare's serious plays in a bar downtown. Anne was no great fan of the histories, but the venue was enough to pique her interest.

William came to pick her up, as planned, but not in his car. "The roads are still too busy," he explained, "and it's a bar. If I have a drink or two, I shouldn't drive. I've got a taxi waiting." He was dressed casually, in dark jeans and a pale grey turtleneck sweater under a tweed blazer. Once more, he looked like he had stepped out of a magazine. Anne glanced down at her own outfit of fine corduroy trousers and a loose tunic sweater and hoped she was suitably dressed.

The bar was long and narrow, and with all the tables pushed to the very edges of the space forming two long rows of seats with the entire centre of the space clear for the actors, it was hard to know what it might look like on a normal night.

The establishment itself was open for business as usual, however, and after they selected their seats, William went to order some drinks. Anne liked a beer every now and then in the summer, but tonight she was more in the mood for a cider, which seemed to be on tap. She opened her program to read through the actors' biographies and the company's vision statement, and she was quite lost in the program when William returned.

He was not alone.

"Look who I ran into! Meet Abdulmalik and Danny." He introduced a couple he knew from somewhere or another, and all the polite things were said. This happened often enough that Anne was starting to wonder how many people William knew. They hardly went anywhere anymore where he didn't end up running into friends or acquaintances. All of them seemed to know about Anne, and all seemed quite thrilled to meet her.

This particular couple took the seats behind theirs for the performance, and they talked all through intermission as well. The play was well enough done, given the unusual setting, but all Anne could think about was that she was the one at a metaphorical centre stage, always the object of curiosity and speculation, an exhibit to be gaped at or a talisman to touch for good luck.

Still, if people got some strange pleasure out of shaking her hand and if they could amuse their friends with tales of *you'll never guess who I met the other day*, who was she to spoil their fun? And so she smiled and chatted and tried to be as interesting and amusing as possible. And William, in turn, beamed at her as if she had hung the moon.

CHAPTER TWENTY-THREE
Presto

Over the next few weeks, Anne saw very little of Fred. His prior commitments as guest conductor for various orchestras around the world had to be met, and he was away more than he was at home. Anne followed his tour on his Twitter feed: Vienna, Edinburgh, New Delhi, Adelaide, Santiago, Austin... She hoped he was accumulating frequent flyer points. Such was the nature of his career, but she knew how exhausting the constant travelling must be.

While he was abroad, a series of guest conductors took the podium with the National Philharmonic. This had been part of the orchestra's program long before Fred had been brought on board; this too, was part of the business. It was not part of Anne's official duties to attend every concert, but tickets were made available to her and it was suggested that it would look good if she appeared every so often in the audience.

This was also the case for board members. They generally donated enough to the organisation to more than cover the price of tickets, and they, too, had access to a certain number throughout the year. William took advantage of these tickets, and often purchased others for his use. As often as not, he invited Anne to join him, and she always accepted with pleasure.

They made a handsome pair, she knew, arriving in style at the concert hall. William wore a tuxedo like it was created for him. His light hair and eyes were a perfect contrast to the stark black and white of his clothing, like the keys on a piano. White and black, silence and tumult, peace and chaos. Against this backdrop of extremes, Anne felt comfortable wearing a bit of colour. Sophia's gentle haranguing had led her to buy a few more items that were not dark blue or black, and at times she would appear beside William in her green dress, or with a splash of red, or in the pale yellow gown that Soph had all but forced upon her. She had to admit, looking at herself in the mirror before leaving home in that frock one night, it was a good colour on her. Paired with delicate gold earrings and a dark gold shawl, the dress brought out fresh colour in her cheeks. She could even imagine that she looked quite pretty these days.

Of course, and not surprisingly, as often as they attended a concert, they met somebody William knew. A colleague, an old school friend, a client, a former business associate—so many seemed to be patrons of the arts and music lovers, and William poured on the charm from the moment he saw them. One evening they saw the Gaultiers, the couple she had met at that fine restaurant several weeks ago. Pierre started to talk to William about the venture he had just invested in. "You certainly convinced me," he started, "and I decided to throw in a couple of hundred thousand..." At which point, Anne and Monique found something more to their interests to discuss until the men had finished talking business.

At another performance they saw Abdulmalik and Danny, from the strange Shakespeare production at the bar. Just as William so often ran into acquaintances when they went out on their own, so did he meet people at the orchestra concerts. "All part of the package," he winked to Anne when she questioned him about the curious coincidence after one such evening.

"I run in the same circles as these people, and we have similar tastes and interests. It might seem a bit odd, I suppose, but it's a bit of a small world, really." And he had dropped the topic, asking her instead about her new piece.

It was now near the end of November, and Anne and William had been out once again, this time to hear a small band at an upscale pub. They met Abdulmalik and Danny once more, but now by arrangement. It had been Danny's suggestion. He was a devotee of all genres of music and had seen the video of Anne improvising with the jazz band back in early September. He wondered, so William conveyed the message, if Anne was a great fan of jazz as well, and invited her and William to join him and his partner one evening. Anne agreed at once. She had liked the two men when she met them at the play, and was always happy to listen to new music.

This particular band was a quintet and their specialty was early jazz, reminiscent of the 1920s and '30s, all Great Gatsby and Speakeasies. They promised a varied program with new compositions based on the old favourite style, with some standards thrown in to keep the audience humming along. The group was made up of keyboard, drums, string bass, saxophone, and trumpet, with the trumpet player switching to vocals as the music called for it. Anne had heard this singer before. She had a rich sultry alto voice that would fill the cosy pub with melted caramel warmth, perfect for the music and the venue.

It was the first time since her outing with Jasmine and Connor that Anne had heard live jazz. Come to think of it, that particular evening had also been the first time in several years that she had gone to hear music at a bar. She recalled Fred enjoying several types of jazz, from big band to modern. Sometimes, after a long day studying some great symphony, after she had completed her own work for the day, Fred would close all the books and turn down the lights and just let some jazz flow through their tiny shared apartment.

What did he listen to now, she wondered. What sounds filled his space when he wasn't preparing for his next concert? Did he go to the classics that he conducted? Did he still enjoy the change of genre, a break for the mind? Or did he find respite in silence, for his whole career involved sound? What he would think of an evening like this, just a small gathering of friends in a dark and comfortable venue, with good food and drink on the table and good music on the stage.

And then she chastised herself for thinking of Fred when she was here with William.

They found their table where Danny and Abdulmalik were already seated, ordered some rather classy appetisers, and chatted with the waitress briefly about the drinks on offer. It seemed too snazzy a space for beer, although Abdulmalik chose a stout from a local microbrewery. If the music was from the 1920s, shouldn't the drinks be likewise? And that meant cocktails!

After some discussion, she settled on an Old Fashioned, with the intention of having a Sazerac later. She liked a good whisky, and these drinks seemed perfect both for the evening and for her tastes. William bypassed the cocktails entirely, ordering a single malt Scotch, and Danny selected a cognac.

They ended up in a delicious conversation about the history of different drinks and about everyone's favourites, and Anne was almost disappointed when the band filtered into the stage to begin their set, so delighted was she with the company. She could well imagine becoming good friends with the couple they had come here to meet.

They shifted their chairs in preparation for the performance. The table was set up so that they could all see the stage just by turning their heads, but it would be easier on the neck to angle a bit towards the musicians. Danny snuggled up next to Abdulmalik and took his hand, sending his partner a smile that almost curled Anne's toes.

Then, to her surprise, William pulled his chair right next to hers. He was just moving it to see the stage, wasn't he? But as the lights dimmed a bit and the bass player tried a few notes on the large instrument she picked up from the stool, William snaked a hand around her shoulders and pulled her against his side. It wasn't the first time he had made an obvious display of affection in public, but it was the most intimate. Until now, he had danced attendance on her but had kept to a strictly-PG code of behaviour, almost out of a Regency drawing room. Now he sat here in this busy bar with his arm draped behind her, cuddling her close. From the corner of her eye she saw Abdulmalik's expression, a sort of "ah, yes, I thought so." He should get together with Sophia to trade tips on how best to deliver *the look*. They were both experts, it seemed.

"Do you mind?" William's voice tickled her ear. His lips were so close to her neck they almost touched her skin, but he kept that sliver of distance.

Did she mind? She wasn't ready to fall into the man's lap, but his embrace was nice, and he had been considerate enough to ask. She felt safe with him. Comfortable.

"Not at all." She leaned a bit more into his side and relaxed into the feel of his arm on her shoulders, his hand against her arm, as the set began.

The group was very good. "They were a huge hit at last year's Montreal Jazz Festival," Danny explained when the quintet took a break. "Ab and I went for a few days and you could not get a seat to hear them unless you arrived ages early. *Très populaire!*"

Abdulmalik grinned, his teeth brilliant white against his olive skin. "Turned me into a jazz fan, and I didn't much fancy the music before. If they go back next year, we'll be there to listen."

The group ordered more food, and William took Anne's hand in his, toying with her fingers as they waited for the platter to arrive. By the look on their friends' faces, it did not go unnoticed.

"Thanks for coming along. I had a lovely evening." William stood in front of her building later on, the taxi waiting patiently. He was close, just inches away, facing her. He was not as tall as Fred, but he still had several inches on her and she had to crane her neck to look up into his eyes.

"I enjoyed it. I need to listen to more live jazz. Most of the concerts I see are classical, and it's good to have a change. I think I might experiment with some jazz riffs, too."

"Danny and Abdulmalik like you. You really charmed them. They're thinking of buying into my Lake Simcoe development, so I've been seeing a lot of them. Maybe we can get together again soon."

She smiled. Had he moved even closer? "I'd like that. They're really nice. Ab tempted me with his boasts about his whisky collection."

Yes, he had definitely moved closer.

"Let's not talk about Abdulmalik and Danny right now. I'm much more interested in Anne Elliot."

The wind was cold and a light drizzle had started falling, but Anne hardly noticed as William closed the final wedge of space between them and kissed her. Not a full-out passionate kiss, but certainly more than the butterfly touch of lips he had bestowed on her before. This was definitely *A Kiss*. With capitals and italics. Sophia would do her mind if she saw this.

And, to her surprise, Anne found herself kissing him back.

"Do you like him, Anne?"

Sophia's voice sounded from the other end of her phone.

Anne had not intended to call her friend, and certainly not to discuss William, but after an almost sleepless night, she needed to talk through her emotions. Her dreams, such few that she had, were not filled with romantic interludes with William, but instead were full of doubt and confusion.

"Do I like him? You ask that as if you don't."

There was a pause on the other end of the line. "I wouldn't say I don't like him. He's very charming. What's important is whether you like him." Another pause. "Do you, Anne? You wouldn't have called if you were completely certain."

She sighed. Her coffee was cooling in its mug and she picked it up, letting the dark liquid swirl around before setting it back on the kitchen counter. "I don't know. I think so, but there's something going on that makes me... not wary, but confused. It's like there are two parts of me, my head and my heart. My head says yes, and my heart asks if I'm sure."

"Hmmm," Sophia murmured. "Has he done anything to disturb you?"

Anne shook her head, although she knew her friend couldn't see her. "No. Not at all. As you say, he's very charming. He's handsome and cultured and he dresses well, and he's so attentive and unfailingly polite. He's everything a girl should dream of. Right?"

"But...?"

"But… But nothing."

"Tell me, Anne, you and Fred were together a long time ago. How many boyfriends have you had since then?"

"You mean going out on-a-date-type boyfriends?"

"No, I mean relationship-boyfriends."

Silence.

"It's eight years, Anne. Surely you haven't been alone all that time."

"I've been busy. And I'm not a very outgoing person."

"You mean William is the first person you've gone out with more than a couple of times since you and Fred broke up? How did I not know this?"

She wished she had something to hide behind. Curse the transparency of the telephone. She couldn't deflect the conversation to a safer topic. "I just don't like talking about myself. You're right. I'm being an ass, that's all. I'm just creating trouble where there isn't any. Maybe I'm still a bit unsettled with Fred being back in my life in some way, so it's making me uncertain about relationships in general. I mean, I've been going out with William in one way or another for months now. It's hardly like he's pressuring me or anything, and I really enjoy the time we spend together. I need to stop holding back. It's just…" She trailed off and there was a moment of silence on the other end of the line.

"Yes?" Anne could picture her friend on the other end of the phone line, eyebrows raised, *that look* on her face.

"I'm being silly, Soph. Ignore me and my insecurities. The problem is me, not him. I like him just fine." *But he's not Fred.*

With Christmas coming up, Anne's schedule became, if possible, even busier. She had almost finished the score to *Impressions* and was working on some final details so she could print parts for the orchestra. Fred had completed his round of guest conductor gigs and was expecting to have a first rehearsal of the piece in a week's time. Anne, of course, would attend. She was looking forward to hearing her piece as the orchestra read through it for the first time, but she was also anxious. This would be the first time she would see Fred since he had started his tour, since William had made his more romantic overtures towards her.

As well as her days being busy, so were her evenings, for the annual array of Holiday and Year End parties was about to begin. The first of these obligations was in early December, and it was not even a party she was invited to. Rather, Charles had asked her to watch the boys on this night while he and Marie were at his office's party. It was the day after the first rehearsal for *Impressions*, and Anne could think of no reason to refuse. With the score delivered to the musicians, her duties with the orchestra were over for a few weeks, and she was always happy to play with her nephews. The week after Charles' office party was Marie's. Her company had arranged for an afternoon affair, heading into the evening, and she had asked Anne to pick up the boys from school that day. Anne assumed she would still be expected for her weekly babysitting duties, and planned what little time she had free accordingly.

There were, of course, all manner of other holiday events. Every year Charles' parents hosted a big family gathering, to which Anne was always invited, and she was expected to attend two or three parties at the University. As well, Sophia and Jeremy always held a small but lavish do for their select friends, and Jasmine and Connor had invited her over to their house for dinner one night.

And then there were the parties connected to the orchestra.

The board of directors were holding their year end gathering two weeks before Christmas. While she was not required to attend, she knew her presence would be noted and expected. And then— and this *was* a command performance—the orchestra was doing a fundraiser, an elaborate affair for any who had the funds for a seat at a finely set table, with performances by small ensembles consisting of orchestra members, and a short presentation by Fred on the progress on Anne's symphony to date. She would be expected to play short excerpts on the piano, or from pre-recorded snippets that she would create from the music notation program that she used.

The software had a robust set of sound samples and while a clip could never sound like a live orchestra, she could program it to give a very good suggestion of what a performance might offer.

That was the easy part.

The hard part was more personal. William had called up to ask her to attend with him as his date. His 'companion,' he called it. This was not the first event Anne had attended on his arm, but it would certainly set tongues wagging afresh. She accepted, of course, and immediately called Sophia to ask for help in selecting, or possibly purchasing, a suitable outfit.

The next day, Fred called with exactly the same invitation.

The night of the fundraiser arrived more quickly than Anne could have imagined. She was not used to being so much in demand, and with her calendar full, the days slipped away.

The first read-through of *Impressions* had gone well. There were some tricky passages for all the musicians, but they were a first rate crew and did a creditable job for not having seen the music before. Fred had some questions for her and the musicians made a couple of comments, but in all, there was very little for her to do other than sit back and enjoy the rehearsal.

This never failed to thrill her. No matter how often it happened, there was something wonderful about hearing her music being brought to life by others. She recorded the session with Fred's permission; she would use the tape to refine a couple of short sections and to guide her development as she moved on to other pieces. And, of course, she would play a clip here or there for Sophia and Jasmine when next she saw them. Perhaps this was her version of baby photos.

On the following night, she watched her nephews while Marie and Charles were out. There were no more disasters, no emergencies, and after the boys were in bed, she took advantage of the quiet house to read a book she had been neglecting for far too long.

Then came dinner with Jasmine and Connor. Connor had invited his friend Jamal, the jazz bass player, and his partner, and they spent a lovely quiet evening talking about all things musical. This was the first time Anne had been in the Smiths' home. They had a small apartment in a less fashionable part of town, but their furniture was all very fine, some looking like excellent antiques. The expensive interior did not match the somewhat shabby outside. Of course, it made sense; her friends had, not so long ago, been far better off than they were now. She wondered what it had been that had toppled Connor from the career he had built for himself and forced the couple to live on what Jasmine could bring in from teaching. It must have been quite dire. And, not for the first time, Anne wished she had some means of helping. But that was beyond anything she could do.

CHAPTER TWENTY-FOUR
Con Fuoco

Almost before Anne knew it, December was nearing its end. She had never been so busy, her calendar so full of social engagements. Between the parties and dinners and babysitting nights, she felt she had hardly been home a single night this month. And this evening was the orchestra's fundraiser gala. One more event to suffer through, although this was as much a working event as a celebratory one. Somehow that made it better to contemplate; putting on her social face for her career was easier than trying to be gregarious for its own sake.

Regardless, she must make an excellent impression tonight. This, too, was part of her job, and she stood by her mirror, turning slowly this way and that, hoping she looked acceptable.

On Sophia's recommendation, she had bought a new gown for the occasion. It was a rich gold jacquard with a soft shimmer to the silk fabric. The square neck framed her face and gave the frock a nostalgic look, which was emphasised by the fitted bodice and flared skirt. 1950s meets Renaissance, she had joked to her friend, but the dress suited her well. No simple jewellery for this one. She had borrowed some spectacular pieces from Sophia for the evening: topaz and chocolate diamond earrings, with a matching choker necklace and a string of chocolate diamonds at her wrist.

In her brown satin clutch purse (that matched the diamonds, of course), she had placed her keys, a tube of lipstick, and her phone, which now held the four clips from her symphony that Fred would discuss in his lecture. She checked again. The gadget was charged, and she had a connecting cord, despite all assurances that the sound system would connect through Bluetooth.

She fluffed her hair, re-cut and coloured just that morning, and contemplated herself as she waited for William to arrive.

She had, of course, explained to Fred that she had already accepted William's invitation to attend the gala with him. She wondered if the guilt she felt seeped out into her voice. Fred had said everything proper and assured her that he understood, no hard feelings. They were, after all, just friends. But she knew him too well to ignore how hurt he was by her refusal, no matter that she really had no choice. And she wished he had called first.

He had then changed the topic at once to discuss which excerpts he wanted for his lecture. She had not seen or spoken to him since.

William was waiting for her when she arrived downstairs. As usual, he was dressed perfectly, like he had stepped off a magazine cover, and he greeted her with a gentle peck on her lips. "I won't spoil the lipstick," he joked, "yet."

He handed her into the car and manoeuvred the vehicle through the city streets to the Royal York Hotel, the venue for the evening. They left the vehicle with the valet at the main doors and walked, arm in arm, into the lobby, up the richly carpeted grand staircase, and into the ballroom.

The grand hall was already abuzz. Large circular tables dotted the carpeted floor, the ivory hued linens a perfect foil to the intricate painted ceiling, all punctuated by a veritable forest of fabulous potted trees that towered above the guests. Stately and verdant, they projected upwards, brown and green, like piano chords, straining for the azure expanse above. Tall arched windows extended the entire length of the long wall opposite the door, and in the very centre of them stood a lectern, a grand piano, and a gathering of music stands for where the chamber groups would sit to entertain the diners. Swirling through this symmetrical maze of furniture and accessories, the *crème de la crème* of Toronto's arts patrons ornamented the space. This was the new *haute ton*, the Upper Set. There were ladies in ball gowns, men in tuxedos, and the occasional kilt or sari, beautiful and sophisticated, a symphony of class and style. Anne could all but hear the musical notes suggested by the sight of it all. The room was only about half full now; when all five hundred or so guests were present, the waiters would have a more difficult time weaving in and out with their trays of drinks and canapes.

Despite the crowd that had already gathered, Anne heard William's name called almost at once. Kevin Walters came striding through a small knot of donors, a glass of whisky in his hand. "There you are, William, and with the beautiful Anne Elliot as well. If I'd known what a looker we had with you, I'd have put you on the front of the season's brochure. Come, let's find our table. I believe we're together. Anne, you know Penny, my wife? Of course you do. The others will be some special donors, real supporters of the orchestra, just falling over themselves to meet you. Come along, let me find them and introduce you now. I've seen them here somewhere."

He grabbed Anne by the arm and all but pulled her through the gathering crowd. She swivelled her head to look at William over her shoulder with pleading eyes. He gave an apologetic shrug and turned towards a waiter with a tray of drinks. She thought she saw Penny Walters there as well. At least he'd have someone to talk to.

With Walters at her side, Anne was trotted around the room like a prized heifer at a country fair. Everybody came by to gawk at the specimen on display, for all that they were garbed in silks and diamonds rather than plaid and denim. They cooed and said erudite things with twenty-dollar words, and she smiled and flashed twenty-dollar words back at them, and then they drifted off looking like they had just won a hunk of cheese or a slab of beef at the raffle stand.

She fought a yawn as Walters pointed to yet another couple he knew. She must smile and play along, this she knew. These people were the donors whose huge contributions kept the orchestra alive and vibrant, and if shaking her hand led them to maintain or increase their contribution for the next year, she would plaster on a smile and do what was necessary to make herself charming and agreeable.

She tottered behind the CEO, careful to avoid tripping on a tablecloth that touched the carpet. Her eyes were on her feet and she almost walked into one of the massive potted trees. She stopped short and stepped to the side, bumping into something hard.

Someone hard. He put his arms out to help her keep her balance and she, out of instinct, reached back, putting her weight against his chest.

She knew this body, tall and solid, all too well.

Fred.

She should step back at once and cut this contact between them, but she could not move. She was transfixed, held there by some force she could not identify. For a moment, all she could hear was the beating of her heart, all she could see were his eyes, deep and brown, bottomless, enticing. Her feet, rooted to the floor, hummed with an unknown energy that sent a thrill through her body. It was as surprising as it was eye-opening, and she had to catch her breath. Here were all the thrills, all those little jolts of electricity, that were absent when William held her. Here was the spark that went beyond the physical, that connected her to his soul.

Being held and kissed by William was nice. This, this accidental contact with Fred, unexpected and transitory, was not "nice." It was elemental.

She staggered back before she said or did something untoward. Like running her fingers through his carefully combed hair, or kissing him senseless in the middle of the ballroom. Or declaring herself still in love with him.

Instead, she stepped backwards and said thank you.

His smile was polite but cool.

"Anne."

Double cheek kiss, but just for show.

"Fred. How are you tonight?"

"Are you ready for the lecture?" So no friendly chatter. He was too professional to be rude, but he was not pleased. She could hardly blame him, although it was no surprise to anybody that she had come with William.

She patted her compact purse. "I have my phone in here. I should set up the Bluetooth connection before too many people arrive. And the music is already on the piano, even though I don't need it."

"Let's go, then."

She found Walters and excused herself from the next introduction, then followed Fred to the lectern. Within minutes, they had completed their little task. A black-clad techie walked them through the steps to connect the phone to the Bluetooth speakers, although they didn't need his assistance. Anne could now play the synthesised clips from her symphony for the gala's attendees. And she could sit at the piano to play other shorter sections to illustrate Fred's talk. It was all very proper and clinical, nothing like that jolt that had all but seared her when she bumped into him a few minutes before.

She was certain he had felt it, too. Now, with the distance of a moment to contemplate that little accident, she recalled his arms tightening about her for just a second, the sudden, short intake of breath. He, too, had not wanted to let her go. Had he? When tonight was over, after the lavish meal and the presentation and the dancing afterwards, she would ask him if they could talk.

If he was really finished with her, she would have to live with it. But if there was still a chance, she had to know.

"There you are, Anne." William slipped through the crowd, a smirk on his face. His light blue eyes went cold as ice as he looked at Fred. "And Maestro. Good evening. Getting all set up for the presentation? Can I help with anything, Anne? No? Good. Let's find our table. I believe they're serving the salad course before your lecture."

He grabbed Anne's hand again and pulled her with him, not giving her a chance even to whisper a word to Fred.

The evening, as a holiday party and fundraiser, was a great success. As befitting such a high-end venue as the hotel, the food and service were exceptional, and throughout the meal, small ensembles brought together from the orchestra's musicians filled the air with the sort of music that aids digestion and encourages conversation. Before each new course, the background music was replaced by a more challenging piece for the guests to attend as concert goers and for the musicians to display their skills, and the rhythm of this variation was perfectly planned to keep the evening interesting and engaging.

As per the schedule, Fred stepped up to the lectern before the entrée course to present his thoughts on Anne's new symphony, and she took her place at the grand piano at his side.

"We have the incredible fortune," he began, "to have with us, both tonight and for the next two seasons, one of the world's finest young composers. You have all heard her brilliant *Preludes* and the score for *The Butterfly's Kiss*, and our first concert in January will feature the world premiere of her new work, *Impressions*. You surely already know her, but please help me welcome Dr. Anne Elliot."

The hall erupted into applause, and Anne rose from the piano bench and bowed. There, at one of the tables near the centre of the room, she saw Sophia and Jeremy. Her friend's encouraging smile was enough to buoy her through these disliked necessities.

"Tonight, however, we are going to talk about her first symphony. This piece is still in progress, and one of our great projects this year is to work together towards its completion. The composer, the orchestra, and the conductor—that's me." He paused to let the trickle of laughter settle. "But the bones of the piece are there, and they are fine. More than fine. We are working together on minor details, the musical equivalent, perhaps, of finding the right colour cushions for the couch. But the house is built and it will be the star of the neighbourhood."

And so he went on. He talked about the grand introduction to the symphony, the massive block of sound that dissolved, incrementally, until just one solo instrument remained to take up a plaintive melody. He described it, and then Anne touched the appropriate icons on her phone and music filled the room.

He talked about the thematic material, which Anne played on the piano, and about the use of traditional elements and counterpoint, harmonic devices and large-scale musical forms, and between the piano and her phone, Anne painted the musical pictures to demonstrate the meaning of his words.

The short lecture ended with an even wilder rush of applause, and it was several minutes before she was able to fend off the surge of fans and questions shouted from the floor and return, at last, to her table. She felt warm, but whether from the pressure of being up on stage or from exhilaration, she could not quite say. Either way, she was certain her face was red. She took her quick bow and slid back through the labyrinth of tables to her seat.

"Well done, Anne." William leaned over and pressed a kiss on her cheek. He took her hand in his and rested it upon the table so all around could see. Several eyebrows went up. Oh, there would be chatter.

During the break between the main course and dessert, Anne was swept away by Sophia. The board members were all at different tables, the better to mingle with the other attendees and talk up the wonders that were the National Philharmonic. This was, therefore, the first time Anne had a chance to chat with her friend.

"I want you to meet a couple of people," Sophia dropped a conspiratorial whisper in her ear, "but first, you and William? Things look like they're heating up. I saw how he held your hand. That was positively possessive!"

Sophia was, as always, the pinnacle of style. How she managed to make a simple black sheath dress look so wonderful was beyond Anne's reckoning. Perhaps it was the glorious shawl she wore with it, in dark tones of green and blue, shot with flecks of silver. Perhaps it was the cluster of light that shone from the jewels in her ears and on her fingers. Perhaps it was just the perfect cut of the dress. It flowed gently over her trim shape, hinting at an elegant figure, without being so snug as to be suggestive. Anne wished, not for the first time, that she had a small portion of her friend's innate taste and fashion sense.

Anne tore her eyes from Sophia's gown and glanced over to where William sat, talking once again with Penny Walters. "Yes. I... I wasn't expecting that, but he has been more, er, demonstrative recently."

Sophia batted at Anne's arm. The graceful folds of her beautiful shawl fluttered with the motion. "Demonstrative? You sound like some heroine in a historical novel. He laid down his cloak on the ground so you could walk across a puddle? He swept you away to Greece for a luxury weekend? He tied you to the bed and—"

"Sophia!"

"Okay. No tying anyone to furniture. So...?"

"Just kisses. Long, lingering kisses. He's very romantic." She tried to sound enthusiastic. Or dreamy. Or something. The look in Sophia's shrewd eyes told her she wasn't quite succeeding.

"Do they make your toes curl?"

Anne rolled her eyes.

"I see I won't get any deep confessions out of you this evening. Come and say hello to Jeremy, and then I'll throw you in front of the Nordheimers."

She paraded through the space, stepping around little clusters of people wherever she went. Everybody was up and moving about during this break between courses. In a few minutes, the musicians at the front would put away the Haydn and pull out something a bit splashier to demonstrate their skill. Not that Haydn was easy, Anne reminded herself, but its intricacies were more subtle, more noticeable in their absence rather than put on full display for an audience.

She followed Sophia's gesture towards the couple that was their destination, and let her eyes quickly scan the room. Yes, there was Kevin Walters, schmoozing with someone who looked like he ate hundred-dollar bills for breakfast, there was Pierre Gaultier, and there other members of the board whom she had met on several occasions. And there was Fred, standing aloof and alone. His eyes caught hers and she tried to smile, but he turned away almost at once.

With a sigh, Anne hurried her step to catch up with Sophia and paste on her socially adept-genius smile as she was introduced to the Nordheimers.

Soon enough, it was time to return to the tables for the performance and then dessert. Kevin Walters ambled up to the table and glared around with a stern look before taking his seat, and soon the others began to assemble as well. Penny hurried in at the last minute from somewhere, looking a bit flustered, and one of the other couples at their table didn't stop chatting until the quintet at the front of the room were well into a performance of the third movement of Brahms' opus 34. Only William was missing.

He slid into his seat just as the applause was dying down after the short performance. "Sorry," he whispered into Anne's ear. "Got caught chatting and didn't want to interrupt the show. Great piece, the Brahms, isn't it?" He reached over to kiss her cheek, then took her hand again and brought it up onto the table top until the dessert arrived, so everyone could see.

Anne took in a deep breath. She smelled the coffee and the flowers in the centre of the table, the scent of five hundred washed and primped bodies, and something else: the scent of a woman's perfume that sent flashes of colour through her head. She leaned a bit closer to William, and the scent grew stronger.

He turned to beam at her as if she were the most important thing on the planet, but the germs of uncertainty had started growing in Anne's mind.

After dessert, the formal part of the gala dinner came to an end, but the night was by no means over. The musicians from the orchestra packed their instruments and left, to be replaced by a small ensemble that would play old standards and some waltzes for anyone who wished to dance. And it seemed by the number of people pressing at the edges of the dance floor that was now being prepared, there were plenty of that mind.

Anne was no dancer and refused William's invitations to join him a couple of times.

"It's not hard, Anne. No one is watching. It's just a waltz. It's slow and there are only four steps. Your fingers have learned to play all those marvellous notes on the piano. I know your feet can manage this."

All sorts of memories of high school dances came flooding into her mind, standing there under the black throb of bad speakers, feeling the bass thump from the soles of her feet to the ends of her hair, clinging to some boy she didn't particularly like as the reek of sweat and bad body spray assaulted her nose. Dancing had no good connotations, no matter how lovely it could be to watch.

"No, thanks, but I'll sit out. If you want to ask someone else, I'm sure any number of women would be happy to have the opportunity."

And it was true. He cut a fine figure, and his natural elegance promised grace and finesse on the dance floor.

"If you're sure...?"

She assured him she was quite certain and stood for a moment as he surveyed the crowd. He walked over to where Kevin and Penny Walters were talking with somebody, exchanged a few words with them, and then led Penny on to the floor.

They danced well together, and when the waltz ended and a foxtrot began, they remained on the floor. They were both accomplished ballroom dancers, and they must have danced together before. Anne watched with a twinge of jealousy, but not, she realised, of Penny. Rather, she envied their skills on the dance floor. It must be nice to be able to move like that, to feel the music not just in her fingers but through her whole body.

Perhaps, when her current pile of commitments was over, she would look into taking lessons. It would be strange going to classes alone, however. Could she go with Sophia? Or Jasmine? No, that would be strange too. After all, who would lead?

Maybe Fred...

Her eyes fluttered closed as she pictured him before her, tall and strong, one arm extended in invitation to pull her out onto the dance floor.

"May I?" His voice was so clear in her mind, she could swear it was real.

"Annie? Are you in there? They're playing another waltz. Come. Please."

She opened her eyes. He was real. He was there, in front of her. She blinked, and he must have taken that as an acceptance, because before she knew what was happening, he had pulled her to her feet and led her to the floor.

"I can't dance," she protested, but Fred tutted.

"Put your hand here, and your other one there, and then relax. Feel the music and let me lead, and enjoy yourself."

She didn't have time to refuse again, because he had already started to move, and she was swept up in his wake.

Where did Fred learn to dance like this? Was it part of conducting school lessons? Was it something he learned in Italy when he wasn't memorising symphony scores? He certainly hadn't been a dancer when they were together all those years ago. But here he was, leading her about the floor. Or rather, stumbling around the perimeter of the floor. Despite his calm assurance, she knew she was hardly acquitting herself well, but neither was she falling onto her backside. Perhaps this wasn't so terrible, after all. She relaxed into his embrace just a bit more and let him guide her into another half turn.

Really, this was quite nice. She liked being held by him. She liked the feel of his arms around her, of his body so close to her own. She could almost feel his heart beat, like back then, before everything went wrong.

If she spoke, if she told him how much she had missed him, would he listen? He was the one who had abandoned their marriage eight years ago, and he was the one who had made love to her and then left back in the summer, when Dylan was hurt. She had no reason to imagine he wanted anything more now. No reason other than his continued friendship, his hurt expression whenever William's name came up, and the heat that emanated from his body, so close to her own.

She must say something. He might reject her, but how much worse would she be than she was now? She took a deep breath, hoping it would give strength to her resolve.

"Fred?"

He looked down at her from his superior height, his dark chocolate eyes pools of question.

"What is it, Annie?"

"I... that is, we..."

She never finished her thought. A figure loomed up behind Fred and tapped him on the shoulder. William.

"May I cut in? Thanks, Maestro."

Without waiting for either of them to respond, he pushed Fred out of the way and took his place, pulling Anne closer to him than Fred had dared. And there, in front of everybody, he pulled her into the middle of the dance floor and kissed her, long and deep, until applause broke out all around them.

CHAPTER TWENTY-FIVE
Fantasia

All that night, the evening's conclusion played out in her thoughts. She had stumbled backwards the moment William released her from his grip and muttered something about being exhausted, then dashed off to find a taxi before he could object. Of Fred, she saw nothing other than his retreating back. She should have gone to him then, but her head was too much in a whirl to think straight.

What had she been thinking, allowing William to kiss her like that, and in front of so many people? At first she had been taken by surprise, almost in shock, and hadn't had a moment to react. And then, with everybody standing around and watching, had she pulled away or stomped on his foot, it would have provoked a nasty scene.

It wouldn't have caused her to lose her position with the orchestra, and it wouldn't have cost her any of her current commissions, but it would have damaged her reputation. *Troublemaker. Uppity. Unfriendly. Cold.* Social skills were not really on the list of things an ensemble or film director might be looking for in a composer, but at the same time, being known as difficult never helped anybody's career. And whether it was his deliberate intention or not, William had known that. Known that she wouldn't resist.

And then realisation had hit, and she was mortified. This was something that happened to other people, that subtle but pervasive pressure to put up with sexual advances at the risk of losing a great deal. She never imagined it would happen to her. *Me too.*

And so Anne had suffered through the kiss.

When the self-recriminations ended, other questions started flooding her mind.

What had *he* been thinking? What was William's point in kissing her so publicly like that?

Was it really something benign, like wanting to show everyone how much he cared for her? She played with the notion for half a moment before rejecting it. He had, until tonight, been the perfect gentleman, always asking her before taking the next step, moving slowly and with every consideration of her feelings. And she had happily allowed his advances before. In private. This, on the other hand, was very public and very much imposed upon her. It was quite unlike everything she had known from him before.

It seemed more likely that he was trying to make a point. Just as when he had clasped her hand and brought it up onto the table for everyone to see, he was claiming her. It wasn't affection. It was possession. He was trying to make a point to somebody, but to whom?

Could it be jealousy? Had he noticed somebody else with an eye on her? That hardly seemed likely, for Anne had hardly spent the last eight years beating men off her doorstep. The only other man she was even a bit close to was…

Fred.

Was William jealous of Fred? Is that what all this was about? He had, after all, interrupted their dance, and swept her out of Fred's arms and into his own. Did Fred, perhaps, care more about her than she thought? Her hand reached out for the telephone to call Sophia, but she stopped short and let out a great sigh.

No matter what his intentions, William had doomed himself in her eyes. That little germ of question that had poked up when he arrived at the table smelling of perfume now began to grow stronger. He looked the gentleman and he acted the gentleman, until he chose not to. There was something about William Barnett that was starting to bother Anne a great deal.

Morning brought no answers, only a headache and bleary eyes from too little sleep. She needed to talk to somebody.

She wouldn't call Sophia, since Jeremy had to work with William on the board, and stories would travel. But she could call someone else. She grabbed her phone now, and called Jasmine Smith.

It was too cold to walk by the lake, and Anne did not want to bare her soul in an impersonal coffee shop. Instead, she invited Jasmine up to her flat. She had a poppy seed babka in the freezer, which she took out to thaw, and set about engaging in some culinary therapy by turning flour and butter and sugar into flaky shortbread.

"Mmm, it smells like a bakery in here!" Jasmine inhaled and smiled as she walked inside the apartment. "I brought some chocolate. It's not fancy, but hey, it's chocolate!" She handed Anne a bag and then shrugged off her winter coat.

In a moment, the kettle was on and Anne brought out some plates and the small tray of goodies she had prepared. She put the chocolates into a pretty glass bowl and added it to the tray, which she set out on the low coffee table. Then she prepared the mugs for their drinks (apple cider for Jasmine, chai tea for her), and waited for the water to boil. Soon, the women were comfortably nestled into their seats with steaming mugs and plates of goodies at hand, ready for a good chat.

"What happened last night? You've always been so private. It must be pretty serious if you want to talk about it." Jasmine sniffed her cider but didn't drink.

"I've been seeing this guy." She stopped. Why was she so reluctant to speak about it? What was this sense of guilt that weighed so heavily on her shoulders? She felt somehow dirty, although she had done nothing wrong. Silence hung in the air, leaden and tight.

"And?" Jasmine's voice was so low the word was more breath than sound.

Anne let out a long sigh and put her mug on the table. No hiding this time.

"I've been seeing this man, kind of. It started off as a casual thing, more like someone to do stuff with than anything else. And it sort of grew." She told her friend about taking photographs of birds in the parks and attending concerts, and the small gestures of affection that had developed into something more serious.

Jasmine nodded at the right times and murmured little sounds that Anne took as encouragement.

"He even invited me to look over one of his property developments up north on Lake Simcoe."

Anne saw Jasmine stiffen. What had she said?

"Is everything okay?"

"Yeah. Everything is fine. You didn't tell me his name. Is this the same person you were out and about with last summer?"

"William? Yes. That's him."

"Hmmm." Jasmine took a long drink of her hot cider. "I saw all those photographs in the press. Barnett, right?"

"I'm surprised you recalled his name."

Jaz stared into the plate of treats on the table. "It's come up a few times about... about other matters. Connor's business, you know."

Anne remembered their conversation a while back. There seemed to be some bad business between her friend's husband and William Barnett. She mumbled something and Jasmine forced a sad smile. "Don't worry about it." She picked up another biscuit and took a nibble. "So, what did you want to talk about?"

There was something in her eyes that bothered Anne, a wary look, not quite defiant, not quite scared. But it was enough to disrupt all her plans. Jasmine knew something about William, and all of a sudden, Anne felt she could no longer confide in her friend.

There was too much else happening, a part of the story she didn't know, but that would make it all but impossible for her to be completely candid.

"Nothing, I guess. It was such a busy night, so much happened... I guess I was just overwhelmed a bit. I went with William, as his date, that is. I think a lot of people have started to see us as a couple. That's really it."

Jasmine's eyebrows rose in question, but she said nothing.

They talked a moment about the weather, Jasmine and Connor's plans to visit his parents over Christmas, and about Anne's new piece, *Impressions*. Anne had asked Kevin Walters about Jasmine attending the dress rehearsal, and she now made that invitation. The violinist was delighted and dived into her purse to check her teaching schedule for that day. It was clear of other appointments, which thrilled her even more.

They then talked about finding some music to play together in the new year, with Jasmine on violin and Anne on piano. They decided to start with the Bach sonatas for violin and harpsichord, and then try some Mozart before venturing further into the repertoire. Anne pulled up some scores on her tablet and they settled on the fourth sonata, and they lost themselves in the world of music for a while.

The time passed quickly, and soon Jasmine had to get ready to leave.

"Students?" Anne asked.

Her friend shook her head, sending her cascade of hair swaying. "No, not tonight. Somebody is writing an article and wants to interview Connor. Something about his investment days." Jasmine looked a bit uncomfortable again. "Well, I need to go. I'll find that music and start practising. It will give me something to do at the in-laws when Con's mother starts getting on my nerves! I'll call when we're back in town, and we can make a music date."

They hugged goodbye and exchanged all the appropriate wishes for the season, and Jasmine disappeared down the hallway to the elevators.

And Anne still didn't quite know how to sort out her feelings about William.

Christmas was now just days away. Anne had spent a great deal of time searching for the perfect gifts for her family and friends, but the biggest present she herself expected to get was some solitude. A few days with no calls, no command performances, no last minute invitations would be welcome.

William had left a message the day after Anne's almost-confession to Jasmine, wishing he could see her but full of regretful apologies for an unexpected absence from town.

Anne dear,

So dreadfully sorry about this. I had been hoping for months to spend the holiday season in your company, but some desperate business matters have arisen that I have to attend to. I cannot imagine worse timing, but there it is. I will make it up to you. I hope you like tanzanite.

Thinking of you every minute,

William

Anne's fingers hovered over her phone, itching to type in a short message telling him not to bother, but she could not type the words. No matter her discomfort with his actions, he deserved to be told goodbye in person and not by text.

Likewise, Sophia and Jeremy were away for a few days at their cottage, and Marie and Charles were busy with Musgrove family events. They had invited Anne to spend Christmas itself with them and her own parents, but she anticipated spending much of the intervening time alone.

This rather suited her. She enjoyed her family and friends' society a great deal, but she was also happy in her own company. She had a large pile of books waiting to be read, another pile of movies to watch, and a kitchen full of treats and ingredients to cook and bake. She was absolutely content.

She also decided to spend the time completing her piece for Ben and Louisa's wedding.

That couple, she heard from Ben through a quick email, were flying to England to meet his family. Afterwards, he wrote, Louisa would have to return to Toronto for the first orchestra rehearsals of the new year, but Ben himself would be away for another two or three weeks, doing some work on a project he was working on.

She felt a flash of regretful envy. Clearly, distance and temporary separations didn't bother them at all. Heck, Ben had even suggested that if they were forced to be separated for a year before they got work and immigration issues ironed out, it would be alright.

If only Fred had been of that mind. But there was no point lamenting this now. Spilt milk and all that, she reminded herself.

What Fred was doing over the break, she had no idea. She hadn't asked and he hadn't volunteered the information. He had family in town, his parents and a brother. Presumably he was doing the big Italian Christmas thing with them. She had spent a couple of years in their company, and while it was a very different celebration to the restrained affair her family would do, she had enjoyed those parties of so long ago. She recalled lavish meals and far too many sweets and grand gestures of welcome. The exuberance was foreign to her, as much a product of their personalities as their traditions, but she had loved the warmth and, quite frankly, the fun of the season with them.

But that was all in the past. She would not be spending Christmas with Fred or the Valores this year.

She closed the door on those old memories and settled herself into her chair with her tablet in hand to work on the new composition.

Anne was to spend New Year's Eve at her sister's house, babysitting the boys while Marie and Charles went to a party hosted by a friend in the neighbourhood. She had expected nothing else.

"You will come." It was a statement, not a question. Marie presented her with this information at her house on Christmas day, as Anne set about washing a sink load of dishes after dinner.

"Are you busy, Anne?" Charles came up beside her to take the large crystal serving bowl from her hands. "Pity this can't go in the dishwasher. Do you have some lavish society affair to attend?"

She gave him a twisted half-smile. "No, it's alright, Charles. I don't have other plans. I'm happy to spend some time with the boys."

"Well, of course you are." Marie's voice sounded from the other end of the kitchen where she was directing her mother-in-law as to the best way to put away the leftovers. "What else would you be doing? It's not like you have anyone else to go to."

Anne bit her lips but stayed silent. Charles took up her case instead. "Now Marie, that's not true. She's got her good friend Sophie—"

"Sophia," Anne corrected, but no one heard her.

"—and she's been seeing that businessman, haven't you, Anne? Bill someone? Will...?"

"William. William Barnett. But—"

"Right. And there's her old friend from school she's met with again."

"Please, Charles. Anne has better things to do than associate with poor violin teachers. They're really a dime a dozen. And Anne's famous."

"Jasmine is my friend," Anne began, but Marie had started talking again, and clearly hadn't heard a word.

"So you'll come on New Year's Eve. We're going to the Grajos, just on the other side of the park, in the big house with the white pillars. They do such a nice party every year. I even dress up."

Brenda Musgrove's voice now sounded from the table where she sat with her plastic tubs, sorting leftovers into suitable containers. "Anne, dear, you looked lovely in the photographs from the orchestra gala. Marie, didn't Anne look lovely? I was so proud to show the pictures to my friends. 'That's Anne Elliot,' I told them. 'She's a famous composer. And she's so pretty too.' You had on such a beautiful dress."

"What about my dress? It's every bit as beautiful as Anne's, I'm sure."

"Of course it is, Marie dear. You will be the loveliest woman at the party. My Charlie will be the envy of all the other men with you on his arm."

"Well. Yes. Let's put the sauce in this container. No, the glass one, so the plastic doesn't absorb the smell. No, the other one."

Anne rolled her eyes and went on washing the serving dishes.

By New Year's Eve, her piece for Ben and Louisa's wedding was all but complete. As planned, she spent the night at Marie's house with her nephews, for Charles had insisted she sleep over in the spare room. She knew this meant she would be expected to wake up early to make some sort of treat for breakfast, but she didn't mind. It would be nice to bake for more than just herself. She planned on making cinnamon buns, which she would start as soon as the boys were in bed. The dough could then rise in the fridge overnight and be baked hot and fresh in the morning.

Marie and Charles left for their friends' party just after eight, Charles in a suit and Marie in a really sweet red dress that did look lovely on her. Anne glanced down at her worn-in jeans and tired fleece sweater with a grimace. Oh well. Jake and Dylan loved her, no matter what she wore.

They read stories and built towns from wooden blocks for a while before preparing their own little celebration. There would be ice cream and party hats, and even some streamers that Anne had brought along. When the clock struck nine, they brought in the New Year (albeit a bit early) and then went through the normal bedtime ritual. Anne was happy to let the boys drag it out for a bit. Favourite Aunts had some leeway in these things after all.

Now the house was quiet. Anne found her tote bag and pulled out her tablet, then went to find a comfortable armchair in the living room. She curled up with a throw blanket about her shoulders, got out the stylus, and set to work on the last touches of her music for Ben and Louisa's wedding.

It was not a long piece, only about five minutes or so, and it was scored for just two instruments instead of a full choir or orchestra. She was pleased with her progress on the work, and hoped to finish it tonight, before her sister returned home from the party. The melodic material had come to her almost at once, and before Ben had left for England, she had begged a peek at some of his poetry for a bit more inspiration.

Although she did not plan to set the verse to music, she did allow it to shape her thoughts and her notes until the piece for piano and cello could almost be sung as a song. Perhaps she would rework it one day for tenor and orchestra, but for now, it would live in its current form. As the clock on her phone app chimed midnight, ringing in the new year, she played through the composition one more time and closed the music notation program on her tablet. She let a smile creep over her face as she contemplated her little creation.

It was not the most challenging music she had written, but it was deeply personal to her, not because of her friendship with the groom, but because of its performance. Despite Fred's coolness to her since the gala, he would be the one performing it with her. It would be his long, capable fingers coaxing melody from wrapped wire and horsehair, teasing magic from a carved block of wood. Knowing his skill, both technical and musical, she had allowed herself some fun with interweaving harmony and melody, creating an intricate web where one line bled into another until the line between the parts became blurred.

When she first began the composition, she had looked forward to the rehearsals. They would need some time, she and Fred, to negotiate the intricacies of the lines so the melody could soar. Hopefully, by the time they met to go over the piece, Fred would have lost the coolness that marked their last parting. Perhaps, if she dared explain herself, he might listen with an open mind and an open heart.

The clock on the VCR in the corner flashed 12:32. Marie and Charles would still be out for another half hour or so, perhaps longer if the past was any predictor of the present. Anne put away her tablet, checked on Dylan and Jake one last time, and then took herself to the guest room to go to bed.

CHAPTER TWENTY-SIX
Duet

The first rehearsal for Ben's wedding piece was at Fred's place one early afternoon in the middle of January, the day after the premier of *Impressions*. The concert had been terrific and Anne had taken her bow, but then had slipped back into her seat. She had not spoken with Fred afterwards.

It was strange being in Fred's home without their 'chaperon,' but it was the logical place to practise. Ben was still out of the country, working on whatever his new investigative project was, and Fred had more room in his apartment than Anne did. Furthermore, Fred's piano was nicer than her own, and she hoped that he would be comfortable enough in his own space that he might open up a bit.

She had printed out the music, but had also emailed a PDF of the score to Fred. He had it set up on his tablet when she arrived, all propped up on his music stand. Anne, likewise, had her tablet with the music to set on the piano. Some musicians, she knew, preferred to read all their music this way, and had special large tablets and stylus pens to make notes on the electronic devices, never going near a sheet of paper. She was happy with music in whichever form it came, but knew that for the wedding they would be better using paper so it didn't glow in unwanted places on photographs.

They exchanged the basics of polite conversation, all form and no content.

"Nice Christmas?"

"Yes. Thanks."

"Parents good?"

"They're well. Charles and Marie? The kids?"

"All good."

Then came the obligatory chatter about the previous night's concert and the premier of *Impressions*.

"Your new piece was a great success. I heard so many favourable comments. The orchestra did very well."

"You brought out the best in them."

"I didn't see you at intermission."

"Sophia and Jeremy insisted on buying me a drink." Pause. "The Brahms was excellent."

"Thanks." Silence. Then, "The third is an underrated symphony."

When they ran out awkward nothings to say, they settled into the rehearsal. Maybe afterwards they could talk a bit.

The first step was to play through the piece, to get a sense of how it sounded and to identify areas that needed attention. As expected, they stopped here and there to clear up some confusion, and once - to Anne's chagrin - to fix a mistake in the score. "It should be a B-flat, not an A-flat. Sorry!" There would be a few notes to learn and more rehearsal in order, but it was a good start.

There was no time to talk, however. Fred had a meeting with the board that had just come up, and he needed to leave early. His apology seemed genuine, though. Perhaps he had wanted to talk as well. Maybe next time.

The second time they met was at Anne's place. Ben had just arrived back in Toronto from his travels and was once more taking up temporary residence in Fred's spare room. It seemed odd to Anne that Ben should hear the piece of music she had written for him before it was ready for performance, although she could not say why. Perhaps it was pure superstition transposed. Just as the groom isn't supposed to see the bride on their wedding day until the ceremony, so he was not supposed to hear the music that was composed entirely in his and Louisa's honour. He knew it existed, of course, but the exact piece itself was to be a surprise.

When she voiced her feelings to Fred, he concurred at once. "Yes, of course. I agree. Your place then?"

They arranged for Thursday night. The orchestra was performing, but they had a guest conductor for this program and Fred was not engaged in any tours of his own at the moment. She thought for a minute about inviting him for a light dinner before rehearsing, but changed her mind. She didn't want to come over as pushy. Or needy. After dinner would do fine. And then, perhaps, coffee and cake afterwards. She had something in her kitchen in anticipation of a good, soul-clearing conversation.

And so, at the appointed hour, Fred arrived at Anne's apartment with his cello case in hand, ready to play.

This time, with sheets of printed music before them, they did more detailed rehearsing. "These lines here," Anne mentioned a section, "where it sounds like it's just harmony at first, that is where we should really pass the passage back and forth. Then the melody will emerge from the two instruments. Let's give that a try."

"Yes. I see what you've done, using the different registers of the cello to function both as the melody instrument, as well as to fill in for the figured bass part when the piano takes over. It's masterful. And more importantly, I think, it sounds lovely. Alright, let's try that section again. Is this the transitional note here?" He played a couple of bars and they discussed the structure of the piece before playing together once more.

It was nice. It was more than nice. Anne knew she was a competent pianist, if nothing special, and had played in several ensembles through the years. Sometimes she had played with singers for wedding gigs, or with a violin and cello to make up a piano trio, or with slightly larger groups such as piano quintets. There was something she particularly loved about these small ensembles. They were intimate, the company of musicians more akin to a gathering of friends, the music itself more of a conversation, rather than the grand pronouncements of a larger work such as her symphony.

But playing with Fred was something beyond even that. They completed each other's musical thoughts. He was a particularly fine cellist, but moreover, he was a first-rate musician. He understood music like it was his mother tongue. Not the Italian of his childhood home, not the English he grew up with in the city, but music. Pure, unadulterated, blissful music. Pitch, rhythm, melody and harmony: these were his most essential thoughts. The musical phrases came as naturally as the words he spoke, his fingers and bow speaking more eloquently than Ben's admittedly fine verse.

How she had missed this, playing music with someone who understood her almost as well as she did herself. They might have to stop playing to work out a transition or to refine a detail, but the essence of the music, the vital communication, the meeting of hearts and minds, was there intact from the beginning. Making music with Fred was as sensuous and intimate and elemental as making love with Fred. It was a connection at the deepest level, beyond words and beyond thought. It was the merging of souls.

"It's a beautiful piece." Fred leaned back in his chair and balanced his cello on one leg as he loosened the hairs on his cello bow and rubbed some loose rosin powder from the wood. "It deserves to be heard more than just once." He stood up, stretching out his shoulder muscles from the physical work of playing.

"Oh. Thanks." Anne gathered her sheet music into a pile and slipped it into the folder she had assigned for the purpose. "It's a simple enough melody, but I was pleased at how the interwoven lines turned out. What I hear in my head doesn't always work out in practice." She watched as Fred placed his cello into the solid fibreglass case. He rubbed satiny wood with a soft cloth, caressing the instrument's luscious curves, like a lover touching his beloved. Her body ached in memory. She gave herself a mental shake and returned to matters more mundane.

"Can I make some tea? I have a poppy seed babka from the bakery around the corner. Or would you prefer coffee? I've got espresso and decaf..."

She was rambling. She had so much to say, and she was so afraid of how it would come out. Of how he would react. But he surprised her by his own announcement.

"Annie, we should talk." He closed the case and walked over to her at the piano. "Let's have a tea and a chat." He moved to the kitchen and put on the kettle. Of course. He knew her apartment, knew where things were kept.

She followed him and got out two mugs and some plates for the babka. They moved at their tasks in silence, comfortable and tense at once. How many times had they done this, worked side by side in the kitchen, making a meal or preparing a snack? It was as if they had never been apart, and yet it was strange and unsettling in all the best ways. Words kept taunting her tongue, promising eloquence before dissolving into nothingness before she could give voice to them. Did he feel the same?

She glanced over. He looked so calm, so at ease. Perhaps this was all in her own mind. She chastised herself for her silliness and dedicated herself to finding a suitable plate for the babka and bringing out the sugar bowl for tea.

At last, settled on the couch, side by side but not touching, Fred took a sip of tea and broached the topic, the elephant in the room.

"What do you feel about it?"

"About what?" She knew exactly what, but needed to understand his intentions perfectly. It was only when playing music, it seemed, that she could sense his every thought.

"Ben and Louisa. Us. But for now, Ben and Louisa. It's very sudden."

Was he trying to avoid the topic they both knew was lurking, treacherous reefs just below the placid-looking surface? She swallowed and nodded. "He seems very sure, like every roadblock in the world is just a little snag to be worked around."

"Mmmm. I hope he's not being too precipitous. A few months ago, he was ready to starve himself to death on the floor of my empty flat in Rome because of Claudia. When I found him, he hadn't eaten in days. Now he's marrying somebody else. To go from such black despair to such elation doesn't seem normal."

"He certainly isn't the same man I met last August. I thought it would start raining inside every time he entered a room. Now he's Mr. Sunshine and Rainbows. Is this sort of mood swing usual for him?"

Fred shrugged. "Not from what I've ever known. He's always been a bit melancholy. I sometimes wondered if it was real or affected, if he was trying too hard to be the tortured poet."

Anne laughed. "That is exactly what I thought when I first met him! I wondered which particular Romantic Poet he was trying the most to personify."

"He seems genuinely happy now. Almost like this is the person he's had inside him all these years that I've known him, finally given the freedom to come out." He took a bite of pastry. "It's as if Louisa was the key that set him free from this affected persona he had created for himself. For the first time since I've known him, I feel like he isn't pretending."

"Do you think he's right? That this will really work between the two of them? You know Louisa better than I do." After all, although she didn't say it, he had been all but a couple with her for much of the summer.

Another shrug. "I hope so. I would never have imagined them as a match, but perhaps there really is more to Louisa than I discovered. Perhaps they really are just grabbing at what life has bestowed upon them. Love, after all, is not something one should throw away. Who knows when you might find it again."

His eyes bore into hers. What was he saying? Was this some sort of apology? Was he asking her something? Or was it another accusation?

This was the time. This is when she had to stiffen her spine and speak. Tell him how much she had missed him, tell him how much she thought only of him. She knew he believed she and William were a couple, and she could not really blame him. William certainly had been working hard to give that impression, and she, she admitted, had not taken any steps to counter it. If Fred thought she and William were in love, it was only her own fault. He could not know that she had hardly thought of William at all since he had dashed off on business before Christmas. She didn't even know when he was expected back in town. How could he know if she hadn't told him?

She had been devastated by his desertion eight years ago. Was he now feeling that she had abandoned him? His eyes, dark and veiled, met hers and then flashed away. Perhaps he still cared. Perhaps there was still a chance.

The weight of the moment was too much to bear. She had to say something. She took a fortifying gulp of tea and a deep breath. "Fred, I—"

Her phone rang. Damned device. It was loud, too. They had been using an app as a metronome and the volume was set high and it resonated through the bluetooth speaker by the piano.

She wanted to ignore it, but the synthesised tones sliced through her thoughts, breaking her focus for just that moment. It was enough. She stopped mid-sentence, unable to go on. The words stuck, part way between thought and execution, and she couldn't find them again.

"Where is the phone? I'll refuse the call and turn it off. Where did I put it?" She jumped up, almost spilling her tea. Her eyes darted about the room in search of the offending item. The bluetooth connection to the speaker made it impossible to locate the device by sound.

There. There it was, on the small set of shelves by the piano. In a moment, she reached for it to turn off the ringer.

"It's alright. You can answer it." Fred looked deflated. There was resignation in his voice and gesture. Had he known what she wanted to say? Or had he dreaded something else?

Anne glanced down, her eyes moving without her permission. "It's William." She spoke without thinking. For some reason, she tried to avoid mentioning William in Fred's hearing, and vice versa. It wasn't a matter of trying to hide infidelity, more one of conscience. Still, as by some sort of arrangement with herself, she refrained from talking about William in front of Fred, and she never mentioned Fred when she was with William.

Fred's reaction confirmed the wisdom of her actions. His face went hard and blank and he began shifting about. He put his half-finished plate of babka aside and stood up.

The phone stopped ringing and a moment later, another beep informed her of a message.

"It's okay. Return the call. I need to get going."

"Please, we need to talk. This can wait."

She stared at the now-silent phone, but Fred was already dragging his cello to the door. "I'll call you about the next rehearsal." He found his jacket in the small front closet and wrestled himself into it, then shoved a woollen hat over his thick hair. In a moment he was gone, leaving Anne staring alternately at the door and at her phone.

CHAPTER TWENTY-SEVEN
Crescendo

Anne pushed her faux-fur-trimmed hood off her head and waited for the last droplets of melting snow to drip onto the mat. She caught a glimpse of herself in her hall mirror. Those tendrils of hair that looked so cute in the summer were less fun now that winter clothing was necessary. Hats, hoods, scarves… they all kept her nice and warm, but were unkind to her hairdo. How did Sophia manage it? No matter the season, her friend always looked so put-together. She could step inside from a blizzard and look like someone had just spent an hour making her look just right.

Perhaps it was time for another visit to the salon. Or perhaps she should just invest in some hair bands and cute indoor hats until the weather was more conducive to her new look. It was late January, almost February. It would only be two or three more months of winter headgear, right?

She tossed her hat onto the rack by the front door, hung up her heavy winter coat, and then took her tote bag to the couch. This morning had been busy with another session with the orchestra as they did more collaborative work on her symphony.

As arranged through a series of emails, Fred led the orchestra through the first movement, playing it and doing some spot rehearsing where technical or musical issues were obvious. Then, after the break, he had convened a sort of round-table to discuss it. This was one of the new initiatives with her position. She didn't know if it had ever been done before, and it was... illuminating.

At first the musicians had been quiet, no one wanting to say anything even remotely negative about her piece. It had taken a great deal of coaxing on her part, and some initial comments from Fred, to break the ice and get the orchestra members to speak up.

"At the very beginning," he had begun, "when the big wall of sound starts to break up to reveal the melody, do you not think it's still a bit dense, harmonically speaking? I can ask these talented people to lighten up even more, and they will do a fine job of it, but this symphony is terrific enough that it won't always be in the hands of such excellent musicians. Would it be worth thinning the parts a bit more so a... a less accomplished crew would still produce the same effect?"

"Oh, thank you!" the first oboist responded. "I didn't want to say anything, but I did feel like I couldn't play quietly enough to suit the music and still be heard."

There followed a discussion about the intent behind this introductory passage. The symphony began with a great block of sound, every instrument playing at once in a grand triumph of harmony, a great edifice of sonority, before, one by one and section by section, they died down and dropped out, leaving only the barest harmonic cushion upon which the solo oboe melody could float.

But not bare enough, it seemed. Anne had agreed. The orchestra could indeed do what she asked to create the desired effect, but it felt strained. She had said as much to the orchestra and taken some notes, and the discussion had grown from there.

And so it had gone for over an hour. It was sobering to hear these thoughts, especially as the orchestra had warmed up to the idea and had stopped trying to polish their points into something perfectly harmless and palatable. She was used to hearing critiques from her professor and the two or three other composers with whom she shared thoughts and ideas; from most people she usually heard only raves. But it was also edifying. They had not been cruel or dismissive at all, their comments only paving the way to a better piece of music.

She would be a better composer for hearing what they had to say.

She threw herself onto the couch and pulled out her tablet and made a few notes, hoping she had written down all the pertinent points the musicians had raised.

And this was, after all, what she had hoped for in accepting the position. She had accepted the role of composer-in-residence, part of a collaborative project. It was exactly what she wanted and needed.

Fred had been everything professional and courteous. Since that night last week when William had called during their aborted *tête-à-tête*, he had not contacted her, other than to discuss plans for this morning's session and to arrange for a final rehearsal before Ben's wedding. The conversations had been short, almost to the point of rudeness. There had been no comfortable chats, no familiarities.

She couldn't blame him. But she missed him, nonetheless.

This time when the phone rang, she answered it right away.

It was Ben.

"Let's grab a cuppa somewhere. Things are about to get busy for me and we haven't had a good chit-chat in a while. I've got so much I want to talk about. Can you spare an hour or so for me?"

He sounded excited and a little nervous. Was he having second thoughts? If nothing else, Anne knew how to listen and be a good friend.

"No problem. Name the time and place. The only time I'm busy is Wednesday evening when I'm babysitting my nephews. Tomorrow morning?"

"Brilliant. Louisa has a rehearsal, so it's a perfect time. That place we've been to before? Ten o'clock, see you then."

He was waiting when she arrived. She ordered a cup of coffee and some fresh toast with cream cheese and took her breakfast to Ben's table. He had an empty cup in front of him and went to get a refill before settling in for a chat.

"You sounded anxious on the phone yesterday," Anne began. "What's up? Getting cold feet? You've got two weeks before your wedding. There's still time to run away."

Ben laughed. He didn't sound anxious now. "No! Nothing like that at all. I've never been more certain of anything in my life. She's wonderful, Anne. I've never known anything like this connection I have with her. I thought I loved Claudia, but I know better now. I was gutted when Claudia left me. I thought my life was over. But really, leaving was the best thing she could have done, because that's why I met Lou."

"It's not just a rebound? Sorry, but I had to say it."

Ben's expression was hurt. "You don't mean that, Annie. Not really. No, this is real. This is what I was missing all that time. When I'm with Louisa, I feel complete, and I never felt that with Claudia. No," his eyes lit up, "now my life is perfect."

Anne had always imagined that brides glowed with incandescent joy. She had seen Louisa at the rehearsal yesterday, and she seemed happy enough. Her smile was wide and genuine and she exuded an aura of absolute satisfaction with the world, from the sparkling sapphire ring on her finger to the tips of her now-magenta hair. But even her overt happiness was nothing to what Anne saw from this beaming, radiant man who sat across from her. He was the bridegroom and not the bride, but it made his joy no less palpable.

"Then I am delighted for you." She did not say that she once felt the same way about his best friend. Maybe still did. "So, what did you want to talk about? Anything specific, or did you just want to gush about your bride?"

He leaned back in his chair, balancing briefly on the two rear legs before settling back onto solid ground. For a moment, his face took on that dreamy look that she thought only existed in novels. "I could talk about her all day, I could! But no, that's not what I had in mind." He grew a bit more serious. "I want to talk a bit about you. You and this bloke you've been going with. William Barnett. Tell me more about him."

She frowned. "About William? We're not— Why?" Suspicion at his motives stopped her words.

Ben gave a one-shouldered shrug.

She narrowed her eyes. "What did you want to know? He's on the orchestra's board of directors. That's how I met him. And he's a fascinating man. He's well read and knows a lot about art and music. He minored in art history at university and played in the university orchestra for a while. He certainly knows a lot more about art than I do, and when we go to exhibits or shows, his comments are often much more interesting and informative than the official plaques on the walls."

She cocked her head. Was this what he wanted to know?

"Does he have a favourite artist, or a period of art that he really likes?" Was it her imagination, or did Ben look like he wanted to take notes? This didn't seem like a casual chat about someone's boyfriend. Or not-boyfriend, not that anybody seemed willing to listen to that part.

But there was no real reason to hold back. She only had approving things to say about William, after all, and she didn't want uncomplimentary words coming to haunt him, and the orchestra by association. And so Anne talked a bit about what she thought were William's favourites, although, she had to admit, she did not know for certain. He had never really mentioned any particular likes or dislikes, or even discussed one piece of art or artist with more fervour than the next. Perhaps he was a general lover of things beautiful, with only enough knowledge to satisfy his general interest. Or perhaps he only took her to exhibits he knew a great deal about. He had never expressed his real opinions to her. Of course, it would take a lot of guts to be the one to confess, "I never understood the fuss about Renoir, anyway."

Likewise, his interest in drama. He could talk knowledgeably about the particular show they were seeing. He knew the playwrights and the plots and enough about the history behind them to supplement her enjoyment of the productions. Anne herself had little more than a passing knowledge of theatre. She knew more than most, perhaps, but certainly not enough to consider herself anything close to an expert.

"Does a person need to understand art at an intellectual level to appreciate it?" She asked Ben this question sincerely. "You're a wordsmith. I'm guessing you have more than a passing acquaintance with English letters through the centuries. Does knowing about Sheridan's personal history bring you any more enjoyment of his plays? Or Shakespeare, even? Do you need to understand his social position and his relationship to the crown to really appreciate his comedies?"

"Oh, his histories, certainly!" Ben returned. His face grew animated, and he leaned forward in his chair, his coffee forgotten in the excitement of the turn of conversation. "Take Richard III, for example, or the Henry plays..." He launched into a long spiel about history and power and the role of artists in creating authority, reframing the past, and defining the present. There was more power and passion in this impromptu lecture than ever Anne had heard from William, even though the latter had more data and information at his fingertips. It was a fascinating discussion, and for a moment Anne saw what might connect this unusual man to his intended bride. If Louisa responded to this sort of discussion with even half of Ben's zeal, they must have some wonderful and stimulating exchanges indeed.

They talked for half an hour about art and its contexts before Ben turned the conversation back to William.

"But he doesn't make his living through the arts. He's in business. How much do you know about that?"

Anne turned her attention back to her cup of coffee, which was now empty. Ben jumped up and returned a moment later with another cup for both of them, then repeated his question.

"What does he call it? Property development. You were up at that place on Lake Simcoe where Louisa had that terrible accident." Ben's face went pale, and Anne let the words hang for a moment. Neither wished to remember that awful occasion.

Eventually, Ben cleared his throat. "I wish I had never seen it, wish it had never happened. But it was as she was recovering that we really got to know each other. I liked her a great deal before, but wondered if she still had a thing for Frederico. But each time I came to visit her, she asked me to come back, and that's when we really fell in love."

There was another moment of silence, this one reflective rather than strained.

"What else does your friend Barnett do? Does he have other projects on the go? I'm always interested in what keeps people busy."

This was curious, but again, Anne had no reason not to speak.

"I'm not exactly sure, but he's always flying down to the Caribbean to check on the progress of something there. I suspect he's very well off and he has a lot of well heeled acquaintances. He always treated me very well when he took me to a show or to dinner, and we met a lot of rather affluent friends of his. That's why he's on the board—to help bring in donations and procure new donors. Why? What's with all these questions?"

Ben's face was inscrutable. "I'm just looking out for you, Annie. There's been talk, you know…" He shrugged again with a half smile starting to crack through.

"Talk? Was it the gala? What sort of talk?"

Another shrug. "Just… talk."

"Did Fred put some ideas in your head?"

He put his cup on the table and leaned forward. "Speaking of Fred, I think we also need to chit-chat about him. He saved my life, quite literally, and while he was one of my best friends before, he is even more so now. What is your history with him? I know you were friends back in the day. I also know I'm missing something. He won't say another word, no matter how much I nag him, but his interest seems to go a lot further than mere friendship, if you know what I mean."

He rocked back again and gazed at Anne through half-closed lids. He remained silent, just staring at Anne through half-closed eyes. Should she respond to this? What did he want her to say? He helped her along by explaining.

"To answer your unasked question, he didn't put ideas into my head. I put them there myself. Still, Fred obviously cares a great deal for you, and, as I said, he is my best friend. Your happiness is his happiness, and his happiness is mine. So I need to know, are you and William...?" He made a rather rude gesture with his fingers.

"Ben, really!" She was shocked he would even suggest this. It was the twenty-first century, sure, and Anne was no prude, but some things should remain private.

"So are you?" His voice teased, and he flashed a conspiratorial grin, but his eyes were stony and serious.

"It really is none of your business. None of yours and none of Fred's." Suddenly, every idea of confessing her heart to Ben, in hopes that he would pass along something of her message, vanished into the ether. That very personal and suggestive question put pay to any such thoughts. Anne returned his stare. "He had his chance."

"Oh ho! So you two were a pair? When was this? What happened?" He leaned forward now, elbows on the small metal table between them.

The steam rushed out of her. "If he hasn't told you the details, I won't break his confidence. But I suppose it's no secret. Yes, we were together. We aren't anymore. It's over. That's all."

The forced smile now grew shrewd. "I'm not so certain it's all that over."

Jasmine came over to Anne's place one morning the following week. January had come to a shivering end and February seemed to promise no more warmth, but music and good friendship could thaw even the bitterest of winters. The two friends sat for a half an hour with some mugs of hot chocolate before moving to the piano to play music.

As they had decided before Christmas, they began with some Bach. The music was interesting and challenging, but well within both women's capabilities, and they were able to work through some interpretive aspects of it as well as the purely technical. This was something Anne loved: making music purely for pleasure. There was no need to produce anything, no pressure of performance. It was music for the sake of music.

And Jasmine was a good violinist. Not quite, perhaps, at the level of the musicians in the National Philharmonic, but close, and better than many out there who made their livings on the instrument. She played with a sweet tone and with the agility and flexible musicality that Anne appreciated. Would Fred be amenable to playing some piano trios at some point? Violin, cello, and piano, a venerable combination that had inspired the composition of a wealth of first-rate music. She should mention it to him... But no. Something had happened, and they seemed not to be communicating again.

Yesterday's conversation with Ben flashed across her mind. What had he told Fred about her? Surely he thought that she and William were a couple, destined for something more serious. His questions and his vague, "there's been talk," suggested he had some firm notions about Anne's future, and Anne's protestations had been met with a disbelieving eye. Fred would never want to rebuild a friendship now. She pushed these unwanted thoughts from her mind and concentrated once more on the music before her.

All too soon, they reached the final bars of the piece and they beamed at each other for a moment as the echo of the last notes faded.

"Oh, that was wonderful!" Jasmine's face almost split in two from the width of her smile. "I haven't played like this in far too long. What a magnificent piece! It gives you energy rather than taking it."

Anne, too, was buoyed by the music. It was energising and calming at the same time, bringing with it a profound sense of peace and completion. "I am so glad we did this! And we'll do more. I can't believe it took until now to play together." She glanced at the clock in the corner. "I know you have a busy schedule, but is there time for another cup of something before you need to leave?"

Her friend nodded. "Thanks. I do have a few minutes."

Jasmine put her violin away and then followed Anne into the kitchen.

"I ran into Fred the other day." She made the offhand comment as Anne turned off the boiling kettle. "I was so surprised he remembered me at the dress rehearsal before your concert a few weeks ago. He's a really nice guy. You'd think fame would have gone to his head, but it really didn't. You too, I suppose. You're also famous, and as nice as they come."

Anne felt the blush creep up her neck. "That's sweet of you. I don't always feel nice. More invisible." She poured the water into the teapot. The scent of bergamot began to waft up from the spout. "Fred really is down to earth, isn't he? He's as happy in jeans at a baseball game as he is in a tux on stage. Where did you see him?"

A chuckle. "It was almost like he'd planned it. I was just leaving the community centre where I teach on Wednesday afternoons, and there he was at the corner by the subway station. He didn't seem surprised to see me. I suppose he knew what my teaching hours were. We went for a very quick coffee."

Oh?

Jasmine must have seen the surprise on her face and explained. "We just stopped into the Tim's at the corner. It was fifteen minutes at most. He asked about my teaching and then asked about Connor. Does he know something about the financial mess we got into? About that awful investment deal that stole all our savings?" She sighed. "I suppose it's not a secret. He must have looked me up after the rehearsal. I would have done the same thing. I'm easy to find because I need to be available for new students. And it's not hard to get to Connor and all that stuff through me."

Anne poured the tea, and they went to sit for a few minutes. "What did he want to know about? I had a strange tea with his friend Ben the other day, too."

"Just some general stuff. Where had Connor been working when it all went haywire? What was the project that we invested in, the one that the developers sold out from under us? That sort of thing. I didn't know Fred was into investing."

"He has a lot of interests, I suppose. He was certainly busy enough when we knew him all those years ago."

"Hmmm." She gazed at Anne through her liquid dark eyes, her thoughts inscrutable. A thousand questions rushed through Anne's head, none stopping long enough for her to grab it and form it into words to ask. Each impression melted into the next, leaving her with nothing but a sense of mild consternation. Something odd was going on, and she had no clue what it was.

They drank their tea quickly, and then Jasmine had to leave for her students. Anne, too, had a class to teach that afternoon, and she followed her friend out the door and to the subway, where they parted ways with a promise to repeat the Bach next week and perhaps move onto some Mozart.

But more and more questions buzzed through Anne's head like a swarm of busy bees.

CHAPTER TWENTY-EIGHT
Seconda Volta

There was a message waiting for Anne when she returned home from teaching her class. It was from William. Had she even known he was in town? The last she had heard from him, he expected to be in Barbuda—or was it the Dominican Republic? No, the Caymans—for another few weeks working on his latest property deal.

Anne, darling,

I'm back at last. Things with my project wrapped up quite suddenly, and the next thing I knew, I was on a plane. I can't wait to see you again. Dinner? I'll pick you up at seven.

Dinner. It was a summons, not an invitation. She thought about calling back and refusing on principle. She reflected on that awkward kiss on the dance floor at the year-end gala for the orchestra. That, too, had been something of a summons rather than an invitation. And yet she had gladly accepted his kisses before, and had not objected at the moment. He had no way of knowing she was not quite so pleased this time.

Perhaps she should accept tonight after all. A dinner would be a good place to talk, to approach the subject gently and find out exactly what he had been thinking. And, she admitted, she did usually enjoy his company. He was always interesting and he would almost certainly have some fascinating tale to tell from his business trip down to the islands. The gala had been quite out of character for him, and he had sent her some sort of note or message every day that he had been away, even if he hadn't said when he was likely to return.

It must just have been that she was confused at being at the gala with both Fred and William, wanting to speak to one, yet socially obligated to the other. That internal conflict was surely the reason she had been so shocked by his behaviour. Wasn't it?

Still, she knew she did not want a relationship other than friendship with William. That she had decided quite firmly during his absence. Dinner would be a very good time to discuss it.

She dressed carefully, hoping to give the impression of friendliness without crossing into flirtatiousness. In the end, the weather had the final say in her choice. Black woollen trousers, a light grey turtleneck, and simple silver hoops in her ears would have to do. Her one nod to her decision was to replace the red lipstick she first reached for with something more subdued in a soft pink. Pink for friendship, not red for passion. She hoped he would understand.

He arrived in a taxi, explaining that he was too tired to drive, and asked the cabbie to take them to a popular Italian restaurant near the entertainment district. It was something of a change from his usual selection of exclusive and high-end venues, but for once they did not meet some colleague or friend or associate of his.

The food was good and the ambiance lively, but while it was not too noisy to talk easily, it was also not the quiet setting for the conversation she hoped to have.

Still, William was once more at his gentlemanly best, not pressing, not assuming. He did indeed tell grand tales from his weeks away in the sun, entertaining her between bites of squash-filled ravioli and fresh spinach and berry salad.

"...and that is how we discovered that the chef we planned to hire for the catering service really had no idea how to prepare lobster!" He settled back into his chair with a satisfied smile. Anne returned his laughter. She could all but picture the disaster William had painted in words, of terrified serving staff running around the kitchen trying to avoid the escaped creature's pincers, while the chef staggered backwards from the shock of having to submerge another of the live creatures into the pot of boiling water.

Thank heavens she had not opted for the fish today!

He explained his prolonged absence and the unexpected snags that kept him away for so long, and then the sudden resolution of a mountain of issues that allowed him to return without any warning.

"Have I mentioned Adam? Adam Wallis? He's one of my partners in this development. We've worked together on and off for years. He arrived out of the blue with a briefcase full of documents. It seemed that while we were trying to solve all our problems on the ground, he was haunting the lawyers' offices in Toronto and Cockburn Town and got half our headaches ironed out with a couple of signatures. So he stayed to see everything properly implemented, and I hopped on the first flight home.

"It's lovely being in the Caribbean in the middle of winter, but there was a lot here in Canada that I missed too much." He levelled his eyes on her, but made no other advances.

The conversation lapsed into that moment of silence that so often happens. Anne once heard that this was a phenomenon that happened regularly at twenty-minute intervals. The room would be all abuzz with chatter and then, almost on the clock, it would fall silent.

Across from her, William seemed unaware of the lapse. He sat back in his chair, eyes almost closed. His usually animated face was lax; he must be tired.

But he had also finished his account of his trip. This was the time to raise the topic. She might be misunderstanding him, but she had to clear matters up. She took a deep breath to fortify herself.

"William, I…"

He blinked.

"Sorry, Anne. Where was I?"

"There is something we need to talk about. Something I've been thinking about for a while."

He tried, but failed, to stifle a yawn. "I'm afraid I'm not much fun tonight. Can this wait?"

This was not going well. "Not really. I—"

He spoke on as if she hadn't said a word. "I thought I was well enough rested. I did sleep on the plane, but it seems I was wrong. I'll call you a taxi. I hope you'll forgive me. We didn't even have time for dessert, but I just can't keep my eyes open. Another time?"

The fire rushed out of her again.

"Yes, of course."

"Look, Anne, I was thinking…" He rose from his chair walked her to the front where they had left their winter coats. Was he going to break it off? Would he save her the anxiety? But no, by his eager body language, this wasn't going to happen.

"There's a small do on Friday night, a last-minute thing at the Carterets. From the orchestra's board. You know them, right?" She nodded. "It's just a little cocktail party. Come with me."

She sighed as they walked out onto the street. "I'm not sure. Perhaps..."

But he brushed her words aside once more. "We've found a new potential donor who has been asking to meet you, and Kevin Walters was going to call with an invitation. I told him I'd bring you with me. It's always good to rub elbows with these people. Good for the organisation, good for you. I know your term with the orchestra is for another two years, but afterwards, who knows what sorts of contacts you'll make through some of these lovely folk. They have fingers everywhere. You'll come? Good. Semiformal, I think. Let me pick you up at eight. Will that do?"

She opened her mouth to speak her concerns, but as she was about to say *No*, a taxi drew up and William shuffled her in, then gave the driver her address and money for the fare. And just like that, the evening was over, with another date planned, before she could summon the strength to tell him she didn't want to go out with him anymore. Somewhere, somehow, she had neglected to order a backbone. Perhaps next Christmas.

Between her teaching obligations and some music she was working on for a short television documentary, Anne kept busy over the following two days. Soon enough it was Friday evening, the night of the Carterets' cocktail party.

William was correct. As distasteful as it seemed, being on good and sociable terms with well-provisioned and well-connected people was part of the business she was in. The documentary for which she was writing the opening theme, after all, had come her way through another board member who knew someone who knew the director. She suspected that her name had helped the director procure some coveted government arts funding for the project, which in turn would pay her bills for a month or two. And while not part of her contract, her appearance was requested by the boss, and it would not do her career any favours to refuse.

And so she took her usual pains to look as presentable as possible. Her green lace dress, gold and topaz jewellery, and too much time with a hair dryer and curling iron, all combined to create a more than acceptable result. She put her shoes into a small bag, stepped into her winter boots, and dug her nice coat out from the corner of the closet. It was not as warm as her everyday coat, but she would be in and out of William's warm car, and appearances were more important than comfort tonight.

He, as always, was dressed impeccably. Did he have a whole closet full of dinner jackets? Or a local dry cleaner to ensure his suit was perfectly pressed every time he needed it? No matter. Whatever she thought of her future with or without him, it was no shame to be seen in his company.

The expected crowd was there. Being purely social, there was no pressure for everybody to attend, and only about a dozen couples milled about the spacious great room of the house. A grand piano stood in the corner, black and polished, but no music sat open on the stand. Was it an instrument that somebody played often? Or was it more of an ornament, a symbol of class and wealth? Anne knew the Carterets a bit. Eleanor, who sat on the board, was always polite and friendly, but carried about her the air of an arriviste. Could it be the latter? Was the piano merely for show? Then a dreadful thought occurred to her: Did they expect Anne to provide some music for them? No, surely not. She really must get out of the mindset that everybody wanted something from her. She was spending too much time with her sister.

Eleanor greeted them warmly and invited them over to the bar to choose their drinks. Anne scanned the room, looking to see who was present. Kevin and Penny Walters were among the guests.

Being professional staff rather than a volunteer on the board, Kevin didn't really fit with this well-heeled crew, but if this possible donor was on the guest list, it made sense for him to be there, just as he had requested Anne's attendance. This was all part of hobnobbing with donors and board members alike, and being on good terms with one and all could only make his administrative tasks easier. Still, Anne wondered if his presence tonight was due to social or political reasons.

No time to consider this now. The Walters had seen them and were walking over, drinks in hands.

"William, Anne," Kevin reached out a large red hand. He might just be the hired manager, but he looked every bit as comfortable in these surroundings as did William. "Good to see both of you. William, you must tell me about your latest adventures. We're thinking that a spot in the sun might be in the budget after all."

"Hello, Anne." Penny's voice was always cool, but it was her nature and no personal slight. She leaned forward a bit to offer the traditional double cheek kiss where one missed one's target on purpose, but made the appropriate motions. Anybody who had lived in Montreal knew it intimately. Mwah, mwah. Left side, right side, hand gently on the upper arm, cheek not quite brushing cheek, kissing sounds in the air. Then it was over.

Anne took a deep breath...

And stopped.

She knew that scent.

"That's a lovely perfume," she offered, though her heart had started racing.

Penny smiled and named something Anne had never heard of and most likely could never afford. But it didn't matter. She had smelled that before, and she knew where.

Back before Christmas, at the orchestra's year-end gala, when William had been late to their table before dessert. She had smelled it then. On him.

Her eyes widened, and she fought to maintain her calm.

Suddenly, a pile of little pieces that she had never thought much about fell into place. William at Sophia's soiree in September, chatting with Penny. William at the reception after the first concert of the season, chatting with Penny. William at the fundraiser gala, chatting with Penny, dancing with Penny... What else had he been doing with Penny? There was no point at all letting the other woman know that Anne had guessed her and William's secret, but her own course was now quite firmly set. This would be her very last outing with William under any guise.

She disguised her shock by asking more about the perfume and then steering the conversation elsewhere—anywhere—until the little foursome broke up. All the while, her heart hammered in her chest and she felt her hands dampen.

Don't wipe them on your dress. Not on the dress. She excused herself to get another drink—just ginger ale this time—and a serviette with which to mop up the sweat on her palms. One of the other board members saw her and sidled over to ask about some music and generally chat, and she had never been so grateful in her life to be an object of curiosity. It meant she needn't spend more time than necessary with William.

And Penny.

Oh God.

Perhaps she could make some excuse about not feeling well. She could take a taxi home. William could stay and do... whatever it was he thought he was doing.

What was he doing? Why go to all this trouble to woo her, drag her around town, kiss her like he had at the gala, if he was involved with Penny? Could she be wrong? Perhaps they had just been chatting outside the main hall that night like old friends do. There was nothing wrong with that, was there? Surely she was over-reacting.

But how would that perfume have clung so strongly to him if he had not clung to Penny? Her head began to swim. Maybe claiming to be ill wouldn't be so much of a lie after all. Yes. She would find Eleanor and have her pass a message to William. She could call a taxi or Uber from the foyer where her coat was. She swivelled about, looking for her hostess.

"Anne, there you are." William's voice sliced through her conviction. She had to find her spine and just face him, tell him she needed to go. But before she could draw breath, he had his arm around her shoulders, a possessive gesture if ever there was one. She tried to shift, but he pulled her closer.

"I was telling Walters and Rob over there," his voice a little louder than it ought to be, "just how much I missed you when I was away in Turks." He emphasised the last word just a bit. What was going on? Was he trying to deflect something? Convince Kevin that he had been in the islands the whole time? Hadn't he been? Where was he then? Had his story of coming home with hardly any notice been a lie? And where had Penny been?

But there was no time to think. William was still talking. Performing, more like, the room his audience. "I missed you a lot, Annie. More than you know." He moved in front of her now and in a single, practised motion, pulled her towards him with one arm while pressing a long kiss to her lips. Then, as she stood in shock, trying to find her feet beneath her, he straightened up and smirked to the room as if to say, *Yes, I have conquered.*

And at that very moment, Jeremy and Sophia entered the great room. Sophia's eyes met Anne's, and she grinned. Oh God. This would be a most uncomfortable discussion!

The great reckoning came far too early the next morning. Anne had claimed a sudden headache after William's display, which had not been entirely fictitious, and she made her apologies at once and called a taxi.

Both William and Sophia had offered to drive her home, but she refused. She really was not up to any sort of company. Instead, she peered out of the taxi window through half-closed eyes all the way to her building, as the car slipped along icy streets decorated with the reflected glare of too-bright lights. At last she unlocked her apartment door and staggered inside before collapsing on her bed, the beautiful green lace dress a crumpled heap on the floor.

Now her night of fitful sleep was shattered by the din of her phone. How much had she had to drink last night? It really had not been a lot, but her head throbbed in earnest, a reprimand after the semi-feigned headache she had claimed.

Would that phone not stop its relentless shriek? She groped on her bedside table and made contact with the cool slab of technology. The racket ceased, but she couldn't stop her eyes from looking at the name on the screen.

Sophia.

She would have to call her back at some point. There was no avoiding this discussion.

The phone rang again. With a groan and clenched eyes, she answered.

"Annie, are you alright? What happened last night?"

"Grmsxl."

"Oh. I see I've called at a bad time. Look, sweetie, let's not get into it now. But on Monday, you've got to tell me. There's a story in there and I have to hear it. Call me if you need me. And Annie?"

"Hmmm?"

"Go make yourself some coffee. Jeremy sends love."

The phone went silent.

She was awake now. Sophia's suggestion made as much sense as anything, and so she stumbled to the kitchen to put on the kettle. No time for brewed coffee today. Instant would have to do. She could brew a pot later if she needed it. Which, she was certain, she would.

She ignored her email and phone all the rest of the day, taking a bracing walk along the ice-crested lake and then devoting herself to her documentary score instead. The following day, she had agreed to spend with Marie's family and there would be no chance to work. This time it was Brenda Musgrove's birthday, and she had sent a special request that Anne join them in a day of celebration. She had planned an outing to the aquarium with the boys, and then had ordered in a meal of pizza and ice cream. Anne suspected this celebration was much more for Jake and Dylan than for Brenda, but such was the woman's devotion to her grandchildren that she surely enjoyed it as much as they did. Their pleasure was her pleasure, no matter how much Marie might complain.

And then it was Monday. There were no more excuses, no more ploys to avoid contact with the rest of the world.

She set aside the three unheard phone messages from William and two emails from Jasmine for later, and got ready to meet Sophia instead. Today's trip was to a high-end fabric outlet, where Sophia was hoping to select new coverings for her dining room chairs. "The current upholstery is looking so tired, Annie. It's got to be ten years old. You have an artist's eye. Help me find something perfect."

Anne had rolled her eyes. Sophia's taste was far more sophisticated than anything Anne could summon up, but she accepted the ruse with good grace. And now she stood in the small warehouse in a light industrial part of town near the 401 highway, surrounded by floor-to-ceiling stacks of rolls of the most luxurious and expensive fabric she had ever seen.

Sophia had not mentioned a word about the cocktail party all morning. It was coming, Anne knew, but her friend was biding her time. "What about this one?" Sophia fingered the edge of a rich golden brocade. "Too much? Perhaps something a bit less flashy. Dark red? We can paint the walls..."

"No, the gold is good. It's only for the seat cushions, and most of the time no one will see them. They'll just be a splash of glitz when people pull out their chairs to sit down."

Sophia grinned. "I knew I brought you for a reason, Anne. Let me get a small swatch and pin it to one of the chairs for a few days. What colour tablecloth would match, do you think?"

Whew. Was this going to be the worst of the interrogation? Perhaps Sophia would leave her in peace for another day or twelve.

"I think it would match something in apricot or light pear. The china has a gold rim, so that would go. And what, exactly, is going on between you and William Barnett, after all? After that big newsflash about Fred, now you're all but married to one of the members of the board! Anne, why didn't you say anything?"

All but married? Her mouth opened, but no sound emerged. So much for the reprieve.

"Not now, Annie. Collect your thoughts. I'll just buy this swatch and then it's coffee time. Or would you prefer a glass of wine somewhere? I need this story."

They ended up at a small place on Avenue Road, a few minutes' drive away. It was a bar with excellent food... or was it a restaurant with a first rate drinks list? Regardless, in the evening, this eatery would be bustling, but now in the middle of the afternoon, it was all but empty and the perfect place for an interrogation.

Sophia leaned forwards over her pinot grigio and the plates of edamame beans and bruschetta that filled the table between them. "So, no more avoiding the topic, Anne. Talk."

"William…"

Sophia's head bounced up and down, her pendant silver earrings swaying with the motion.

"He is very charming…" Anne began.

"Oh, he is. He can be a bit too suave, but it's his manner. I think that beneath that too-perfect exterior, he's a passionate man."

Passionate. For Penny, perhaps. The thought of him preferring another woman to her was not troublesome. She had never been so enamoured of him that she felt his loss. But to be used as a decoy, that was painful. Because it was exceedingly clear to her that William's advances had only been to deflect attention from his affair with the CEO's wife.

"You're silent, Anne." The repressed smile on Sophia's face suggested she quite misunderstood Anne's reticence. "I understand if you'd rather keep the details quiet for now. But you really must know, William was quite raving about you after you left. He could talk about nothing else. He's quite besotted with you. Can I use that word? It seems so old fashioned, but it suits him somehow. He didn't say as much, but I wouldn't be surprised if there are wedding bells in your future."

"Oh, Soph, no…"

"You don't have to be coy, Anne. I won't say anything to anybody else, but they probably all suspect the same thing. Has he said anything to you?"

"You don't understand…"

"No, no, it's okay. I'll let him keep his plans secret. I'm sure he's got some *grande geste* planned for when he asks you. He's a real catch. Rich, handsome, sophisticated, an art lover… you'll be jetting all over the world, and in first class, too."

"It's not like that…"

Anne wanted to disappear into her chair. Is this what everyone thought? Oh God. Her face must have fallen, because Sophia's expression changed completely.

"Is everything alright, Annie? I'm sorry. I shouldn't have said anything. I know you're very private about these things. Let's talk about something else." She reached down to her purse and brought out three more swatches of fabric that she had just bought. "For this one," she gestured to a delicate moss green, "I was thinking of the kitchen. Wouldn't it be nice to recover the kitchen chairs with this? It looks pretty resilient too, and I might do the balcony chairs at the same time. But then this apricot is also a lovely colour, and so fresh…"

And Anne never did explain to her friend that marrying William was the last thing in the world she wanted to do.

CHAPTER TWENTY-NINE
Sotto Voce

Jasmine came again on the next Wednesday morning, her violin case slung diagonally across her back by a sturdy nylon strap. Anne was ready with a small box of breakfast pastries and the kettle fresh off the boil, hoping for a quick chat before they brought out the music. But Jasmine seemed somehow distracted.

She set her violin down by the keyboard and opened the case, revealing the shiny golden-hued fiddle inside, but her eyes kept darting about the apartment and she eyed Anne curiously, long searching looks replacing her usual cheerful demeanour.

"Coffee or tea? The kettle is hot." Anne began to move towards the kitchen.

There was a moment of silence. Jasmine was usually so voluble, so ready to talk. "No thanks. Perhaps later. Not now."

Those curious eyes flashed around the space again. What was she looking for? Maybe something else?

"Glass of water? Or maybe some juice? I think I've got apple juice."

Jasmine shook her head. "No, I'm fine." More silence. Then, "Mind if I use the washroom?"

"Of course. Down the hall. You know where it is."

Jasmine was gone for a couple of minutes. She returned with a slight frown on her face, disappointed almost. Something was going on.

"Is everything alright? You seem... distracted."

Her friend smiled. It wasn't quite the open laugh Anne was used to, but it didn't seem entirely feigned. "Everything is fine. Quite good, really. Let's talk later." She moved to her fiddle and removed the bow to coat the long white hairs with a kiss of rosin.

Anne screwed up her brow for a moment. "Oh. Alright. Should we look at the Bach again, or do you want to move right to the Mozart?"

They settled on the Bach they had played the week before. Both had gone over some notes and a few difficult passages, and this week's endeavour produced something more like a performance than last week's play-through. There were still a couple of sticky moments that needed more attention, but the result was more than acceptable, and both women finished the piece much more at ease than when they had started.

Next, they made a first attempt at reading through the Mozart they had chosen, the violin sonata in E minor. It was a short piece, with only two movements, and not particularly challenging technically, but the frequent unison sections, where violin and both hands of the piano played the same notes, required them to pay close attention to each other's subtle gestures and musical suggestions. Then the music moved into the development section of the first movement, with first the piano and then the violin interrupting the other's musical line, a statement and argument, and then the reverse, before settling back into a comfortable closing. Then came the second movement, song-like, first gentle and then more fiery, and when at last they played the final chord, it was with the joy of music salving some unknown wound.

Now, when Anne offered coffee, Jasmine nodded. The sparkle in her eye was back, and her smile relaxed and open once more.

"I bought a selection of danishes," Anne pushed the box across the table. "I couldn't remember if you preferred poppy seed or fruit, or maybe cinnamon, so I got a bunch of little ones. We can sample and do a taste test."

Jasmine contemplated the offerings, and then placed a blueberry pastry onto her plate before reaching back with a cheeky grin and taking a poppy seed one as well. "I suppose you will be able to buy all the pastries you want soon." She glanced up after that cryptic remark.

Anne tilted her head and frowned. "Sorry?"

"You don't have to play coy with me. I've… I've heard things."

Another frown. "What things?"

"About you. You can tell me. It's alright."

Anne shook her head. "I'm sorry, Jaz. I have no idea what you're talking about."

"Connor heard it from someone he used to work with. A fellow named Adam Wallis. Surely you know him."

Wallis? Where had she heard that name before? It was familiar, tantalising, but not there. He was certainly not anybody she had ever met. Had she heard someone mention him? With her dreadful memory for names, it must have been recent, perhaps just this last week or so. That was when William returned…

"Wallis? Yes! That's where I've heard of him. William's business partner. He mentioned him in connection to some deal in the

Caribbean. St Somewhere? Or was it Something Town? Oh, I'm terrible with names."

"Cockburn Town. In the Turks and Caicos." Now Jasmine looked directly at her. Asking... something.

"That's right." Something was going on that she didn't quite understand. "What do you know?"

Jasmine sagged a bit. "You and William. Wallis told Connor that you are going to be marrying William Barnett."

Anne's coffee cup clattered on the table. "What? Me marrying William? Why does everybody think I'm marrying William Barnett?"

Jasmine bit her bottom lip. "You're not?" She seemed surprised, confused, and relieved. What in the world was going on?

"No! You are the second person in so many days who thinks so, too. What has he been telling people?"

"You have been seen together all over town, and for months now. I've seen the photos on social media. Everyone has. You can't hide it."

"I'm not denying that. But it's a big jump from going to a gallery opening to getting married! We're just friends."

Jasmine pushed her cup around in a small circle on the table. "Is it? All those shows and plays and dinners out? And I heard about the gala. That kiss didn't make it into the newspapers, but someone pulled out a phone. That didn't look *just friendly* to me." Her eyebrows rose in accusation.

Anne cringed. That kiss, that unwanted kiss, was coming back to haunt her in so many ways. It had, she now knew, been the beginning of the end, the first real warning bell that tolled the demise of whatever it was between her and William.

"Annie? I'm sorry. I didn't mean to say something hurtful. But you must understand what people saw."

"It wasn't like that, Jaz. Or, it was, but I didn't mean it. That is... Oh, I'm just not making any sense at all." She closed her eyes and sighed.

"And then I heard about the cocktail party last weekend."

Anne's eyes popped open. "Oh God. From who?"

Her friend took a sip from the almost-empty cup. "That's where Adam Wallis comes in. It's a long story. Wallis and William Barnett are business partners—"

"Okay, that much I know."

"And Wallis and Connor have worked together in the past, and not always amicably." Her look was pointed. "Connor has been back in contact with Wallis, trying to get some details worked out about... well, I'll tell you in a bit. But back to this. Wallis told Connor that William told him that you two are all but married. Something about a big announcement at the cocktail party, but that you got sick so had to leave early before he could say anything publicly. But he was pretty certain..." She shrugged.

Anne glanced at the clock. Eleven o'clock in the morning. Too early for wine. But not too early for more coffee. She staggered up to move to the kitchen to grab the carafe from the coffee maker and bring it to the table.

With her cup full once more, and another pastry on her plate, she chewed over this story for a moment. How to make sense of it all?

"I think," she began, "there's been a huge mistake somewhere. I don't know who has been telling what to whom, but I'm not marrying William. I'm not even sure I wish to be his friend anymore. I've... I've discovered some things that I don't like."

"But you did love him?"

"What? No! I liked him. He was all dashing and romantic, and I tried to find something more than just friendship, but no, I never loved him. I couldn't. If people thought that, it was all just a mistake. A big mistake."

A wave of relief passed over Jasmine's face, so clear it was almost palpable. "Oh, thank heavens!" She looked at the box of pastries and took two more. "This calls for a celebration, I think, and an explanation."

If Anne had been confused before, now she was beyond fuddled. "I'm listening. But I don't understand at all."

Over more coffee and the rest of the pastries, Jasmine told her story.

Five years before, Connor had been working as an investment advisor and had heard, through associates, of this phenomenal opportunity in Turks and Caicos. It was to be a five-star development that could be a permanent home, a vacation home, or an income property for vacationers. It was guaranteed to be a money maker one way or another, and after due diligence, Connor had invested everything he and Jasmine had into the project, forgoing thoughts of purchasing their dream home in Toronto for this opportunity.

And then the development company pulled the brakes. There was no construction, no planning, no work at all. The consortium always had an excuse - missing permits, lack of suitably skilled workers, environmental assessments - but the result was the same, namely nothing. After four years of this, the development consortium announced that the project would not proceed after all and sold all the land and plans to another company. And that company had announced it was, indeed, proceeding with the development but at double the price. Everyone who had put money into the project could continue with their plans, but they needed to find the extra cash, and quickly.

Now the Smiths, and all those like them, had both lost the use of their fortunes that had gone into the first project, and were unable to afford to buy into the resurrected project. Inflation had made their initial investments relatively smaller; there was little they could now use that money for. In the five years since they had invested, housing prices at home had almost doubled.

Worse, a little bit more digging turned up some nasty business. The new consortium that had bought the project and land from the original group was composed of almost the identical set of people. In other words, they bought the project from themselves, doubled their take, and left a lot of people hung out to dry. When this came to light, the case ended up as the subject of court cases and governmental probes, and any money that might have gone back to the original lot of investors was now tied up in a bureaucratic mess that would take years to resolve. So not only was the initial investment worth so much less, the investors didn't even have access to the money they had poured in.

And this had left Jasmine and Connor living in a tiny apartment in a not so nice part of town, trying to survive on what she could earn as a violin teacher.

"I knew a bit about this from the newspapers," Anne shook her head, "but the details are awful. I'm really sorry. But... but how does this relate to William and me?"

"One of the people involved up high in both consortiums was William. William Barnett is the man who basically robbed us of half a million dollars."

Anne felt she had been hit. Her jaw went slack, and she stared at her friend, dumbfounded.

William? William would do this to people? Oh God. She knew he was a determined businessman, but to do this on the backs of trusting investors was appalling. How could he live with himself, knowing his wealth had pushed others into poverty? Every bite of pastry threatened to make itself known to her again. She swallowed hard.

"Are you okay, Anne? You knew nothing about this?"

"No." The walls swayed around her. "Not a thing. I knew he had business there, but... I never suspected. He always seemed responsible, even if not the most open person ever. But..."

But Penny. But he had been using Anne to hide his affair with the orchestra CEO's wife. That was morally repugnant, and she felt ill again.

"I'm really sorry, Anne. I knew all of this, of course, but when I thought you liked him, I kept quiet. I never wanted to hurt you, and if you loved him, I could live with this secret. You're more important than he is."

Another gulp. "What else is there, Jaz? I can see in your face you're not telling me everything."

"Wallis bragged quite a bit to Connor. It seems our friend William has been using you in all sorts of ways. All those dinners out you've had with him? Did you ever run into his friends?"

The art gallery, the Shakespeare play, the restaurants...

"Yes. Often. All the time, really. It was almost uncanny, the coincidences."

"Not coincidences. William planned it all. At least, that's what Connor got from Wallis, who I presume got it from William himself. He planned it, all of it. It's not hard, if you know the right person's secretary or personal assistant. 'Can I call So-and-So tonight?' 'Sorry, sir, he's out. I just made reservations for him at Chez Somewhere Fancy.' You know how it goes."

"But why? What possible reason could he have?"

Jasmine cast a sympathetic glance over the top of her mug. "You're a star, Anne. You're his endorsement. If William is in company with the brilliant, talented, charming, and totally reputable Anne Elliot, then he, too, must be totally reputable. He'd meet with these people, use you as his entrée, get them talking, and then sell them stuff. Connor thinks that's also why he's on the orchestra's board. It's like street cred for the very well-to-do. Act like a good guy in public, and people will think you're a good guy in private."

Something wet trickled down Anne's cheek. Was she crying? Oh, don't be crying! He's not worth it.

"He's a rat, Anne. When you told me you didn't love him, I was so relieved. He's got a black heart. He has no conscience. He thinks only of himself, and would do anything he could as long as it didn't put a blot on his supposed good character. I can't think how many people he has ruined, and I am just beyond relieved that you're not one of them. Oh, hon, you're leaking. Don't cry. You should celebrate being smart enough to see through his pretty shell."

In a moment, Jasmine had Anne wrapped up in her arms and Anne let the tears fall, long and hard.

Soon enough, the flood stopped, and Anne grabbed for a paper serviette to mop up the evidence. "You said you had good news too," she sniffled. "I could use some good news."

"Come. Let's sit again. It's pretty simple, really. Basically, we're getting our money back. It won't make up for the loss due to inflation and any interest we might have accrued on it, but it's half a million we never thought we'd see again. We're pretty pleased."

The lead ball in her stomach lighted a hair. "Pleased? I'm sure you're more than pleased! That's wonderful news. But how? How did this all happen so quickly?"

Jasmine blushed. "It was your friend Ben James, really, who did it. I told you I ran into Fred the other week?"

Anne nodded.

"Well, he put us in touch with Ben, who was doing an investigative piece on property market scams. It seems this particular project was high on someone's radar, and he took a deep dive into it. He was even down in the islands looking through the records and files there."

"Ohhh... So that's where he disappeared to after Christmas. Fred just said that he was working, but I didn't know where. That's... interesting. What happened? What did he find?"

A wide smile spread over Jasmine's pretty face. "He's the one who dug up the information about the new consortium being the old one in sheep's clothing. He wrote up a long piece for some prominent global publication, and approached a few of the folks involved at the top, offering to tone down some of the more accusatory language if they would start to return the money they effectively stole. I know we were owed the money in theory, but when things get tied up in legal cases, it was a guess as to whether we would have seen a penny of it. Now they are paying up."

This time, the hug was one of joy.

"So it was Ben who did this? Who helped you get your money back?"

Jasmine beamed. "Ben, but really Fred. From what Ben said when we met with him, it was Fred who told him about the scam, and Fred who sent him to us. Without Fred spearheading the whole idea, we would still be looking for old crackers behind the sofa cushions."

The celebration that followed was short. Jasmine had to leave to teach her violin students, and Anne had her own class at the University to lead. But both women parted ways with much lighter hearts.

Anne was free of William. Despite the pain her friend's tale had brought, the knowledge was its own relief. Jasmine and Connor could start to rebuild their lives, and Fred had proven himself to be one of the best men of her acquaintance. To do this for somebody he hardly knew was evidence of his truly good nature. She must call him and thank him from the bottom of her heart. She would have to do exactly this as soon as she got home from teaching. She carried on to her classes with a smile on her face and a sense of calm she had not felt in far too long.

It was only later, as she returned home that afternoon, that a heart-stopping thought occurred to Anne.

If Sophia and Jasmine thought she was in love with William Barnett and probably about to marry him, what did Fred think he knew?

CHAPTER THIRTY
Cantabile

Three days. It was three days before Ben and Louisa's wedding. So many emotions, relentless and insistent, washed over Anne that she could hardly stand. Thursday and Friday had slipped by in an endless daze, and now the weekend gaped before her. She called Marie to beg off watching the boys on Saturday evening, and stared at her blank tablet and piles of manuscript paper, unable even to lift the pen or stylus to write.

Music was usually her refuge where she could pour out her heart, a tacit therapeutic outlet that would never divulge her most private thoughts. But now nothing would come. Not a note. Her muse had forsaken her.

She was delighted for Ben and Louisa, mortified at Jasmine's tale and her own unwitting role in William's deception, relieved at the reversal in Jasmine and Connor's fortunes, and heartbroken over the loss of a friendship even if she had no wishes for anything deeper.

What should she do about William? Despite everything, she could not break up with him by text... not that they were a couple, at least as far as she was concerned. But the thought of contacting him to suggest a meeting was even more impossible. He would assume she wanted to pursue the relationship, and who knows what else he might tell people. Time and again, she wrote this email and that, trying to find the right words, but each time she deleted every letter and ended up staring at the same blank page she had started with.

She tried to phone, but it went straight to voicemail, although she knew from Jeremy that he was in town. Perhaps he was too busy with Penny to answer her call. In the end, she sent a few words thanking him for his friendship, but saying she couldn't go out with him again. It was unsatisfactory, but it was all she could manage, and the weight of his deceit and expectations sat heavily on her shoulders.

But the worst of all was the dread that suffocated her when she thought of Fred.

Fred. His name had been at the forefront of every thought that had passed her fevered brain since Jasmine's visit. When she closed her eyes, it was his face she saw. When she tried to listen to music, it was his baton that led the band, his voice that filled her ears, his thoughts that invaded her mind.

What did he believe? What did he think he knew? Was he also deceived into thinking she was marrying William? She had to talk to him, had to tell him the truth. Had to somehow let him know that if she loved anybody, it was him. She sent an email begging him to call, then left a voice message on his phone. But she heard nothing back from him and her read-request notification on her email suggested he had not opened it at all.

On Sunday morning, she received a short text from him. It was brief and quite disheartening.

> *I hear congratulations are in order. We still need to practise once more for the wedding. I am busy, but can make time before the orchestra rehearsal on Monday morning. That should be enough for the wedding in the evening. I'll be at the theatre at 9:30.*

That was all. No personal gestures, no kind words, no queries as to her feelings. Was he angry? Hurt? Just tired of her? God, why wouldn't he answer his phone? She needed to talk to him for five minutes.

Maybe before their rehearsal on Monday. Maybe if she arrived a bit early... but no. The theatre wasn't open until 9:30. She had spoken to the custodian Kostas several times in the past, and she knew his schedule. And afterwards there would be too many people around. Even at 9:30, the tech crew would be in, getting the stage set up for the orchestra. Maybe he would agree to talk later that day.

She hoped.

After a fuzzy weekend of too little sleep and too much coffee, Anne arrived at the theatre exactly on time on Monday morning. Hopefully, she would be able to nap in the afternoon. The wedding, later on in the day, was going to be a small evening affair. Ben had found a non-denominational officiant to perform the ceremony in a private room at a rather nice restaurant she had heard of but never been to, and they would remain there for a celebratory meal afterwards. According to Ben, it was a beautiful and intimate space with high ceilings, exposed brick, crystal chandeliers, and a prominent fireplace, with a rather good grand piano at one end. It all sounded lovely. Except that Fred would be there. *Please, let us sit beside each other*, she prayed to the universe, while at the same time pleading, *please don't let us sit beside each other.*

Of course, with only a dozen or so people invited, avoiding Fred would be impossible, all the more so since they were performing together at the ceremony.

And that was why she was here now, she reminded herself: to do one final rehearsal of the piece she had written.

She pushed open the heavy glass doors and waved to Kostas, who sat in his office-booth near the front. He called out his greeting and pointed to the one side door that was unlocked. She passed through it and into the dark theatre.

As expected, the stage crew were there, getting set up for the orchestra. The grand piano was already in place at one side of the stage, and Fred's cello sat on its side next to it. Of Fred, she saw nothing. She walked down the closest aisle and up the three stairs, then tossed her coat onto a chair and pulled her music out of her tote bag. She ran her fingers up and down the keys, warming them up after the cold February air outside, working out stiff joints with some scales and arpeggios, and then a short passage from her piece.

Nine thirty-three. No Fred. Nine thirty-six. No Fred. Was he not coming? Surely he had to be coming. He had a rehearsal to lead in a few minutes.

Then he appeared as if from nowhere. He looked at her sternly and cut her attempted greeting short. "No time now, Anne. I've asked Kostas to keep everyone but the tech guys out until we're done, but we only have a few minutes. I don't think we'll need more. Let's start. I'm already in tune."

He sat down and placed the instrument between his knees and looked at her to start playing.

He might not want to talk to her, but he still connected with her at a musical level. There was very little work that needed to be done, and Anne knew they would play well together this evening. At ten minutes to the hour, Fred stood, thanked her for her time, and informed her that they were finished for now.

"Until this evening." He turned away before she could say another word.

The wedding was lovely. It was short and personal, filled with snatches of Ben's poems and little stories about the couple that brought a smile to every face in the room. The officiant had clearly done her work in getting to know the newlyweds. Anne and Fred played the new piece before the ceremony started, and then again as the couple signed the official paperwork before being pronounced married. They received nearly as many congratulations as did the bride and groom themselves.

Then the small party drifted to the far side of the room for a celebratory cocktail as the serving staff began shifting the chairs and tables into position for dinner. Would it be possible to speak to Fred now? There were not so many people present, no more than a dozen, and they were bound to be close enough to exchange a few words, weren't they?

Of course, this was not the time or place to bare her soul to him; she would not do anything to upstage the two stars of the evening with her own little drama, but perhaps a word in his ear that she wanted to talk, that it was good, would be possible. She accepted a glass of something sparkling from the young man behind the bar and moved towards where Fred stood alone in a corner.

His eyes met hers and went cold, and he stepped a few feet away to insert himself in a conversation between one of Ben's best friends from school and Louisa's mother. It seemed there would be no such luck for her now. Maybe at dinner. With so small a group, Ben and Louisa had arranged for three tables of four people each. "Don't make yourselves too comfortable, though," Ben had announced to the assembled gathering. "We'll switch around for each course. We want a chance to mingle and chat with everyone."

Perhaps there would be an opportunity to sit with Fred after all, even for a few minutes.

For the first course, Anne sat with Louisa's parents and Ben's childhood friend. They were pleasant people and had a great deal of good conversation. All expressed both surprise at this hasty relationship and marriage, but at the same time, commented on how well suited the bride and groom seemed to be.

"I thought she was joking," Louisa's mother commented around her salad. "Some English chap from Italy! Would you have imagined it? I was ready to tell her she was crazy, especially if she needs to leave the orchestra to be with him. All those years she studied, practising till midnight, auditioning everywhere. But I trust her. I know I raised her right, and I trust her judgement. If she wants to be with Benjamin, if she's happy with him, then what else could a mother really want?"

Louisa's father grunted his agreement before her mother babbled on some more.

"And Ben is such a nice man. I wasn't sure what to expect of someone who would ask her to throw her career away, but it's not like that at all. Even if they have to leave Toronto and move to England, she'll always have her music. But she wouldn't always have Ben. That, I think, is a sacrifice well worth making. A gamble well worth taking."

Just like Anne gambled when she refused to join Fred in Europe. Yes, she won her career. But what did she lose? If only Professor Russell had been more like Louisa's mother! Perhaps they could have found a compromise. There was so much water under that bridge.

From the corner of her eye, she noticed Fred, sitting at another table almost exactly behind the mother-of-the-bride. He was very still as the lady spoke on. Was he listening? Could he hear her? What was he thinking? Anne's hands grew damp, and she fumbled for a serviette before she wiped them on her skirt and damaged the pale green silk.

The salad course was removed and people rose for a moment to mingle and refresh their drinks and then change tables. Now Anne was with Ben and Louisa and one of Louisa's sisters. Again, by accident or by design, Fred was directly behind Ben.

The conversation was animated and jovial, all celebration and sunny, despite the cold, dark February night outside. As Anne expected from the restaurant's reputation, the food was exceptional, and somebody—a sommelier or perhaps Ben or Louisa—had chosen the perfect wine to match the meal.

Fragrant tomato sauce, rich with basil and olive oil, provided the perfect coat for an artistic pile of grilled eggplant and portobello mushrooms, with fish, lamb, or tofu as the focus as the diner wished. On the side, the potatoes were perfectly roasted, and even the Brussels sprouts were good. Anne usually hated Brussels sprouts. She sipped her Baco noir and let the conversation fill in the spaces between bites.

Louisa held court, telling her friend and Anne about the honeymoon she and Ben had planned. She talked about warm beaches and fine restaurants, all a world away from a frigid Canadian winter, and both women gushed their approval of the plans.

"I've taken a short leave for the next concert," Louisa explained, "so we can enjoy ourselves for a week or two. Just long walks on the boardwalk and no pressures. I might even take some pencil crayons and see if I can still draw."

Ben gazed at her with nausea-inducing adoration.

"You should be taking notes, Anne," he turned to her when Louisa had finished. "If rumours are to be believed, you'll be next."

Behind him, Anne saw Fred's head twitch.

She laughed, trying to toss it off as a joke. "Rumours are funny things, but not always true. In this case, about as far from the truth as you can get."

Fred's head now went very still.

"But everything I've heard about you and William Barnett—"

"—is some sort of story that somebody cooked up. I cannot imagine how this is getting about at all. There is absolutely nothing to it. Nothing." She pitched her voice a touch louder than necessary, loud enough, she hoped, for every word to carry to the man sitting just behind the groom.

"But what about all those photos of the two of you, and the gala before Christmas?" Louisa leaned forward, the rich cream of her sleeves now resting inches from the tomato sauce on her plate. "I wasn't there, but I heard about it from Kristen, who saw it from a couple of metres away."

Another laugh. "No, he was just showing off. Really, I think it meant as little to him as it did to me." She became more serious now. "It certainly made me realise how much I dislike being put on display like that. I never want to be anybody's trophy, even in jest."

"I had some ears at the cocktail party the other week, too," Ben interjected. "Didn't he try something similar? Who was it who told me? I left my notebook at home."

"And a good thing," Louisa quipped, her smile wide and her eyes sparkling.

"I think," Anne mused, "that I've been a lot of things to a lot of people over the years, but mostly as some sort of commodity. It's taken me a long time to realise this. I grew up just being Anne, the boring kid who doodled music notes on her math worksheets and who preferred practising piano to watching television. When people started paying attention to my jottings, it never occurred to me that they might have designs on me that weren't about me as a person."

"But surely this fellow liked you for the person you are." This was Louisa's friend. "I've just met you, but I can tell you're interesting and worth knowing completely apart from your music."

"I hoped so at first, that he wanted to know plain boring Anne, but I also think I always suspected something, even if I couldn't put it into coherent thoughts. I never could understand what a smooth, urbane businessman like that would find in socially awkward and bumbling me. I know now that it was never me at all that he wanted. Not the real me. Just my name."

"Aw, Annie, you're selling yourself low." Ben reached over to place a hand on her forearm, his new golden wedding band glowing in the subtle light. "You're worth a thousand of him. He's all show. You're substance."

She gave him a half a smile. "You're a gem. I hope you know how lucky you are, Louisa. You've found a good one here. No, I've had a few fabulous friends over the years. You know Sophia Croft, and you've met Jasmine, right? But if we're talking love, the sort you two have, that's only happened once. There is only one person who I think loved *me*. Not the composer, not the musician, but Anne. And there's only one person I have ever loved. And that was over long ago."

Ben gave her a curious glance, but the others knew nothing and Anne did not elaborate.

Louisa sipped her wine and asked, "But surely, over the years and with all the amazing people you must have come across in your career, you've met someone equally suited to you. Or do you believe in soulmates?" Her eyes drifted to Ben, and she dissolved in a beatific smile.

Anne lightened the mood again. It was a wedding, after all. "I don't know about the concept of soulmates, but he was one if they exist. My career... yes, I've met some really fascinating people, it's true. But you imagine my life is a lot more exciting than it is. Really, I don't get out all that much. I mostly stay at home. All of the adventure happens in my head. I correspond with people by email and text, of course, but it's all business. My career isn't one that takes me out into the public eye a great deal. Not like..." She could see Fred's head behind Ben, still motionless as she spoke. "Not like some people's."

"So when that fellow, William, started wining and dining you?" Louisa asked.

"I was flattered. It was nice to be the centre of attention for a change. Me, not my music, but me. But it wasn't me after all that drew him. Look," she shook her head and raised her glass, "this is a time to celebrate you. A toast to Ben and Louisa! I wish you everything good in the world."

Louisa's friend raised her glass too, and soon the whole room was toasting the happy couple, and the sad topic and Anne and her lost love was abandoned.

But hopefully, just hopefully, Fred had heard enough that he would at least read her emails. She gulped down the rest of the wine and sent a small prayer to whoever might be listening.

Soon enough, the dinner dishes were cleared away and the party all rose to mingle for a few minutes before finding their new seats for dessert. Anne was swept up at once by Louisa's mother, who cooed afresh about how thrilled she was for her daughter to have found such happiness. There was no regret at Louisa possibly leaving Toronto, no clucking about abandoning a great career with the symphony, just pure joy.

Then Ben's brother was at her side to rave about the piece she had written, followed quickly by his father with equal words of praise. When she found her new table for the final course of the meal, she realised Fred was nowhere to be seen. His seat at the next table was empty, but his cello still stood silent in the corner by the piano. He had not left. But where was he?

The waiters started to bring in dessert, an assortment of little cupcakes for each table, piled high on a multi-tiered wrought-iron serving dish. There was one iced in pale blue with silver sprinkles, one that looked like strawberry shortcake, another that seemed to be a Black Forest confection, and more. Enough, by her quick count, to have one of each, perhaps more. She licked her lips in anticipation. Then came a tray of cheese and fruit for the table, and coffee and tea.

And still no Fred.

The four around her table had just finished discussing the selection and making their first choices when a motion to her side caught her attention. He was back, sliding into his seat at his own table.

"Sorry," she heard him mumble to the others. "Urgent message. I had to deal with it quickly." He rubbed his thumb and forefinger together, as Anne knew he used to do when agitated. Hopefully, it wasn't anything serious.

The chatter now was as light as the delicate cakes they ate, and as delightful. There was no more opening of the heart, no pouring out of lost longings. But it was a most pleasant end to a meaningful wedding. There came more toasts, more coffee, and then it was time to leave. Tomorrow was, after all, a weekday and many of the guests had places to be early in the morning.

She kissed the bride and groom on the cheek and offered her most sincere wishes one more time, as well as her hopes for a wonderful honeymoon, and went to find her coat and bag in the little cloakroom near the door.

Fred strode across the room, cello case slung over his one shoulder.

"You forgot your music, Anne."

He handed her a sheet of paper, and she took it out of reflex. Was it hers? Surely she had packed her music earlier. A frown crept over her brow, but the pleading look in Fred's eye kept her silent.

"Thank you." She placed it in her tote bag without looking. She would have all the time she needed to peruse it later at home.

Was it a final order to leave him alone? A renewed recrimination of past wrongs? Something else? Whatever it was, she could only read it in private.

She buttoned her coat and waved at the newlyweds, and when she turned around all she saw was Fred's back disappearing out the door into the frigid snowy night.

CHAPTER THIRTY-ONE
Espressivo

Anne's hands shook all the way back to her building. That sheet of paper that Fred had given her was a millstone in her tote bag, both hampering her every step and propelling her home as soon as she could get there. Anticipation, trepidation, and plain curiosity warred within her as she trudged the final few steps down her hallway and into her apartment.

Her coat fell onto the floor as she flung herself onto the sofa, tote bag clutched in shaking hands. She reached inside and withdrew that single sheet of paper. It was music, after all, one of the first sheets she had printed out, before making nicer copies to use for the performance. But it was not the printed side of the paper that drew her anxious eyes. She turned the sheet over to see Fred's familiar handwriting all over the back.

This must be what he was doing when he was late for dessert. The paper burned in her hands as she read.

I cannot listen in silence any longer. I have been afraid to speak, afraid to say what I want to say. I left you once and broke your heart, and my own, and when I thought you had found happiness with Barnett, I promised myself not to destroy your life again with my selfishness.

But now I hear that I was wrong, that you are not marrying him. I cannot speak to you tonight, my thoughts being where they are, but I have to try to be heard. You pierce my soul, Anne. You leave me in agony, but also in hope.

I once told you I was no poet. But for you, I will try.

There once was a very proud man
Whose life went according to plan
But he learned his success
Always felt somewhat less
For it wasn't the same without Anne.

I was wrong, and I lost more than I knew. Is there any chance of a future for us? Being here with you, unable to find the courage to talk to you, is almost more than I can bear. Tell me, Annie, show me somehow. My fate is in your hands.

How many times she read and reread the short letter she could not tell. But reread it, she did until every word was etched into her brain.

He loved her. He still loved her! And he hadn't said anything because he wanted her to be happy with William. He was willing to sacrifice his own hopes for her. He had put her future ahead of his own. If it was possible, she loved him even more for it.

She reached for the phone to call him now. Her fingers trembled as she touched his name on the contacts list, but it went straight to voicemail. Email, then, or a text...

No.

At once, she knew what she was going to do.

It was late, and she had another session with the orchestra tomorrow afternoon to workshop some elements on the third movement of her symphony, but there would be little sleep tonight.

She read Fred's letter once more, placed it in her file of Very Important Papers, and got to work.

Giving full attention to the orchestra's attempt at her symphony was one of the hardest things Anne had ever done. She had finally fallen asleep as the sun rose and had forgotten to set her alarm. Only her stomach reminded her to wake up, and she was nearly late for rehearsal. There would be no time to let Fred know what she had in mind.

Partly giddy with anticipation, partly terrified, she slipped into the auditorium and took her seat, notebook in hand. Fred turned to greet her, eyes blank, and she nodded solemnly back. Then he asked the orchestra to turn to the appropriate passage, and they started to play.

Following the play-though came the feedback session. This was becoming a source of genuine pleasure for Anne, as she heard the thoughts of the very people whose skills would bring her imaginings to life. Just as she was growing comfortable with the questions and critiques, so were the orchestra members growing comfortable with her.

After a productive conference about the movement in question, one of the trumpet players threw out a joking question. "So, Anne, what is up with these five sharps? Couldn't you have written this movement in an easier key? You're making me work hard for this!"

The orchestra laughed. Very few people enjoyed negotiating all those sharps and flats, and with the transposition required for the instrument, these black-note keys were a particular challenge for the trumpets. Anne laughed with them and apologised, but then gave a serious answer.

"Sorry about that, Rick, and this might sound strange, but that's the key that's the right colour. It needs to be that soft metallic brown that we get with this key signature. B major is no one's favourite, I know, and I feel bad about the section in D-sharp minor, but if I transpose it up a semitone, it gets all orange and brassy, and if I take it down, it just becomes a sad shade of limp green, like old wilted lettuce."

The sea of faces before her took on all manner of expressions, from confused to incredulous, and one or two, she was certain, thought her downright crazy. But the colours were there, and she had to write the piece as she wanted to hear it, in the proper colour.

"Tell you what, Rick. If you want to transpose your own part of the D-sharp to E-flat, I won't tell anybody, as long as I can't hear the difference."

This received a round of applause mixed with laughter, and some of the musicians began shifting in their seats, a sign that they thought this session was over.

It was. Almost.

"We have about ten minutes left," Anne went on before the orchestra got too many ideas about an early dismissal. "With Maestro Valore's permission, I would like to try one more short work today. I do not think it's too difficult, and I would like to hear it."

The sea of faces nodded, almost as if they had rehearsed the move in unison.

"Maestro? Do you mind?"

He peered at her from his seat at the edge of the stage, a quizzical look on his handsome face, although his eyes were still veiled.

"Of course."

"May I borrow your baton? I promise to return it in good condition."

A tight smile. He rose and handed the slim painted stick to her. The handle, a slightly elongated ball of cork, was warm from his hand and she revelled in the feel of it for a moment.

She reached into her bag and pulled out sheets of music, which she sent around the group. One pile for the first violins, one for the cellos, one for the winds and brass, and so on all through the orchestra. "Everything is in order, so just pass them along.

Whenever you're ready. You will please forgive my skills here. It's been a while since I was on the podium, and you are all quite spoiled by your maestro. I beg your indulgence. It is an offering, of sorts, to a friend."

In a moment, the musicians were sitting at attention, eyes on her, waiting for the downbeat.

She raised the tip of the baton in a gentle arc to set the tempo, and music began to fill the hall. It was not new music, not to her. But it had never been heard before like this, played by a symphony orchestra. It had, until last night, only existed in a form for piano and cello.

She had studied conducting, long in the past, and was competent if not exceptional at the art. But this music she knew intimately. Every note had been born within her, part of her soul. It was her declaration, her offering. Her plea.

She turned towards the double bass section, then the violas, who began the gentle swell of rippling harmony that would support the tune. Deep purples of colour rose from the orchestra, matched and contrasted with flashes of pink from the oboes and deep blues from the bassoons, satin and velvet and silk. Then the violins added their voices to the cushion of sound, sending slivers of silver into the sonic mix, until the cello section at last took up the refrain in their rich burnished gold.

As the line passed from instrument to instrument, as it had previously passed from piano to solo cello and back, the melody emerged, now a multicoloured tapestry woven from the shimmering threads of the orchestra. It glowed, iridescent and tangible, bright and clear, with strong underpinnings in rich oak, the harmonic structure set by the lower voices, then moving through the musical forces, and back again.

It was a concerto for orchestra, her gift to the musician whose instrument was that ensemble, the maestro, the one who made the music sing. Her gift to Fred.

Fred had been reclining in his chair near the back of the violins, and as the music began, she saw him come to attention and sit straighter in his seat. She wished she could watch his face instead of looking at the orchestra. She ached to see his eyes as he heard this piece of music that she had written for Ben now being played for him. She had spent all night orchestrating it for these musical forces before her, and she sent a prayer into the universe that he understood.

A glance showed her that her efforts were not entirely for nothing. He was sitting quite upright now, as still as the grand piano beside him, his eyes wide and his jaw slack. He knew she had done this for him. She hoped.

Too quickly the piece was over. It was not long, after all, only five minutes or so. A few voices called out kudos from the orchestra, but the sounds scarcely registered in her consciousness. All of her attention was on one man, the tall conductor, still sitting immobile in his chair.

Before anybody could move, she turned back to the orchestra.

"Thank you. You played beautifully. I should let you all know that this piece was set with a poem in mind. It was written by a friend. May I read it to you? It won't take a moment."

She pulled out the text and held it in front of her. Were the words on the paper so fuzzy last night? No, silly. It was her eyes that were watering. She blinked, and the letters swam back into place.

"It's called *Pieces of Us*.

> *We are, the poet said,*
> *All of us made of pieces.*
> *Pieces of joy,*
> *Pieces of pain,*
> *Pieces of others,*
> *Pieces of ourselves.*
>
> *We try, the poet said,*
> *To rearrange our pieces.*
> *To grasp our dreams,*
> *To light our fires,*
> *To find our loves,*
> *To find ourselves.*
>
> *And when, the poet said,*
> *We find all our pieces*
> *And lay them before us*
> *A picture of our lives,*
>
> *A space appears*
> *That we had not seen,*
> *That was somehow missed*
> *In the sortment we were given.*
>
> *You'll find, the poet said,*
> *Another with his pieces,*
> *That fit with yours,*
> *That fill the void,*

That make you whole,
Both whole, together."

She breathed the last syllable. The auditorium was silent, white emptiness of sound but filled with anticipation, electrical. And then, as one, everybody took a breath and the crackle of tension in the air disappeared.

"That was lovely," someone said. "Almost as beautiful as the music."

"Almost as beautiful as the composer," whispered a voice just behind her, words meant only for her ears.

She turned to face those dark eyes, so familiar, so loved. There was nothing veiled about his gaze now.

Aloud, he said, "I believe, Dr. Elliot, that we have a couple of things to discuss about... about some music. Perhaps you have time?"

And she turned to him with as wide a smile as she had ever felt upon her face, "For you, Maestro, I have all the time in the world."

What time was it? Was the sun shining or were clouds obscuring any remaining daylight? Was it snowing or was it clear? All these considerations were nothings, nonsensical trivialities. What mattered now was Fred.

She walked beside him through the streets, a hair's breadth of air between them, not quite touching. There would be time for that later. First there must be words. If she wanted it, the merest shift would have her in his arms, nestled in the crook of his shoulder. A turn of her foot would rub her side against his. But she kept that sliver of distance. Though there were winter coats and hats and gloves between them, even a brushing contact was too much... for now.

This time, they would do it right. They would talk, clear away eight years' worth of pain, these last few months of crossed purposes. She ached to hold him and have him hold her, ached to feel his lips, so familiar and so missed, against hers. But not quite yet. When their time came, it would be better and stronger for this solid foundation. Bass notes, steady and sure, the harmony holding the music together. Treble and bass, him and her, Anne and Fred.

They talked, at first, of lighter matters: Ben's wedding, Louisa's parents, the choice of wine. The streets disappeared beneath their feet as they threaded their way through the city, their destination a tacit decision, undiscussed but sure. Across the street, past the row of fashionable shops, behind the new theatre, past the coffee shops, and at last to Anne's apartment.

Now, at last, divested of their winter coats and sitting angled towards each other on the sofa, they could approach the heart of the matter, their bodies not touching, but their hearts, at last, united.

How to broach the subject? What to say? Anne stared at him, so close, but still untouchable. His dark eyes met hers and she knew he understood, even if he too was not quite ready to put words to so many feelings.

For this moment, it was enough to be close and in harmony, to drink in the knowledge that he was here. His dark hair, mussed by his winter hat into something intimate, the long limbs, strong and elegant, those deep eyes that never failed to entrance her, they belonged here, not necessarily in her living room, but in her life. She let her eyes flicker closed for a second, just to allow his presence to envelop her, and she breathed in deeply, sensing the remaining remnants of his citrus shampoo. This, for now, was enough, and she let her senses celebrate in this unexpected glow.

At last, she opened her mouth. "Do you sometimes wonder if we...?" She trailed off, letting the silence speak instead.

"If we gave up too easily?" His voice was warm. There was nothing recriminating in it, only rueful.

She turned her eyes on him, but said nothing.

"I'm not angry, Annie. Not anymore. We needed different things then. You needed to finish your degree—yes, I know that now—and I needed to study with Buscagni. No, please, let me finish. If you had done what you said at first and come with me, and had not listened to Professor Russell, you might have finished *Preludes*, and it might well have been the fabulous piece it is now. But who would have heard it? Maybe some little provincial orchestra somewhere. You would certainly ever have come to the attention of the guys behind *The Butterfly's Kiss*. He was at one of those workshops you gave. You'd never have become famous. And I think you would have known that you were missing out on something, even if you didn't know what it was. You would have been relegated to the role of The Conductor's Wife, always playing second fiddle. And you would have come to resent it. To resent me."

His thumb worried his forefinger as he spoke, but his voice was tender as he continued.

"I *was* angry at first, so angry. I don't know if I was angry with you or with your professor, but all I felt was the anger. I know now that she only did what she thought was best for you—"

Anne interrupted. "To be honest, it helped her career as well, being known as the mentor who honed all this." She gestured mockingly to herself.

"Don't sell yourself short, Anne. You are... you are incredible. All that talent, that sheer gift of music, within a beautiful wrapper, and coupled with the kindest soul I can imagine, that's nothing to deprecate. You are amazing."

He shifted in his seat. Was he now closer to her? He had made no attempts at physical contact yet. He must know as well how important it was that words come first.

His voice, when he spoke again, was so low it was a vibration as much as a sound. "I really believe now that she had your best interests in mind, or what she thought were your best interests. And you have grown into yourself and your music in a way you might not have otherwise.

"I was young and arrogant and I could not accept that you might put your career ahead of me, even for a year or so."

"And I," Anne's eyes met his, "was too easily led. Why could I not have worked out a way to finish my degree from Europe? It would have been possible, I'm sure of it. But she somehow convinced me I needed to be here, in person. If we had..."

"If we had not let our egos and tempers take charge, we could have talked it through and made a plan. I would have liked you by my side."

Now he did shift a bit closer to her. "I thought of you, Anne. Almost every day I thought of you. I wondered what you were doing, who you were with, where you were. Every time I met a new orchestra or travelled to a new city, I wished you were with me. I was a sad and lonely man."

She cocked her head. "You must have had other... friends to share things with."

His eyes fluttered closed. "Dalliances, a few dates here and there, yes. But there was never anything serious. No one could live up to you. There has always only been you."

Her hand reached towards his and he grasped it with the fervour of a drowning man clutching a rope. Those long fingers, warm and smooth, intertwined with hers, every touch sparking amber flecks of love.

"And for me," Anne breathed, "there has only ever been you. You are the final piece that's missing from me. You make me whole."

"And now?" His chocolate eyes were inches from hers.

"And now we try again, but with no egos and no anger."

Fred laughed, rich tumbles of sound in the dark apartment. "I am a conductor. My ego is my stock in trade. But yes. Between us, no egos, and lots of discussion and accommodation."

"We're lucky, you know." She had shifted to face him directly. "We lost each other, but we found each other again. I loved you so much, Fred, and I never stopped loving you."

"As I love you, and always have." He was so close, his eyes capturing hers. His free hand floated towards her face and he let his fingers rest on her cheek for a moment before moving to thread themselves in her hair. "Come," he whispered, his voice hoarse, "come to me, Anne."

The last inches disappeared between them, and he pulled her into his chest, arms around her back as hers snaked around his. For a long time they just clung to each other, him half turned on the couch, she with her knees curled beneath her, leaning onto that strong body she had known so well. Just being here, for now, was enough. It was the start of something new, emerging from the old, fresh growth appearing on long-dormant branches, stronger now for the deepening of roots.

It was a phoenix, arising from its own ashes, fierce and fiery, ready to soar again.

Then she felt his head move next to hers and light pressure fell on her brow. A kiss, gentle as a drop of rain, and as welcome after a drought. Then another, not demanding, not asking, merely giving.

She pulled back a bit to look at him, letting her eyes meet his. Was her smile as broad as his? Did her face glow with that same joy and contentment?

His hand reached up to cup her chin, and she nodded at him before pressing her lips to his. A gift, an offering. Her love, as pure as it could be. He accepted it and returned his own, and they fell into each other.

This was joy and contentment, not that panic-filled passion of the day of Dylan's accident. This was the end of their estrangement and the start of something new and better: a prelude to a grand new part of their lives.

And, in the morning when Anne opened her eyes, Fred was there beside her, a look of pure serenity on his handsome face. They would be torn apart no more.

CHAPTER THIRTY-TWO
Finale

"Are you sure she won't mind?"

Fred hugged Anne to his side as they rode up in the elevator to Sophia and Jeremy's condominium unit. His arm felt good around her shoulders; it was exactly where it belonged. She leaned into him and looked up with a grin.

"She won't mind at all. When I texted her earlier, I said I was bringing a friend to her little tea party, and her only concern was whether my friend preferred chocolate or fruit. And no, to answer your next question, she doesn't know it's you. I want to see her face when we tell her. I'm quite sure she thinks I meant William."

"William who?" he teased.

She raised her eyebrows at him. "I have no idea. I don't remember any William at all."

This was met by a kiss that only ended when the elevator gave its gentle rock, telling them they had reached their floor.

"Minx. I'll deal with you later."

Anne giggled. "Only after I deal with you. Is my hair a mess?"

Fred's gaze was dreamy. "In my eyes, it's always perfect. But you are perfectly tidy for your adoring public, too. Come along. Let's go and meet our fate."

Jeremy answered the door. He kissed Anne's cheek and gave Fred an assessing stare before inviting both inside. "Come on inside. Soph will be out in a moment. It's still cold for a February evening, so we have a tureen of hot apple cider as well as the usuals. Let me take your coats. I'll let Sophia know you're here."

They were the first to arrive, by Anne's planning, and for now, they had the spacious living room to themselves. They stood a bit apart. They had no need to touch physically right now. They were connected at a far deeper level. The air around them was warm and tingling with quiet electricity. They were, in all essential ways, one.

"Anne, darling!" Sophia's voice came from down the hallway. "What little gem do you have to tell me? Who—" She sashayed into the room and stopped short. "Frederico! What a surprise. Did you run into Anne coming over? Did you...? Oh!"

Understanding dawned.

"Annie, darling? I expected you in tears, not like this. Tell me there is a reason you're glowing so brightly I don't need the lights on. What little secret do you have? I don't think I've ever seen a smile like that on your face." Her eyes assessed Fred more keenly than had her husband's, and she returned to them both with a look of great pleasure. "The two of you...?" Her eyebrows moved suggestively.

Anne just grinned in response.

"And William? What was that all about? You two seemed like you were heading somewhere." Her face clouded momentarily. "Have you heard…? I was afraid you'd be devastated—"

Devastated? What did her friend know? No matter. William was hardly a memory now.

"I tried to tell you, Soph. It was nothing with William. It never was anything. He was all style and no substance. And I recently learned some things about him that quite convinced me I wanted nothing to do with him at all."

A sudden look of relief rushed over her friend's face. "After what I heard today, Anne, I think that is the wisest thing you've ever said. Well," looking from Anne to Fred and back again, "perhaps the second. Come and sit. We've had news that affects both of you."

Jeremy was at the bar and in a moment, the four were sitting with drinks at hand. Jeremy took up the tale.

"It seems there have been some, er, irregularities with our friend, Mr. Barnett. His business dealings were not all quite above-board, as they say."

"I know. I think we have Fred to thank for that."

Jeremy's face took on a shrewd look. "Is that so, Maestro? Interesting. You can explain later, but I suppose we should thank you."

Fred shook his head. "Not me. A friend of mine did the legwork. I just suggested the direction he should start looking. I have to admit, I was not quite expecting the dirt he dug up. It might prove embarrassing to the orchestra, and I'm sorry about that."

"Never you worry, Fred. We'd rather know. This way, we can be proactive. He's already been removed from the board, and if we need to address this, we can say we acted as soon as we learned there was something shady going on. There are rumours about criminal charges coming forward as well for fraudulent activity. One of our members is a lawyer and said something about his accounts being frozen, but, well, rumour is just rumour. Still, our old friend is facing a bit of trouble, it seems."

Sophia pinched her lips. She clearly had more to say.

"There is something else you should know. I... I heard this about Kevin Walters. It's a bit of a grapevine, but my sources are usually trustworthy."

"You'll keep this quiet?" Jeremy phrased it as a question, but it was an order. Both Anne and Fred nodded.

"It seems that Walters' wife, Penny, has, er..."

"Run away with William Barnett?" Anne finished.

Jeremy and Sophia turned to her with wide eyes. "How did you know?"

Anne laughed. She had not found this at all amusing at the time, but now, just a week later, it seemed inane, ridiculous even. How could she ever have thought enough of William that she was surprised by this? She wasn't even hurt anymore. A bit angry, perhaps, at having been used so cruelly, but she knew now he had never had enough of a hold on her heart to injure it.

"I smelled her. That gala, before Christmas, when William came back late after one of the courses, he smelled of perfume. It was a very distinctive scent, blue and purple, with flecks of amber. When I shook hands with Penny at the gala, I smelled the same perfume. It was unmistakable. You can't transfer a scent like that by shaking hands. They must have been... more intimately involved behind some potted plant somewhere." She paused and sighed. "Poor Kevin."

Sophia clucked. "That must hurt. But if that's the sort she is, he's better off without her."

There was a moment of comfortable silence between the four. Then Sophia sat up pertly in her chair. "We have a few minutes before the others arrive. Sarah is in the kitchen getting everything ready, so you can spill. You two? What? How?"

Anne beamed at her friend. "The 'what' is simple. Us. We are what. It's always been us, despite all those years apart. I always knew I'd never find anyone like him." She reached across the small space to take his hand again.

"And how," Fred's face took on that blissful expression again, "is a story for our grandchildren. Anne," he leaned forward conspiratorially, "wrote me a love song!"

Sophia clapped, and Jeremy called out his approval.

"And she had the orchestra play it for me. She stepped up to the podium, took my baton, and waved it at them. And they played the music she set in front of them. They had no idea what was happening, but I knew, from the first note, I knew. No one has ever written a love song for me before." His eyes met hers and she was lost in their deep brown depths. With an effort, she pulled herself away to return to her friends.

"Perhaps I did," she confided after a moment. "But that was only after he did what he said he would never do. He wrote me poetry!"

"A poet? How lovely. And romantic." Sophia's voice was everything enchanted.

"Oh no! My poetry is dreadful. I am far better with a stick than with a rhyme. But it was enough."

"What's next for you two? You have a past, but I don't want to assume..."

"We're taking it slowly," Anne replied, "not because we aren't sure, but because we want to do it right. We want to make sure we are both completely ready for every step, no matter how or when it comes. When Fred goes to Vancouver next month for his guest conductor gig, I'll join him..."

"And when Anne goes to New York in April to talk to the people there about the television miniseries they've approached her about, I will join her."

Jeremy clucked his approval. "So, none of my business, but will you get married again?"

Anne turned to Fred and the two of them burst out laughing. "You tell them, Annie."

"No, you can."

Fred turned on his brilliant grin, the one that delighted audiences around the world, and announced, "we can't do that. You see, we never really divorced. We started proceedings, but we never finalised the paperwork. It's still sitting in some lawyer's office somewhere, waiting until it was necessary. We've been married all this time."

"Then a toast, before the others arrive." Sophia leapt from her chair. "To Fred and Anne. May you always make beautiful music together."

"To Fred and Anne. Congratulations!"

And as the doorbell rang and Sarah in the kitchen started bringing out hors d'oeuvres and little cakes, Anne stepped into the arms of the man she had loved for so long and gloried in the feel of him.

"To us. This was our *introduzione*, our beginning. Now on to the symphony of our lives. To you, Fred."

He didn't reply because he was too busy kissing her.

EPILOGUE
Glorioso

The concert hall still rang with the reverberations of the ultimate chord of her symphony, bold and triumphant. The musicians had not yet breathed their release after that final exultation of sound and perched on their chairs in that exquisite moment between action and repose, frozen in time, a tableau to be captured. Apart from the fading echo of that great, triumphant chord, the hall was absolutely silent.

On the podium, Maestro Frederico Valore took a deep breath and lowered his baton, and at once, the crystalline stillness exploded into a tidal wave of applause. Where a second ago, full silence reigned, now the massive space rang with the thunder of a thousand hands and cries of *Bravo!* from all parts of the auditorium.

Fred turned around to face the crowd and take his bow. His face was exultant, his brow shining with the beaded perspiration generated by the energetic command of a forty-five minute long oeuvre. Anne's symphony.

The waves of applause continued and the orchestra members stood to take their own bows, first the entire ensemble and then section by section. Fred motioned for particular soloists to stand for the audience's adulation—the oboist, the concertmaster, the principal violist, Louisa in her role as first French horn, the first trombone—and then he brought the entire group to their collective feet once more.

And still the applause rang with no sign of slowing.

"Go up!" Sophia nudged Anne's side. "He's gesturing for you. It's your turn." She all but pushed Anne from her seat in the front row of the audience. Anne was ready for this. It was quite expected, after all, and she was prepared for her moment in the spotlight.

Behind her, Jasmine and Connor called their words of encouragement, and even Marie, to her other side, looked impressed. "It was really rather nice, Anne. I don't think I could have done that."

Anne rose to her feet and strode to the stairs at the side of the stage, then climbed them in three easy steps. She looked good tonight, and she knew it. No more dark blues and muted blacks. Black was for the performers. Tonight she wore bright red. Sophia had convinced her that this shade was all but made for her, and even Anne had to agree. The brilliant colour brought out the delicate beauty of her complexion rather than overshadowing it, and she felt... powerful.

She bowed to the orchestra and mouthed a huge "thank you" before continuing to the podium. Once there, Fred grabbed her hand and turned her to the audience, lifting that hand high above their heads in a gesture of triumph.

If anything, the thundering appreciation grew louder. Red to match her dress, sparks of gold and flashes of emerald green, the sound rushed through her and boosted her. Could she smile any wider?

The orchestra joined in the applause and a little girl in a lacy white party dress danced onto the stage from the wings to hand Anne a huge bouquet of flowers. And beside her, Fred stood tall and beaming, his sweat-damp face a picture of pride and elation.

"You did it, Anne." He whispered, although with the noise from the seats there was no need to be quiet. "Your symphony is a masterpiece."

"And you conducted it perfectly. Every note was exactly as I hoped." Could the audience see the adoration in her eyes? She hoped so. Everyone should know how much she loved this man.

Fred caught her hand in his again and raised his arm in appreciation of the applause and in glory. The ring on Anne's finger caught the bright spotlight and sparkled in a cascade of sound and colour.

Soon they would go to the reception. Soon they would make the announcement of their official celebration of marriage, albeit eight years after the fact. Soon they would speak to their fans and celebrate with their friends.

But now, for this moment, they stood here together, she and her beloved Fred, on stage between orchestra and audience, together in music and together in love, and life was truly wonderful.

The End

NOTES

This novel has allowed me to explore some of my great loves: music and the world of the orchestra, Toronto, where I live, and my favourite of Jane Austen's fabulous novels, Persuasion. Through the creation of this work, and through my research, I also discovered some new loves, including the poetry of E. Pauline Johnson.

I am a musician and have played in orchestras since I was a child. From those very early student groups to professional ensembles playing Brahms and Mahler, orchestras have fed my soul. I have not written much about individual pieces of music (other than my protagonist's fictional ones), but I have referenced several. Here is a list of some of these pieces, if you wish to look for recordings. All are readily available on various streaming platforms.

J.S. Bach - Brandenburg concertos

W.A. Mozart - String quartets (all of them. They're wonderful)

G. Holst - The Planets

L. van Beethoven - Symphony #5

J. Brahms - Quintet for piano and strings, op.34

J. Brahms - Symphony #3

J.S. Bach – Sonata #4 for violin and harpsichord

W.A.Mozart - Violin Sonata No. 21, E Minor, K. 304

I moved to Toronto as a university student, and had no real love for the city at the time. It was big and brash and soulless, or so I thought. But the passage of time has changed these first impressions, and I have come to see the city for what it is beneath the glass-and-concrete exterior. It is a network of communities that welcome you in, a multicultural hub where the world is just a subway stop away, and a thriving centre for the arts. From movies and television, to first-rate theatre, to a fabulous music scene, Toronto has everything at a world-class standard. It is no stretch to believe that a famous young composer could live here, or that my fictional orchestra could attract a principal conductor with a global reputation.

Updating Austen is a most delightful challenge. Her characters are so beautifully drawn they are timeless, and those same loves, losses, heartbreaks and victories that her characters experienced two hundred years ago still resonate.

Still, some changes must be made to reflect the current times and settings of a modern interpretation. Some of those changes in this novel are the names of some characters. Where Miss Austen gave us no name, that was easy. But in other cases, I had to make some decisions.

Frederick Wentworth, for example, is no longer a navy captain, but an orchestra conductor. Given the glorious heritage of music in Italy, and Toronto's huge Italian community, I have made him Italian, born in Canada to an Italian-speaking family, full of love for his city, his heritage, and his music. But Wentworth is not an Italian name. So, I translated it, or, rather, part of it. "Worth" translates roughly as "Valore," and that became Fred's new name. Move over Captain Wentworth. You are now Frederico Valore.

William Elliot was another challenge. In Austen's world, marrying within families was not at all uncommon, and especially in the case of Persuasion, where cousin William Elliot is in line to inherit Sir Walter's baronetcy. That would strike readers as odd, if not creepy, in a modern novel, and so I made him a stranger. And what to call a man who wants to be a baronet? Barnett, of course. And thus, my handsome businessman was born: William Barnett.

Other changes are simpler. Mary becomes Marie, which is just a bit more in keeping with modern fashions for names, and Captain James Benwick is now Ben James. Hopefully a few different names will not impede anyone's enjoyment of the story.

E. Pauline Johnson

Anne Elliot is a Canadian composer, and I wanted her to base one of her commissions on Canadian poetry. I wanted something steeped in tradition, but also modern and forward-looking. And I wanted poetry that sang to my soul. I hunted and I searched and I scrounged and found nothing that really called out to me. And then I saw a name I knew. E. Pauline Johnson.

I'd heard of her before and certainly knew her photograph, but had never really taken the time to read her poetry. So I sat down with a collection and began to read. Oh, how glad I am that I did! This was exactly what I wanted. Her poetry is rooted in the land and in her indigenous North American traditions, while still speaking to European sensibilities. And most importantly, it sings. It sings to my soul. I am not a particular aficionada of poetry, as much as I appreciate it, but sometimes something just reaches out and grabs me. And this is exactly what happened. As I read her words, melodies formed in my head. I can just imagine the fabulous riches a real composer could find in her work.

Emily Pauline Johnson was born in 1861 in what is now Ontario, Canada. Her father was Mohawk and her mother English, and she often went by her Mohawk name, Tekahionwake, meaning Double Wampum. Despite the inherent prejudice her parents faced from their mixed marriage, she was brought up in comfortable and culturally rich circumstances. Her father, George, was chief of the

Six Nations, spoke English, French, German, and the languages of the Six Nations Confederacy, and worked as an interpreter and cultural liaison between the federal government and the indigenous peoples of the area. Her mother, born Emily Susanna Howells in England, came from a family known for their interest in the literary arts. Due to a large extent to George's reputation, their home was often host to quite distinguished guests, such as the Marquess of Lorne, Lord Dufferin, and Princess Louise, and Pauline's elegant manners owed much to this aspect of her childhood.

As might be imagined, Johnson's life and work were greatly influenced by her dual heritage. She received a good if modest European education from her mother and from Brantford Collegiate Institute, where she graduated in 1877, and learned about her Mohawk background from her grandfather Chief John Smoke Johnson, whose dramatic talents inspired many of Pauline's poetic works.

When George died in 1884 the family was forced to leave their home and move to nearby Brantford. Pauline turned to writing as means of supporting herself. She had been writing poetry since her teens, and between 1884 and 1886 published several poems. Four were in *Gems of Poetry* (New York), eight were in *The Week* (Toronto), and several occasional pieces appeared elsewhere, including a poem written for the retirement of Seneca orator Red Jacket in 1885 and the dedication of a statue of Joseph Brant (Thayendanegea) the following year. By 1886 she had acquired a considerable reputation and it was now that she began signing her works as both E. Pauline Johnson and Tekahionwake.

In 1892 she was invited to participate in an evening of poetry sponsored by the Young Men's Liberal Club in Toronto, which she did to considerable success. Here her childhood lessons in elegance, manners, and deportment came into play, along with the dramatic gifts and lessons from her grandfather. The audience was delighted with her recitation of her poems, and she soon embarked on a tour of towns and villages across Ontario. She had become, if not the serious poet she wished to be, successful as a popular performer of her own poetry.

Over the next seventeen years she toured Canada and parts of the United States, and presented a series of successful recitals in London, England. While there, she arranged for the publication of her first collection of poetry, *The White Wampum* (London, Toronto, and Boston, 1895). Her second collection, *Canadian Born*, was published in 1903, and *Flint and Feather* was published in 1912.

She continued touring and writing poetry until ill health forced her to retire in 1909. She chose Vancouver, British Columbia, as her new home and it was here that she died of breast cancer in 1913, three days before her birthday.

Johnson's poetry really celebrates her heritage and her home and is rich in early expressions of Canadian nationalism. She turned the styles and techniques of English poetry to the landscapes and scenes that she knew: gurgling brooks, towering pine trees, purple sunsets, and a lover in a canoe. She extolled the glories of the wilderness and wrote ballads with episodes drawn from First Nations history. Hers was not an easy life, having to straddle late Victorian expectations as an unmarried performer, societal and institutional racism as an Indigenous woman, and just surviving as a woman artist in a time when women's rights were more fantasy than reality.

ABOUT THE AUTHOR

Award-winning author Riana Everly was born in South Africa but has called Canada home since she was eight years old. She has a Master's degree in Medieval Studies and is trained as a classical musician, specialising in Baroque and early Classical music. She first encountered Jane Austen when her father handed her a copy of *Emma* at age 11, and has never looked back.

Riana now lives in Toronto with her family. When she is not writing, she can often be found playing string quartets with friends, biking around the beautiful province of Ontario with her husband, trying to improve her photography, thinking about what to make for dinner, and, of course, reading!

If you enjoyed this novel, please consider posting a review at your favourite bookseller's website.

Riana Everly loves connecting with readers on Facebook at facebook.com/RianaEverly.

Also, be sure to check out her website at rianaeverly.com for sneak peeks at coming works and links to works in progress.

MORE FROM RIANA EVERLY

Much Ado in Meryton: Pride and Prejudice Meets Shakespeare

A tale of friends, enemies, and the power of love.

"Thou and I are too wise to woo peaceably."
– Benedick, Much Ado About Nothing, 5.2

Mr. Darcy's arrival in Meryton raises many people's disdain, and Elizabeth Bennet's ire. An insult at a dance is returned in full measure, and soon the two find themselves in a merry war of words, trading barbs at every encounter. Matters go from bad to worse when Elizabeth and Darcy find themselves living under the same roof for a time, and their constant bickering frays everybody's nerves.

Will a clever scheme by their family and friends bring some peace to Netherfield's halls? And what of Mr. Wickham, whose charming presence is not quite so welcome by some members of the party? When the games get out of hand and nastier elements come into play, will everybody's chances for happiness be ruined forever?

This clever mash-up of *Pride and Prejudice* and Shakespeare's *Much Ado About Nothing* casts our beloved characters in fresh light, uniting Jane Austen's keen insight into love and character, and Shakespeare's biting wit.

Please enjoy this excerpt from **Much Ado in Meryton**.

CHAPTER ONE
Only you excepted
(Benedick, 1.1)

Fitzwilliam Darcy shifted in place as the carriage bounced over another rut in the lane. It was quite black outside and the curtains were drawn, allowing nothing of their surroundings to be seen. Surely they must soon be at their destination. Beside him on the squab, his friend drew his own curtain aside enough to peer through. He gazed into the void for a moment, then turned back to the occupants of the carriage with a broad grin.

"Surely you cannot see anything, Charles. There is no moon and we are facing backwards. The lamps will show you nothing." Darcy shifted again, trying to stretch out his long legs without disturbing the women sitting across from him. He had spent a great deal too much time in a carriage today. Perhaps if he had insisted upon using his own for this short ride, he might be more comfortable, for his coach was both longer and wider than Charles Bingley's. But his men and horses had made the drive up from London that very morning and they deserved a rest. His friend's carriage was adequate. Just.

His young friend widened his grin. "I own it is full dark, but we shall be there very soon. Look! There is the first house." He drew the curtain open to reveal a small cottage with lights flickering behind two windows. "I do believe I shall like this town very much indeed."

He smiled indulgently. Then, turning a worried frown to his tall friend, asked, "Darcy, you will be polite, will you not?"

A very pretty young woman on the forward-facing bench gave a delicate sniff. "Mr. Darcy is unfailingly polite. When it is merited."

The other woman beside her tittered. Her carefully contrived ringlets bounced against the hat that marked her as a married woman. "I doubt he shall have to exercise those skills tonight, Caroline. I cannot imagine a single creature here who is deserving of Mr. Darcy's charm. Really, Charles," she turned to the beaming young gentleman, "why have you brought us here? London is far preferable at this time of year. Could you not have found a more..." she turned to the closed window and sniffed, "civilised place to let an estate?"

Caroline nodded. Her face, lovely though it might be, was not made lovelier by the disdain that crept across it. "Surely, Mr. Darcy, London is your preferred place. Why, you stayed an extra three days after the rest of us came up to this sad part of Hertfordshire." She batted her eyelashes at him.

The rumbling of the carriage wheels turned to a jostling bounce that suggested cobblestones rather than a packed dirt lane. They must be well within the village now. It was not so large a place, this market town called Meryton, but prosperous enough if they had stone streets, and Charles had spoken of a rather grand set of assembly rooms.

"My personal business kept me in town," was all Darcy replied.

Bingley added, "And Darcy was most gracious in cutting that business short so he could attend the assembly with us." His smile became more serious. "I do thank you for this, Darcy. I have met many of the gentlemen of the area, but this shall be my first introduction to the local society as a whole and I am pleased to have you at my side. Not that I am nervous, but I wish to make a good impression." Then he turned back to the two women who sat across from him. "And I shall assume the same excellent behaviour from you as you expect from my friend. This is my home now, and for all that you are my sisters, I shall be quite put out if you turn the people against me with your high and mighty ways."

Caroline sniffed again. "You are so easily led, Charles. One man tells you of a grand estate to be let, and you are ready to sign the lease before setting an eye on it. Another tells you Meryton is as fine a town as any in England, and you accept his very word as truth without question. You are always so determined to like a thing that you never consider it for yourself. I shall see for myself whether these people are worthy of my consideration."

Her sister, Louisa Hurst, said not a word, but beside her, her husband gave a snort. "Good wine and food, you say? Cards and good hunting? Jolly good. Then we shall get along very well."

By now the carriage had pulled to a stop and the party of five alit from the vehicle to get their first sight of the assembly rooms. The edifice that faced them was grander than anything Darcy had expected and looked really rather fine from the square. Finer than he had expected, to be honest. The building was large and rectangular, with two short wings on either end and a Grecian portico over the large double doors. The style was of the last fifty years, and it looked, in the light of the burning lamps about the square, newly painted and in excellent repair. Darcy suspected the building functioned more often as a space for town meetings and local business than for assembly balls. Tonight, however, it was the centre of local society, to judge from the number of carriages lining the square and the sounds of revelry from the tavern across the way where any number of drivers and footmen must be whiling away the hours until they were needed again.

Bingley and his party promenaded inside the building and divested themselves of their outerwear, then proceeded to the main doors that led to the grand hall. Darcy could hear the noise from inside abate even before the doors were fully open. Of course. Their arrival must have been long anticipated, and speculation as to their names, numbers, and bank accounts must have filled the air since the building saw its first guests that evening.

True to his expectations, no sooner had the party of newcomers set foot into the grand hall than the whispers started. "Five thousand..." came one voice. "No, ten! And an estate in Derbyshire!" came another. He even heard someone suggest, "Related to the king!" This last was quite ludicrous, but it was not the strangest thing Darcy had heard. He was well used to being the subject of such whispers and rumour. In fact, whilst he despised it, he rather expected it. This *sotto voce* rush of words provided the carpet upon which he walked into a room, and likewise provided the insulation he so often relied upon to protect him from an onslaught of false admirers. It was easy to avoid conversation when one was seen to be so much above one's company. He straightened his spine and raised his chin a bit, so as to peer down his nose upon those around him. This was the armour he donned to protect himself from the rabble, and the armour was all but impenetrable.

A man came rushing up to the group as they moved into the assembly hall. He would have been elfin had he been smaller; his gestures and physiognomy seemed more suited to a little creature than this large man. But he bowed prettily and spoke with cultivated tones as he offered his greetings.

"Mr. Bingley!" he gushed as his fingers danced in the air. Was the man trying to cast a spell? Darcy clenched his jaw and exhaled slowly as the man prattled on. "Delighted that you have come. Delighted! The whole town is anxious to meet you. And what charming guests you have brought. Capital, just capital! Please, if you will?"

Bingley made the introductions. The man was Sir William Lucas, former mayor of the town of Meryton and self-appointed master of local society. He was, Darcy grudgingly admitted, a pleasant enough person, if a bit overblown in his own self-importance. Darcy pulled himself to his full height once more and returned the older man's bow.

"And my sisters," Bingley continued the introductions, "Miss Bingley and Mrs. Hurst, and my brother Mr. Hurst." Bows and curtseys were exchanged in a most formal manner before Sir William grabbed at Bingley's arm like a schoolboy to pull him into the room.

"You must allow me to introduce you to..." His words were lost in the growing din of the gathered company. For lack of any alternative, Darcy followed.

The next half hour seemed interminable. Every face looked the same, every coat and gown interchangeable. There was too little of fashion and taste, and too much of vulgarity. The ladies' gowns were dated enough that even he knew they were last year's styles, and not a single gentleman, other than Sir William himself, wore the latest cut of waistcoat and collar points. Furthermore, everybody talked too freely, too loudly, like farmers at a harvest festival. These—*these*—were the haute ton of local society? What had Bingley got himself into?

"...my daughter, Charlotte."

Darcy blinked and brought himself back to the present. Sir William was still speaking, introducing the new arrivals in the neighbourhood to everybody in the space. Darcy turned to take in the woman now before them. She looked sensible enough, and about his own age of twenty-seven, but she had no particular charm or beauty. Was she married? No, it seemed not. Bingley greeted her, saying, "A pleasure to see you again, Miss Lucas." To be unmarried still at her age did not bode well for her future felicity in life. He must take care to find a good husband for his sister Georgiana to save her from this same fate; although his sister, at least, had the sort of fortune that made spinsterhood a choice rather than a sad fate.

But he had no time to worry about ageing spinsters. Sir William and Bingley were weaving their way through the throng once more and Darcy must follow them. Sir William was still talking. "You have, I believe, previously met Mr. Bennet of Longbourn, Mr. Bingley. He is not here this evening, but do not fear! Pray, allow me to introduce to you his lovely daughters. This way, I see them together by the fern."

He traipsed behind Bingley and Sir William as they waded through the crowd, which parted before them like the waters of the Red Sea before Moses. Everywhere he glanced, he met an ocean of fascinated eyes. The whispers were quieter, but they had not stopped. One ruddy country face after another looked upon him with variations of awe, reverence, and other intimations of being in the presence of a superior creature. He held his head high, not deigning to meet any one person's eye, certainly not daring to smile. He was not one to crow about his place in the first circles in London, nor to bask in the glow of his noble relations, but neither would he lower himself to befriend these rustic imitators of society. For Bingley's sake he would be coolly polite, and even civil should he find himself in suitable company, but these people were not of his class, and they must know it.

He glided across to where Sir William was now introducing Bingley to a matron and a gaggle of young women, all similar enough in feature that they must be sisters. One or two were rather pretty. But not of his class. From their giggling and gestures, they seemed quite countrified. There was no suggestion of elegance, no lingering benefit of a dancing master's tutelage in the finer points of deportment and carriage. Except for that one. One of the sisters had caught his eye. He stood still whilst Sir William introduced them all, allowing his eye to linger on the elegant one for a moment.

The matron was Mrs. Bennet. She was a handsome woman, old enough to have five grown daughters, but still striking enough that Darcy could see she must have been quite beautiful in her youth.

"A pleasure, Madam!" Bingley's smile lit the room. "I had the pleasure of meeting Mr. Bennet when I first came to the neighbourhood two weeks ago. I am delighted to meet you."

The lady fluttered and cooed, and Darcy stood as rigid as a statue as he received her exaggerated curtsey. Her motions were fussy, like an overly decorated doily, with a great deal of flounce and frill, but no taste and less elegance. Then came the sisters. "Miss Bennet," Sir William began with the eldest. She was the one who had caught Darcy's eye. She was rather pretty. No, he corrected himself, she was particularly lovely. Tall and slim, she had the sort of figure for which the fashions of the day were created, and she moved with an innate grace that a good dancing master would turn into a sort of art. Likewise, her face was a model of classical beauty, symmetrical and regular, her skin perfect alabaster tinged with rose, her expression everything pleasant. Neither by feature nor by appearance would she be out of place in any fine soirée in London. As Darcy glanced over to his friend Bingley, he noticed his friend all but gaping at this lovely creature. It seemed, by the look on Bingley's face, that Miss Bennet would equally be welcome in his salon. If not elsewhere in his home.

There were three other sisters gathered about their mother, whose names Darcy only half-heard. Mary, Catherine, and Lillia... no, Lydia. He was tired from his long day of travels, and his interest in these silly looking creatures was minimal. He blinked his eyes and nodded his head in greeting and then excused himself to stalk towards the wall where he might stand and watch the proceedings. The band had reassembled on the dais and a dance was forming in the centre of the room. He closed his eyes for a moment and stifled a yawn. As he took a deep breath to return himself to the good regulation that was his pride, he scanned the crowd again. Was that Bingley, leading the eldest Miss Bennet to the line? So it was. And Sir William was gesturing them to the head of the dance; they were to lead, it seemed.

"Had you asked me, I should now be calling the dance." A voice sounded at Darcy's shoulder.

"Miss Bingley." She was beautiful to gaze upon until she began to speak. "But I did not ask you, and therefore that honour belongs to your brother and Miss Bennet."

She tilted her head in the manner she had, whereby she seemed to look down her nose at him despite his superior height. "When you ask me to dance later, we shall show these... people... what excellent dancing is." She tapped his arm with her fan and drifted off, leaving Darcy gazing once more into the crowds.

The people avoided him, afraid to come too close. Most had not been introduced, after all, and his stern demeanour (so he had been told) deterred any who might dare break the conventions of polite society. Their eyes still landed upon him with their expressions of reverence. He abhorred the attention, but quite depended on the acknowledgement of his superiority... but what was that? There was one face in the crowd that seemed to look upon him with blatant disapproval! It moved behind one head and in front of another, and all he could tell was that it belonged to a young woman. A young country woman, scarcely more than a girl. Curling her lip at him! The impudence!

He squared his shoulders and stood taller, making himself all the more formidable, and thus he stood alone and unmolested all through the long country dance until at last Charles Bingley delivered his lovely partner to her mother and sisters and came to find him once more.

Bingley's forehead was aglow with the tinges of healthy perspiration and his smile was as wide as ever Darcy had seen it.

The young man's eyes flickered constantly to where Miss Bennet was now in a tight group with her mother and one or two young ladies her age from the town.

"She is pretty," Darcy opined. There. That was his attempt at friendly civility this evening. He wished nothing more than to be back at Bingley's newly leased estate with a warm fire before him, a good book on his lap, and a brandy at his side. But he knew his duty to his friend and he would make some effort.

"Pretty? She is more than merely pretty. Look at her, man! She is everything lovely. And charming too. I have already requested a second dance later this evening. See how she smiles at me!"

Darcy deigned to cast his eye in Miss Bennet's direction. She was, indeed, smiling. She smiled at Bingley, she smiled at her mother, at her friends. "Yes, indeed. But she seems rather indiscriminate with the bestowal of her smiles."

"Really, Darcy, you are a bore! I like her, and you cannot tell me not to wish to further my acquaintance with her. But have you not danced? Not at all?"

Darcy stifled a yawn. The day had been long, far longer than he had hoped. "I was up very early to conclude my business with my agent before departing London."

"Yes?"

"I wish only to stand here."

"And disappoint all these charming ladies hoping to meet you? No, indeed! Come, Darcy, this is quite wrong. I must have you dance. I hate to see you standing about by yourself in this stupid manner. You had much better dance."

His eyelid twitched. He had hoped to avoid such a discussion, but there was nothing for it. He was weary and not well pleased by his circumstance, and that look he had seen on that one girl's face, that look of derision, had set him quite in a foul temper.

"I certainly shall not." Somewhere, a twinge ran up his calf from sitting too long in the carriage. "You know how I detest it, unless I am particularly acquainted with my partner. At such an assembly as this," he narrowed his eyes as he peered around the room, "it would be quite insupportable. There is not a woman in the room whom it would not be a punishment to stand up with."

Bingley rolled his eyes, a habit Darcy had not been able to rid him of. "You are a bore indeed! I would not be as fastidious as you are for a kingdom. I have never met with so many pleasant girls in my life, and there are several of them who are uncommonly pretty."

Perhaps there was something in Bingley's statement, but Darcy was now set against the very idea. It was bad enough that he would have to dance with Miss Bingley later. "You," he said at last, "were dancing with the only handsome girl in the room."

"Oh, she is the most beautiful creature I ever beheld!" Bingley cried. *Indeed*, thought Darcy, *not since the last ball we attended in London*. Bingley was somewhat lacking in constancy. But he said nothing, and Bingley continued. "But there is one of her sisters sitting down just behind you, who is very pretty, and, I dare say, very agreeable. Her name, I believe, is Elizabeth. Do let me ask Miss Bennet to introduce you."

Heavens! Not another Bennet sister. Was there no end to them? "Which do you mean?" he asked. He turned around and saw none other than that country girl who had turned up her nose at him earlier. A wave of anger rippled through him. That impertinent chit must learn her place. He looked again. She was sitting with a friend—Miss Lucas, if he recalled—but it was most assuredly her. Her! One of the Bennet girls. This was most unpleasant. His jaw grew tight again.

He looked at her for so long that he caught her eye, and in that moment that she returned his frank gaze, he sensed her sneer once more. He withdrew his eye and said with all the ice he could muster,

"She is tolerable, but not handsome enough to tempt me." Had she heard him? He certainly hoped so. "I am in no humour at present to give consequence to young ladies who are slighted by other men. You are wasting your time with me."

Bingley gave another great roll of his eyes and stalked off to return to Miss Bennet and her friends, and Darcy shifted his weight, the better to withstand another tedious country dance. Then, to his side, he caught a flash of motion as the annoying Bennet sister rose from her chair and walked towards him.

She stopped in her path and pivoted to glare at him directly. Her dark eyes flashed and her chin thrust forward as she scrutinised him in the manner of a distasteful piece of meat left out in the sun for too long. Then she stated in clipped syllables, "How fortunate it is that I have no interest in dancing with you. Any lady of quality must have her standards, and I only dance with gentlemen. And you, sir, despite your airs and wealth, are no gentleman." With which, she turned her back on him and melted into the crowd, her friend scurrying behind her.

Miss Elizabeth Bennet, so it seemed, had just declared war.

You can read the rest in eBook or paperback.

https://books2read.com/muchadoinmeryton

Other books by Riana Everly:

Teaching Eliza: Pride and Prejudice meets Pygmalion

A tale of love, manners, and the quest for perfect vowels.

Professor Fitzwilliam Darcy, expert in phonetics and linguistics, wishes for nothing more than to spend some time in peace at his friend's country estate, far from the parade of young ladies wishing for his hand, and further still from his aunt's schemes to have him marry his cousin. How annoying it is when a young lady from the neighbourhood, with her atrocious Hertfordshire accent and country manners, comes seeking his help to learn how to behave and speak as do the finest ladies of high society.

Elizabeth Bennet has disliked the professor since overhearing his flippant comments about her provincial accent, but recognizes in him her one opportunity to survive a prospective season in London. Despite her ill feelings for the man, she asks him to take her on as a student, but is unprepared for the price he demands in exchange.

"With her clever mash-up of two classics, Riana Everly has fashioned a fresh, creative storyline with an inventive take on our favorite characters, delightful dialogue and laugh out loud humor. Teaching Eliza is certain to become a reader favorite. It's a must read!" – Sophia Meredith (author of the acclaimed *On Oakham Mount* and *Miss Darcy's Companion*)

https://books2read.com/teachingeliza

The Assistant: Before Pride and Prejudice

A tale of love, secrets, and adventure across the ocean

When textile merchant Edward Gardiner rescues an injured youth, he has no notion that this simple act of kindness will change his life. The boy is bright and has a gift for numbers that soon makes him a valued assistant and part of the Gardiners' business, but he also has secrets and a set of unusual acquaintances. When he introduces Edward to his sparkling and unconventional friend, Miss Grant, Edward finds himself falling in love.

But who is this enigmatic woman who so quickly finds her way to Edward's heart? Do the deep secrets she refuses to reveal have anything to do with the appearance of a sinister stranger, or with the rumours of a missing heir to a northern estate? As danger mounts, Edward must find the answers in order to save the woman who has bewitched him ... but the answers themselves may destroy all his hopes.

Set against the background of Jane Austen's London, this Pride and Prejudice prequel casts us into the world of Elizabeth Bennet's beloved Aunt and Uncle Gardiner. Their unlikely tale takes the reader from the woods of Derbyshire, to the ballrooms of London, to the shores of Nova Scotia. With so much at stake, can they find their Happily Ever After?

https://books2read.com/theassistant

Through a Different Lens: A Pride and Prejudice Variation

A tale of second glances and second chances

Elizabeth Bennet has disliked the aloof and arrogant Mr. Darcy since he insulted her at a village dance several months before. But an unexpected conversation and a startling turn of phrase suddenly causes her to reassess everything she thought she knew about the infuriating and humourless gentleman.

Elizabeth knows something of people who think differently. Her young cousin in London has always been different from his siblings and peers, and Lizzy sees something of this boy's unusual traits in the stern gentleman from Derbyshire whose presence has plagued her for so long. She approaches him in friendship and the two begin a tentative association. But is Lizzy's new understanding of Mr. Darcy accurate? Or was she right the first time? And will the unwelcome appearance of a nemesis from the past destroy any hopes they might have of happiness?

Warning: This variation of Jane Austen's classic Pride and Prejudice depicts our hero as having a neurological difference. If you need your hero to be perfect, this might not be the book for you. But if you like adorable children, annoying birds, and wonderful dogs, and are open to a character who struggles to make his way in a world he does not quite comprehend, with a heroine who can see the man behind his challenges, and who celebrates his strengths while supporting his weaknesses, then read on!

https://books2read.com/throughadifferentlens/

The Bennet Affair: A Pride and Prejudice Variation

A tale of secrets, sweethearts, and spies!

Elizabeth Bennet's bedroom in the ancient tower of Longbourn has always been her private haven. So what are those footsteps and shuffling noises she's now hearing from the room above her head? Drawn from her bed one dark summer night, her clandestine investigations land her in the middle of what looks like a gang of French spies!

William Darcy's summer has been awful so far, especially after barely rescuing his sister from a most injudicious elopement. Then he is attacked and almost killed nearly at his own front door in one of the best parts of London. Luckily his saviour and new friend, Lord Stanton, has a grand suggestion—recuperate in the countryside and help uncover the workings of a ring of French spies, rumoured to be led by none other than country squire Thomas Bennet!

Drawn together as they work to uncover the truth about the Frenchmen hiding in their midst, Elizabeth and Darcy must use all their intellect as they are confronted with an ingenious code machine, a variety of clockwork devices, ancient secrets and very modern traitors to the Crown. And somewhere along the line, they just might lose their hearts and discover true love—assuming they survive what they learn in the Bennet affair.

https://books2read.com/thebennetaffair

Love mysteries? Don't miss the Miss Mary Investigates series, starring Mary Bennet and her friend, investigator Alexander Lyons.

Miss Mary Investigates

The Mystery of the Missing Heiress: A prequel novella

Death of a Clergyman: A Pride and Prejudice Mystery

Death in Highbury: An Emma Mystery

Death of a Dandy: A Mansfield Park Mystery